GLEN ROBINS

Chosen Path

First edition

ISBN: 978-0-9863517-8-5

This book was professionally typeset on Reedsy.
Find out more at reedsy.com

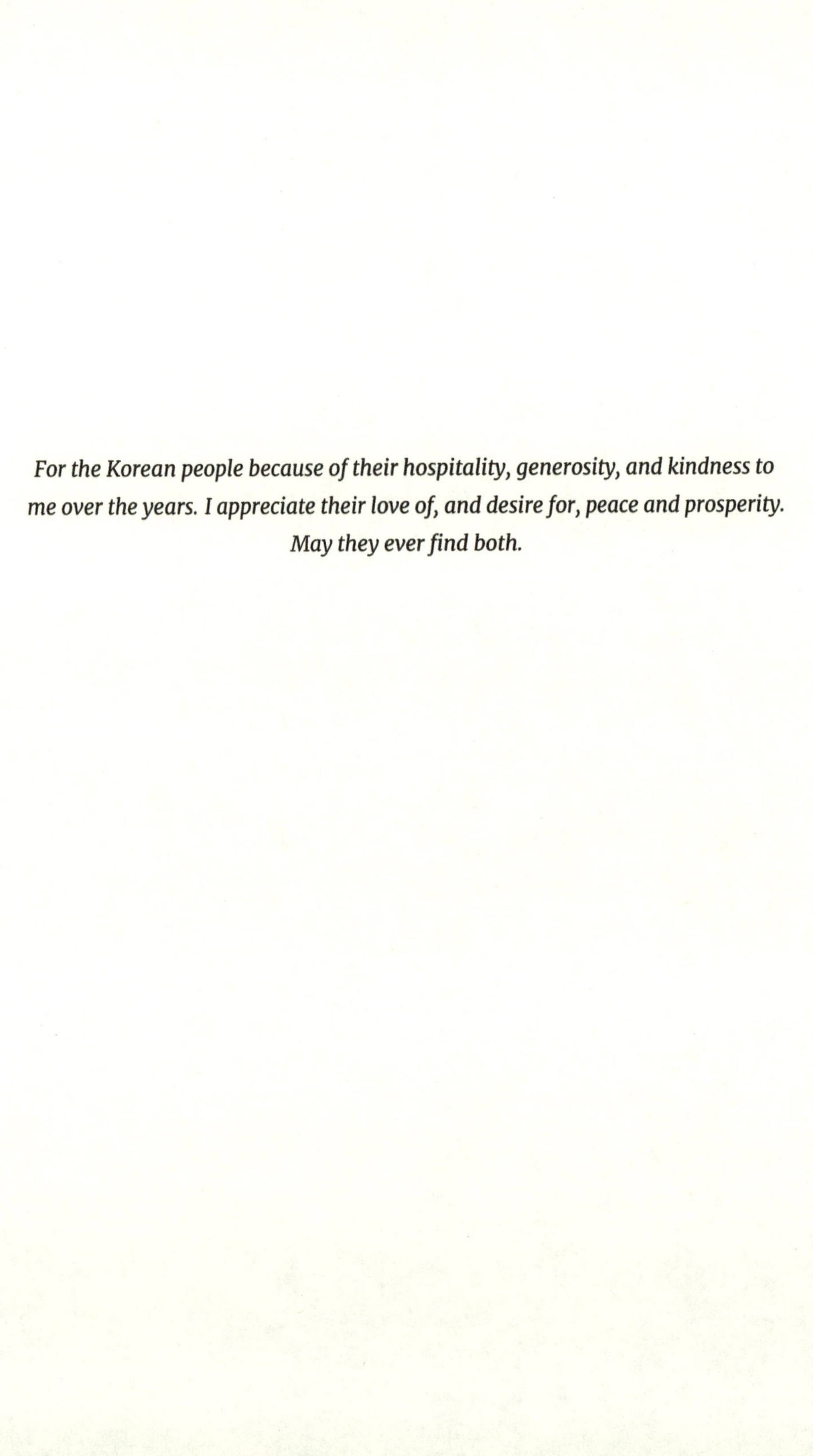

For the Korean people because of their hospitality, generosity, and kindness to me over the years. I appreciate their love of, and desire for, peace and prosperity. May they ever find both.

Contents

Prologue	iv
Chapter 1	1
Chapter 2	8
Chapter 3	13
Chapter 4	20
Chapter 5	27
Chapter 6	33
Chapter 7	39
Chapter 8	43
Chapter 9	47
Chapter 10	53
Chapter 11	59
Chapter 12	64
Chapter 13	72
Chapter 14	80
Chapter 15	84
Chapter 16	92
Chapter 17	96
Chapter 18	102
Chapter 19	108
Chapter 20	114
Chapter 21	121
Chapter 22	124
Chapter 23	129
Chapter 24	139
Chapter 25	143

Chapter 26 147
Chapter 27 153
Chapter 28 157
Chapter 29 162
Chapter 30 172
Chapter 31 177
Chapter 32 183
Chapter 33 190
Chapter 34 196
Chapter 35 202
Chapter 36 204
Chapter 37 211
Chapter 38 216
Chapter 39 223
Chapter 40 226
Chapter 41 232
Chapter 42 234
Chapter 43 239
Chapter 44 243
Chapter 45 248
Chapter 46 251
Chapter 47 255
Chapter 48 260
Chapter 49 262
Chapter 50 267
Chapter 51 270
Chapter 52 278
Chapter 53 280
Chapter 54 284
Chapter 55 288
Epilogue 291
Before You Go 293
Born Into Espionage – Sneak Peek 294

Born Into Espionage – Chapter One 299
About the Author 304
Also by Glen Robins 306

Prologue

Northbound 405 Freeway, Orange County, California
June 6, 4:54 a.m.

It had been the worst twenty-four hours of my life, yet I felt oddly satisfied. Exhausted and depleted in every way and yet relieved, thanks to a relatively successful outcome.

For the second time since waking up early the previous morning, I found myself in handcuffs in the back of a law enforcement vehicle. This second time, I was OK with it.

I deserved to be there. What I had done was morally reprehensible. And illegal. I had violated several laws, including provisions in the Geneva Convention.

Yet, my conscience was at peace. I closed my eyes and leaned my head against the seatback, settling in for the long car ride back to where this adventure—or misadventure, depending on how you looked at it—began. I needed to catch up on my sleep, knowing there would be more grueling hours ahead of me.

If you were to judge my day's performance strictly in a numerical sense, I guess the highest grade you could give me would be a B-. I had been 80% successful in what I set out to do.

I take that back. I accomplished 100% of my original goal. However, my task was multiplied by five as the day progressed, and not because of anything I did. That's just the way things went. Once I decided to be vigilant, my day, and I suppose my life, took a sharp turn away from the expected and into a role I never thought I would be in again.

If I had done nothing—if I had remained in my seat in the airport waiting area like everyone else did—almost sixteen hundred more people would have lost their lives. Myself included. But if I had somehow been able to act faster or more effectively, another four hundred people would still be alive. I'll wrestle with the decisions I made and the results I attained for the rest of my life, I suppose.

I chose a course of action today that altered not only my personal plans but, perhaps, world history. I don't suppose, however, that more than a handful of people will ever know the full story of what transpired. The events of this day are not the kind of things those in authority, especially elected officials, want the public to know. The things I did to earn my B- are not things you talk about. There's no pride in recounting them.

I've been told that terrorist plots get thwarted from time to time, but these incidents get swept under the proverbial rug because we can't have the public living in fear. It ruins the economy. It tilts elections. It snuffs out joy. And if that happens, the bad guys win. No one wants that. At least, none of the good guys.

When I got up from my seat at LAX this morning, I stepped onto a path that would lead me to places and decisions that I could never have foreseen.

I did what I did because there were hundreds of lives on the line, not to mention careers and reputations. What I did wasn't pretty. It's barely defensible. But it was effective. Mostly.

Would I do it the same, given similar circumstances? Yes, if it meant achieving the same or better results. Saving innocent lives often requires unspoken sacrifices. Most assuredly, mine will never be written in the annals of history or spoken of at dinner parties. My sacrifices involve moral morasses on a societal level.

I sold my soul in a way in order to save hundreds, if not thousands, of others. In the final analysis, I can only hope the means are justified by the end result.

Chapter 1

Tom Bradley International Terminal, Los Angeles International Airport
June 5, 9:48 a.m.

Something about these two guys didn't look right. It didn't feel right. Something was off, which triggered a response in me—a soldier's response, I suppose—that was almost as innate as breathing, compelling me to take a closer look. They caught my attention, and my internal alarm went off.

Despite the crowds milling to and fro and the noises and confusion of one of the country's busiest airports on what felt like an unusually busy day at the start of the summer travel season, two men stood out of the crowd. Of all the people moving about in the cavernous corridor of the International Terminal at Los Angeles International Airport at a quarter to ten in the morning, these guys made me notice them. Everyone else carried on with business as usual. No one paid them the attention that I felt they deserved. But that's understandable. I used to get paid to detect threats and to notice unusual things. It had been a few years since I was relieved of my duty, but the tendencies drilled into me in my prior life as a border guard still remained.

Our plane wasn't scheduled to depart for another two hours, not that I was counting down. Another one of those military things.

My small group was congregated in the waiting area not far from our gate. We had decided to beat the wildly unpredictable traffic between Orange County and LAX and get through airport security ahead of schedule to reduce stress on everyone, especially me. It's just easier to manage youngsters without all the typical chaos that ensues when thousands of people are all scrambling to make their flights. Besides, I was the teacher, and I was trying to teach a life lesson by example. In my Tae Kwon Do classes, one of my many mantras was, "Show up on time and be in the moment."

We had made our way through security, grabbed some food at various food vendors in the airport, and found our places near our assigned gate. The kids were now settled in and quiet, amused by whatever apps they had on their phones. Games and social media, I suppose.

We had arrived even earlier than I had planned, thanks to the carpool lanes. That's why I was sitting there people watching at the airport, sipping coffee with two hours to spare, thinking about how my life had turned out so much differently than I had planned, trying to relax so I could prepare myself for my first return trip to Korea, my homeland, since I had left in shame six years before.

The first thing that came to my mind was the argument my wife and I had had about this trip. I started involuntarily replaying the scene in my head. My wife was upset about my not bringing her and our two children with the group. She had wanted to take a vacation as a family. Great idea, maybe, but that would have meant an obligatory visit to my parents' house. Talk about awkward. I was not prepared for the stress of dealing with my father yet. My wife was eager for me to patch things up with him. Despite the fall out between us and his difficulty accepting her into the family, she wanted our children to have a relationship with both sets of grandparents. But I needed more time.

Even as I contemplated my life and the mess it currently felt to be in, my eyes kept returning to the two guys and the way they comported themselves.

Watching them lurk about for several minutes had me even more on edge than the argument. Maybe it was the way they were dressed. They wore thick-soled work boots and what looked like mechanics' one-piece zip-up uniforms under unzipped hooded sweatshirts. The uniforms were the customary dark blue. I could just see the edge of some sort of embroidered patches on the left chest area on each uniform, outlined in red. The boots were the typical black. The hoodies were dark gray. Nothing odd about any of that, except for the fact that they matched perfectly, and it all looked brand new. Not a scuff on either pair of boots. The pant legs were stiff and still had perfectly straight creases. The sweatshirts were practically shimmering with that fresh-off-the-shelf look. Even the point at the top of the hoods looked starched. Both of them. They looked like twins whose mother had dressed them in their brand-new outfits before sending them off to work.

A casual observer might say they were showing up for their first day on the job, but as I watched them, that seemed less and less likely.

Something was amiss. Both men had a familiar bearing about them, the type of bearing that comes with specialized military training. There's a kind of hyper-awareness about operatives. It's subtle, but noticeable to the trained eye. They were scoping the place, getting the lay of the land, surveilling. That's what my instinct told me, even after being out of the game all these years.

The first two times they passed by me they were empty-handed. That's not unusual. But the way they walked with purpose and determination told me they were up to something. The two men continued on down the corridor and I tried to push the thought of them out of my mind. I stood and went to the restroom. On my way back, I stopped in the little convenience store just a few meters from where my group was seated. I needed some Advil and wanted one of those bottled smoothie drinks to wash it down. A headache was the last thing I needed before we even boarded the plane.

When I walked into the store, the same two guys with their freshly bought outfits were there. I overheard them speaking in my native tongue with the clerk behind the counter when I walked in. Their conversation quickly ended, and they walked to the far corner of the shop, which only served to further raise my hackles. They pretended to be interested in the American newspapers and paperback books, but I caught them in my peripheral vision peering over the racks, as if waiting for me to leave.

I spoke very few words to the clerk, all in English, as I paid for my items. I glanced back at the two characters as I headed out of the store. They were watching me, so I focused on looking casual, clueless, and unconcerned.

Returning to my seat, I tried to tell myself I was being paranoid. I swallowed a couple of the pain relievers and pulled out my phone to check my newsfeeds when I noticed the two guys emerge from the store. There was something different about them that I was sure no one else noticed: they were no longer empty handed. This was a significant development, one that triggered afresh the alarms in my head.

The smaller guy dragged a medium-sized, nondescript black roller bag behind him, the same kind of luggage as half the other passengers in every airport I've been in. But this bag appeared heavy. He struggled to keep the handle in his grip and the way it clacked as it rolled along the shiny marble floor betrayed its mass. His head swiveled often and purposefully. The big guy muttered frequently, but not to the shorter guy. The shorter guy never responded and paid no attention to what the big guy was saying. He was watching for watchers. It didn't take a genius to realize these guys were up to no good.

I knew they were Korean, like myself. I could tell by their features and by what little I had heard of their conversation with the clerk. I'm not in the habit of suspecting my fellow countrymen of wrongdoing, but experience told me something was brewing.

As they exited the store, I got the sense that they had received their assignment. The familiar look of a soldier with his marching orders was painted on each of their faces. They never checked departure or arrival times on the giant display screens, yet it seemed to me like they were anticipating something—something big.

I kept watching them.

I had the perfect seat to do it, too. At the end of a row of conjoined armchairs perpendicular to the direction of foot traffic, I sat closest to the tiled concourse that led from one end of the terminal to the other. I could sit and observe them without moving a muscle. I played it cool, though, slouched in my seat looking bored and sleepy. With my phone held in front of me as a decoy, I observed them walk past my position without registering the fact that I was watching them and recording them with my phone. I flipped the camera on my phone so that I was recording over my shoulder as they moved away from me, still hyper-aware of their surroundings.

Their demeanor had shifted now that they had this bag in tow; their alertness amped up a notch or two as they made a beeline for an unmarked door halfway between two stores.

Vigilance is an interesting concept. People talk about it. Authorities ask for it. The public is warned that it is necessary for their own protection and security. But what is it? What does it entail?

In this case, vigilance meant that I had to stand up when I would have preferred to stay sitting. It meant that I had to shake off the weariness and stress of the past several weeks leading up to this trip. It was a big deal to get these kids ready for it. I was nervous, as were they. The Advil had not yet kicked in. I needed a few minutes of quiet time, but it was becoming clear that I wouldn't get it. I couldn't ignore these two suspicious characters.

My entire upbringing had taught me to be wary, alert, and vigilant. You always do your duty, do it well, then your conscience lets you sleep at night. A lesson, a mantra, a way of life drilled into me, sometimes forcefully, by my father.

I shook my head to clear my thoughts, but I couldn't shrug off the nagging instinct tickling the back of my neck.

At first blush, mine was a difficult choice. I had two competing responsibilities battling for supremacy within my beleaguered brain: follow the two odd dudes to make sure they were not a threat to the safety of everyone in sight or stay with my sixteen Tae Kwon Do students and the five accompanying chaperones.

I quickly determined my course of action. All twenty-one of my charges were zoned-out to some extent. They would be just fine if I left them for a few minutes.

Urgency prompted my decision. The two quirky dudes had ducked through a door about ten meters behind me and across the wide corridor. As they approached the door, about one stride from its handle, I watched them don black gloves. Even though there was a security lock that required the swipe of a card key, neither of them swiped, but the door opened when they pulled on the handle. Before the door closed behind them, they pulled the hoods of their sweatshirts over their heads. What further prompting did I need? Apparently, mine were the only eyes that caught this cagy little exploit.

The door they pulled open, entered, then pulled shut, did not appear to be a doorway for use by the general public. There were no markings or placards on it. No signs anywhere explained the use of that door. It was even painted the same pearl white as the adjacent wall, probably so that it would blend in and not be mistaken for an available exit. But these guys, without ID, disappeared inside.

Hordes of people ambled to and fro, oblivious to the potential menace. Most were too concerned with getting somewhere. Many were staring at their phones. Others were talking with each other or wrestling children or focused on finding the right place.

I sat no more than fifteen meters away, arms folded across my chest, slumped down in my barely padded seat at the end of a long row of connected chairs, phone in hand recording the whole thing. My legs were stretched out in front of me as I watched it all unfold. Once the door closed, I sat straight up and twisted my head in all directions to see if anyone else was going to do something. I detected no movement, no signs of recognition that anything unusual was taking place. Why was someone not reacting to this apparent breach of airport security? Did these guys really belong there? Did they have permission to enter that passageway?

I couldn't be sure one way or the other. Part of me wanted to ignore it. After all, it wasn't *my* job. Getting my kids on the plane for their competition was. But the soldier in me with all the training on defending the home country and protecting the innocent wouldn't—couldn't—sit by idly and let this pass. There were too many oddities to suppress the internal alarms.

There were no security guards or police officers or even TSA agents in sight. By the time I explained the situation over the phone, these two would be long gone. It was time to act, not time to talk. I had missed that chance. At this point, I had no other choice but to follow them.

I looked at my students, the select group that had qualified to participate in the World Tae Kwon Do championship in my hometown of Seoul. Two from each of my eight mid-level to advanced classes. One winner and one runner-up. The youngest two, seven and eight years old, were cute, smart, and sassy. The two oldest were seventeen and all teenager. Shaggy dyed hair, hoods over their heads, slumped in their chairs, earbuds in, eyes closed. That was the façade a Korean kid living in America had to put on to fit in, I guess. Inside, however, I knew them to be diligent students, respectful of their parents, aware of their culture and history, and proud of it. They had mastered not only the skills of Tae Kwon Do, but also the principles. Discipline. Respect. Self-Mastery. The other students ranged through the intervening age categories. All were good kids from good families, trying to bridge the gap between keeping the values of the old country while assimilating to the new.

The competing stirrings within me grew stronger. I was in charge of all these kids. I shouldn't leave them. But I also knew something was about to go down and I had the capability to stop it. Therefore, I also had the duty to act—another lesson I had been taught at home. In the end, that would provide more safety than merely being present with my students. If something big were to happen and I didn't do anything to stop it, I knew I would regret it for the rest of my life.

Vigilance called, and I answered.

Chapter 2

Los Angeles International Airport
June 6, 9:52 a.m.

I hopped to my feet, briefly pulling the attention of a handful of my students away from their electronic devices. I waved off their concern and looked to one of the other adults who was sipping coffee as she read a book. Using a few clipped words and hand signals, I indicated that I would be right back. She nodded her understanding. My assistant coach was strolling the concourse burning off nervous energy, so I couldn't leave him in charge, as I normally would have.

I was hopeful that this would be just a quick and easy check to put my mind at ease.

After glancing up and down the corridor one last time to verify that no one else was going to act, I darted in the general direction of where I had seen them disappear, continuing to surveil the area as I crossed the bustling concourse. There was no response from any sort of security personnel. I thought about that little wrinkle as I weaved through foot traffic. My mind went immediately to the worst-case scenario, like I was trained to do. Hope for the best, prepare for the worst. Two guys in newly purchased maintenance uniforms going through a secured door without security cards had big implications. It meant that these guys had inside help of some sort, most likely the clerk at the airport store. I filed that away in the back of my mind and proceeded to the unmarked door.

The handle was locked, but the door swung open freely with only the slightest pressure. A quick look revealed clear packing tape across the latch.

Beyond the doorway, a short, wide hallway extended maybe ten meters. Dull yellow paint on the walls. A door on each side, which I assumed led into the backs of the airport stores. Tubular fluorescent lighting, two per rectangular fixture, spaced every three meters along the plain white ceiling. Matted gray carpeting, the low pile kind they put in high traffic areas that lasts forever, stretched out in front of me, bending left with the walls.

Moving slowly, I side-stepped the first ten meters, tensed and ready for anything. As I crept along in full stealth mode, there was no sign of the two shady characters. I recognized the buzz traveling through my nervous system. It wasn't just paranoia. Those two did not belong there and I had to figure out what they had planned.

My past was colliding with my present, my former duty to protect prodding me onward and my current lack of authority giving me pause simultaneously. It was like those waves at the beach that sometimes meet as one is rushing towards the shore and the other pulling back out to sea. The result is a mash up that looks all out of whack. That's how I felt inside. It was both exhilarating and stupefying at the same time.

I had no business trolling a couple of guys through some restricted-access back hallway at LAX just because I thought they might be acting in a suspicious manner. Not as my present self, a Tae Kwon Do instructor from Costa Mesa.

But my past self knew I was doing the right thing for the right reason. Once upon a time I was a highly decorated commander of an elite border patrol along the most heavily armed border in the world. My training and my upbringing would not allow me to be passive in a moment like this.

Of course, I hadn't finished the soul-searching that I had started back there in the waiting area, but I figured I could do it on the plane ride. Thirteen hours in a tin can with wings would give me plenty of opportunity for some long overdue self-reflection.

The hallway kept going, following the contour of the impossibly large building. The right wall split at a sharper angle to the right—a soft "T" intersection. The right branch ended with another door just a few meters beyond the split. I continued down the corridor to the left. As it bent, I could only see a few meters in front of me. I kept creeping forward but could neither see nor hear a thing. Part of me expected an ambush, but there was no place for them to hide, so I had to continually dismiss that nagging worry.

Windows replaced the dull yellow paint on the wall opposite from the one I had my back pressed against. The windows started at about waist height and went all the way up to the ceiling. They looked out to the West, but also gave me a view of LAX's northern-most runways. All I could see was an eerie fog, typical for the Southern California coastline in June. It shrouded and obscured everything. The evenly spaced orange glow of diffused lights around the working areas below spread in every direction. Only one plane, with its flashing wing lights and bright forward beams, was in motion on the outer fringes. Its hulking mass indistinct as it lurched through the pea soup, maybe a kilometer away from my position. Based on the color scheme of the fuselage, I knew it was a UPS plane moving toward the cargo sorting hangar on the airport's western-most edge.

I kept my back against the left-hand wall as I continued my stealthy pursuit. Something banged against a wall ahead of me. I froze in place. Unarmed, I was an easy target for someone with a weapon. The noises echoed, making it hard to pinpoint the distance between me and them.

Looking out the window, I saw them in the mottled light, two hooded figures crouched next to a parked vehicle. They pulled off the sweatshirts, stuffed them in the roller bag, and started darting between vehicles and equipment with their heavy suitcase in tow. They were running toward the Korean Airlines plane my students and I would presumably be boarding in less than an hour. I watched them disappear from sight under the belly of the 747.

Why was no one doing anything to stop them? Didn't the ground crew see them? What about Airport Security?

That's when it donned on me. I looked up at the ceiling and saw the familiar blackened bulb that hid the security cameras. It was mounted on the ceiling just a meter or so ahead of me. Another meter beyond that, I could see a door between two of the windows. My guess was that their teammates had hacked the camera feeds to mask their intrusion, but, most likely, had me in their sights. *Oh, great*, I thought as I stared at the bulbous, technological eyeball.

I pushed aside the creepy feeling of being watched by the bad guys and dashed to the door. On the other side was a metal staircase leading down to the tarmac. I bounded down and caught a glimpse of the dark shapes moving through the gloom. The taller one was now dragging the roller bag with some exertion.

I darted to the vehicle they had used as cover and ducked behind the back bumper, peering around it so I could keep an eye on them.

They stopped. Another figure approached. The new arrival pointed at the bag. The tall guy relinquished the handle to the new guy and the threesome split up.

I tried to keep an eye on my two original targets and the roller bag at the same time. The new guy disappeared into the fog beyond the 747 with the suspicious suitcase. The two odd ones peeled off and disappeared while I kept my eyes on the roller bag.

I moved closer to the plane, staying low and sprinting to the side of another vehicle without losing visual contact with the bag. I was under the massive left wing, an engine partially blocking my view. The new guy hoisted the roller bag onto a conveyor belt that was hauling baggage into our plane on the opposite side of the fuselage. There was only one way to find out what was in that bag and if it was dangerous.

There were several baggage handlers in the immediate area. Two were unloading suitcases from three covered carts connected to a towing tractor painted the same blue color as the plane, the Korean Airlines symbol emblazoned on the side of the vehicle. That tractor had hauled the passengers' luggage from somewhere under an overhang and was now parked alongside the body of the plane. Several men were hauling the bags from the carts and placing them on the moving belt. One was sitting in the driver's seat of the tractor, checking his phone. Two others were walking back toward the overhang of the terminal.

I had no time to formulate a plan. My only objective was to stop that bag from getting on the plane. Within a few short seconds, it would be out of my view, mixed in with a whole bunch of similar-looking luggage. Once inside the cargo hold, I knew my chances of finding it would shrink to somewhere between slim and nil.

As I rounded the end of the vehicle that was shielding me from view, keeping my eyes glued to the indistinguishable bag, I bumped into something. When I looked up, I was staring into the menacing gaze of the big guy I had been following.

Chapter 3

Los Angeles International Airport

June 5, 10:04 a.m.

Whatever advantage I may have had in terms of the element of surprise or my use of stealth was gone, as were my chances of grabbing that bag.

Their surveillance guys probably saw me with the big black eyeball and clued them in.

The two guys in their fresh-off-the-shelves work clothes brandished no firearms, which is what my mind expected in the milliseconds it took to process what was happening. That was a definite plus. Makes sense, since carrying them through an airport would have been nearly impossible.

Instincts kicked in, clearing my mind and channeling years of army and Special Forces combat training. Defensive maneuvers, offensive tactics. It all came back like an express train charging out of a tunnel.

The big guy was larger than most Koreans, probably about 6-foot-3 and a muscular 225 pounds. He regarded my 5-foot-9 frame like he would a coat rack blocking his path. I was a nuisance and nothing more. Like tossing me aside wouldn't take more than a flick of his arm.

His reflexes were quick, but mine were quicker. In a flash, his meaty right paw was going for my neck and I was dodging away from it. Most people would move to their right, the attacker's left, to avoid the incoming strangulating hand. But I ducked down and to my left, giving me more options to stunt his offensive. His left arm was already moving into position at the center of his body, ready to secure his prey. By moving to his right, I was out of reach of both hands momentarily, thus neutralizing his left hand. Doing so gave me the split-second advantage I needed to overcome the size difference. Years of training and practice had made these kinds of maneuvers, and the instantaneous decision-making behind them, second nature.

The surge of adrenaline flowing and the awareness that I was now in a life-or-death struggle awakened every nerve and synapse in my body and brain. I felt more alive in that moment than I had since being engaged by the enemy during border skirmishes.

My stunt placed me in a perfect position to disable my attacker. Being on his right side, away from the natural swept of his right hand and out of reach of his left, allowed me to grab his right wrist as he extended it with my right hand so I could pull his arm away from his body and throw off his balance. As soon as my feet were set half a second later, I twisted my torso and smashed the heel of my left hand into his elbow, unleashing all my energy and using his momentum against him. Strength from every muscle group from my legs, my torso, my arms, and my shoulders converged on the poor guy's elbow before he could muster any resistance. The opposing forces from my right arm straightening his arm as I pulled it upward and my left hand crashing downward broke the joint with a sickening snap that I felt reverberate down his arm. All tension from his muscles stopped, and his arm went limp as I held the wrist. I released his ruined appendage and repositioned myself as he screamed in agony, clutching his ravaged elbow, the forearm swinging unnaturally as he writhed.

I knew he was incapacitated, but I needed him immobilized as well. And quiet. I was acting on the teachings instilled in me to crush your enemy before he had the chance to regroup.

Things happen fast in combat. If you stop to think and plan, you lose. Quick, decisive action and aggressive adherence to age-old rules of engagement wins the battle, and, eventually, the war. Using Sun Tzu's philosophy, I had to subdue him with overwhelming force. Therefore, I did not relent.

A split second later, I had recoiled and rebalanced my weight on the balls of my feet. Without hesitation, I bounced and struck out with my right foot, landing my toes directly beneath his sternum. There is far more strength in the legs than in the arms, so landing a kick with the force generated by the largest muscles in the body can inflict greater damage, especially when properly placed. My victim was defenseless, which may make some people hesitate to finish the job. I had learned that that was precisely the time to unleash the fury. The opportunity was ripe, so I pressed my advantage. Knowing the first rule of close combat is to remove the immediate threat, I had to take him down hard.

The blow to his sternum jolted the big guy's system. All his breath was forced out as my foot connected with his solar plexus. The force of a blow to this sensitive region, especially because it was unprotected by the tensed abdominal muscle group, paralyzed the diaphragm, sending it into a spasm. While his brain was processing the pain and the lack of oxygen in his lungs, he dropped to his knees, let go of his useless arm, and tried to grab the new pain center. Unable to draw in even a single breath, the big guy toppled shoulder first in a twitching heap. His eyes widened like doors thrown open. Panic had set in due to lack of oxygen. He was incapacitated.

The most immediate and dangerous threat had been neutralized.

It was time to dispatch the next one.

Before doing so, I scanned the area quickly to assess the situation. I wanted to make sure there weren't more of them. I was also curious about potential onlookers. There was no one around and, thanks to the vehicles and the fog, we weren't visible to anyone in the area.

Without delay, my attention moved to the shorter guy, who was lunging at me from my left.

I popped into a defensive posture with my right leg slightly behind me, feet shoulder width apart as I quickly shuffled backward several paces. My fingers curled until my fists were like compact hammers, raised to chin level, cocked and loaded. It took about a millisecond.

This changed his line of attack. He had been targeting my vulnerable blind side. My retreat caused him to pause, as if to reassess his options and angle of attack.

The fear in the smaller guy was palpable. His eyes were wide open, as was his mouth. I could almost see the decision-making gears whir inside his head. Fight or flight? His survival instinct must have kicked in knowing there was nowhere to run and that I'd catch him anyhow. Falling back to his own training, he eyed me like a tiger eyes a rival. Taking the aggressive approach, the guy led with his right foot flying at my face. At the same time, he released a primal scream. It was aimed at intimidating me while also conjuring up courage and inner strength. It didn't faze me because I had experienced it many times before.

I stayed my ground and thrust both arms up, catching his heel in my cupped hands and pushing upwards as high and as fast as I could. That maneuver cost me my balance, sending me backwards, while pinwheeling him. He crashed to the ground. It looked like he landed on his head and shoulder, but he managed to tuck into a ball just before impact, thus diffusing much of the force. I staggered and spun on my heels but didn't fall.

The smaller guy regained his feet as I recovered my balance. The side of his face was scraped, and a trickle of blood had started down his cheek. His eyes were unfocused, and he blinked hard and fast. I decided to end this swiftly and get back to searching for that weighty piece of luggage.

I stunted left, then right, the left again. He followed my every move with just the slightest delay, trying to be ready to block and parry. I made a move like I was going straight in for the kill. He took a step back, his eyes trying to focus on my flying fists as I faked jabs and strikes to keep his attention on my upper half. He took another step back, but I closed the gap in a blink and juked to my right as I dropped to the ground and executed a lightning-fast leg sweep that he must not have seen coming. I hit the back of his heels hard, thrusting upward after making contact, which brought him crashing down to the ground with no resistance. His arms, which were in the process of striking out at me, barely had time to try to catch his fall. The back of his head absorbed the full brunt of the impact. I heard a crack as his skull collided with the concrete.

At first, there was no movement at all. Then, his body began to convulse—the sure sign of serious brain trauma. Most likely he wouldn't make it without immediate medical attention.

Now I had two problems. These inert bodies sprawled out before me and an unmarked bag with unknown contents loaded into the cargo hold of the plane that would carry somewhere around four-hundred unsuspecting souls, including myself and my students, across the great Pacific. Our flight was scheduled to leave in roughly an hour and fifteen minutes. Boarding would commence in about twenty minutes.

The fog and the noise of the jets must have masked our deadly sparring match. No one approached the scene. Without further thought, I raced to the baggage loader, intent on retrieving that bag. I had no idea how I would find it, but I knew I had to try.

I ignored the baggage handlers as they yelled at me and climbed onto the conveyor belt. I hopped over luggage and ran upward into the massive hull of the 747. The cargo hold was almost as big as a high school gymnasium, though not as tall. The two guys working inside looked surprised. The Caucasian started to shout at me that I didn't belong there or something along those lines. Being fixated on my objective, I moved past him and went in search of the bag like a hungry dog who knows there's a steak in the vicinity.

When two big Tongan guys blocked my way, I tried my best to explain to them quickly and succinctly what I was searching for and why. My English is not perfect, but I am good enough to carry on a conversation at almost any level with a native speaker. Despite my proficiency, I could see a complete lack of comprehension on their faces.

That's when I noticed a third man in the cargo area. He stiffened as he finished shoving a medium-sized black suitcase into place. It seemed to have required significant energy to maneuver, so I knew it was the one. The way he straightened and turned his head when I started to speak caught my attention. He was Asian and roughly my height. When I glanced at him, our eyes locked briefly, and a look of recognition passed across his face before he ducked behind the loaded luggage holder.

One of the Tongans, who seemed to be the boss, either didn't understand what I was saying or didn't care. His gloved hands were planted firmly on his hips and his eyes blazed with indignation. I pointed to the bag the Asian man had just put loaded on the rack and began moving toward it. The Tongan boss-man said simply and powerfully, "Don't move another inch." His voice conveyed authority and distrust.

I halted immediately, though I desperately wanted to remove the bag and inspect its contents to prove my point.

I tried slowing down and explaining in more detail. "If you'll just let me check that bag right there, I'm sure we can resolve this issue."

"No way. Not on my watch. That is a violation of Federal Aviation law," said the Tongan boss. He had to be twice my size. "I could lose my job."

As he spoke, several other workers joined in, entering the aircraft while I was busy talking. They formed a circle around me inside this hollowed aluminum hull. I don't know where they came from, but each one of their facial expressions was serious and menacing. Brows were knit, mouths pulled tight. The words were terse. My mission was nose-diving toward failure as they looked at me like I had tried a comedy routine at a funeral.

"I'm telling you," I continued. "There is something suspicious in that bag. Is that a chance you want to take with the lives of your passengers? I will accept responsibility for whatever happens. I'll take the blame. Just let me look inside, I'm begging you."

As I continued to plead my case before this rough and tumble crowd of baggage handlers, the LAPD Airport Division showed up. Two cars screeched to a halt just outside, under the wing. Four doors opened, one after the other. I could hear them announce themselves and ask for everyone to show their hands. Then they wanted to know where the suspect was. They entered the plane the same way I did, guns drawn.

I stopped and stood still with my hands in the air, palms facing the group as a show of trustworthiness, pleading for someone to take me seriously and search that black roller bag. "Please, somebody just open that one bag." I pointed to where I had seen the Asian guy put it. It was gone, and so was he.

They all glared at me and stepped forward, some raising an eyebrow at me like I was certifiable.

The four police officers spread out, quickly taking control of the situation.

The lead baggage handler pointed at me and said, "Out of the blue this lunatic just climbs up our loader and starts talking about a black suitcase that he has to look through. Says there's something suspicious about it. He points over there, you know, and says it's right there." The guy indicates the empty space where the bag was. "Problem is, Officer, I got a lot of black suitcases in here and they've all been through the scanner. This guy's nuts."

As the officers moved in, I grew frantic, knowing take-off was fast approaching. Knowing my sixteen students would be boarding soon. Knowing I wouldn't be with them and they would be confused. Hoping my assistant, Jin Sook, would do the right thing.

I had answered the call to vigilance. Now I would answer to the local authorities for it.

Chapter 4

L*os Angeles International Airport Police Station*
June 6, 12:08 p.m.

I sat waiting, a song I had heard on the radio playing in my head. I liked it. Sung by a duo of popular artists from different musical genres, their voices blended beautifully. The tune was upbeat, rhythmic, and catchy. It repeated a line several times that I found fitting for this occasion because it talked about not getting caught up in the middle of it and how not saying anything is sometimes the best thing to do.

Maybe that would be the best thing for me to do in the situation in which I had found myself.

I was in a jail cell, roughly two and a half meters wide by three and a half meters long. The mattress on the lone bed that resembled a large steel shelf cantilevered from the left-hand wall was thin and stained. The paint on the walls dull but clean. Not the worst place I'd ever been, but not where I wanted to be in that moment. Thankfully, I was alone with my thoughts. A chance to do the reflecting I had planned to do earlier, but it took forced concentration to get back in the mood to ponder my life.

Thinking was difficult because I was starving. I hadn't eaten anything since I left home.

I thought again about vigilance and wondered why it had tapped me on the shoulder. Why me? Why that morning?

Vigilance had pulled my attention away from my deep reflections upon my chosen path in life, my marriage, my destiny, and my shattered career. I had hoped to use that hour near the departure gate and the thirteen hours on the plane to gain some perspective. Instead, I was filled with dread at the prospect that my hunch may have been right, and those three fellow Koreans had somehow managed to hide a bomb onboard the plane that my students would soon be boarding.

I feared that I had made some critical mistakes. Maybe I should have trusted the local authorities to handle this. Maybe I should have called them when I first noticed the two guys. And maybe I shouldn't have gone full force on them. Keeping them conscious so they could answer questions probably would have been a better thing to do.

Two other things that kept interrupting my brooding over these mistakes was that flash of recognition in the eyes of the Asian guy in the cargo hold and the one phone call the law allowed me to make, which hadn't gone well.

First, I tried to figure out if that look of recognition was really that. Why would he know me? Had we met before? It was odd, like the two guys I had followed, the two that started this whole nightmare. Something about him gnawed away deep in my subconscious. Something in those eyes conjured up a memory that I couldn't quite pull out. I pushed the thought to the back of my mind for the time being.

Instead, I thought about the second occurrence more intently, trying to sort out what went wrong and how I could have handled that conversation better. My one phone call had been squandered, I felt. Jin Sook Lee, my assistant coach at the Do Jang I owned in Costa Mesa, was young, dynamic, and sincere. He really enjoyed his work and cared about the students. In a word, he had the kind of qualities that allowed him to connect well with the teenagers. He was a great coach and the kids loved him. Beyond that, he was relatable and a source of inspiration for things beyond Tae Kwon Do. He was a living example to them of one who had successfully navigated the dangerous waters of being a first-generation Korean. He was a twenty-five-year-old master's candidate at the University of California–Irvine, studying Microbiology. Tough, smart, and a born leader, I both trusted and distrusted Jin Sook. I trusted him to teach the kids well and show them how to live the principles we taught. The distrust came from his penchant for taking more credit than was his due and being bullheaded about doing things his way. He had an impetuous streak a mile wide.

When I called him, I told him that our students would have to bow out of the competition in Seoul and go home because something had come up that required my full attention for the foreseeable future.

He was understandably shattered and expressed strong feelings about my decision and asked me over and over, "Where did you go? Why did you just leave like that?"

I tried explaining that something came up, an emergency that I had to take care of, but he wasn't buying it.

"The ajuma's saw you go through a door next to the convenience store," he said in our native tongue, referring to the students' mothers. "Then there were the police cars. Then I get this call from a number I don't recognize in the 310-area code, and it's *you*. There's something going on that you're not telling me."

This kid was smart. Not that I ever underestimated him, but it surprised me how quickly he put the pieces together.

"Listen," I said as calmly as possible. "I'll explain everything later. Right now, I just need you to call the shuttle service back and have them come pick you all up and take you all home."

"After all their hard work, you're going to dash their hopes at the last minute like this?" He was speaking through clinched teeth. "That's just cruel. It's mean, and it's not right. This is completely not OK. How could you even think to do something like that?"

"No, it's not about dashing their hopes. It's about preparing to fight another day." I had to be careful with my words. I had been warned by the cops that I was not to raise any alarms with my "made-up" story about the mysterious bag. Warning my students of an unverified threat could trickle out to others and eventually lead to widespread panic that could spin wildly out of control, upsetting the delicate sense of security necessary to keep the traveling public traveling. Saying anything that could potentially lead to a disruption of airport operations for an extended period of time would not bode well for my situation, they told me before the call. Making a false threat was a felony and opened me up to not only criminal, but also civil prosecution that could make me liable for the airlines' lost income. Probably a staggering amount that I could never wrap my head around, so I agreed to play nice.

A Korean American police lieutenant stood nearby, listening in to our conversation to ensure my compliance.

"Is this your fear of failing again coming out?" Jin Sook's tone was derisive. He was not good at hiding his displeasure when met with unexpected disappointment. We had been working on his reactions to such things in the year and a half since I had hired him, but still had a way to go.

I tried to calm his temper and make him understand that boarding that plane was not a good idea. "I will explain the situation in full later, when the time is right. Right now, I need you to get our group back home and keep them calm."

Jin Sook sucked a breath through his teeth. "How can I do that? What would I say to the kids?"

"You need to be a strong leader right now," I said. "They will listen to you if you say it with conviction. Trust me. It's the right thing."

Another long pause before he spoke again. "What happened to you? Where are you, anyway?"

"It's long and complicated. I'll explain later, I promise."

"I can't tell these kids we're going home with a promise to 'explain things later.'"

He was right, but his tone and his obstinance frustrated me. The fact that he didn't trust me implicitly and obey without question made my blood boil. "Look, something very important came up and I couldn't ignore it." My tone was firm and authoritative, but it didn't back him down.

"*What*? Something more important than the competition we've all been preparing for since last Fall? Something that got you a ride in a cop car?" Instead, he was backing *me* down.

"I told you I can't talk about it right now, but I will later," I said. "It's not what you think. I had something very important to do. I just did it the wrong way and the cops got involved. I'm sorry."

"You decide *now* that there's something more important to you than these kids and their dreams?" He breathed hard a few times, then continued. "That's messed up. Whatever you did, you messed things up. Not just for yourself, but for me and for all of these kids and their parents." He paused again, still huffing loudly as he breathed. "We're going to be boarding that plane, with or without you."

"Please don't. Just do as I say." My words were forceful, but that was the wrong tack to take in the heat of the moment. I had reverted to my role as a military commander where subordinates simply obeyed. I had issued an order when I shouldn't have. Frankly, I was intellectually and emotionally incapable in that moment of using words alone to lead him in the direction I wanted him to go. I found myself in the familiar position of knowing more than I could share and yet trying to explain to someone who wasn't allowed to know what I knew why they needed to act on information that only I had. I tried to soften the blow. "I'll explain later. I can't talk about it right now."

My attempt to use words and logic and reason backfired on me. Again.

He did just what I would have done at his age. He told me I was crazy and that he would make sure that these kids had the chance to show the Tae Kwon Do world what they were made of. "You're too afraid to be here with them. You're afraid that they won't win and that will reflect badly on you. Either that, or you're afraid to face your father. Either way, these kids will feel that you don't have the confidence in them that they deserve. But I will do everything in my power to give them the inner strength to triumph despite your fear of failure. I will lie to them this time and this time only. I will tell them you became very ill. It's for their own good. And if you want to fire me, that's fine. There are plenty of other Do Jangs that will appreciate my talents. I might even start my own."

With that, he hung up.

That's what I liked about him. He had the same fierce loyalty to "the cause" as I did in my earlier years. His cause at the moment was far different than mine was back then, but the fire inside was similar. But it was also the part about him that made me crazy. Even years after the end of my military career, I found myself incapable of tolerating insubordination.

First, my anger flared, and I cursed out loud as I slammed the phone receiver back in its cradle. I was furious that he wouldn't obey me, that he wouldn't listen to what I was saying. Then I thought about what I was saying and realized I gave him no reason to pull the plug on our long-anticipated trek to the world championship. He was justified in refusing to march those kids out of the airport and tell them they couldn't go. He couldn't do that without a good explanation. I couldn't have, either. If our roles were reversed, I certainly would have done the same thing.

Then, as I remembered the overweight roller bag and its mysterious contents, my heart nearly stopped beating. I felt the blood drain out of my head and had to steady myself against the wall next to the relic of a phone I had just used.

Though the Asian baggage handler had removed the heavy suitcase from the cargo hold, I felt that I had failed. It seemed certain he would find a way to sneak it back onto the plane, the same plane where sixteen of my best students and four of their mothers and Jin Sook would soon be seated. I was helpless to save them. Sixteen sweet, innocent kids brimming with pride in their accomplishments, ready to show the world their skills and courage. Eager to compete. Eager to win. Eager to conquer whatever challenges life threw at them.

Except this one. They didn't stand a chance against what I feared was in that bag.

Once again, words were my undoing. They didn't come when I needed them most, when they were my only hope. Not on the phone with Jin Sook. Not in the plane's cargo bay with the cops. Not in front of the Army tribunal six years earlier.

This failure would be even more dreadful and would cost more than the lives of the eleven dedicated soldiers who died when I failed back then. This time there would be over four-hundred lives in peril because I could not seem to get anybody to listen to my words and believe what I was trying to tell them. And that didn't include the devastation to the families, friends, and businesses that would be affected by their loss.

It had been forty minutes since Jin Sook hung up on me. I sat with my head in my hands, reviewing the events of the past ninety minutes and comparing them to the events six years earlier when a sharp clang brought my attention to the bars of the jail cell. The words of the song in my head stopped abruptly, just like on the radio, reminding me that sometimes it's best to say nothing at all.

My back stiffened, and my shoulders squared out of habit. A military man must always maintain his composure, his sense of self, and understand his power to triumph.

"Mr. Noh," said a calm and steely voice. "Come this way, please. The Director of the Transportation Safety Administration for Los Angeles International Airport would like to have word with you."

Chapter 5

C*osta Mesa, California*
June 6, 12:12 p.m.

She knew something was wrong as soon as she saw Jin Sook's name appear on her phone's caller I.D. *He should be on the plane with JT*, thought Stephanie Noh, as she double-checked the time on the over-sized faux-retro clock, visible from the kitchen on the family room wall. *They should have taken off by now.*

Since her husband, Jeong Tae, had not called her to say good-bye before boarding, the tendrils of her nervous system were already sizzling with anxiety, like electricity through a downed power line. The tension from their early morning blow up was still hanging in the air.

"What is it, Jin Sook? What is wrong? You guys should be on the plane," she blurted all at once.

Her fourteen-month-old baby, Matthew, sat in his highchair and played happily with his food. She glanced at him to make sure he was OK. He was blissfully ignorant, busy trying to get kernels of rice from his tray into his mouth with his chubby little fingers. Sophia, her three-year-old daughter, had finished her lunch moments before. The familiar sound of her footsteps skipping down the hallway upstairs echoed softly against the walls and floors, giving away her location as she headed to play with toys in her room.

Jin Sook hesitated. She could tell he wasn't ready for so many questions right off the bat, and she'd thrown him off his prepared script. "Ah, I called to say there is a problem," he said gingerly. He was inexperienced in the ways of the world, sheltered by hovering parents. A great Tae Kwon Do coach, Jin Sook lacked the interpersonal skills required to build a successful gym, or Do Jang, the way JT had. He was, however, exceedingly proud and grateful for the opportunity to work with her husband, a renowned champion. "Our flight has been delayed. There is a problem at the airport. The police have to investigate."

Jin Sook was being careful with his words. Stephanie knew that. She also heard cars honking and people clamoring in the background. An announcement blared loud enough for her to hear. It said it was now safe to re-enter the terminal. She scurried around the corner of the kitchen counter into the family room and lunged at the remote on the end table next to the couch. Her hands were already shaking. She gripped the remote tightly, knowing she would drop it otherwise, as she switched on the TV and found one of the morning news channels. "Is it serious, Jin Sook? Are you in danger? Where is Jeong Tae? Why didn't he call me?"

Again, Jin Sook hesitated. "There is no danger. Everyone is OK. Our flight was delayed while the police checked out a hoax." Ordinarily, Stephanie thought Jin Sook's careful cadence was adorable. Right now, she wanted information and his obvious caution was hindering that.

"Where's JT? Why hasn't he called me?"

"Mr. Noh had to leave," he said. "He told me he was attending to something very important and he didn't know how long it would take."

She tried to make sense of what he was saying, but it didn't compute. Something about his tone gave away his angst. He was unhappy but was trying to hide it with a forced calmness in his voice. Besides, there was nothing more important to JT than those kids and the world championship in Seoul. It was all he talked about for the past two months. "What do you mean he had something *more important* to attend to? What could possibly be more important to him than getting those kids on that plane for the World Championship?"

Jin Sook hesitated before responding. "I don't know what to say. He told me that something came up, but he didn't explain in detail, only that he would call later. He said, 'Don't worry, it will be OK.'"

Stephanie looked up at the ceiling trying to work out the meaning—not of the words, but the implications of what Jin Sook was saying. "When will we know something more?"

Jin Sook sucked in air through his teeth. "Honestly, I don't know. Our conversation was very short, but he promised me that he is OK and that he will call as soon as he can." Jin Sook paused. "They just announced that our flight is boarding. The students are anxious. I need to be with them and keep them calm. Can I text you from the plane?"

"Of course," she said, and ended the call. She turned up the volume on the TV and flipped through the channels until she found one reporting from LAX. At the same time, she speed-dialed her husband's number. As expected, it went straight to voice mail. She hung up and gave the story on the news her full attention. The reporter, a dashing young man with perfectly combed hair and a stylish zip-up jacket displaying the station's logo, stood in front of the Tom Bradley International terminal at Los Angeles International Airport with crowds of people, mainly foreigners, tussling and moving about behind him.

". . . for nearly two hours. The police are being tight-lipped so far, but the indication from the passengers in the terminal was that someone had gotten past security and approached the underside of a plane as the luggage was being loaded into the plane's cargo hold. We don't know the details or why the airport has been closed to all arrivals and departures since roughly 10:30, but one man tells me he saw something unusual." The reporter paused while the camera zoomed out to a young Asian man wearing a UCLA sweatshirt. "Can you tell us what you saw?" asked the reporter.

"Yeah, it was weird," said the young man. "Two men, Asian dudes, wearing hoodies and gloves, opened this door that I didn't even know was there, behind one of the food places there near the waiting area, you know. Then another guy, he was Asian, too—probably Korean, like me—followed them like a minute later."

The earnest reporter continued retrieving any salient information from the younger man. "Did you see anything else?"

"Well, there are windows, you know, over to the side, that look out at the planes all lined up there. I went over there to see what was going on, you know. But it was really foggy. Plus, the view is really limited. It was hard to see anything. But after a while, a bunch of cop cars came racing up with their lights on, so I watched for a long time to see what was happening. Then I heard the security announcement over the loudspeakers in the terminal telling us all to exit the building and go to the curb, but I stayed until the security guys came and made us leave."

"Before you left, what did you see out there by the plane?" the reporter urged.

"I couldn't see much with the fog. Just a group of people moving around, you know. Then the cop car took off again with its lights going."

"What did the third man who entered that hallway look like?"

"I don't really know. I didn't see his face, just his Dodger's jacket. But I think I saw the cops put him in the cop car."

The camera shot tightened, showing only the reporter as the witness stepped away. "As you can see, we don't have the details of who was arrested or what exactly happened, only that three men were able to gain access to the loading area of the plane, causing airport officials to lock down the runways and evacuate the International terminal while they evaluate this potential threat. After confirming with airport authorities, we do know that one man has been placed under arrest and that the apparent threat, whatever it might have been, has passed. One airport official told me moments ago that the 'All Clear' has gone out and they will return to normal operations just as quickly as possible. We will bring you more information as this story unfolds. Reporting live from LAX . . ."

Stephanie switched the TV off and let out a deep sigh. JT was involved, she knew from the eyewitness description. A Korean guy wearing a Dodger's jacket, while not that uncommon, fit him. To satisfy her curiosity, she dashed up the stairs and checked his side of the closet. Yep, his Dodger's jacket was gone.

Her insides started to sink as the implications and complications began to manifest themselves. Had he gotten himself into trouble? Not likely. Had he tried to stop something he thought was not proper? Quite possible. After five years of marriage, she knew his sense of duty would never allow him to let something untoward go unnoticed.

What would this mean for her and their family? How long until she could talk to him and sort out what was going on?

Matthew started squawking as she reentered the kitchen. What remained of his lunch was now spread all over the tray, on his hands, in his hair, and on the floor. She had to push the big question mark about Jeong Tae out of her mind and take care of the kids. After taking them to her mom, she would walk to the office behind the house and ask her dad for his advice. He would know what to do.

As she washed Matthew's face at the kitchen sink, she thought about the hurt look on JT's face when she confronted him again that morning about not taking her and the kids with him to Korea. "If you're still too ashamed of me to be seen together in your hometown, fine. We don't have to go anywhere near your family or friends. I would just like to check out the places you liked growing up."

"It's not that," JT said.

"Then what?"

"We can't afford it," he muttered.

"We have the money. You're just making excuses."

"Maybe we do, but we need to be careful. You never know what could happen. The business isn't growing like we need it to."

"Then work harder," she said, a stern rebuke in her voice.

"I've tried." His tone was softer, and he wouldn't look her in the eye. "It's no use."

"Then advertise or go to the schools to recruit like you used to do. Ask the other merchants in town for referrals. Just do more marketing."

JT shook his head and looked at the floor. "I don't know how much longer I can keep this up." The look of dejection and uncertainty had given Stephanie pause, but she was too disappointed to try to pull the truth out of her husband. He was upset and in a hurry. It was not a good time to have the difficult conversation they needed to have. "I've got to go. The shuttle guy will be at the Do Jang soon."

"Wait and I'll drive you down."

"No time for that." He checked his phone. "An Uber will be here in less than a minute."

With that, he had walked out the door, hanging his head. She knew she had bruised his pride.

Matthew put his arms up in the air and tried to squirm free, bringing her back to the present. Stephanie finished drying his hands and face, then set him down to walk. She had been a jerk to her husband, and she felt sorry. She knew JT needed her help now. She knew it was him who'd gone into that doorway and been put in the cop car, but she had no idea what kind of trouble he was in. The only thing she knew was that her children's father could not go to prison. They could not afford the cost of an attorney, nor the damage to his reputation and standing in the community. Something like this could ruin them and their business and everything he had built. There had to be a way to fix this situation quickly and quietly.

She hated to do it, but Stephanie Noh could think of only one option to solve what would likely be a complex legal problem with potential federal charges. JT wouldn't like it. That much she knew, but she also knew her idea would be supremely effective in getting him out of whatever mess he had gotten himself into. She pulled her cell phone out of her pocket and opened up her contacts, searching for the right number.

Chapter 6

Los Angeles International Airport
June 6, 12:42 p.m.

Two uniformed officers stood at the entrance to my cell and ordered me to stand and place my hands through the slot in the bars. I did, and the second officer clamped cuffs on them. I stepped back, the door slid open, and the three of us marched single file down the hall, with me in the middle.

I was escorted into an interrogation room within the airport police station. It was not so different from other interrogation rooms I had been in. Except for one other time, I wasn't the one being interrogated before. Plus, this was a new country and it would be in my second language, so this was a new experience.

The guard who had cuffed my hands led me by the elbow around a scuffed up wooden table with dark mottled stains on its surface. As in most interrogation rooms, a mirrored window dominated the wall to my right. The room behind it was probably filled with people and video recording equipment. They were most likely watching my every move, looking for signs, clues, anything that would tell them what they wanted to know about me.

Despite the scrutiny, I imposed calm on my countenance. I knew everything about the process was designed to instill fear, or at least, uneasiness. The accused should feel hopeless and helpless, to the point of despair, unless they chose to cooperate. That was always the golden carrot dangled before the desperate and discouraged: cooperation.

Despite knowing this, desperation was beginning to creep in. When you believe a bomb has been planted on a plane and no one is taking you seriously, it's natural to start feeling anxious and desperate.

As I entered the room, I contemplated the role reversal. It wasn't so many years ago that I was on the other side. Therefore, I was able to anticipate every move and comprehend the purpose behind each element of my surroundings and the theatrics that would soon play out.

I felt an urgency to hurry the process along but knew I had to let things work their way out in the prescribed manner. Any deviation would ruin my credibility and place me at a disadvantage. I didn't want that. The passengers on that plane needed me to be strong. Maintaining *kibun* would be vital to gaining a positive outcome. There is no direct translation for the concept of *kibun*. The closest description is "face" or "dignity" or "pride." I had to keep up a certain appearance, a certain mystique, until they realized that I was an asset, not a liability.

While this wasn't the first time I had been on the wrong side of an interrogation, I vowed to myself that I would use the lessons I learned last time and create the necessary result. Words, gestures, body language, and confidence would need to combine in just the right way to earn my freedom and gain the cooperation needed to save hundreds of lives.

Walking to my appointed chair, the one bolted to the bare concrete floor, I focused on my facial expressions and my breathing. I wanted to radiate calm. No reason I shouldn't be at peace. I hadn't done anything wrong. I drew in a deep breath and followed it with a long, patient exhale. No twitching. No movement. Koreans were good at the stone face thing. It was part of our culture, part of being a man in my home country. Of course, the hooded eyes probably helped me appear more nonchalant than I felt. I had learned to show my opponent nothing. Displaying emotions was a sign of weakness. And one should never show weakness in front of an adversary.

A long time passed. If my internal clock was still working as it should, I had been seated for thirty-five minutes. Following my training, I had mentally cocooned myself so as to shield my emotions and override physical discomfort. I was semi-catatonic.

Finally, I heard the clicking of shoes in the hallway and the turn of the knob, which woke me from my trance. A tall man in dark blue slacks, well-worn lace-up dress shoes, and a light blue shirt stepped in and closed the door behind him. I noticed his sleeves were rolled, top button undone, and his red-striped tie had been loosened. His expression showed that it had already been a long day for him. "Director Alan Robinson from the Transportation Safety Administration," he said. He flashed a badge, then held me in his steely gaze as he walked slowly in a half circle to the far side of the chair opposite me, across the meter-wide table. He dropped a thick manila folder on the edge of the wooden slab, then stood back, staring.

Alan Robinson had thick dark brown hair with steel blue eyes and stood about six foot two. I would place him somewhere in his late thirties, maybe early forties. An athletic Caucasian with a dark complexion and large hands. A serious man with a stern face.

"Your file," he said, shooting a glance at it. "Impressive. We've learned a lot about you in the past hour." He kept looking at me, those steel eyes boring through me, like he expected that single statement to act as some kind of lever to pop open the can. Maybe he was expecting the contents to come spilling out spontaneously. "Four years at the American High School in Seoul. Graduated top of your class. Graduated from Yeonsei University, one of Korea's top schools, again with Honors, in just three years, while simultaneously going through special forces training. Eight years of distinguished service in an elite border patrol unit, the last three of which you were the commander of said unit. Promoted at the earliest possible opportunity in every case. Stellar marks all around—education, leadership, physical fitness, IQ tests, language capability, marksmanship, martial arts master, proven combat skills, medals for valor, sacrifice, and merit. Did I leave anything out?"

I gave a slight shake of my head without looking up.

I wanted to mention that my colleagues and superiors always said I had more *noonchi* than anyone else they knew. *Noonchi* is the ability to read people by listening to them and watching their movements so you can discern their moods. I was good at it, but I kept that to myself.

Robinson continued. "Plus, it looks like you worked closely with American troops in several capacities during that time. So, I assume you don't need an interpreter. That seems pretty obvious." He waited for me to acknowledge, which I did with a slight head movement. "Anything you'd like to tell me?"

"Beyond what I told the LAPD Interrogators?" I asked.

"Yeah. Any points you want to elaborate on? Any details you may have forgotten to share?"

I gave him a similar once-over. I thought about asking for a lawyer but decided to find out what Director Robinson had in mind first, see how things went before adding a new dimension that would cause delays. I wanted to use what time we had to save the people on that plane, not to protect my legal rights. These guys wanted information, not an arrest. Robinson and the others whose job it was to keep their airport safe had at least as much to lose as I did. They needed to get their collective heads around this problem, and fast. I needed the same thing. Asking for a lawyer would slow things down, further complicating an already complicated situation. Cooperation would likely be the best strategy, but I didn't want to play my best card first. I decided to ask the question just to see his reaction. "Will I need legal representation?" I asked in the humblest tone I could conjure.

Alan's face softened. "No, Mr. Noh. No need for a lawyer."

"But you have me in handcuffs. That must mean you intend to indict me." When I spoke English, I could still detect an accent. Some of my consonants still sounded harder than when Americans use them. Same with the "oh" and "ah" sounds. Too harsh to be considered a native speaker, but not too far off. Twelve years of studying English in primary and high school, plus evenings and weekends with tutors, eight years working closely with American soldiers, and six years in this country had helped with my pronunciation and usage. It needed more work still. I noticed it more than ever in this setting.

I pondered the fact that the cops had not found the two bodies I'd left behind the food service truck. Where had they gone? This left me with very little in terms of evidence that things had gone down the way I had explained them.

No surprise that the police also did not have any video footage of the two weird guys and me in the food-service hallway. Chances were good that whoever was behind all this had hijacked the airport security cameras and now had my image on their drive somewhere. That could only spell trouble. I was a known quantity on both sides of Korea's Demilitarized Zone.

Robinson's eyebrows shot up like he hadn't realized I was cuffed. "Tell me what I want to know, and I'll consider removing the cuffs."

That got me thinking and strategizing my best move. Humility. That was the card to play right now. Asians were good at humility, better than Americans. They knew how to use it to their advantage when the situation demanded it. "I've told the policemen who interviewed me everything they wanted to know. I am happy to cooperate."

Robinson stared hard. "They tell me you explained to them why you were in that hallway and why you trespassed on government property. They also reported that you entered the cargo bay of an airplane saying there was a bomb on board. Is there anything you forgot to mention in your answers to them?" He stepped back and waited.

I remained expressionless. "I never once used the word 'bomb.' I said they needed to check the bag I saw those two men take down that hallway. They looked suspicious to me and that bag seemed very heavy. When I saw one of them lift it—with some difficulty, I might add—onto the conveyor belt loader, I tried to stop it from getting on that plane."

I then rehearsed for Robinson—and the people behind the mirror—the whole incident, from beginning to end. Every detail, every nuance. My thoughts, my observations, my motivations. I told them I felt confident, based on years of experience, that the two men I had taken down were from North Korea. I told them I was quite sure there was something harmful in that bag and that we needed to ground the airplane and do a more thorough search.

"It's too late to ground the plane, I'm afraid. It departed fifteen minutes ago—after a complete rescreen of every bag in that cargo area. We also sent in bomb-sniffing dogs. We found nothing. Not even a trace of residue."

My stomach sank at those words. Dread crept into every muscle of my body and my head drooped until my chin met my chest. I had failed my students and everyone onboard that aircraft.

Chapter 7

Seoul, Korea

June 6, 6:11 a.m. Local Time; 1:11 p.m. on June 5, Pacific Daylight Time

President Jang Ho Shin rose as the General entered the room. Once rivals vying for their party's nomination to the office which Jang now held, the two had developed a mutual respect and working relationship. Shortly after taking office four years earlier, President Jang asked the General to be Chief of Staff of the Republic of Korea Army, a job for which he was well suited. The General was a trusted military advisor and planned to run for the presidency in the general elections in one year's time. Since 1988, the President of Korea was only allowed to serve for one five-year term. The General had been forced by Party officials to bow out of the previous race during the exploratory phase of candidacy due to a scandal involving his son.

"Good to see you this morning, General." President Jang, gracious and polite as ever, bowed slightly at the hips and held out a hand. "You're up early, as usual, I see."

"Yes, sir," said the General, clasping the outstretched hand with both of his, bowing slightly deeper than the President. As he rose and pulled back his hand, he added, "This is normally my favorite time of the day. I enjoy the calm of the morning and the stillness prior to sunrise. Thank you for agreeing to meet me at this early hour. I trust you have eaten this morning?"

President Jang smiled. He, too, was a morning person. His reputation for working long hours matched the General's. Early morning meetings were not unheard of between the two of them, but this morning's arrangement was hastily made. "Is all well with you, General?"

The General cocked his head and sucked in a breath. "Well, sir, that's what I had hoped we could discuss."

"What's troubling you?"

The General spoke in halting words, exercising caution. Unsure of whether to share the communication he had received from the National Intelligence Service Director, General Noh treaded carefully. "We have a situation that has both national security and personal implications, sir. It needs to be handled swiftly and quietly, but not necessarily in secret. For the sake of the public, it is best if we contain the information to as few people as possible. However, I know because of the personal implications, that doing so will create the illusion of a cover-up. I am being forthright with you, sir, because I trust you will understand the gravity of the situation."

President Jang furrowed his brow. "Please explain."

The General told the President everything he knew, but did not disclose his source, nor did President Jang ask. The General would have been embarrassed to explain the phone call his wife had received.

The President clucked his tongue against the back of his front teeth to signal his understanding of the delicate situation. "I trust you have been successful in making contact with your son."

"Not directly, sir. However, my office relayed all of the information in his file, as requested by the Americans."

"Do they have someone who can read it, General?"

"Perhaps they do, but we sent the English translation just to be sure. We always have both English and Korean files for soldiers who interact with the Armed Forces here in-country."

"That is good. Time is of the essence, I'm sure."

"Yes, sir, especially if what my son told the TSA is to be believed."

President Jang's eyes widened. "Is that even possible? I mean, after what happened before, it seems it would be difficult to believe his story, based on his prior record. Surely they have read his file and know of the incident in question."

General Noh Tae Sung lowered his head, averting his gaze to the ground rather than allowing his President to see the anger and disappointment in his eyes. His jaw muscles flexed involuntarily as he stifled the rising emotions within. "Mr. President, sir, my son is an honorable man. I am sure there's an explanation behind his being inside the cargo hold of that airplane. The transcripts from his interview indicate that there was suspicious behavior that warranted him following through. As for his prior incident, I have my regrets in regard to what happened that night and how I handled the aftermath, but that is a discussion for another day."

"Yes, I suppose it is. I heard about his arrest just before you arrived. My assistant alerted me after they received a call from the TSA. Your son still carries his Diplomatic Corps ID and the Americans wanted to be sure we knew they were treating him with the utmost respect." President Jang paused, tapping his desk with all five fingertips of his right hand as he stood next to it. He watched his own hand moving up and down. His cadence matched the movement of his hand. "It's a very unfortunate situation we have here. Unfortunate for him that nothing was found onboard. Unfortunate for you that you are once again dragged into a highly sensitive security situation. I assume that is why you requested this meeting."

"Indeed, it is, Sir." General Noh took a deep breath and held it for a beat. Despite their amicable working relationship, he sensed Jang, a career politician, was posturing. Since there was nothing left for him to accomplish in the political realms of South Korea, the General assumed force of habit caused Jang to always exert the upper hand. He ignored it. "As I said before, I believe what my son told the Americans. He would have no reason to breach a secured area otherwise. He is too smart for that. He knows right from wrong; legal from illegal; suspicious from strange. He knows civilians like himself cannot be in the baggage loading areas. Only the strongest premonition would cause him to do such a thing. If his premonition was that strong, I must trust his instincts and offer whatever support we can offer ... using the proper channels, of course."

President Jang scratched his chin. "Of course. But proper channels may not be enough. We should consider asking for diplomatic immunity."

General Noh bowed his head and nodded. "Yes, I think you're right. I was hoping not to use his diplomatic status because that can lead to some very bad press if the media were to learn of it. All I know, sir, is that I cannot leave my son without support. Not again."

"Something like this could have very damaging effects on your status as the leading presidential candidate at the next election."

"I realize that, but it's a chance I must take. I believe the damage to my relationship with my son last time has been far more devastating to me than having to relinquish my candidacy. I cannot stand by idly watching this time. I must do something, anything, to help him. I know his heart. It is in the right place. He is not a criminal, nor is he in league with any terrorists."

"You are an honorable man, General Noh. If this gets out, the press and—therefore, the public—will not see things the way you do. I believe your son is innocent of wrongdoing, but without all the facts, his actions could be branded as rash and even foolish. But if we do this and ask for this favor, the press could eat you alive. Are you willing to put aside your aspirations to run for the presidency for the sake of your son who has already shamed you once before?"

"With all due respect to you and the office you hold, my son is ultimately more important to me than the office I seek."

President Jang considered the General for a long moment, nodding in appreciation. "Very well, my friend. I will contact my counterpart personally and make a request. I'm sure we can arrange something with our ally."

Chapter 8

Interrogation Room, Los Angeles Airport Police Station
June 6, 1:24 p.m.

I was struggling to keep my cool while worrying about my wife, my children, and especially about my students aboard that doomed plane. In my mind, there were too many question marks about that plain-Jane black roller bag. I couldn't help but think that we were wasting time repeating the same questions and the same answers. I didn't care that their scanners didn't pick up on any explosive material residues. I know plastique, also known as C4, could be handled in such a way that it was nearly impossible to trace.

Thinking it through, I was convinced that the three men I had encountered were North Koreans. The few words I had heard them speak clued me in. My opinion of the North Koreans and their abilities and determination rose sharply. They must have been committed with a full team in place to pull this off. I just wished that I could get someone to believe me. So far, nothing I said seemed to influence anyone's opinion. These American cops must have thought I was nothing more than some crazy Asian chasing an imaginary enemy.

The only things that had changed in the past hour and a half while I sat in this chair were that the plane, and all other flights coming and going at LAX, had been cleared for take-off and landing. Airport operations were trying to get back to normal. Robinson had said that the Korean airlines flight I should have been on was underway. I prayed that the mysterious bag, which was not in the rack where I had seen the third guy put it when I pointed to it for the arresting officers, was not onboard.

The longer this questioning lasted, the frailer my story became. The constant haranguing from the interrogators had managed to plant a tiny seed of doubt in my own mind. I began wondering if maybe I *was* crazy. Were my suspicions about two random people completely unfounded? Had my longings to return to my days on duty overcome my sense of rationality?

I sensed that that was the sentiment among the American authorities. Because nothing unusual or suspicious was found in any of the bags onboard the Korean Air Line 747, and because the dogs didn't smell anything, I was now treated as a veritable nut case.

To further solidify this fact in the cops' minds, no bodies had been found. How could that be? I left them right where they fell, and they were far from ambulatory. I was pretty sure I hadn't dreamed up the confrontation. But, without proof, who would believe me? It was apparent that no one had seen anything, either. I was completely out on a limb, alone and defenseless.

Again, my assessment of the North Koreans ratcheted up. Their team was more committed and more focused on details than I would have ever guessed possible.

During our conversation, I said to Robinson, "Check your security camera footage. I'm sure you'll see something that will corroborate my story."

"No such footage," said Robinson.

"Isn't that strange to you? Your footage doesn't even show me in a secured area?"

Robinson had thought about that for a moment, then left the room.

When he returned, he simply said. "We're looking further into that."

It was time for me to assert myself. I knew I had to be subtle, yet persuasive. "You found the tape on the door I went through, just as I had said, right?"

Robinson nodded.

"I could not have entered that door otherwise, right?"

He nodded again.

"There's a camera in that hallway, right?"

"I see where you're going with this, Mr. Noh," he said. "But it doesn't explain why we didn't find anything the way you describe. No mysterious, overweight bag. No bodies laid out on the concrete. No blood, even. Not even an Asian baggage handler matching the description you gave on duty this morning."

"No? Did you ask the other baggage handlers who were with me in the cargo hold? One of them must have seen the guy."

Robinson shook his head. "That's the only thing you've got going for you so far. Two of them say they saw an Asian guy. But they all said they knew him. A Mr. Lee, they said. He's their supervisor. Nothing unusual about him being in or around the aircraft."

"OK. That's a starting point. There are cameras in the baggage loading area. I saw them myself. You should have footage showing me climbing up the loader," I said. "Should be easy to determine it was tampered with if I never appear on your security video. Your guys will just have to look for an anomaly. It should all fit in the timeline."

"They're working on it now."

"And there's no blood on the tarmac?" I asked. "No sign of a stain?"

"We've got someone looking into that, too," he said, waving an arm at the space between us, as if slapping away the very idea.

"If I'm right, doesn't it look to an orchestrated mission with some serious resources? They have covered their tracks thoroughly."

"Yes, they have," Robinson agreed. "And that's a problem for you."

"And those passengers. Four hundred of them. The longer you keep me here telling you the same story over and over, the less time we have to save lives and figure out what is really going on here. Agreed?"

"We? Let me remind you, Mr. Noh, that you are being detained on suspicion of terrorist activity on a passenger aircraft."

I didn't flinch. "Let me remind you that there are four hundred lives on the line, and I have the experience, knowledge, and skills to help you evaluate the situation and act on that evaluation better than anyone else you're going to find. Anywhere. Look at my file again if you don't believe me."

Robinson just stared, didn't say a word for a long time.

Neither did I. If I were to speak first, I would lose. I knew that. He probably did, too.

The stand-off ended when the Korean lieutenant burst into the room. "Director Robinson, sir, I've got something for you."

Robinson turned his gaze to the lieutenant and huffed. He slammed the door shut behind him and left me to my thoughts, which were jumbled. *Deep breaths*, I told myself. *Control the facial expressions.* I had to avoid unwanted scrutinizing from those who watched me from behind the glass. If something went wrong, I knew they would analyze the video footage of me to bolster their claim of my guilt.

When he returned three minutes later, consternation mixed with defeat enveloped Robinson's face. He paced in a full circle between the door to the mirrored wall, stopping at the chair opposite me without saying a word. At length, he repeatedly jabbed the manila file folder still sitting unopened on the corner of the table with his long, thick index finger but didn't say anything for a full minute. Then he said, "We need to talk."

Chapter 9

Southbound Interstate 405, Garden Grove, California
June 6, 1:37 p.m.

Traffic was snarled. Typical and to be expected in the metropolitan Los Angeles area, especially on this freeway. It seemed that nothing could go right today. Not since that South Korean soldier had showed up.

Crawling down the 405 Freeway slower than he could walk was not helping Kim Yong Byun's rising anxiety. It only exacerbated the sense of doom that was closing in around him. The morning started out fine. Everything was going according to plan until that guy in the blue jacket showed up. It took some fast thinking and brave actions by one of Yong Byun's teammates to salvage a yet-uncertain victory. Only time would tell if that teammate had successfully reinserted the explosives on the plane. Either way, Yong Byun knew his future was in jeopardy.

The more he thought through the problem, the more he realized he was doomed regardless of the outcome of the overall mission. He had not pulled off his part flawlessly and undetected, as the Council demanded. There would be hell to pay—but only if they could find him.

After months of painstaking planning to "line up the dominoes," as the leader of the planning council had called it, "*Chammae Boksu*," the name of the mission now in question, was the North Korean dictator's pet covert project. Chammae referred to the Northern Goshawk, the national bird of North Korea. Part of the raptor family, it was known as a fierce and resourceful hunter and revered in Korean culture and history as a symbol of strength. Boksu meant revenge. Thus, the Americans would start calling it "Raptor's Revenge."

Officially, the Supreme Leader had no knowledge of this mission. Plausible deniability on his part had been fastidiously built into every facet of the mission. But in reality, everyone involved knew it was his brainchild. They also knew that anything short of flawless execution could only end in another sort of execution—one that no one would ever find out about unless Yong Byun's bones were dug up in some remote desert decades from now.

Inside, his emotions were like a witch's potion brewed from all manner of toxic components. His nerves were so raw that he couldn't discern what he was experiencing, other than dread.

At first, it was panic. When that South Korean army man with the Dodger's jacket showed up, Yong Byun's whole world felt like it had imploded. He saw the guy running up the conveyor belt and into the belly of the plane. Who does that? And why? The guy came out of nowhere, demanding the very bag Yong Byun had just personally carried to the back of a nearly full rack. He had just hefted the fifty-kilogram suitcase into place when his fellow baggage handlers stepped in the way, blocking the wild man's approach. Yong Byun had used the ensuing confusion as cover so he could pull the bag and sneak toward the open cargo door. No one could ever see the contents of that case. He had to remove it unnoticed and the confusion brought on by the group of his fellow workers provided just the cover he needed.

The three packets disguised as portable computer battery chargers inside the black case each weighed sixteen kilos and held enough C-4 plastic explosive material to blow the plane into oblivion and, if the projections were correct, inflict significant damage when it exploded over Seoul. The blast radius was calculated to be over three hundred meters. The flying debris from the fuselage would add several hundred more meters as flying shards became deadly shrapnel.

But that now depended on his team member finding a way to stow that bag on the plane.

Yong Byun escaped the cargo area during the confrontation, dragging the heavy roller onto a scissor lift and lowering himself and the bag to the ground.

But his escape wasn't entirely clean. While four of his colleagues were yelling at the intruder and preventing him from getting his unauthorized hands on any passenger luggage, which could cost them all their jobs, Yong Byun caught the attention of the Korean guy in the Dodger's jacket. He was just stacking the bag into place when they locked eyes. That's when he realized he knew who the man was. Yong Byun wondered if the intruder recognized him. No matter. Yong Byun planned to never see the son of General Noh ever again.

Before his narrow escape, Yong Byun had overheard the man explain to the other baggage handlers that he had knocked down two men, whom he identified as North Koreans, near the left wing. Hearing that made his heart drop. The General's son had interfered and severely altered the plan. Each member of the team had specific assignments and if two of them were sidelined, the plan would surely fail. That was when Yong Byun realized his survival was at risk. He decided then that he would give his best effort to the cause regardless, but if he could not find a way to bring down that plane as directed by the council, he would abandon all and save his own life.

Darting out of the plane, Yong Byun had found a pick-up truck that lacked a driver near the baggage cart tractor. He hefted the loaded suitcase into the back and surveyed the area for witnesses. Seeing none, he climbed in behind the wheel, relieved to see keys in the ignition. As he started the truck's engine, he spoke into to the top button of his coat. "Mission compromised. Initiate counter measures and move to alternate stage. Repeat: Abort mission."

Each member of the team had instructions known only to them on what to do if something went wrong before the mission plan was completed. But he already knew that he had to revert to a self-preserving strategy, one he had devised just in case things didn't work out. As the leader of a failed portion of the overall mission, there was no hope of survival if he followed the prescribed pullout drill. A return home meant shame, humiliation, and punishment. Although he had been tediously trained and indoctrinated; had professed his fervent devotion to the cause and pledged to do all in his power to make it successful, nagging doubts had crept in, forcing him to think about his own best interests—in the event he or his team failed.

His time in America had opened his eyes to new possibilities for his life. A newfound hope had sprung up inside and survival instincts had edged into the space where the desire to kill the enemy had resided. Over the past several weeks, as the final pieces of the mission came together, Yong Byun had experienced pessimism about its success, which blossomed into full-blown fear for the first time since he volunteered for it. There were too many variables and too many unknowns and the grand council was pushing too hard to make it happen on June 6, the South Korean Memorial Day. Contingencies had begun to manifest themselves, making him realize that each step in the plan was lined up just so. If all went right, no problems. But it would only take one misstep and things would collapse like a row of dominoes. That one misstep had occurred with the unexpected appearance of General Noh's son. Now, if Yong Byun was going to survive past the end of the week, which he wanted to do more than ever, he realized he had to devise a strategy to save his life in the event he could not return home a glorified hero.

"Raven, this is Eagle. Raven, this is Eagle. Do you copy?" Yong Byun heard the words through the comm unit in his ear.

"Copy Eagle. This is Raven."

"Confirming two Comrades down under the port side wing. Evacuate them immediately. Repeat: evacuate downed Comrades immediately."

"Roger. On my way."

Yong Byun's heart sank, the last rays of hope obscured by a new kind of fog. If two of his men were down and unable to escape on their own, let alone function according to plan, the mission was surely destined for disaster. This knowledge only fueled the growing desire to break away on his own and start a new life. But he couldn't just abandon his teammates. It would hurt his chances of escape. The gears in his head spun and caught and began to churn out new ideas even under the pressure from his collapsing mission imperatives.

Yong Byun threw the truck's gear lever into "Drive" and maneuvered toward the underside of the left wing. His blood ran cold, and his hands shook as he realized everything he had worked for was unraveling and he would soon have to launch himself into unchartered territory.

There must be a chance to score a victory for the homeland, he thought as he drove the truck toward his fallen Comrades. Maybe, just maybe, they could make something work. Maybe he could salvage this thing and return home with honor despite the setback. He tried to keep hope alive in those few seconds.

As he steered the truck around the tail of the plane, Yong Byun's heart dropped. His two incapacitated teammates lay on the ground, a pool of dark blood under the smaller guy's head. He knew that wasn't a good sign. But Un-Chul, the big guy, was struggling to get up. He was in a bad way when Yong Byun arrived on the scene, but at least he was moving. He cradled his right arm with his left hand, pinning it against his body as he knelt with his forehead against the pavement, struggling to breathe. When Yong Byun helped him to his feet, the man hissed and grunted in agony. All the while Jung Min was motionless, spread eagle on his back.

Un-Chul was no help to him as he wrestled the smaller man's frame into a position where he could get a better grip on him. Moving and lifting the dead weight of the unconscious man was difficult, but years of rigorous training had made him strong and the surge of adrenaline did the rest. By the time he had maneuvered the inert body into the bed of the truck, the big guy had scooted his hind end onto the tailgate, a grimace of pain etched on his pale countenance. With significant aide from Yong Byun, he was able to get his legs and torso into the back of the truck. After pushing Jung Min's legs to the side, Yong Byun covered them with a tarp.

Before leaving the scene, Yong Byun pulled a large orange water jug from its rack in the truck's bed and poured its contents on the spreading pool of blood. A broom in the truck bed helped him scrub the stain and spread the water around, dissipating the colored liquid across the dark grey concrete. No sooner had he closed the tailgate, then the Airport police came rushing past with their red and blue lights flashing through the fog.

Yong Byun hopped in the driver's seat and smashed the gear shift into drive. With forced calm, he resisted the urge to tromp on the accelerator and race out of there. Instead, he let his foot off the brake and eased the truck slowly toward the next plane to the north. Checking for any signs that he was being followed and, seeing none, he continued around the tail-end of that plane and toward the next. Following that pattern until he was at the northern end of the International terminal, Yong Byun had successfully navigated to a vehicle access road just south of the northern-most runways. Lights from other trucks and delivery vehicles moved about all around him in an eerie, loosely orchestrated mechanical ballet.

Un-Chul, the big guy, spoke through the com unit in Yong Byun's ear. His voice was raspy and shallow. "Is the package secure?"

"No It is in the back of the truck with you."

"Is it armed?"

Yong Byun's insides knotted. "No. I had to get out of there. I took the bag with me so it wouldn't be discovered."

Un-Chul spoke with great effort. "Our mission cannot reach its glorious destiny if we do not arm the devices and load them onto that plane. Let me out here and I will complete the mission."

"How will you do that? You only have use of one arm."

Through a series of halting breaths and strained whisperings, he protested. "That is none of your concern. Leave it to me. I know what to do."

"I can't leave an injured Comrade behind. Too risky."

A pained cough through his earpiece was followed by, "You must. I have planned for this possibility. I know what to do."

"You are severely injured," said Yong Byun. "I will go and complete the task."

"No, I can manage with just one good arm. It must be done. There is no other choice," Un-Chul hissed through gritted teeth, the pain obvious with each syllable. "You must report to the council. Now, go with honor."

"We cannot leave a trail for them to follow."

"Don't worry. I won't. And you mustn't either. Dispose of Jung Min and disappear, as planned. I will likewise disappear when my role is completed."

Yong Byun didn't reply, the gears inside his head spinning but not catching.

Un-Chul continued. "There will be no rendezvous. Trust me. I will finish the job and leave no trace."

Chapter 10

Interrogation Room, Los Angeles Airport Police Station
June 6, 1:55 p.m.

Robinson had disappeared. He'd been gone for ten minutes. No doubt he was conferring with the others behind the glass, trying to figure out how to best apply whatever leverage they felt they had on me for some purpose I could only imagine. I was beginning to feel this situation tilting out of control. It made me uncomfortable. That and the hard, wooden chair I'd been cuffed to for the past two hours.

This was all part of the ploy. Interrogation protocol was designed to inflict fear, doubt, regret, and impatience. Make the subject so eager to get out of that room that he'll say anything and give up any advantage he may have had going in. Not me. I wasn't about to fall for it. I knew better, having been on the other side of the table so many times before.

Patience and experience would work to my advantage. After all, the ticks on the clock were working harder against the Department of Homeland Security than against me. I didn't have to answer questions to the media or to Congress as to why the airport had been shut down for two hours or why all the bags on that 747 had to be re-scanned.

And if catastrophe struck, at least I would be able to say that I tried my best. I also wouldn't be the one to blame if and when that plane blew up and killed all those people. Yes, I would be devastated by the loss of those I cared about, but I wouldn't be answering to an outraged public for not taking the threat more seriously.

This salient fact was my main bargaining chip and I planned to use it appropriately.

The thought of the grim possibility I had potentially uncovered made my stomach turn. There were twenty-one people on that plane I cared for, that were my responsibility. It brought me full circle, back to where I started: If something happened to them, I'd never forgive myself for not doing everything I possibly could. My best had to be better. I had to save that plane.

A groan worked its way to the surface, but I prevented it from escaping. I needed to get out of there. I needed to find that baggage handler—the one that recognized me in the plane. My innate *noonchi* told me by the look in his eyes that he was up to no good and that he was scared of what I might do. It also told me he had information. At this point, that is what I needed most. That and more time.

Flight time between Los Angeles and Seoul was about thirteen and a half hours. I also knew that there would be enough fuel to last another three hours. So, it felt to me like an hourglass had been turned over with sixteen hours' worth of sand in it.

The thought unnerved me, but I was careful not to let my expression change.

A few more precious minutes ticked by before Robinson sauntered back into the room, a trace of benevolence mixed with condescension on his face. It was all posturing. I knew it but doubted that Robinson knew that I knew it.

Whatever Robinson had learned during his ten-minute absence would not be forthcoming. He'd bluster about how things were not looking good for me before he got around to the "big reveal."

As I listened, I had to suppress a smile. It was amusing to see someone do things that I had done to my prisoners in the past. Maybe these guys didn't know as much about me as Robinson had indicated earlier. My file was three inches thick, so I'm sure no one had had the time to read it all the way through or comprehend what it meant to be the youngest-ever commander of a border patrol unit along the DMZ. When you guard the boundary between a hostile Communist neighbor who employs the largest standing army in the world, your learning curve on the job is steep. If you survive, you are forever changed and forever wary.

Robinson had already shown his ignorance by supposing out loud that I had advanced because of my father's high rank. In reality, the opposite was true. I could have stayed in a normal unit and been promoted even faster had I chosen to ride my father's reputation and clout. But I had chosen the most difficult career path so as to avoid the very accusation which Robinson had hurled at me.

No one chose to serve on the DMZ, at least no one in their right mind. The unit had the highest death rate, although that was never publicized. Suicides were more common, though swept under the rug or blamed on the enemy. Combat was far more likely as skirmishes broke out frequently in the area between the fences when the testosterone-laden, highly trained, and fully armed soldiers that patrolled both sides of the four-kilometer-wide line that divided the once-united nation of Korea encountered each other. Most young men in Korea wanted to fulfill their mandatory time in the army somewhere far away from the DMZ, learn something that would be useful in their future careers, then get out as quickly as possible and go on with their lives as normal citizens.

I could have chosen that option. It was open to me. A life of relative ease and comfort. Had I chosen the easy route, my path to the top was all but paved. Honors, promotions, and accolades would surely have followed and all I would have had to do, really, is show up for work and do the job I knew how to do without thinking.

But that would have been too easy and would never have made me happy. I loved a good challenge. I loved the idea of gaining a reputation on my own. Building merit because of what I did, not because of what my father had done. Choosing the least desirable duty in the Korean military had been just the beginning.

Robinson looked somber, resolute. The act was almost convincing. I bit my tongue as he told me that he really wanted to help me, but only if I was able to help him first.

"Mr. Noh, you're in a world of trouble here. You know that, right?"

I squinted my eyes and held his gaze.

He paused and looked as if he was analyzing my reaction. "We can do this the hard way, or we can do this the easy way. Which is it going to be?"

I kept eye contact. "What's the hard way?"

Robinson shook his head as his eyes dropped to the file on the table. He waved my question aside with his hand. "The easy way is to describe for me the reasons you left a high post at the most prestigious unit of the Korean Army."

He glanced at me, but I kept my stone face going, so he continued. "The hard way is for me to read every word in this here file while you continue to sit in that chair with your hands cuffed behind your back."

I inhaled and held it. "It's not that easy. You probably wouldn't understand the situation with all the cultural nuances. It's very complicated."

Robinson's eyebrows rose with intrigue. "Try me."

I looked to the ceiling as I tried to decide how far back to go. Time was working against me—against us and the passengers on that plane—so I had to choose my words carefully while still giving him the complete story. Words were not my strong suit, even though my English fluency was very respectable.

"In high school," I started, "I was teased by the American kids about being a spoiled Army brat. My father was a public figure, a very high-ranking officer with an innate gift for public speaking. He was always a very visible and accessible leader. The news media loved him for it. In fact, in many ways he was the face and the voice of the Korean Army."

When I paused, Robinson cocked his head and said, "I'm listening. Go on."

"I decided at a young age that I wouldn't live my life in his shadow. I'd do things my way while maintaining the family name—the family pride, you know? I love my father and would never want to bring dishonor to him or to the rest of my family. That included not taking the easy way out and just going along with the safe assignments that would likely be offered. No. Instead I signed up for the border patrol as an enlisted man. A normal grunt."

"Why didn't you go to Officer Candidate School?"

"I didn't want any type of favoritism. When I was in high school, my father had been promoted to Lieutenant General and was handling press relations and liaison duties with the American Armed Forces stationed at various bases north of Seoul. He helped coordinate the training exercises as well as communicate with the Americans, the press, and the National Assembly.

"I was always intrigued by the stories he would tell us, when he could. Most of his stories, I found out later, were highly classified. But the stories he could tell us were all about the men who patrolled the DMZ and their great acts of valor and bravery. He would praise those men saying they represented the best of our country."

Robinson squinted at me. "So, you chose to go into one of those units to win his praise?"

"I guess you could say that. His and my friends' praise, both Korean and American. The Korean friends would all go on to do other things after the military. Some became doctors, many went into the high-tech field, some went into animation or game design or started small businesses. But in my family, the military is what you do. My father, my grandfather, and even his father, were all military officers. It was almost as if I had no choice, so I made the one choice I felt was open to me: I signed up for duty in the Lightning Brigade."

"They're the border guards, are they not?"

"Yes. They live in the most remote parts of the country, isolated in the mountains, patrolling the fences, and occasionally receiving and returning fire with the North Koreans."

"So, not the best conditions?"

"Not at all. It's very cold up there in the mountains during the winter and very hot and humid and swarming with mosquitoes in the summer. It's the most miserable place in our country. The gear we had to wear weighs over 22 kilos – that's 48 pounds of armor, weapons, ammunition, and supplies. We train in that gear sometimes eight hours a day, sometimes eight days in a row with no break while on field operations."

"I take it you wanted to prove that you're tough? That you're not some pampered son of a high-ranking officer?"

"I guess so. Mostly, I wanted to serve my country and bring honor to my family."

"Did you ever regret your decision?"

I paused. It was a loaded question. I could feel the eyes boring into me, both from Robinson and from the other side of the glass. My credibility rested on what I said next. "I had days where I questioned myself, but there was really no time for that. Conditioning, training, and rigorous field exercises kept me focused on the task at hand. Most mornings, I arose thirty minutes before anyone else and did push-ups, sit-ups, and isometric strength exercises. I also listened to American talk shows on my headphones while I worked out. Being fluent in English would help me shine. My goal was not just to survive those grueling tests; my goal was to rise to the top. I wanted to be the best by a long shot, so I had no time for regrets. That's not the way I want to live my life."

"And from your file, I know that's what you did. You have commendations up the Ying Yang. 'Fastest recruit to ever reach Sergeant Major,' it says here."

I didn't say anything, just nodded my head in the obligatory humility hard-wired into Asians.

Robinson continued. "From there you were sent to Officer Training School."

Again, I nodded.

"You graduated with honors, passing both physical and academic requirements with flying colors. On top of that, you passed all English fluency tests, no problem. Seems your hard work paid off."

"Hard work comes with the territory. It runs in the family."

"Ah, so you do take after your father?" Robinson peered at me in disbelief before he dropped the proverbial bomb. "Then why did he have you court marshalled and essentially exiled?"

Chapter 11

L*aguna Niguel, California*
June 6, 2:12 p.m.

Stephanie Noh was winding her way up the hill toward her parents' house, passing one stately home after another, when the call came in. Matthew was asleep in his car seat. Sophia was happily engaged at her daycare center at the base of the hill. It was time for Stephanie to confer with her father and let him in on what was happening. She needed his support, if nothing else. Ever the optimist, he had a way of coaching Stephanie through every difficulty she had faced.

The morning had been nothing but bad news. Any information, comfort, or guidance she could get from her dad might help replace the feeling of being in the dark and helpless. She had made phone call after phone call trying to learn something, anything, about what was going on with JT and with his flight. Korean Airlines, the LAPD, the TSA, and the Korean Embassy had all given her vague non-answers, each saying things like, "There is an active investigation. We are unable to share any information with you at this time."

Her best hope for information was for the first call she had made to be returned. It was a shot in the dark, a calculated gamble, that could upset everything. Or, it could illuminate everything.

What she learned through the numerous phone calls was that the plane had been delayed but was in the air. However, no one would confirm whether her husband was onboard or not. She had been told multiple times that they were not allowed to give out that information. Not knowing where he was or what he was doing compounded her sense of disconnectedness.

The call coming in would, she hoped, provide more information than the American officials had been willing to share. The "82" country code on the Caller I.D meant it was coming from Korea. She took a deep breath and answered with her best Korean accent. "Yeoboseyo."

The voice on the other end was stern and official sounding. "Mrs. Stephanie Noh, please," he said in lightly accented English.

"This is she."

Stephanie continued driving past an estate where the gardeners were blowing leaves and pulled her minivan to the curb around the corner where it was quieter, so she could safely focus on the call.

"Mrs. Noh, please hold the line for General Noh."

Her heart skipped a beat. She had only had two encounters with her father-in-law in the entire six years she had been married to JT. Neither one was pleasant.

The first came shortly after she and JT had eloped. Not knowing that she spoke and understood Korean quite well, he had asked his son why he had brought "this mongrel" into his house. "Mixed breeds are not acceptable, Jeong Tae," he said. "Why do you shame me this way?" JT had glared at his father, grabbed her hand, and left the house.

She closed her eyes and swallowed hard, gently shaking her head. She let out a sigh and sucked in another deep breath.

A deep gravelly voice came on the line, speaking clipped English with an air of power that seemed to permeate the radio signal that carried his words. "Stephanie? This is General Noh. I want you to know that my office was informed of Jeong Tae's arrest earlier this morning. We are working with the Korean Embassy in Los Angeles to make arrangements for his release."

She squared her shoulders and lifted her chin as she spoke, projecting every ounce of confidence possible. "Thank you very much, General. I appreciate your help. Do you have any information about his condition or why he's being held?"

"As far as why he's being held, I'm not at liberty to say. This is a very delicate diplomatic matter. The allegations are very serious and the evidence against him immutable. However, there are special circumstances that I cannot discuss with you. We have certain legal grounds to challenge his detainment, so we are working through diplomatic channels to have custody remanded to his country's embassy as soon as possible."

The General's tone was all-business—no small-talk or familiarity.

The emphasis on "his country's embassy" did not go unnoticed.

She paused, clinching her jaw muscles for a beat. "I'm glad to hear that, sir. What can you tell me about his condition? Has he been harmed in any way?"

"The Americans promise me that they are treating my son well and that he is in good health and good spirits."

"Do you think there's any way I can talk to my husband?"

This time, it was the General who paused before speaking again.

"I can't say. The Americans only allow one phone call, which he has already used. Unfortunately, he did not think to call me first."

She cocked her head at that response but stayed silent.

The General continued. "Our diplomats are in constant contact with the American TSA office in Los Angeles. They will pass any information they have to my office. My office will relay pertinent information to you."

Her eyebrows lifted involuntarily. She clinched again, then responded. "That's very kind. I appreciate that."

"You're welcome—"

"There must be something I can do?" she blurted. "Do you think it would help him if I drove up there and talked with someone?"

There was a long pause. Stephanie gulped, putting her hand to her face.

"My office and the Korean Embassy in Los Angeles are working on a diplomatic solution. We have tried to make the Americans aware of Jeong Tae's considerable prior experience and talents, as well as his status. His considerable skills can and should be put to good use in the ongoing investigation. This, we hope, will elicit his release."

During the few conversations Jeong Tae had had with his father since leaving Korea, each had revolved around him wasting his significant talent on teaching Tae Kwon Do to Americanized kids. If this conversation with Stephanie was a boxing match, the General had scored on several jabs that connected to vulnerable spots. Stephanie's return jabs were not as insulting.

Even though the General was busy and condescending, it was her first ever one-on-one conversation with him. Tense though it was, it was a connection, and she didn't want to break it for fear she would never get another chance.

"Sir, I don't know what to do. I want to help free my husband. My children need their father. I can't have him go to prison. He doesn't deserve that."

Another pause. Longer than the first.

"I understand. This is a very difficult situation, but I have hope. You must also keep hope. Please do not tell my grandchildren that their father has been in prison. That would cause them shame. He will be released very soon. Let the children think he is away on business, as was planned. This is not something they need to be concerned about."

Those words and the gentler tone in his voice stopped her in her tracks. This man had never acknowledged that her children were his grandchildren. He had only seen them twice for five minutes each time. Two disastrous attempts by JT to form a relationship between a grandfather and his grandchildren. No affection was shared other than a pat on the top of each of their heads as he said good-bye.

"OK," she said, nodding. "I will hold on to hope. Please keep me informed. That will help."

"Very well. We will do everything we can from the government side. Meanwhile, stay strong. Pray for him ...and I will pray for him, too."

The line went dead.

Stephanie stared at the phone, tears welling in her eyes. She put her hand over her heart and drew in another deep breath.

Matthew squawked from his car seat behind her, snapping her focus back to the present. He was waking up from his nap now that the car was not moving and would soon be screaming. She knocked the gear shift into drive and pulled away from the curb, blinking hard.

Maybe this crisis would be the chance Stephanie needed to prove to her father-in-law that although she was of mixed race, she was not a "mongrel" or a second-class citizen.

Her father was full-blooded Korean. That should count for something. Her mother was half Thai, half African American—the result of a weekend fling between a US soldier on leave in Bangkok during the Korean Conflict and a naïve waitress. Stephanie had come to terms with her heritage and felt no shame being of mixed race. The only shame was never having known her grandfather, because her mother never met him, either. One of the many abandoned half-breeds left behind at the end of the war. The man probably never knew he'd fathered a child. According to her grandmother, there was no further contact after their encounter. She never saw or heard from him again.

Jeong Tae had told her he didn't mind her mixed bloodlines, either. He reminded her constantly that he was intoxicated with her beauty and her "I-don't-care-what-people-think" demeanor. She knew who she was and overcame the scorn with thoughtfulness, intelligence, and a practiced grace she inherited from her mother.

Chapter 12

Southbound Interstate 405, Garden Grove, California
June 5, 2:13 p.m.

It was a risk he had to take. There was no choice, not if he was going to escape. Chances were good someone knew. They had to know. Or at least suspect.

He had called through his comm unit to abort. The operation was botched, and everyone was now in scramble mode, acting on their own unique set of instructions prescribed by mission command. Everyone except Yong Byun. He was following a self-created plan, one that would free him from the consequences of failure as well as the dismal existence in which he had grown up. And if they knew he wasn't where he was supposed to be, they could be at the control house, waiting for him. If so, his life would be ended. Probably in a horrible manner. And probably after weeks, if not months, of long and drawn-out tension or torture or both.

But without his passports and some money, it would only be a matter of time before he met the same fate anyway. Getting to Mexico was his best chance at survival. He had to have his passport to enter the country and he needed money to live, as well as to swap vehicles. It was very likely his control agents had a tracker in the car, so keeping it wasn't an option. He had to chance it and try to find his papers and some cash at the safe house.

The car he drove was one of the team cars, one they kept in the warehouse near the airport, the warehouse he had burned down along with the truck he had stolen, and his mortally wounded Comrade. He had no other choice, not with a tight timeline. He hadn't had time to follow the original guideline and sanitize the warehouse. Plus, he needed to get rid of the body. Burning the place down was the only way to hide the evidence and possibly buy himself some time.

Driving the speed limit through the neighborhood in Garden Grove, an hour south of LAX, Yong Byun passed the little house halfway down the block on his left that matched all the other little houses on the street. He saw nothing out of the ordinary. No cars in the driveway and none in front of the house. The curtains were still closed. The porch light was on. That could mean the other team members left in a hurry, or that no one had returned since the night before. As he turned at the next corner, another thought entered his frazzled mind: what if it was a trap?

If the guardians were watching, they would surely recognize the car as he drove past.

He dismissed that thought. If there was a tracker, they were already monitoring his movements, so what did it matter?

Nothing looked suspicious or out of place during his second pass, either. Even so, his guts were tied in a knot. He knew of this safe house, knew the address, but didn't know who lived there or what function they fulfilled in the grand scheme of this operation. He knew there were "observers," but he had never seen them. They called in his grocery order every night. They talked to people at his apartment complex. They seemed to know everything he did and everyone he spoke to.

Tracked or not, he had to go inside and find the items he needed. Getting out of this country was his only hope for surviving. Even in Mexico they could find him, but he liked his chances better there.

The third time down the block, he gritted his teeth, summoned all of his courage, and drove straight into the driveway. He stopped suddenly and shoved the gear selector of the non-descript, four-year-old Honda Civic into Park. Feeling completely exposed and targeted without a weapon or body armor, he sucked in a deep breath before swinging the door open.

Yong Byun got out of the car, leaving the engine running, and listened carefully for any sounds coming from the house. All he could hear above the Honda's idling was a dog barking somewhere in the middle distance and cars on the boulevard which was just over the wall of the tiny back yard. He carefully punched the code, which was 9948—the date North Korea became its own nation—into the garage door opener keypad. Once the door was three feet above the ground, he ducked under it and ran to the interior door, still listening for sounds of movement or activity inside the house.

At the door, Yong Byun paused fifteen seconds to listen before carefully turning the handle and pushing the door open a crack. Another fifteen seconds told him there was no one moving. His heart pounded. A patient sniper could be silently sighting on the entry, waiting for him to step inside. He held his breath and entered in a crouched position to minimize the target area.

The house was darkened. Muted sunlight entered through cream-colored drapes in an outdated living area ahead of him. To his right was the kitchen. Louvered blinds on a window over the sink created a semi-bright glow in the room.

Convinced that he was alone, Yong Byun moved quickly, feeling the pressure as time continued to march forward. He whipped open the refrigerator door and reached for the gigantic jar of kimchi. Nerves got the best of him as he pulled it from the shelf and the jar slipped through his hands and crashed on the ground, spilling its pungent contents all over the linoleum. Pickled cabbage and briny water seasoned with garlic and red pepper paste spread out across the floor. Amid the shards of glass were two quart-sized sealed baggies stuffed full of hundred-dollar bills.

Yong Byun snatched the two bags of cash. In his haste, a piece of glass the size of a baby's tooth, lodged into the fleshy part at the edge of his hand, between his pinky finger and his wrist. Blood seeped out in large crimson drops. He winced. A flare of pain shot through his system as salty water entered the wound. He inspected the cut and found the culprit. Using his fingernails, he dug the razor-sharp chunk of glass out and dropped it in the pile of kimchi. He grabbed a hand towel laced through a drawer's handle and wrapped it around the hand as he dashed back out the door and jumped in the car.

He dropped the transmission into Reverse with the toweled hand and got part way out of the driveway before he realized he was missing something. The car lurched back up the driveway when he jerked the gear shifter back into Drive just to slam to a stop a few feet later.

Once again, he ran through the garage. As he did, it occurred to him that he had also forgotten to close the garage door on his way out the first time. Panic was setting in, causing him to slip. He needed to slow down, but how could he with the clock ticking? Someone could show up any time. Then his troubles would multiply.

He skidded on the slick surface in the kitchen but used the counter to keep himself from falling as he ran toward the hallway where the bedrooms were. Opening the first door, he found nothing but a mattress on the floor and a few clothes hanging in the closet.

The second room looked like the control room. Computers and monitors and wires and racks of machines with blinking lights.

He found what he was looking for in the third bedroom. A desk was pushed under the window at the far end and another was set up along the adjacent wall. Each had three drawers. He found a dozen file folders in the large bottom drawer of the first desk. His name was on the tab of one of them. He yanked the file out and found three passports, including the one he had used to enter the United States through Mexico. Each passport had his photo but a different name. A few other documents were printed with various official-looking seals. He didn't take the time to inspect them.

Something underneath the file folders made it difficult to move them. It was a large lump in a brown bag. He pulled the bag out and discovered another wad of cash, eight neatly bundled stacks of hundred-dollar bills. Jackpot.

Time was ticking, and his nerves were more on fire with each passing second, but he rifled through the other folders, noting the names on their tabs. He recognized Un-Chul's and Jung Min's names, but none of the others.

A dark cloud passed through him as he thought about Jung Min, who had died because of that miserable son of the South Korean general and his interference. He bit back the rising bile as he thought about what he had had to do to hide evidence of their treachery.

* * *

Los Angeles International Airport
Two hours earlier

Following Un-Chul's instructions, Yong Byun stopped the truck near the terminal building where they both knew from the blue prints they had memorized there was an entrance to the baggage processing area where Un-Chul could sneak through. *The man must be in immense pain*, thought Yong Byun. *What a true hero.*

Un-Chul gingerly eased himself down from the tailgate Yong Byun had lowered. The hard plastic on the back of the black roller bag made a blood-curdling scraping sound as he dragged it across the dirt and debris littering the truck bed. He carefully maneuvered it to the lip of the gate using his one good arm. The bag nearly knocked the big guy down as it slammed into the side of his leg.

Wincing with pain, the ashen-faced hero bid Yong Byun success in fulfilling the rest of his role in the mission and hobbled through the fog, one arm tucked carefully in his jacket, tied in place with a piece of rope Yong Byun found in the bed of the truck and had used to create a makeshift sling. The other arm tugged the handle of the heavy roller bag.

Yong Byun shook his head in admiration and disbelief as he hopped back in the truck and once again fought the urge to speed away. It was all he could do to keep the truck under 15 miles per hour as he slowly meandered, like so many of the other vehicles in sight, toward the employee exit.

Going from memory, he worked his way past a group of tall fuel storage tanks and turned south on a narrow access road between two employee parking areas. Weaving his way between long buildings and past rows of trucks similar to the one he was driving, hoping the whole time to not draw any attention, Yong Byun was grateful for the thick fog that blanketed the entire coastline.

Finally, he found what he was looking for: World Way—the road in and out of LAX for grounds crew and mechanical staff. He turned west, toward the ocean and drove slowly, trying to make it look like he was going about his normal operational duties when really all he wanted to do was floor the gas and get out of there as fast as possible. He worked his way past the maintenance hangars and the security office and the other buildings that dotted the perimeter of the airport. Lucky for him, there was just enough activity to mask his escape. Food service trucks passed him going the other way, toward the congregation of parked aircraft. The pick-up truck a hundred yards ahead of him turned to the right between two buildings as another truck pulled out from his left and headed back toward the terminals. Each vehicle he saw made his breath catch in his throat.

After what felt like an eternity, Yong Byun arrived at the unmanned security gate. He swiped his badge, knowing there were cameras that his tech guys had probably not disabled. They were probably on the run. The original plan called for Yong Byun and his team to exit through this gate much later in the morning. His face would be seen, but there was nothing he could do about that. Escape was the only option. The sooner, the better.

Yong Byun exited the airport onto southbound Pershing Drive, a road that skirted the airport's western edge. He applied the gas in an even acceleration until he neared Imperial Highway, where he turned left to head east, parallel to the southern runways.

Yong Byun continued east as Los Angeles's newest freeway, Interstate 105, rose from ground level to several stories above Imperial Highway. Driving in silence, thinking through his escape plan, Yong Byun then turned right from Imperial Highway into the maze of industrial buildings that ringed the southeastern flanks of the country's third busiest airport. The structures along Imperial Highway were mostly tilt-up concrete affairs, new and well-lit, with corporate names and logos proudly displayed in plain view. Many of the larger airlines had operations buildings in this area, as did many of the food service providers for the airlines. Two turns onto smaller side streets brought him into the less flashy part of the warehouse district, where the structures were older and the signs were faded and the company names unrecognizable to the common citizen.

Halfway down the block of one of these side streets, a twelve-foot chain link gate surrounded a squat concrete building, its paint faded and peeling. The faux stone veneer around the front entrance spoke of its early 70's construction. Its decorative rock and juniper landscaping riddled with weeds and litter gave an air of neglect. This had been their rented mission headquarters for the past four years. Yong Byun thumbed a code into his phone and the gate lurched and shuddered as the ancient motor tugged at the wheeled assembly at its base. He pulled the truck into the crumbling, deserted parking area and around the side of the building. A large roll-up steel door was set into the north side and a glass entrance framed in aluminum faced the street. Yong Byun tapped his phone again and the corrugated steel entry rolled upward, and he idled the truck into the darkened warehouse. Another tap and it closed behind him.

Yong Byun sighed as he killed the motor, concerns over the success of their mission pulling down his emotions like a drowning victim in a whirlpool. Shoulders hunched forward, head lowered, he shuffled across the dusty concrete floor to a row of red fuel jugs lined up under a filthy window.

He pulled the top off of one and let its contents run out as he traced a line around the inside perimeter of the building. It took two jugs to complete the task. The third jug was poured out inside the office space in the front of the building. With the fourth jug in hand, he lumbered back to the truck. He pulled back the tarp and stared for a moment at his dying Comrade. A fresh pool of blood encircled his head like a black halo. The man moaned as Yong Byun began pouring gasoline on him, soaking his clothes.

After saluting Jung Min, Yong Byun hopped down from the truck bed, created a small lake of fuel on the ground near the gas tank, and continued pouring out a line of gasoline, creating a sort of fuse. He closed his eyes and shook his head. It wasn't supposed to happen like this. The Supreme Council had guaranteed success. Every detail had been planned meticulously. A member of the Council, rumored to be a close relative of the Supreme Leader, had given a speech to the team before they departed their homeland. "Have no fear, Comrades," said the mission leader. "The victory you shall win will bring the respect our country deserves. The whores of the South will have no choice but to bow to our demands."

Yong Byun pulled a lighter from his jacket pocket. He lit a cigarette, took a long drag on it, trying to steel his resolve. This one last act was partly for the cause and partly for himself. It would be a worthy distraction that he hoped would buy him enough time to get to the border.

He inhaled another lungful of smoke, then unceremoniously flicked the burning cigarette onto the liquid fuse. It pained him to do so, but he had to destroy all evidence, including his Comrade.

Yong Byun turned his back and climbed into the team's white Honda Civic and drove it out the rolled-up door. Smoke was just starting to billow from the truck bed as he checked his mirror.

By the time Yong Byun was climbing the eastbound on-ramp to 105 Freeway, a black mushroom cloud was spreading into the sky above the warehouse he had just left.

Chapter 13

Interrogation Room, Los Angeles Airport Police Station
June 5, 2:14 p.m.

Even though I expected the question to surface at some point, it still rattled me. *Why was I exiled from the country I loved and had devoted my life to serve?*

It felt like my insides had been stung by a swarm of bees. Despite the stinging going on inside, I did my best to maintain a stone-cold exterior. I couldn't afford to crack now, not with all these eyes on me and not at this crucial moment.

The answer, however, was not simple. It never is in cases like this. The story was laced with complex interdepartmental situations, cultural expectations, military hierarchal traditions, and, not least of all, my father's political ambitions. My answer was an over-simplification to say the least, but completely true and honest at the same time. "It was the only way to save face."

Robinson cocked his head, studying me. "Explain."

"In my country, there is a concept called *kibun.* Ki-bun, in a few words, is one's personal honor, dignity, and public image. It's very important to Koreans. Americans don't understand it because their culture is so much different. In America, someone's truth sometimes destroys another person's reputation. In Korea, someone's reputation often stifles someone else's truth. I got caught somewhere in between those two forces."

Robinson motioned with his hand that he understood and wanted me to go on.

"When you boil it all down, it was my word against theirs."

"Who are you talking about? Whose word was against yours?"

"First in line was my CO, then everyone in the chain of command above him."

"Was your father in that chain of command?" Robinson's eyes narrowed as he asked the question.

"Yes. At the time, my father was the second-highest ranking officer in the Korean Army." I paused while that settled in. "He was also in the process of mounting his candidacy for President."

Robinson shook his head. "So, you took the fall in order to save your father's reputation?"

"Ultimately, yes."

"That's why you were exiled?"

"I left voluntarily. I didn't want to become a continuing story for the newspapers."

"I see." Robinson tapped his index finger on the file again. "Fill in the details for me. What happened that night?"

"My commanding officer sent my twelve-man unit through the fence on an exploratory 'raid.' We had confirmed sightings on our infrared satellite imagery of several individuals—what looked to be a family, including a couple of kids—breaching the restricted area between the fences, coming down from the North. I was the commander of this special tactical unit and this is what we had been trained for. As we approached the area where the group had stopped, we could see in our night vision goggles two adults and two kids huddled behind a rock. My CO was monitoring the operation back at the command center. He ordered me through the comm system to apprehend them and bring them in for questioning. Defectors were always a great source of intelligence for us, so he wanted them brought in so we could mine information."

"OK. So what's the problem?" Robinson asked, trying to get straight to the point.

"My CO wanted us to take them and return to the fence as quickly as possible. He was very impatient. The kids looked to be around eight and ten. My CO figured they were harmless, and we should minimize our exposure by hurrying. I knew better and wanted to proceed with caution. But he threatened to demote me if I didn't obey his orders promptly."

Robinson held up a finger to stop me. "Why do you say you knew better?"

"I don't know exactly. It just didn't feel right. Something about their body language triggered that reaction in me."

"I see," he said, nodding. "Kind of like the response you had this morning?"

"Yes. When you've been in the field as much as I have, you tend to err on the side of caution. That's the best way to avoid bullets."

"So, you were hesitant because you felt you should exercise more caution?"

"Yes, but I was now under orders to proceed directly to the targets and secure them immediately. So, I ordered my team into defensive formation. We fanned out and approached much more quickly than I would have liked. I was uneasy about the situation, but my CO continued to urge us to speed up before the enemy became aware of the defectors."

"Did you disobey orders?"

"No. I followed them to the 'T.' That's what got us in trouble. You have to understand that this was very mountainous terrain, allowing for plenty of hiding places. The body language, the stiffness, the placement of the family—it was all wrong. As my men maneuvered into position, we were ambushed. The whole thing was a set up. Men in camouflage popped up from hiding places in a semi-circle around the family and opened up. Machine gun fire came at us from all directions. Rounds tore through the dark, killing the man, woman, and children behind the rock and all of my men. I alone . . ."

My voice trailed off, but not because of the emotional impact of sharing that story. I realized in that moment where I had seen the eyes from the cargo hold of the plane earlier that morning. Those eyes and that face had confronted me on that fateful night. The same look of recognition. The same scheming expression. I chose to keep that revelation to myself.

"So, you were court-marshalled for a botched operation," Robinson sighed.

I snapped back to the present but must have sounded far away. "Yes. There were no other survivors. I was the one in charge on the ground level. The lives of those eleven men and those would-be defectors were in my hands. I was responsible for them."

Robinson shook his head. "But you survived? How?"

I sucked in a breath, measuring my words. "As you noted, I had received many commendations. One of them was for marksmanship. One of them was for high scores in combat situations. They call it 'tactical response.' I scored very high on those exercises during training."

"How many 'enemy combatants' were there that night?"

"I can't be sure. It all happened so fast. I spotted three in the trees just beyond the huddled family. I took them out first. Two or three behind rocks at the three o'clock position, two or three at nine o'clock. But I can't be one-hundred percent sure."

"You said you were surrounded. How did you escape?"

I kept my eyes down, not wanting to boast or even appear to be boasting. "I dropped to one knee and spun counter-clockwise, 'spraying lead,' as our American cohorts like to say. There were a few rocks nearby. They weren't very tall, but they gave me some cover. I rolled to one side, then to the other, laying down three-round bursts each time I saw movement. I heard lots of grunts and heard rounds hitting their targets. Some of them hit flesh and some hit body armor. I also lobbed every grenade I had. In the confusion, I dragged my team members to the safety of the rocks I was hiding behind. I then lobbed their grenades as well."

"You were able to stave off the enemy all this time?"

"I did the best I could. Once they started moving, their heat signatures showed up on the thermal imaging read-out, which helped me target my grenades better."

"Were you hit during this skirmish?"

"Yes. My body armor stopped three bullets," I said.

"Many people are injured despite the armor," Robinson said, once again shaking his head.

"Yes, the armor saves you from life-threatening injuries, but not from the pain and bruising of an incoming bullet."

"How extensive were your injuries?" Robinson seemed to already know the answer but wanted me to share with our hidden audience.

"One bullet cracked a rib back here," I said, trying to point my cuffed finger at my left side. "One hit my back between my shoulder blade and my spine. The third hit my chest, right above the heart."

"You must have experienced a great deal of pain. How did you manage to get away?"

"Part of our training included learning to suppress pain and stay in the moment until the mission was completed. I reloaded, called in for support to retrieve my fallen men, and guarded them until help arrived. I simply finished the mission as best I could."

"You're saying that the fact that you survived, were able to escape without leaving your men behind, and took out several enemy combatants didn't sway any on that tribunal?"

I waited a beat or two before I answered. "It would have been wrong in our culture to bring up the fact that my CO, who reported to a major general who reported to my father, had ordered the hurried evacuation of those potential asylum-seekers. Any hint that we walked into an ambush would have destroyed the careers of my superiors as well as my own. I felt that was unnecessary."

"Your father . . . he has a reputation for being a hard-liner, doesn't he? He wants to eliminate the threat of North Korean aggression, doesn't he?"

"In a way, that is true. He takes a hardline approach in the public eye. That's why they are keen on rescuing asylum seekers—it provides intel we can't get any other way. But the truth is, he wants reunification. He pushes hard as a negotiation tactic. You have to understand: his family was torn in two when the Allies and the Chinese drew the border along the 38th parallel. His father and uncles were on the wrong side of the line when the border went up. My grandmother used to speak very reverently about them. We all know, however, that they were likely put to death shortly after Kim Il-Sung rose to power in the North."

"But your father's approach in the public eye has been . . ."

"That we need to eliminate the nuclear option, at any cost."

"Even if that means full-scale war?"

"That's the public perception."

"What's the truth, then?"

"The truth is, there are many who support him politically. He is a military man and believes that everything has a military solution. This invokes a certain nationalistic pride in many, thus winning him support."

Robinson paused again, eyeing me warily. "Your actions that night reflected badly on him, didn't they?"

"You can say that. Really, it was the outcome that hurt him. A family trying to escape North Korea—dead. Eleven men in a twelve-man squadron—dead. The son of a high-ranking general—alive and in need of rescue deep inside the DMZ. It all looked bad. Although there was only limited media coverage, what they did speculate was that I had foolishly and haphazardly tried to save a family that made an unwise choice and had risked the lives of my men to do it."

Robinson squinted and rubbed his jaw. "You took the fall for your CO so there would be no backsplash on him or your father. You were the scape goat and made to look 'foolish' or 'unsuspecting' when you were just following orders."

"The words they used to describe me were 'unfit for leadership due to his penchant for self-aggrandizement over the needs of those in his command.'"

"You were stripped of your command and dishonorably discharged. Did I read that right?"

I took a deep breath. My jaw clenched tight, as did my fists. Hearing those words always produced a visceral reaction. To Robinson, I responded with a simple nod.

"Why the exile?"

I let out the breath I was holding. "Honor. Staying in Seoul would bring nothing but shame to my family. Plus, I would never find employment—anywhere. There was enough media coverage to make my name and face recognizable to most. If they missed it on TV, all they had to do was look into my background to see the dishonorable discharge. In Korea, that's it. Game over."

"Why did you go to Thailand, of all places?"

All of these questions were wasting valuable time. They had nothing to do with the suitcase and finding out what was inside or what the two guys were doing with it or where it was now, but I knew I had to play nice. I could sense Robinson probing to figure out what kind of person I really was. He came in thinking I was a lunatic, but somewhere along the line, his impression of me started to shift. The way his tone of voice gradually changed felt like he was beginning to accept that I was in possession of my faculties after all, so I continued trying to earn his trust. "My high school friend's father knew a guy who had repatriated there during the Vietnam war. The guy made a fortune providing logistical support and supplies to NATO units throughout the region during the war, under the radar. After that, he went into the import-export business. After graduation from high school, he had introduced me to him, so I already had a relationship with him. I contacted him after the trial, and he offered me a job."

"Then you married his daughter?"

Robinson had the basics of my file pretty well covered.

"With his blessing, of course. We had known each other for a while already."

"Then you all moved to Orange County?"

Again, I nodded. "His idea, not mine."

"Where he continued in the import-export business, but you chose to split off and start teaching Tae Kwon Do?"

"My skills are better suited to combat than business, so it seemed a more natural fit."

"You've been quite successful at it, I see. Your students have won three national competitions in the past five years."

Once again, I acknowledged his compliment with a slight bow of the head.

"And today you were on your way to an invitational competition, were you not?"

"Yes," I said. "The world championship in Seoul takes place in two days."

A knock at the door interrupted our little fact-finding session. Robinson stepped out. When he returned, his face was all tight. He shook his head as he looked down at my file.

"Well," Robinson said as he moved around the end of the table. "You must still have some friends in high places. Your ride will be here shortly."

I must have looked confused. He stopped, keeping an eye on me.

"A car from the Korean Embassy is on its way to take you into custody and transport you back to your country."

My bewildered expression only deepened.

"This comes down from the highest levels within our government. I don't have the authority to hold you any longer. 'Diplomatic immunity', they said." He walked around behind me and unlocked the handcuffs. As I rubbed my wrists, he congratulated me. "You're a free man, Mr. Noh. It pays to know people in high places. What, with an election coming up in your country and your father as the leading candidate, I guess it's no surprise."

Chapter 14

Laguna Niguel, California
June 5, 2:18 p.m.

Stephanie burst through the side door, the one located around the corner from the garage and that led into the mud room. From there, a short hallway lined with pantry cupboards spilled out to an open-concept kitchen fully equipped with the latest appliances and stylish accoutrements. The kitchen/family room area was bright and cheery, in stark contrast to her facial expression.

Stephanie's mother stood at the oversized sink built into the large granite-topped island, peeling carrots. From her vantage point, she could see the driveway and approach through a large set of gridded double-hung windows to her left. They were opened slightly to allow the breeze to flow through the house. Unfazed by Stephanie's harried entrance, Anna Choi set her peeler aside, wiped her hands on a nearby towel, and came around the corner of the island with her arms outstretched. "How's my big boy?" she cooed at Matthew.

Matthew stopped his squawking and leaned toward his grandmother with a joyful smile spreading across his face and his arms open wide.

Relieved of both the physical and emotional burden of an unhappy boy, Stephanie set her bulging diaper bag on the long, black-stained pine table and let out a sigh.

"What is it, dear?" her mother asked as Matthew wrapped his arms around her neck and squeezed. Anna's jet-black hair had only recently become adorned with a smattering of grey strands. It was pulled in a ponytail in back and covered with a flowery silk bandana on the top. Her face radiated serenity and contentment as she returned Matthew's hug. She planted a series of rapid-fire kisses on his cheek before adding, "You look like you've seen Krasue," she said, referring to the gruesome apparition of a female head spoken of in Thai tradition.

Stephanie stopped in her tracks and gave her mother a look of exasperation tinged with fright.

"What's going on, Stephanie?" her mother asked again.

Tears welled up in Stephanie's eyes as she contemplated what she should say in front of her son. "It's Jeong Tae, Mother. There's something going on and I don't know what to do. I need to talk to Pappa. Maybe he'll have an idea."

"Let's put a movie on for Matthew in the meeting room while we talk to him. Come on." Anna led the way back through the mud room, out the door through which they had just entered, and walked along a flower-bordered stone pathway that curved through a clump of shimmering willows to the two-story edifice known as the office. In truth, it was a combination warehouse, workshop, storage building, and, upstairs, a properly appointed office space for her dad, whom everyone called "Sunny."

The "meeting room" was an open space adjacent to a Sunny's office. An oblong cherrywood table circled with high-backed leather chairs the color of burnt butter occupied most of the area. One wall was mostly a picture window that looked out over the warehouse and workshop. The other wall was partially taken up by the door through which they had entered and a fake tree in the corner.

The far wall was encased with cherry wood cabinetry and shelving full of books and nick knacks collected during a lifetime of exotic travel. Stephanie opened the cabinet doors to reveal a large flat screen TV. She cued up a streaming animated movie, one of Matthew's favorites, while her mother bounced Matthew in her arms and sang a familiar happy Thai song Stephanie remembered from her childhood. Matthew giggled with each bounce and silly lyric.

Sunny's office walls were half glass, half drywall. Sunny stood near his desk and watched his wife, daughter, and grandson with a bemused smile as he held a phone to his ear with one hand and signaled with the other for them to give him one minute.

Sunny had salt and pepper hair that reached to his shoulders and a mostly gray goatee. His typical attire, rain or shine, was a pair of shorts—sometimes plaid, sometimes khaki, sometimes cargo—with either a T-shirt or, if he was dressing up, a short-sleeved button-up with a flower print. On his feet, he wore either sandals, flip-flops, or, in cold weather, low-cut lightweight athletic shoes or fur-lined slippers. Comfort was king with Sunny Choi.

When Anna's song was over and the movie was ready, Matthew turned his attention to the screen and clapped his hands as his grandmother lowered him into a chair specially prepared for him with a booster seat on it. Stephanie set a sippy cup and a covered bowl of goldfish crackers on the table in front of him, but he didn't notice, he was so enthralled with the opening scene.

Sunny opened the door wide and his arms wider. Stephanie moved in for an embrace, which he gave with enthusiasm. "How's my girl?" he asked buoyantly. Whenever he sensed tension or sadness, Sunny "let the sun in," as he often exclaimed. His exuberance for life was contagious. Everyone who knew him loved to be around him for that very reason. Sunny lived up to his name.

"Daddy, there's something wrong. I think JT's in trouble," Stephanie blurted, her face still pressed against his shoulder.

"Let's figure out what we know and what we can do, OK? Tell me everything."

It didn't take long for Stephanie to divulge every shred of the scant information she had learned from Jin Sook about JT's situation and the phone call with JT's father. There were large gaps in the puzzle, but this didn't bother Sunny much.

Sunny curled his lower lip as he turned toward his office. His smile faded and his "business face" emerged. "Hmm. That's not much to go on, but maybe someone at the embassy can tell us something." He pulled his smart phone from his pocket and spoke to it, asking it to look up and dial the Korean Embassy in Los Angeles. “I still know a few people over there.”

Chapter 15

Interrogation Room, Los Angeles Airport Police Station
June 5, 2:25 p.m.

Robinson held the door open for me, but I didn't move. I stood there at the table rubbing my wrists and staring at the thick file. That file represented everything the US government thought they knew about me based on my history and past performance. That collection of papers and pictures and information, however, did not define me. There was more to me than they could ever read.

Robinson cocked his head. "I said you were free to go. Don't you—"

"You have pictures of all your airport employees?" I asked, tapping my index finger on the table.

"Yeah, it's part of the security protocol—"

"Good," I interrupted. "I need to see all your baggage handlers."

Confusion swept over Robinson's face. "What's this all about?"

"I need to see all the baggage handlers," I repeated. "One of them looked familiar to me. In fact, he recognized me instantly. Now I know how. In any case, he is involved in this. I'd be willing to bet he knows something that could help us."

"What are you talking about, Mr. Noh? Your ride is here. Two young men drove all the way from the Korean Embassy downtown to pick you up. You don't want to keep them waiting."

I dismissed the part about my ride waiting for me with a wave of my hand. "You want to figure out what happened here today, don't you?"

"Yes, of course."

"You want to do everything you can to provide for the safety of every passenger that departs from this airport, right?"

"Yes, that's my job. What are you getting at?"

"I'm sure you're good at your job, but I believe you're going to need my help. I am pretty good at what I was trained to do, as well. I'm more than just a brave soldier, Mr. Robinson. I was trained to protect and defend my country and my people. I was trained to understand my enemy, to think like my enemy, and to understand my enemy's motivations. I'd like to help you, if you'll allow me."

Robinson opened his mouth, then closed it. His eyebrows scrunched together, and his eyes squinted at me.

I continued. "You're going to need all the help you can get to determine if there's something dangerous on that plane or not. I'm uniquely suited for this task."

"I'm afraid it would be impossible—"

"Nothing is impossible if you set your mind to it. If you need some sort of official authorization, I'm certain we can go through the proper channels to get it. Considering the potential national security risk and PR nightmare at play, I think it's worthwhile to think outside the box, don't you?"

"Well, I suppose—"

"Good. Let's go make some phone calls and find those pictures. Where are the two men from the embassy? I'd like to speak to them."

Robinson paused; a look of consternation etched in his facial features. "Moments ago, you were on your way to indictment for breaching national security. A no-brainer. All kinds of eyewitnesses. Now I'm letting you go because I was told to let you go because of your diplomatic immunity. Got any more curve balls for me today, Mr. Noh?"

I returned Robinson's quizzical stare. "I'm telling you, that man from the cargo hold knows me and I'm pretty sure I know him. He was there that night between the fences. I know he was. And I know he knows who I am. You should've seen the shock on his face."

He shook his head. "There's no precedent for something like this."

"I know. You need to trust me."

"Why would I trust you? Why do you think I'd let you be a part of my investigation or spend one more minute in here with me?"

"I'm invested in the outcome. Remember, I know people onboard that plane. Is that not reason enough to trust me, especially knowing my background as you do? Without me, you have little or no chance of finding these guys or figuring out what the danger might be in time."

"Ha." Robinson's hand shot to his hips. "Aren't you an arrogant son of a—"

"No, sir," I interrupted. "The word you're looking for is 'confident.' I am confident I can help. I am capable, well-trained, and have a lot to lose if my hunch is right and there's something dangerous on that aircraft. You have a lot to lose, too, if I'm right about this."

"Your daddy pulled some strings for you—with some very powerful people, I might add—to get you off the hook. Now you're asking me to break more rules to let you work on the investigation? You're nuts, Mr. Noh. Plain and simple."

There was more that he wasn't saying, but I picked up on it.

I shook my head slowly. I held his gaze while my jaw muscles twitched. "I told you, I don't want or need my father to pull strings for me. I'm not interested in doing the *easy* thing. I'm interested in doing the *right* thing. Sixteen of my students are onboard that plane. I believe it is headed for destruction. We need to work together. I am offering my services in order to save my students and all those people on that plane. Is that clear enough for you? Is that noble enough for you to trust me?"

I realized it probably sounded far-fetched. But I was sure I was right and neither of us could afford to underestimate the potential threat.

"Problem is, Mr. Noh, there's no evidence, remember? We searched the plane, rechecked every bag on it. There was nothing. Nothing at all. I can't very well launch an investigation and use up valuable resources chasing something that doesn't exist."

I closed my eyes as I drew in a deep breath. "I know what I saw. I am willing to stake my life and my family's honor on it."

Shaking his head, Robinson's countenance conveyed conflict. I could almost see the gears of his mind working away at this problem. It was an unprecedented conundrum, probably one that he had never dreamed he would encounter. There was no protocol, no playbook. There were also no other viable options. Finally, he said, "Wait here a moment."

Twenty minutes later, Robinson returned with a thin file in one hand. His mouth was tight across his face. His eyebrows were pulled down low, and the creases on his forehead were deep. He opened my file, let out a puff of air, then closed it again. "I don't know what's going on here, Mr. Noh. Nothing adds up. Nothing makes any sense to me."

I looked at him passively, waiting for him to add some context.

"You were court marshalled, dishonorably discharged, and shunned by your government, despite who your father is. They, he, whoever it was, left you out in the cold, sent you packing, disowned you. Whatever you want to call it. For six years you've ..." He rubbed a hand across his mouth, then moved it to his forehead, where it stayed while he continued to think out loud. "Now I get a call from the Secretary of Homeland Security, a member of the cabinet of the President of the United States—do you understand how big that is? How high up this thing has gone? He orders me to not only to let you help, but to fully cooperate with you, and—get this—to follow *your* lead. He says the President of your country, that's right the President of the Republic of Korea, called our President, referred to you by name, and asked not only that you be released, but that you be empowered to lead the investigation into the unfolding threat."

My eyebrows shot up. Robinson noticed.

"That's right," he continued. "Your president and my president having a little chat about you. *YOU*. Now you're supposed to *lead* this investigation?"

"I'm sorry, sir," I said humbly. He looked at me quizzically, like he thought I might announce my real identity as some sort of superhero. "Did you say, 'unfolding threat?'"

"Yeah," he said, shaking his head and blinking his eyes.

"What does that mean? 'Unfolding?'"

"I didn't ask for specifics. Why?"

"Don't you think that's a significant word?"

"I guess the significance of a word or two was lost on me the moment I was told that my suspected felon is to lead the investigation."

"Former suspect, sir. You said it yourself."

He shot me a sideways glance. "Yeah. Former." He stopped talking, but his jaw muscles continued to pulse. When he spoke again it was slow and deliberate, like it was causing him pain to say the words. "OK. Let me be honest. Your president told our president and our president confirmed with our intelligence people ... Your guys have picked up on some chatter."

He looked at me and I raised an eyebrow. Then he continued.

"The chatter is about something big going down. Something that would prove the North Koreans were capable. Something that would cause carnage and be 'awe-inspiring' and 'overwhelming' to the citizens of Seoul. That's what they told me. Just now. So, like it or not, I have to admit that your far-fetched story might have something to it."

I didn't say anything. I just looked down, closing my eyes as I tried to imagine what he was thinking. I couldn't get there. All I could think about was that group of innocent students on that plane. "Can I see those pictures? Of the baggage handlers?" I asked as politely as I could, despite the growing urgency of the situation. I knew he needed his ego soothed, but that would have to happen later. For now, we had to get moving before we lost the trail completely. Time was working against us. "By the way, I'm not interested in taking your job or giving you orders."

He shot me a look.

"And I'll work for free," I added with a shrug and a smile.

Robinson's face twisted and he scrunched up his mouth as he shook his head. He closed his eyes and breathed in. "Right. First you need to sign this." He opened the thin folder in his hand and laid it on the table in front of me. It had the seal of the Transportation Safety Administration emblazoned at the top of the page. Everything about it looked official.

"It's a contract for your services," he said.

My brow furrowed as I took a harder look at the paper. Something stood out to me, but I didn't say anything.

"Please sign it so I can release a statement to the press informing them that the man we arrested this morning is, in fact, a contractor working undercover for this department who was hired to find any security weak points for us and help us close those gaps. We will have to admit that you were much more successful, much quicker than we had anticipated."

I took the pen in one hand and pointed at the discrepancy with the index finger of the other.

Robinson peered at the line above my finger. "Yeah, your employment started yesterday."

I nodded and thought how interesting it is to watch government officials at work protecting both themselves and the people they serve. I signed on the line and dropped the pen.

"Very well. Follow me. Let's go look at some pictures." He punched the screen on his phone and said, "OK. He's on board. Release the statement."

Seven minutes later, after we had speed-marched through hallways, across the parking lot, up some stairs, across a walking bridge over the double-decker road that looped in front of the airport terminals, and up another escalator and down another hallway, we arrived at Robinson's office. Two minutes after that, he had cleared all the security measures on his computer as he hunched over his desk and successfully logged into the TSA employment file system. I quickly realized it was a searchable database, so I asked him to select for "baggage handler" and "Asian" from drop down menus. The results indicated twenty-nine matches. I went back to the search criteria and added "male" from a third drop down and narrowed it to twenty-three.

I scrolled through the pictures but was more focused on the last names as I looked for those I knew to be Korean. The fifth Korean name I came across was Lee Baek Young. The picture matched the guy I had seen in the cargo bay of the plane.

"That's our guy," I said. "If I were him, I would be trying to get away."

"Not necessarily. Plenty of places he could hide," Robinson said. "There are many population centers full of Asians around here. He could just blend in."

I nodded, considering his words. "Yeah, that's very true. But chances are he's paranoid. He won't want to stick around here. He'll want to get out."

"Why would he run, though?"

"Look, these guys are North Koreans. I'm positive of that. Knowing what I know about North Korea and their leadership, there's no way this guy can return home."

"Why not?"

"Their plan failed. Failure is not an option within the North Korean military. The Supreme Leader does not tolerate weakness, so unless this guy has a death wish, he'll be on the run. If I'm right, he'll figure that his government has taken measures to insure none of their operators defect. These government agents will have made their presence and their intentions known to keep him and his colleagues afraid to look sideways. Fear and intimidation—that's how they operate. He most likely believes they will know where to search for him, no matter where he tries to hide. And he might be right."

"You think the North Koreans have infiltrated our country that extensively without our knowing it?"

"Yes, I do. I think whatever happened this morning has been in the works for years."

Robinson shook his head. "That's just great."

Before he could go on, I continued my thought. We didn't have time to get off track. "I also think this guy's been told the US has tight security, cameras everywhere, the whole thing. He's probably more nervous about that stuff than he needs to be, but that should play into our hands."

Robinson cocked his head as if the thought had literally struck him. "Why's that? If he's paranoid, as you suggest, wouldn't he figure out a way to stay away from the cameras if he's convinced we can track him?"

"At this point, he's probably running scared. He knows he's got a head start. He just doesn't know how far ahead of us he is, so he'll be eager to get out of the urban areas and onto the back roads. My guess is that he'll head south. Try to cross the border ASAP." The motors in my mind were now in hyperdrive. "If we enter this picture in your computers, you can use facial recognition to track him, can't you?"

Robinson's mouth turned up. "Yeah, I suppose we can. We just need to get the right resources to help out."

"Well," I said. "Didn't you just say that the presidents of our two countries have agreed to make sure we remove any potential threat?"

"I'm on it," he said as he picked up his phone and began making requests for technical assistance and camera feeds and access to the national facial recognition software registry.

"If you're right, the North Koreans will find him before we do," Robinson said. "What happens then?"

"I think you can figure that one out. Any hope we have of getting the information we need to neutralize a potential threat dies with him."

I waited for Robinson to come around.

His brow furrowed and deep lines reappeared on his forehead. "You say you were trained to think like your enemy? You think you can predict what they will do?"

I nodded, holding his gaze. "Not one-hundred percent, but I think I know how they operate."

"Then I guess I have nothing to lose." Robinson pulled his chair out from the desk and sat down, ready to work. "What are you thinking?"

I suppressed a smile. He had a lot to lose, but he just improved his odds of success by changing his attitude about me.

Chapter 16

Garden Grove, California
June 5, 2:28 p.m.

The price was right, so he counted out the cash and gave it to the kid, who seemed more than happy. A quick and easy deal consummated in front of the grocery store where Yong Byun had spotted the car with the for-sale sign. A phone call and a ten-minute wait is all it took. $3000 for a ten-year-old Ford Focus was not a bad deal. As long as it would run for a few hundred kilometers, he didn't care about the mileage, the paint job, or the interior. Just get him out of here now and carry him to Mexico. That's all he needed.

After the purchase, Yong Byun was left with about $85,000 cash with which to start his new life. Careful planning and judicious spending would give him, perhaps, four or five years of living on the lam. No luxuries. That was a given, but not that much different than the way he'd grown up. Spartan lifestyles by the people of North Korea allowed the country to remain secure and continue its progress toward creating a better state for all. A strong military was paramount, they were told. Farming and industry were all about supporting the troops who protected the nation from invasion. Keeping the citizens safe was top priority. Those were goals set forth by the Supreme Leader and his divinely appointed council that loyal and faithful North Koreans knew to be worth striving for, worth sacrificing for.

That's what Kim Yong Byun had been told all his life. Sacrifice would make the country stronger. Yet, as he grew older, he noticed that the people around him were not growing stronger. They were growing thinner and weaker and more hopeless.

He was taught that all Americans and their allies were greedy, soulless monsters who carried the need for all the trivial things money could buy like a deep-seeded infection that they breathed on each other. The avaricious crawled to the United States like maggots to rotting food. This place was supposed to be full of them, but Yong Byun had lived among them for four years and had come to know that many were quite decent people. Most of the ones he had worked with were not so unlike his country people, though much better-fed and stronger and free from the worries that one false move could change one's life for the worse or end it altogether.

Just like in his home country, the people around him worked hard for what they got while the men in the suits seemed to have all the luxuries and all the power. It felt to Yong Byun like it was the leaders who were being protected, not the common hard-working citizens.

Yong Byun felt he could stay in America among them, if circumstances would allow. They weren't that bad. But that option was off the table. Fleeing south and getting lost in Mexico was his only viable option.

His route to the United States had come through Mexico. He liked the place and the people during his short tour through the country. Living among the people there would require some adjustments, but he was hopeful about the prospects—more so than any place else he knew of. He would allow things to settle down, do some more research, then figure out the best long-range game plan.

Knowing there were many Korean-owned factories just south of the border, Yong Byun decided he would seek shelter and employment in one of the inland border towns. Tecate seemed more remote and out of the way. The lax requirements in Mexico would work to his favor, as would his willingness to work for dirt cheap when the time came. Maybe a year from now, maybe longer. He'd lay low for a while before even contemplating work. The biggest problem with his plan was that he would most likely have to work for a South Korean, the enemy. Though the thought was distasteful, he would do what he had to do to survive. But even they were not as bad as his leaders purported them to be.

He shook his head to bring his focus back to the present. First order of business had to be ensuring he wasn't being followed. Doubling back every few miles as he left town let him know there was no one following him. Having left all of his devices in the rented warehouse near LAX, he knew there was nothing they could use to track him, unless . . .

Yong Byun pulled into a gas station. While the pump did its work, he asked the cashier about a restroom. He was directed to go outside and around the corner and was given a flyswatter with a key cleverly attached to it. Inside the bathroom, Yong Byun stripped everything off. Starting with his shoulders, he used the dim lighting and the scratched-up mirror to inspect every inch of his skin for the tell-tale scar of an incision. Several of his Comrades had had devices implanted. They were mostly the underlings, not mid-level lieutenants like himself.

Finding nothing, he put his clothes back on and was about to head out. The reflection of his hair as he took a last glance in the mirror triggered a thought, so he stopped and leaned in. Methodically massaging his entire scalp from front to back and side to side, he determined that no electronic trackers had been implanted. The only remaining possibility was that he had ingested something. But he couldn't think of anything he had eaten that could have had a tracker in it. He had purchased all his groceries at the same store since he arrived. There was no way the nice lady there could have given him an ingestible tracker, was there?

Assured that he was safe, Yong Byun returned the flyswatter and gathered the change from his gasoline purchase. With a slight bow, he thanked the cashier and headed back to the car. Some habits, he realized, died hard. Bowing wasn't a bad thing. It may not even be that far out of the norm in areas with high concentrations of Asians, like Garden Grove.

He had enough gas now to make it to the border. The sooner he could do so, the better. Certainly, those in charge of *Chammae Boksu* would be expecting him to check in by now. Most likely, they had already started the hunt—or would soon. Undoubtedly, the observation team had noted how all of his devices were in the same location and stopped working at the same time the fire started. That wouldn't immediately be viewed as suspicious since the mission had been compromised. But after enough time lapsed, he knew they would start searching.

The getaway car would surely be tracked. Since he had driven it to Garden Grove, no one would be worried about him going off track just yet. He'd left it in the same parking lot where he'd bought the Ford. That way, the bosses would surmise that Yong Byun was merely stocking up on supplies. That would buy him an hour, perhaps a little more.

His head start was marginal. Un-Chul's determination to complete the mission might draw attention away from Yong Byun if he were to keep in touch with the other team members who would, in turn, keep in touch with the observers. In a way, Yong Byun wished he still had his comm unit so he would know these things. He had to trust that Un-Chul would be true to his word, however he managed to do it.

As he turned over the engine of his newly acquired Ford, Yong Byun pondered his future and that of the family he left behind. His parents were old and tired. Not much life left in them. It might be blessing if the Supreme Council decided to terminate them because of Yong Byun's failure. His sister was in a good situation, one that might save her. The fact that her husband was a respected Colonel in the Army may help her avoid a similar outcome.

His wife was a different story. Part of the reason he signed up for this mission was to get away from her and her complete lack of desire for a better life. She deserved whatever fate had in store for her. She had never and would never support his ambitions.

Despite the outcome of Un-Chul's heroics, Yong Byun knew he had no safe place to go and no one to help him.

Chapter 17

M*inistry of National Defense, Yongsan-gu, Seoul, South Korea*
June 6, 6:33 a.m.; June 5, 2:33 p.m. California time

"It could be worse," muttered Park Moon He, General Noh's recently hired campaign manager. The presidential election was a year away, and preparations had begun. Hiring Park was seen by many an insider as a good first step. It meant Noh was serious. Park had an excellent track record running campaigns for elected officials, including two of the last three presidents. As he considered his next words, he ran a hand over his face to conceal a yawn. "He was not charged with any crimes. I'm told he has been released from custody and sent the embassy representatives back, stating that the TSA Director needed him 'for an indeterminable amount of time.'" He used the English words as they had been conveyed to him, knowing that the General spoke excellent English as well.

Park had been pulled away in the wee hours of the morning from the company of a young and flirty personal attendant from the karaoke bar he was known to frequent. His phone had alerted him of the breaking news involving the General's son. He ignored the first few buzzes and chirps, keeping his eyes on the young lady's silky movements as she danced for him. After the fifth beep, it was obvious something was happening, something that demanded his attention. He shook his head as he snatched the phone off the table. A quick scroll told him there was a problem with a Korean Airlines flight out of Los Angeles. Less than a minute later his top staffer called. "I know you saw the alerts. We need to get on this right away," was all he said.

Park told his nubile companion to get dressed and leave the private room. The sulking pout on her face as she gathered her things was enough to make him regret his career choices for an instant.

Despite it being Memorial Day in Korea, a public holiday, Park had arrived at the office forty minutes later, nursing an obvious hangover and full of pent-up annoyance. His driver and right-hand man saw his behavior and went to fetch black coffee and pastries. Before calling the General or the rest of the campaign staff, Park began working the phones and the Internet to glean as much detail as he could, although details were scarce. Tasked with helping his new boss avert a political crisis before he even formally launched his campaign, Park would draw from his experience at handling crises in this, his first week of work for General Noh.

Park had rallied for the job. Another chance to usher a president into the Blue House would solidify his already stellar reputation and increase his future fees. General Noh was the strongest of all the potential candidates in a crowded preliminary field. But he also had a few skeletons in his closet, as most politicians do. Knowing about the scandal involving his son that had derailed his first foray into politics, Park had joined the team expecting to deal with the past. Long, grueling days would be demanded of him. His skills and acumen would be needed.

The General had a reputation for no-nonsense hard work and a disdain for those who liked to party. Park knew this ahead of time. Today, his prudish driver reminded him, he would have to suffer the consequences of his entertainment choices in the form of a raging hangover to earn his handsome salary.

* * * *

At the head of the impressive mahogany conference table, General Noh Tae Sung leaned backwards in his high-backed leather chair and gazed at the ceiling. "Perhaps they have come to realize that he is not only innocent but can also be a valuable asset," he said, revealing nothing. No one but himself and President Jang needed to know about the arrangement that had been made. Jeong Tae may have uncovered something sinister. President Jang and the ruling party stood to lose a great deal of public trust if indeed there was a terrorist plot afoot. His move was as much out of desperation to save his legacy from ruin as it was a personal favor to the General, who hailed from the same party.

The President and his security council needed facts and they needed them quickly. Jeong Tae may not have been Jang's first choice of field operative, based on his tarnished record, but he was the best choice under the circumstances. President Jang knew Jeong Tae could only be of use to him if he were free, which is why he agreed to call in the favor with the US.

"It sounds to me like a political nightmare." Park was shaking his head, lines of worry etched across his forehead. "If the press finds out what has happened, everything from the past will be reexamined. You will be humiliated all over again."

"He is not to be blamed. None of this was his fault. Not now, not then."

"Maybe. But remember, fault doesn't matter. Image matters. Story matters. It doesn't take much imagination to come up with a really juicy story. In the end, the headlines are what the public will remember. Picture it: 'General Noh's son arrested on terrorism charge.' Can you imagine what that headline alone could do to your candidacy? Your career? Your legacy?"

The General remained quiet. He had been through something similar six years earlier. He arched his eyebrows and stared at Park, so Park continued.

"Let's talk about the difference between being a general and being a candidate for President of the Republic of Korea, shall we? Your job, starting right now, is to curry public favor, which, you would be wise to keep in mind, is a very fickle mistress. You lost it last time because of an issue with your son. Because of your high rank, few details were brought to light, but there were rumors and headlines and photos of him being escorted out of a military meat wagon. Even without the facts, the public assumed he was guilty of wrongdoing. You were very fortunate to retain your position."

Park searched the General's face for reaction. Once again, the General maintained a passive expression, as if this was idle prattling.

Park heaved an exasperated sigh. "The public may have forgotten about your son's court martial but if they learn of his arrest in America ... Well, that's a nightmare scenario for us ..."

General Noh tried to remain above the fray of political machinations. With his sights set on another run for the land's highest office, he knew he had to take Mr. Park's comments more seriously than was his natural inclination. "When the whole story is told, the world will see that there is a logical explanation for his actions."

"Logic will play no part in the public's perceptions. Only the presentation of the story. The headlines will win, so we need to make our own headlines here—and quickly, before your opponents have a chance to run with a negative one."

"But there is no story," the General protested. "His name has not been released."

Park paused, eyeing General Noh warily. "We must be proactive and control the narrative. There are damaging things that can be said and shown. Once the Korean press identifies the man in the newsfeed video, we're cooked." Park winced as he said it.

"Suppose he was working for the TSA to help them identify security lapses? That would dismiss any accusations, correct?"

"Maybe, maybe not. The press will dig deep and find— "

"You just said we need to be proactive and control the narrative. This is how we will accomplish that. My office has received confirmation that Jeong Tae was under contract to find and exploit security weaknesses at LAX."

Park was momentarily stumped. He scratched his chin, squinted his eyes, and said, "The first question I would ask if I were a reporter is: 'Why would a Tae Kwon Do instructor from Orange County be hired to do that?'"

"The answer is simple enough, Mr. Park. Jeong Tae has been unhappy in his current capacity. He is capable of far more than teaching Tae Kwon Do. I believe he has been looking for a better way to utilize his many skills and he found it."

Park frowned at this. "Sir, if I may. The press is only part of the problem. A responsible reporter may indeed dig deep enough to discover what you have just told me. But that part of the story is much less sensational, so it may or may not get the airtime. Perhaps we can still use your clout with them." Park stood and began to pace, rubbing the back of his neck as he did.

"Supposing we can contain the mainstream media, we must turn our focus on the larger problem: social media." He paused for effect and to gauge his boss's reaction. "For the most part, there's no attempt at accurate narrative on the Internet. Only opinion posing as fact. Pictures and videos are shared with no interpretation, only comments from unknowledgeable people based on an emotional reaction. Something like this could go viral. Millions could potentially see your son in handcuffs—again. Maybe his name will get attached, maybe it won't. No way of knowing right now. Everyone who sees it will form his or her own conclusions based on what they see. Containment becomes impossible; the damage incalculable."

General Noh, who was no fan of social media or the untamed frontiers of the Internet, grimaced. "What images are currently circulating?"

"I've only seen footage from the Los Angeles news report. Luckily, your son's face is not visible. I've already placed a call to the LAPD Airport Division requesting a gag order on the release of his name to the press, so I think the information is contained so far."

"Good," said the General. "Then we can move on to other items of business."

"Before we do, let me ask you: Have heard from your son?"

The General cleared his throat. "Not directly."

"Oh, I see." Park stopped there, though his mouth was open as if ready to ask another question.

The General remained silent, a tight-lipped grimace hiding his emotions.

Park squinted at him. "I must ask, sir: How did you obtain the information about your son's ... situation?"

The General kept a straight face. There would be no mention of what he and President Jang had done earlier nor the fact that his wife had received a call from Jeong Tae's wife at 4:30 in the morning. He had learned everything second hand. His only son had not called him directly.

The General's wife had subsequently begged him to believe in their son's innocence and to do everything he could to get him out of jail. She pleaded with him, reminding him of all the good things their son had done and how the General needed to take this opportunity to make up for his mistakes—what he had failed to do—during their son's trial years before.

His wife was rarely as forceful as she had been in the wee hours that morning. When she was right, she didn't back down. The fire in her eyes and the ire in her voice said it all. "You need to put aside your pride and be there this time for our son. It is time to do the right thing for this family, no matter the cost," she had said. A mother's instinct, General Noh had learned, was not a thing to trifle with.

The General knew she was right. His son was not guilty of colluding with terrorists. He knew there was a logical explanation for what he did. But he was not like his wife. He couldn't stake an unfounded claim like that without some substance behind it. If he were to say, "His mother knows he didn't do anything wrong" or "I support my son, based on his mother's intuition" he would be laughed out of the building and, ultimately, out of his job. He needed proof, confirmation, something concrete.

At the same time, the moral obligation to defend Jeong Tae, to advocate for him as both a father and a military leader, weighed on his soul. If there was a chance he could mend his broken relationship with the son who had done him so proud, outside of the one and only blemish on his record, he would take it. The problem lay in the size of that one blemish, and the timing. That blemish had destroyed Jeong Tae's career and standing within his own country. Only by distancing himself had the General preserved his own credibility and retained his position.

Today, perhaps, would provide a chance for both men to redeem themselves.

Chapter 18

T*ransportation Security Agency Head Office, Los Angeles International Airport*

June 5, 2:34 p.m.

I was tired of waiting around in Robinson's uninspiring but functional office. Since I couldn't sit any longer, I walked over to a bank of large windows that looked out over a row of 747s parked at the gates of the international terminal. I stood watching with fascination the constant activity of the ground crews and the kinetic movements of a variety of machines. Specialized vehicles of all types moved in and out of sight, around and between each plane. It looked to me like a loosely choreographed interpretive dance.

The fog had mostly burned off, so I could see a cluster of buildings directly in front of me, several hundred meters to the west. Vehicles moved to and fro between the terminals and those structures. Most of the buildings were low and long, except for the tall white tanks across the tarmac and to my right that I guessed were for fuel. I knew that the Pacific Ocean lay two or three kilometers beyond where I stood. There remained a thin layer of gray between the airport and the ocean obscuring my view of it. I could imagine it would be spectacular when it was clear. I guessed being the Director of the TSA's operations at one of the country's busiest airports got you a corner office with a nice view, but few creature comforts.

As I gazed at the scene spread out before me, I realized that Los Angeles International Airport was like a beehive. Thousands of people and machines in constant motion like a swarm of mechanized insects. It had never occurred to me what a symbiotic cluster of organized chaos a massive transportation hub like LAX was.

From this vantage point, it seemed to me that the chances of one slip up, one mistake, one moment of carelessness happening was much higher than the number of incidents that ever made the news.

I became even more sure of the fact that with all the activity and movement I was witnessing, it would not be so difficult for someone with malicious intent to leverage all of this commotion to do just what I suspected had been done this morning.

It also occurred to me that Alan Robinson was ultimately responsible for the safety of millions of travelers, as well as workers, who came through this place each year. And if today didn't go well, he would be packing up and leaving this office very soon.

Robinson, I had learned, was new to the job, just settling in after being appointed less than a month before. He'd worked his way up the ranks quickly, much like I had before I got derailed. Oddly, I felt a kinship with him and didn't want to see him suffer the same fate I had.

Behind me, Robinson had his cell phone cradled between his ear and his shoulder as he punched the keyboard on his desk. There were stacks of files on the corners of the wooden slab and a few loose papers spread out between his monitor and his keyboard. Robinson was obviously a busy man and the TSA apparently spent its budget on things other than office furnishings for its executives.

As he listened and typed, Robinson gestured for me to take a seat on the opposite side of the desk in one of the wood-framed chairs with the dark blue cloth seats that lacked any noticeable padding. I'd been sitting too long, so I indicated that I'd rather stand.

I stood transfixed, looking out over the very same tarmac where I had taken down the two suspects and where the Korean Air 747 had been. It was gone, of course, and that caused a knot to form in my stomach. In its place was another jet. All I could see was the back half of it due to the building between me and the plane. I relived those few moments I had spent down there and how those few moments had altered the course of my day. Worse yet, I contemplated how my failure to stop those two suspicious characters from loading their mysterious black bag onto my plane could alter the course of thousands of lives. The clock was running. That plane was due to arrive in less than ten hours. It was very possible that something horrible was going to happen before it landed in Seoul.

My thoughts darted from one idea to another, much like the human and mechanical ballet happening below me, but at warp speed. Worried about my students, I wondered what the best solution was to keep them and the other passengers on that plane safe. Could they just dump the contents of the cargo hold into the Pacific Ocean? Had Mr. Lee Baek Young, the supposed baggage handler, removed whatever was in that mysterious bag? If so, where had he put it?

I wondered what Jin Sook had told my wife and what her state of mind was, but I figured she was probably still angry about our argument this morning. If she knew that I had gotten myself arrested, things could only get worse. At this point, I didn't want to throw gas on the fire, so I chose not to contact her until I knew something more. What good would it do me to call her and say I didn't know what was going on, when I'd be ready to come home, or how I'd save my students? At the same time, I knew I couldn't postpone that conversation forever. I owed it to her to provide her with some information, but it had to be solid. I gave myself half an hour to come up with something intelligent to say to my beautiful and smart and inquisitive wife. No way could I get away with half-answers or vague generalities with her. Not in this situation.

For some unknown reason, I thought about my father. Given his position, there was no doubt he had been informed of my arrest. I suspected he had played a major part in getting me diplomatic immunity and the contract I had signed to work for the TSA. What if I failed to thwart the impending attack after all he had done for me? It would bring unspeakable shame. He would have to resign his post. My failure would surely end all possibilities of him becoming the next president of Korea—a noble goal for a man whose heart was, for the most part, in the right place. He had a few things to learn about leading civilians, but he had immense capacity to do good and help make

Korea better. No one questioned his devotion to his country or his desire to make it a safe place for his countrymen to thrive. Why is it, I wondered, his only son got embroiled in national security controversies during the run-up to elections?

The volume of Robinson's voice rose, and his tone became strident. Hearing that snapped my attention back to the present. Although I wasn't paying strict attention before, I had heard him talking about traffic cameras, timeframes, an increased radius, and more eyeballs on the task. He threw out phrases like, "avoiding a crisis," "epic bureaucratic failure," and "blood on your hands and mine if we don't." I knew he was enmeshed in the political and organizational complexities of dealing with an unknown threat from an unknown source, but I couldn't allow myself to be dragged into that swamp.

I didn't miss that part of my former job.

Robinson cursed as he ended another call. "Why is it so hard to get you people to understand what is going on here?" he yelled at the phone in his hand.

When our eyes met, my face must have conveyed deep empathy.

He grimaced. "Yeah, you know all about that, don't you?" Robinson rounded the corner of his desk. "Here's the update: we've got the camera feeds from approximately 9 a.m. until noon. That should give us a good window to start with. We're running all that footage through facial recognition software. I've got the FBI involved. They're sending two agents for now, more later if we get a hit on facial rec. Assuming this moves beyond the confines of this airport, the FBI will take over the lead of this investigation. You willing to cooperate with them?"

I shrugged. "Let's assume Mr. Lee did leave the airport. I don't think that ends your involvement and, given the circumstances, there's no time to do a proper hand-off until we have suspects in custody. I think you still need to figure out what happened within this airport. There had to be other accomplices. You might want to check your footage from yesterday and the day before and see if Mr. Lee met with anyone in or around the airport, specifically employees at that newsstand. That bag had to have come through or around your screening process at some point and I'm willing to bet the clerk that I saw this morning was involved. The two guys I took down didn't have that bag when they went into the store. Once they had it, they moved pretty quickly to the rendezvous with Mr. Lee. The question is whether any of that was caught on camera. Heaven knows you've got enough of them around here."

Robinson shot me a quizzical look. "I thought you were border patrol, not a cop."

"There's a lot of police work involved in what I used to do."

Robinson's phone rang again. His reflexes were lightning fast. He glanced at the display as he brought it out of his pocket. "Tell me you have something good for me." His eyes lit up as he listened. "Good. That's what I wanted to hear. Give me the details . . . Uh-huh . . . OK . . . West? Employee entrance? I see . . . Hmm. Yeah, send over the images . . . Stay on it and narrow it down as best you can. I need as tight a search radius as you can get."

He stabbed his phone's screen to end the call.

"That sounded hopeful," I said, remembering I still needed to check in with Stephanie.

"Yeah. We were searching for this Mr. Lee by name and got a hit. It appears your man left in a hurry, out that west side employee parking area," he said as he pointed out the window. "He swiped his badge at 10:14 and headed south on Pershing in an airport pick-up truck. That prompted a search of the camera feed from that exit booth. They say there's something interesting in the back of the pick-up and want me to look at it." Robinson stepped back around his desk and plopped down in his chair and spun toward his computer screen. He angled it so we could both see. He clicked his mouse until a picture appeared. It was a split screen showing the truck from four different angles.

The top left image showed the front of the truck, its license plate and windshield. It was high enough resolution to allow us to clearly see Lee's face when Robinson zoomed in on it. Next, we checked out the top right image, which was a picture of the back of the truck, showing the rear license plate and the back of Lee's head through the rear window. The bottom left image was the most interesting one. Robinson quickly went to it and enlarged it. This was a top view looking down at the bed of the truck. There was a brown tarp covering some sort of lumpy cargo. Robinson brought the focus in tighter and began to move the cursor around the edges of the tarp. We both gasped at what we saw.

"Would you look at that?" Robinson said. "Not that I ever doubted you, but there's the proof you needed." He quickly caught himself and added, "Potentially."

We were staring at a blood-stained hand poking out from under the side of the tarp.

Chapter 19

Transportation Security Agency Head Office, Los Angeles International Airport

June 5, 2:38 p.m.

"OK. We've got an APB out on this guy, this Mr. Lee. Probably a false name, as you indicated, but that's what we'll call him for now." Robinson was pacing behind his desk now. "Tell me again why you think we should close the borders? Why is it you think he wouldn't just try to lay low and blend in here in the Los Angeles area?"

"First, you have to understand that the leaders of North Korea rule with an iron fist. Literally. There is no room for failure. Failure brings shame. Shame brings condemnation. Condemnation means death—or worse."

"How does that factor in?"

"See, they'll have fail-safes in place—people watching the operatives, keeping track of them. There'll be regular check-ins and protocols for every contingency. If I'm correct, our man is a team leader responsible for planting the bomb onboard. He failed to do so and caused the flight's delay."

"Well, technically, *you* caused the flight's delay," said Robinson with a smirk.

"Right. I became a very convenient excuse and distraction. And I was probably seen by their tech guy who was likely hijacking the video feeds from all your cameras."

"I'd imagine they used the confusion to escape and have no problem letting you take the fall."

"I'm sure it would be like a broken-bat single, to use a baseball reference. At a minimum, he and his cohorts raised the mission's profile and caused the plane to be searched. Right? As a result, as far as we know, their plan was thwarted. At a minimum, it was delayed. But if it was aborted altogether? I don't think I need to spell it out."

"So, you're saying this guy's life is in danger?"

"Yes. And I'm sure he knows it."

"OK. That makes sense." Robinson nodded.

I pulled out a chair across from him and took a seat. "Second, you need to know that anyone and everyone recruited for such an operation has a lot to gain from its success."

"How so?"

"Favors, rewards, advancements. All of the things that will add to their standard of living and status. Desperate people will do anything to improve their lives, but despotic regimes will do anything to improve their leverage on their citizens, too."

"That makes sense, too."

"But, if you fully understood the living conditions for the common man in that country, you would understand what I'm talking about. See, there is no middle class in North Korea. Most of their population is a week or two away from starving. They know nothing other than living day to day. That's it. They wake up each day, go to work for ten to twelve hours. Stand in line to buy rice and vegetables. Go home and eat their meager portions and prepare to do it all over again the next day. At least the working class in South Korea and America have a weekend to look forward to, usually. Not in the North. They have nothing to look forward to and can't buy groceries in advance. People in free countries are also allowed to have religion, which breathes hope into their lives. Not so in North Korea. Very little hope, very little chance of improving their lot in life."

"How does this factor into our hunt for the bad guys?"

"The masterminds of this plan thought long and hard about how to make their plan work. They needed dedicated servants who were bright and clever."

"And desperate," added Robinson.

"Yes," I agreed. "But almost everyone is desperate there. It's finding ones that are sharp enough to follow and execute a complex set of instructions over a long period of time and are willing to believe everything they are told. They need servant-types who will believe that doing a dastardly deed will improve their lives and the lives of their loved ones. They also need those servants to be eager to return home, so they come across the border heavily indoctrinated and ready to do their leaders' bidding."

"That's unbelievable," said Robinson.

"Believe it. Also believe that fear is a powerful motivator. Reprisal is not just for the individual, but for everyone he loves."

I could tell Robinson believed me. Something behind his eyes shifted, as if a puzzle piece clicked into place. A right hand went to his face, thumb and fingers spread out, forming a line between his nose and mouth. His left arm folded across his chest, holding up the right elbow. He huffed, then spoke. His words were slow and barely audible, like he was thinking out loud. "This guy could be anywhere. He's got several hours' head start." He paused and stared into space for a moment. "What's our first step?"

"My best guess says he'll head for Mexico, try to escape the manhunt he knows is coming—both from the US and from his own handlers."

"You said that earlier. You seem pretty sure."

I inhaled deeply as I gathered my words. "Despite all the rhetoric lately, it's still an easily-crossed border, especially going *into* Mexico." I stopped and looked at the wall across from me. "My guess is, he's more afraid of his own people than he is of us."

"Who wouldn't be?" Robinson said.

"One of their greatest fears is defection. Next is detection. So, it's very likely that they have set up precautions against both. Safeguards to keep their operatives from defecting to the United States. It wouldn't surprise me if each of their operatives have a tracking device planted in them. Most likely, there are observers living here in the area, keeping tabs on their movements and activities. Each operative would be keenly aware that they are being watched. I'm sure there's a system for checking in regularly and delivering reports daily, if not twice a day. Beyond that, I'd be willing to bet they have a network of informers in every Korean neighborhood in Southern California. Tight control is the norm with them."

"You're saying the North Koreans have sent over hundreds of babysitters to govern their operatives?"

"No. They have contracted the right kind of people to communicate anything suspicious."

Robinson's forehead wrinkled again. "You're going to have to give me more details."

"The North Koreans will use the South Koreans' paranoia and nationalism to their advantage. They probably have a number of extremely loyal, high-ranking officers who pose as counter-terrorism intelligence officers from the South. These officers go around to the owners of the Korean markets, tea houses, bars, gas stations, night clubs—you name it—in secret, asking for information about certain people. They'll show pictures of their own operatives. They'll simply explain that they have reason to believe these individuals may have ties to the North, knowing the South Koreans, especially the older generations, loathe spies from the North. They will give a number where they can leave anonymous tips."

"So, they use their enemies to spy on their own people?"

"Yes, is there a more efficient way to do it?"

"I guess not," said Robinson.

"It's simple, but effective. We've documented several cases, back when I had a promising career in border protection."

Robinson furrowed his brow and nodded his head. He let my last comment go and stayed focused on the next step. "So, our guy will flee to Mexico?"

"Yes," I said with certainty. "There are several border towns where South Koreans own and operate factories and warehouses. Tecate and Mexicali both have significant Korean populations. He would know that. He would assume that he could blend in there and bide his time."

"Wouldn't the North Koreans have set up a similar network of informants there?"

"It's possible they have, but I'd be surprised if they have as extensive a network down there as they do up here where the action is. It's probable they've made their operatives believe that the network is 'everywhere,'" I explained.

"It's a cheap deterrent, if nothing else. Even if it's only partially effective."

"Common knowledge that your activities are being tracked and recorded instills fear and keeps the troops in line. It scares people into compliance, especially when their loved ones' lives are on the line. But secret knowledge? That's how to trap unsuspecting violators."

Robinson's eyes widened. "So, they make it known to all their covert operatives that they are being watched, just in case anyone gets any funny ideas about defecting over to the US?"

"Correct." I said, sensing the light go on in Robinson's mind.

"But, if the op went sideways . . ." Robinson sat back in his chair and looked at the ceiling, his eyes dancing back and forth. "I guess that makes sense," he said as he exhaled.

"We've got nothing else to go on unless your guys were able to figure out who tampered with the security cameras and how."

"No luck there." Robinson stood and paced; his hands clenched together almost in a prayer position. "There's got to be something we're missing. He must have had other accomplices . . ."

"Too much time has passed now," I said. "They've scattered to the wind is my guess. Most likely, they had some sort of prearranged meeting spot, but finding that will be harder than finding this guy," I said, pointing at the screen. "Surely you've got his cell phone. If so, we can track him using that."

Robinson seemed distant. His hands were pressed together and he was lost in thought, pacing. "Yeah, I've got a team checking on that." He completed another turn, then came to a stop. He gesticulated with his hands as he zeroed in on a line of thinking. "So far we know he's left the airport with at least one body. We're not sure if that one body was dead or alive, which brings up the question of the other body you severely injured."

"My guess is, he's somehow disposed of that body that was in the truck. If we track his cell phone, we should get the answers we need about him. But the bigger question is the other guy, the big one. He most likely survived and it's apparent he didn't leave the airport with these two. Have your guys been able to find the footage around those planes?"

Robinson's phone rang before he could answer my question. He held up a finger as he pressed the talk button and moved the phone to his ear. He listened, then said, "Good work. Let's get some people to the scene. Who's there? . . . LAPD and the fire department? An explosion? Holy cow." Robinson barked out a series of orders having to do with reports and evidence and sharing information and the time-critical nature of this investigation. I barely heard him. My mind was racing in another direction. I was more convinced than ever that this "Mr. Lee" was the linchpin we needed to unravel this mystery.

When his call concluded, Robinson pointed at me. "Mr. Noh, since you are now an agent of the Department of Homeland Security, you'll need these." He yanked open a drawer and fished something out of it. He tossed a badge onto the desk in front of me. "Come with me. We'll get you a weapon and a better jacket. You're not going anywhere until we get this guy."

Chapter 20

Laguna Hills, California
June 5, 2:43 p.m.

Robinson answered another phone call, giving me an opening to call my wife. Knowing she would be upset with me made it that much harder to call her. "Stephanie, listen," I said with an air of dignity and urgency that staunched the flow of questions I knew were bound to come. "Something has come up. I'm working closely with the TSA to resolve some security issues. I'm safe. The kids got on the plane and are on their way to Seoul. Jin Sook is with them, so they're in good hands. I'll join them as soon as I am able."

"Why did you take so long to call?" Her voice was half hurt, half accusing.

"These security issues take time to review and more time to resolve. I've had to answer a ton of questions and repeat my story a dozen times. I just didn't have a chance until now. I took a break to let you know I'm fine and that I'll be busy and may not be able to talk much for the next day or two."

My authoritative tone and my message seemed like a dam that had been dropped in her stream of consciousness, splitting and diverting all of her thoughts and worries into smaller, less forceful streams as they moved around the obstacle. After a moment, though, the streams seemed to regroup into coherent questions somewhere below the dam. "What is going on, JT? I saw something on the news that an Asian man in a Dodger's jacket had been taken away in a police car. Tell me that wasn't you."

I exhaled audibly. "That was me, but it's not what you think. I saw something going down, something that didn't look right to me, and I got caught in the wrong place at the wrong time. It was all a misunderstanding, so they let me go."

"Then why did you say you're working closely with the TSA?"

"Well," I said. "They wanted to know how a normal guy like me was able to slip past their security and get to the tarmac. Once they learned that I'm former military, they thought they could use my input to tighten security. So, I'm lending them my considerable expertise." I tried using a more playful tone.

"Very funny, JT. I know when you're bluffing. What's really going on?"

"I'm telling you the truth. I am providing them input regarding beefing up their security."

"You're telling me the truth? The whole truth?"

I sensed a hidden obstacle that was about to be thrown in my way. "Of course. Why would I lie?"

"That's a good question."

I stayed silent for a beat, trying to anticipate the next question. "What are you getting at?"

"If you're telling me the whole truth, then why did your father call me and tell me he was sending over a delegation from the consulate to save your sorry butt?"

Another pregnant pause while I sorted out the implications of this bombshell. I tried to play it off. "My butt is not sorry," I said with faux indignity. After an audible chuff to show my pretend feelings of disgrace, I added, "And it sure didn't need my dad's help. I've got it all under control. Don't worry."

It's a difficult thing to pull off a lie with one's wife. They have that keen sixth sense and know when you're bluffing. My attempts at humor had not sidetracked her as I had hoped.

"I'm not buying it, JT," she said sternly. "That was the first-ever phone conversation I've had with your dad in the six years we've been married. You can't just blow off a call from the top general in Korea. Why would he call me and tell me he's sending help? There's something more serious that you're not telling me."

There was another long pause. I inhaled through my teeth and said, "Yes, there's more to it. I just can't tell you over the phone. It's complicated and we have very little time."

"Then maybe you can tell me in person. When will we get to see you?"

"When I get back from the World Competition next week," I said. "I'll be on the next plane to Seoul this evening."

Stephanie knew Korean Air's flight schedule better than I expected. "This evening? The evening flight doesn't leave until 7:40. That means we have time to meet up and have something to eat together. That'll give you time to explain what's going on and to say a proper good-bye to your wife and children. Where shall I meet you?"

Stephanie could be assertive when she needed to be. Going along with a ruse was not something she was good at, but confronting me directly rarely worked, either, because I get defensive and shut down usually. But I had left her no other option.

"I don't think I'll have time," I started to say.

"Why not? We have five hours. If I leave now, we'll still have more than three hours to talk. You can tell me the whole story while we enjoy a nice meal together."

"That sounds very nice, Hon, but I'm afraid I'm really busy. Like I said, I'm working with these TSA guys and there's a lot to do to make sure something like this doesn't happen again."

"Well, I'm sure you can wrap things up in the next two hours while I get myself and the kids ready and fight through the 405 traffic to get there." She was not backing down. Not when she knew something was up, something I didn't want to tell her.

After several seconds passed, I knew I couldn't avoid it any longer. In a defeated voice I said, "Fine. Let me save you the trip. The FBI just found a dead body not far from the airport, in a burned-out pick-up truck. Although the body was charred, the injuries to the skull match the ones I inflicted on one of the two guys that I took down."

"Wait, what? You took down two guys? You seem to have left that out of the conversation until now. That's kind of important, isn't it? Why would you do that? What is going on?" The streams were reconnecting and gaining momentum.

"I had to because I thought they were trying to put something dangerous on our plane."

"You're leaving out a lot of details, JT. Why did you take down two guys?" Her voice was starting to quaver. I could tell tears were working their way to the surface. "Who were they?"

"There were these two strange-looking guys in the airport before our flight. Two Korean guys. They looked out of place. They kept wandering around the airport this morning, looking around to make sure no one was watching them."

"But you were watching them, weren't you?"

"I had to. They stood out to me because they were trying so hard not to be noticed."

"What made you think they were doing something wrong?"

"I don't know. Gut instinct, maybe. Then I overheard part of their conversation as they walked by me. They must have thought I was asleep or not paying attention. They spoke with a dialect I clearly recognized once I heard it. They were definitely from the North, Honey."

"What do you mean, 'from the North?'"

"North Korea. I know the accent, the dialect they use. It's different enough to be recognizable. When you've heard it as much as I have, you know. Obviously, that caused suspicion."

"Two guys from North Korea? What would they be doing in Los Angeles?"

"That was my question, too. When they went into a store empty-handed and came out with a heavy suitcase, I knew they were up to no good. So, I followed them through an unmarked door they snuck through. That door led to a hallway with a staircase going down to the tarmac. I watched them take that heavy bag under the plane and hand it to another guy working on the loader. I'm pretty sure he's a North Korean, too."

"How can you be so sure?"

"Again, gut instinct. I followed the third guy and the bag onto the plane, into the cargo area, and got stopped there by four American guys who were loading bags. Actually, two of them were Tongans—big, huge guys. That's when the cops came."

"This is unbelievable," she said, her words slow and methodical. I could tell she was trying to picture the scene in her mind. "OK What happened to the North Korean guy and the bag?"

"He disappeared behind a big luggage rack loaded with suitcases and stuff. I couldn't follow him and get the bag because of the big guys blocking my way."

"Why didn't you tell them what was going on?"

"I did. But, as you can imagine, they thought I was crazy. Plus, you know how bad my English gets when I'm nervous. They didn't give me a chance to explain my story. They just called the cops."

"OK. That explains you being hauled away in a cop car. Let's go back to the other two guys. What happened to them?"

"I don't know for sure."

"Jeong Tae."

"OK, we had a little run-in after they handed the bag to the third guy, the guy who took it into the cargo hold. I lost track of them because I was watching the bag. They ambushed me. It was two against one. I had to defend myself."

"JT."

"It's true. They were coming after me. I did what I had to do to neutralize the threat, but I'm sure they weren't dead when I left them. They were hurt bad, but not dead. We now suspect that the third guy, the baggage handler I followed into the plane, took the guy that was hurt the worst to a warehouse that he then burned to the ground."

"JT, you're skipping some big parts of this story."

"I know. The TSA Director is looking at me. I don't have time to tell you all the details right now."

"This can't be good. This whole thing."

Trying to divert the conversation again, I asked, "Where are you?"

Stephanie was slow to respond. "I'm sitting here in my parents' kitchen."

"Where are the kids?"

"Mom is upstairs putting Matthew down for a nap. Dad should be home any minute with Sophia. Knowing him, he's getting her an ice cream cone down at Chantilly's. Why else would it take him so long to get back?" Her voice, which had trailed off at the end of the question came back with another. "How did you find that burned body?"

"When the building went up in flames and the gas in the truck exploded, someone called 9-1-1. The Fire Chief called the airport police when they discovered the airport logo on one of the truck doors that had been blown off. I've got to go. I'll tell you more later."

"JT, you can't just leave it at that. I'm worried sick about you. What am I supposed to do?"

"Honey, this is all going to work out. You don't need to do anything, except maybe tell my father that I've got things under control." I tried to reassure her by projecting confidence I didn't have. "We're on the trail of the baggage handler. If we can find him, we're hoping to find out what was in that bag and where it is now and make sure we eliminate the threat without causing wide-spread panic. So, you must promise me that you will not breathe a word of this to anyone, OK?"

"Who would I tell?"

"Your parents, for one. I love them. That's why they cannot know about this. It's for their own good. Tell them what I told you: I'm working to help make the airport more secure. That's enough for now. I can't have your dad trying to solve problems for me, too. Also, don't tell the press anything if they call. It would cause us more problems if word got out. I've got to go now. The TSA guys want to talk to me some more."

I hoped she knew I didn't mean the part about not telling her parents. She told them everything. I had a closer relationship with her father than with my own. By far. That bit about not telling her dad? That was supposed to be code. I knew she would go to him for help. And that's what I wanted. If anyone could calm her in my absence, it was Sunny. It would be much better for everyone if Sunny knew what I had done and what I was up against. He could handle the press if they came. He could calm Stephanie and her mother and keep my kids entertained and oblivious.

With Sunny, there was never an insurmountable problem, only ones that hadn't been solved yet. If I couldn't be with my family, I needed Sunny's optimism there.

Chapter 21

M*inistry of National Defense, Yongsan-gu, Seoul, South Korea*
June 6, 7:31 a.m.; June 5, 3:31 p.m. California Time

"We need to leak information to the press," Park the campaign manager said as he paced the floor at the head of the long mahogany table. "Make sure the words 'estranged son' are used. Getting ahead of this mess is the only way to save your chances of winning the nomination." Twenty chairs encircled the massive rectangular conference table, but only three were occupied. General Noh had just reentered the room, hoping for an updated assessment of the situation. Two earnest looking campaign strategists, one in his mid-twenties, the other pushing forty, sat forward in their chairs, pained expressions on their faces. Their early morning vigor quickly fading. "His impeccable timing threatens to once again derail what promised to be a winning campaign. On a national holiday no less—the day we planned to announce your candidacy. Unbelievable."

A third man, the fifty-four-year-old Mr. Song had worked on four previous presidential campaigns. He leaned back and pulled out a cigarette, pressed it between his lips without lighting up. Having been shamed too often for smoking in the office, Song didn't care for all the verbal abuse but never tired of stirring things up. He pushed his chair back from the table and crossed an ankle over a knee as he pulled the cigarette out and eyed it.

Park shot him a warning glance just in case he was entertaining the notion of lighting it, then continued. "Your announcement today could be marred by the revelation of your son's involvement in what seems to be a North Korean plot. Maybe you can enlighten us, General, on any relevant specifics?"

"My son has been released from custody. No charges were ever filed. His name has not been given to the press. There is nothing credible linking him to anything happening in Los Angeles."

"Need I remind you the negligible role truth, credibility, or honesty play in social media?" The older man across the table twirled the unlit cigarette between his fingers as a Cheshire cat grin crossed his face.

General Noh shot Mr. Song an angry glance. His jaw muscles tightened. "The story is that Jeong Tae has been hired by the TSA as a security consultant. Today's incident came about when he exploited a security weakness, as he was hired to do. All of the news stations will be properly briefed if his name is ever brought up. The situation is contained."

Park barely masked his exasperation. "That may be the official narrative, but that guarantees you nothing. It's what people say online that matters most, at least with the younger crowd. Remember, everyone with a phone has a camera and a video recorder. We don't know how many people in the terminal saw and recorded him. A post like that could go viral. Anyone out there could see your son's face and identify him. Then we'll have a real crisis on our hands."

Mr. Song cleared his throat and spoke slowly, as if in deep thought "When it comes to unfortunate newsworthy events such as this, we can manipulate the press and the news media, control the message because we're the ones feeding it to them. It sounds like you've already done that, sir." He paused, cocked his head, and looked directly at the General. "As you may or may not be fully aware, social media is an entirely different animal. It is beyond our control. Sources are often unknown and almost never scrutinized. Someone snaps a picture or takes a video of something inappropriate, potentially scandalous, or just odd and, KABAM, your reputation goes up in smoke. These posts, tweets, snapchats, and stories go out into the ether completely unverified, unfiltered, unchecked. But they are seen by thousands or tens of thousands or hundreds of thousands of people." Another pause for effect. "If someone took a picture or video of your son and his face is recognized ... We may have a bigger problem than we know."

General Noh turned to his campaign manager. "Mr. Park, certainly you have someone monitoring the social media channels. What have they seen thus far?"

Park stood with his hands on his hips. "Nothing that specifically names him yet. But that video of an Asian man in a Dodger's jacket is making its way around. Over one hundred thousand views so far."

Just then, the General's phone began to ring. He pulled it out, checked the screen, and nodded. "Good. That doesn't sound too damaging, especially if he has not been identified. Flood the social platforms with the right story and keep me posted. I have to take this."

With that, the General exited the room as briskly as he had entered.

Chapter 22

Southbound Highway 188, Near US-Mexican Border at Tecate Port of Entry

June 5, 4:59 p.m.

The desert heat was winning the battle with the Ford Focus's air conditioner. Despite having it on "max" with the fan blowing full force, the car felt like an oven. The desert sun streamed in through the windshield in front and pressed inward from the side windows and the metal roof, negating much of the cool air pumping through the vents. That was the problem with buying an old car in a hurry.

Yong Byun wiped sweat from his forehead. He grimaced as he realized he would need to figure out a way to live in this hot, barren, foreign country. The nagging concern over being caught invaded every thought like an unwelcome guest he would never be able to evict. Dread and loneliness, together with the heat, made it hard for him to breathe.

Just a hundred meters and a few dozen lined-up cars lay between him and another new, unfamiliar life. The border crossing into Mexico with its overhead sign and traffic controls was just ahead. On the other side of that sign, the new beginning he had imagined only as his worst-case contingency plan.

Yong Byun's mind was full of questions and fears as he waited his turn to enter his new country. The adjustment to living in the United States had been tempered by the fact that he was surrounded by teammates, bound like brothers in a righteous cause, supported indirectly by their glorious Leader and his Supreme Council. Now, crossing into Mexico to avoid a certain ignominious death at the hands of those who once supported him, Yong Byun felt empty, having no mission to fulfill, and completely isolated with no team to support him. Up to this point, someone else had always planned out his life. Now it was up to him and that realization loomed even more daunting than living amongst enemies in the US had.

Failure had put him in this unenviable position, failure caused by that pesky general's son.

His fake passport sat waiting on the passenger's seat. It had already passed the first, more critical border crossing, the one from Mexico into the United States four years earlier. Because of that success, his confidence was high. Rather than worrying about crossing into Mexico, Yong Byun worried about living there. The food was foreign and didn't match his palate. Sure, it was spicy like Korean food, but in a different way. He hoped his taste buds would eventually adapt.

Then there was the language. He had been sufficiently tutored and had spent long hours practicing both English and Spanish with teachers brought in especially for that purpose. Those teachers had mysteriously disappeared at the end of the group's formal and informal language training. Still, his Spanish was rudimentary at best, which left him anxious. The native Mexicans spoke so fast and with so many colloquialisms that he could not keep up. During his brief time in Mexico, prior to entering America, he had found that most of the people there were kind and patient and spoke slowly enough for him to comprehend most of what they were trying to say. Time would help him deal with the communication issue. He'd get better the longer he stayed.

The biggest hurdle would be blending in. He would have to mix and mingle with the local Korean community. That presented its own set of challenges. During their heyday in the nineties, many South Korean businessmen and investor groups had purchased small factories near the border in Mexico. They made sandals and handbags and leather wallets and cheap trinkets, among other low-skill items, that they then shipped into the United States. These factories kept the local population employed and happy, for the most part. But they were always managed and overseen by South Koreans.

In order to blend in, Yong Byun would have to associate with that group and somehow befriend them. He worried that they might report him as a defector once they picked up on his accent. If his team members were successful in bringing about the devastation the Supreme Council wanted, would he become a suspect? Would they turn him in to the authorities? Or would they welcome a brother from the other side of the border? These questions kept rattling around in his mind, creating an unease that he couldn't shake.

Yong Byun felt a pang of homesickness. The protection of his once simple, yet sheltered life evaporated in the shimmering heat as his little car idled in the line-up. When he signed on for the Chammae Boksu mission, he knew that life would change. He had just never counted on leaving his home country permanently. His dreams had centered around a hero's welcome upon his eventual return and the accompanying financial increase that would move him and his family a step or two beyond the hand-to-mouth living conditions which marked their existence, like that of most North Koreans.

The citizenry of North Korea was taught that their efforts combined to support the greater good of the nation. Everyone had a part to play and if they did what was asked of them, better days would come. Whether they made clothing or shoes in large unheated sewing rooms, or built parts and ammunition for the military, or toiled in the fields to supply rice and vegetables for their community, they were told that their contributions were important underpinnings to the "Great Society." Everyone was an equal. That's what the leaders constantly said. Sacrifice by the individual made the whole stronger.

However, it was well known that there were "special contributors" who garnered extra favor from the overseers. Since no one from his family had ever been chosen to become an official on any level, Yong Byun aimed to become one of those special contributors.

He had volunteered for this dangerous mission because the reward was honor, prestige, and a modicum of comfort for his family. He had been chosen because he had proven his valor and bravery repeatedly during his military service, moving up the ranks of the enlisted. He had volunteered for the most dangerous duties and had performed well, including a few incursions into the hotly contested DMZ.

When Yong Byun returned from his first DMZ mission, he was given a promotion. He spent the next two years doing more dangerous missions to prove himself worthy to participate in this, the grandest of all missions.

Now, sitting in a baking car in the middle of a barren desert, Yong Byun realized all of his efforts, his training, his dreams of a better life, were for naught. They would never amount to anything because his part of the mission had been compromised by one lousy southerner, the very man he recognized and who seemed to recognize him. For the second time in his military career, the General's son had nearly spoiled the plan. The very thought of that man made him seethe.

Months of careful planning and training, months of learning a new language and how to blend in with the enemy's society wasted. So much effort, so much time. The failure would be pinned on Yong Byun. He was the leader of the LAX team on the ground. His family would be eliminated because of it, a grim fact that he had to reconcile in his mind. Saving his own life seemed the only logical recourse because no one would know—or care—about Yong Byun's quick thinking to save the mission or of Un-Chul's bravery. If he succeeded, Un-Chul would never have the opportunity to tell the story.

Despite the apparent failure of his team's mission, Yong Byun was proud of his improvisation in the belly of the plane. Had he not acted quickly, the explosive materials would have fallen into enemy hands. The South Korean was headed for trouble, and that was fine by Yong Byun. No one took the guy seriously. They thought he was crazy. That worked well for Yong Byun until he realized the plane would be delayed because of the intrusion.

As Yong Byun replayed the scene from earlier in the morning, he wondered if the General's son recalled their first meeting. That night long ago was dark and the scene chaotic, but Yong Byun came into close contact with the man, close enough to see the surprise, courage, and resolve in his eyes, similar to what he had seen that morning.

Yong Byun inched the car forward in the line. Soon he would be across the border to the relative safety and freedom of Mexico. His heart felt heavy with shame and sadness, but a kernel of resolve resided there. He did not want to die. Living in America had been more pleasant than he had previously imagined, a fact he kept hidden. The prospect of being completely independent with no safety or support was a daunting one. Fleeing to Mexico was a gamble, but it was the only real choice if he expected to survive past sundown.

As he approached the guard station, he rolled down the window and knew instantly he was in trouble. The look of recognition on the guard's face was undeniable. Before he knew what was happening, he was forced from his car, patted down, handcuffed, and led away into a building on the American side of the border.

Reeling from the sudden turn of events and despairing that, for the second time in a day, he had been within a hair's breadth of triumph and yet had failed, Yong Byun surrendered. Exhilaration quickly turned to abject disappointment. Victory and glory had once again been snatched from his grasp. Instead of ascending to new heights, he was sinking to depths he had never imagined.

Every hope Kim Yong Byun had held for a better life imploded in that moment.

Chapter 23

Onboard Bell UH-1N Helicopter, approaching the Tecate Port of Entry Station

June 5, 7:03 p.m.

Staring out the window of the Bell UH-1N transport helicopter, two things jumped out at me unexpectedly. First, although this was desert country, I had not expected it to be so hilly. We passed several rugged peaks, one of which the pilot pointed out as Tecate Peak. That signaled that we were approaching our destination: The border crossing from Tecate, California, into Tecate, Mexico.

The second thing that struck me was the stark contrast between the US side and the Mexican side. The US side was desolate in comparison. On the southern side of the border, buildings and houses and businesses dotted the hillsides in a semi-organized fashion, whereas the US side hosted maybe a third as many of the same types of structures but spaced farther apart and more haphazardly. Tecate, California, was far less populated than Tecate, Mexico.

As we approached, Robinson pointed to a white building with a red-tiled roof, ringed with trees. "That's the border inspection station. Built in the 1930's and modernized over the years. It's now somewhat of an historic site. That's where they're holding our man, the one you saw in the cargo hold."

I nodded my understanding and approval as I surveyed the scenery.

The helicopter descended. Dust and debris swirled into a cloud under the powerful wash of the helicopter's rotors as we touched down in a fenced-in yard near behind the historic border station. As the engine began to wind down, Robinson nodded to me, a wry smile spreading across his face as he spoke into the microphone of his headset. "This is it, Mr. Noh. This is our border with Mexico. Not quite the DMZ, I'd imagine, but a border nonetheless."

I peered out the window at the rocks and chaparral that dotted the rugged landscape. "Slightly different environment, same goal, I suppose. We have similar mountainous terrain, you know. Just more vegetation to deal with. And I doubt you have the snow and freezing temperatures around here that we have to deal with in Korea."

A twelve-foot-high metal barrier topped with razor lay a hundred meters to our south. It spread east to west as far as I could see. A ribbon of dark asphalt ran southward fifty meters to the west of the landing pad. A line of cars backed up beyond a grouping of guard huts and gates as they passed through the border check point.

Robinson and I were greeted by two smart-looking Border Patrol Guards as the door slid open. They wore crew cuts, wrap-around black sunglasses, and Colt M4 Carbine sub machine guns slung across their shoulders. We received snappy salutes and were escorted quickly to the rear entrance of the characteristically southwestern adobe-style building a few meters away. At Robinson's insistence, I had replaced my Dodger's jacket, jeans, and Nike's with desert camo cargo pants, black boots, and a black synthetic polo shirt with the DHS logo stenciled on the left breast. I looked official but felt like an imposter.

As soon as I stepped out, I felt heat. Although the sun was low in the western sky, the heat came from all sides, including upward from the ground. The asphalt of the helipad and the clumps of rocks strewn throughout the small yard radiated a long day's worth of pent-up solar energy. The helo's rotors simply moved the hundred-degree air around, along with a cloud of dust, causing the grit to stick to my skin as I ran across the dirt lot. Droplets of sweat began to form and capture the swirling dirt before I even reached the building entrance.

"Right this way, sirs," said the tall one with the spiky black crew cut, perfectly squared in the front to match his imposing jaw line and strong chin. He opened the door and stood aside as we entered a reception room. The blond guard entered after us and closed the door behind him. He stopped abruptly and remained at the door. Black Hair nodded at him, then led us down a hallway tiled with large dark brown adobe squares to a closed office door. He knocked, pushed the thick knotted pine door open far enough to stick his head in, then closed it again.

The alcove near the office was furnished with two wide chairs. Both were upholstered in a southwest design and pushed up against an adobe wall. A rustic end table adorned with magazines occupied the corner. Our escort motioned for us to take a seat. "Sergeant Lewis will be with you in a moment."

We waited less than two minutes in silence.

When he appeared in the doorway, Sergeant Lewis filled it almost as well as the door itself. He was tall and thick with broad shoulders that barely tapered to a sturdy waist. There wasn't an ounce of fat on him from what I could see. From the look of him, he could have been made of steel. His face had a no-nonsense scowl permanently etched into it. "Pleasure to meet you Director Robinson," he said in a deep baritone voice. His hand engulfed Robinson's as they shook.

"Sergeant Lewis, we appreciate your cooperation, especially at such short notice. This is Commander Noh, formerly with the South Korean Border Patrol. He's joined my team today to help interrogate the suspect."

Lewis nodded his approval with a tightening of his mouth and jaw.

I gave him a perfunctory bow. Force of habit, I guess.

"Very well," Lewis said as he looked almost straight down at me. "Welcome to the most abused border in the world, Mr. Noh." His mean face cracked into a wide smile. "We do our best here, but we've got almost two thousand miles of fence line between these two countries to protect and hundreds of thousands who want to enter the United States every year in any way possible. We've got a tall task, but we're up for the challenge." Another smile as he straightened his posture to make himself even more imposing.

Robinson chuckled. "You certainly measure up, Sergeant Lewis." More smiles. "This assignment, I suppose, was a bit different than usual."

Lewis cocked his head. "Very true. We're usually trying to keep them out, not in."

"Well," said Robinson, "Your quick response and diligent efforts are greatly appreciated. I'm sure you understand the delicate nature of the situation. We must consider the flying public, the safety of the citizens of both the United States and our ally, South Korea. Plus, the time-sensitive nature of our inquiry."

Lewis nodded. "I completely understand. My men and myself will remain professional and committed to the overarching goal of safety and protection."

"Good," said Robinson. "We don't need word of this spreading, certainly not to the media."

Lewis gave a deeper nod to show his understanding, then gestured for us to follow him around the corner and down another hallway. "We have your man sequestered in a special room down here."

Two armed guards, one stationed on each side of the closed door, saluted Sergeant Lewis as we approached. One opened the door. Robinson and I followed the giant Lewis into a room that was bisected by floor-to-ceiling bars. Our suspect was sitting on the edge of a cot, elbows on knees and head in hands. His posture mimicked that of a deflated tire. He barely looked up when we entered the room. When he caught sight of Lewis, his eyes grew wide.

I chose to stay behind Lewis, out of sight, until the formal introductions.

"Mr. Lee. We have brought someone who speaks your language. He will have some questions for you. I suggest you give him your full cooperation." Lewis stepped to the side and held his hand out, palm up, to introduce me. "Mr. Noh, if you would, please review with Mr. Lee his rights and confirm his understanding of them."

Once again, the man's eyes opened wide and his jaw dropped. More air escaped the tire. His gaze dropped to the floor and his head bowed slightly. I thought that was a good sign, so I did the best I could to recite the Miranda rights in my native tongue. I was reasonably close. I informed him that he had the right to remain silent and had the right to an attorney and all that good stuff. I asked him if he understood his rights. The man looked at me in disbelief but nodded anyway. "If I were you," I added, "I would waive my right to keep silent. The things you say here could very well save you a lot of hardship and difficulty. Telling us what you know can only help you, not hurt. Remaining silent, on the other hand, could prove disastrous for you and a lot of others."

I launched into my prepared interrogation, wasting no time, informing him that I knew that he and the two men I left for dead had conspired to plant an explosive device on Korean Air Flight 134 and that if it went off, his situation would turn from bad to extremely bad in a matter of hours. "The life you thought you were going to lead is over. You need to understand that. You will never live a free life again. Never. You can't go home. You can't stay here. And now, you can't run away to Mexico as you had hoped to do. So, you can fix a very bad situation and avoid the full weight of justice and the guilt that comes with killing hundreds of innocent people, or you can take your chances on the American and Korean legal systems. It's up to you. But, believe me, if you take down a plane, there will be plenty of hungry wolves howling for your blood. And they will rip you limb from limb. How lucky do you feel?"

A false sense of superiority overshadowed his face. "There are no innocent people on that plane. They are all thieves and gluttons."

"Thieves and gluttons? Really? Who have they stolen from? You? Your country? The corrupt regime keeping you and your fellow countrymen starving?"

His countenance clouded over.

"Yeah, I've heard all the radical rants from other captives we've apprehended in the DMZ. It's always the same rubbish. Your poor nation is suffering because the South is flourishing at your expense. Do me a favor. Save your tripe for the trial."

My prisoner looked flabbergasted. I let him stew for a minute while I pulled something up on my phone.

"I'll bet this little video here will make the case for your execution. Want to see it?" I wiggled my phone in front of him.

He shrugged.

"Check this out," I said, moving closer to the bars that separated us, holding the phone at eye level for him to see.

As he watched the surveillance camera video of him escaping the airport in a stolen airport truck, the deflated tire posture returned.

I paused the video at a frame that clearly showed his face. "You didn't know there were cameras there? That surprises me. Or did you just not know that they were High Definition?" I let it play for another few seconds. "See that? That's clearly a body under that tarp. I'm pretty sure I recognize those shiny new boots. This is the smaller guy, right? His boots look just like the bigger guy's shiny new boots, but this lump is too small to be that big guy."

I watched him for signs of realization. He was hiding it well.

"Clearly, this is not the big guy, the one with the messed-up arm. I'm pretty sure this is the smaller guy. I kicked his sorry ass a centimeter short of death. Your two friends tried to ambush me right after he handed off that heavy suitcase to you under the plane. Same guy, right?"

His shoulders rose and fell with the intake and expulsion of a deep breath as I spoke, but he remained silent.

"I can also assume that the big guy is on the loose. Maybe you shot him up with some sort of painkiller or something, then forced him to take the suitcase and get on the plane because you're too scared to do it yourself. You're a damn coward, aren't you?"

Mr. Lee's jaw muscles flexed, and he stared at the wall behind me.

"You're a little boy inside, aren't you? Not quite a man yet. Not man enough to see this thing through. No, you're running away like a scared child."

Still no reaction, just a rigid posture and a stone face.

"You call yourself a leader? Do you even know what being a leader is all about? It's not about forcing your wounded subordinate to do something you're perfectly capable of doing. No. That's what we call cowardice, you pathetic excuse for a man."

The insults finally penetrated his armor. Mr. Lee practically spat as he spoke, his voice so choked with anger the words were barely intelligible. "He volunteered to go, even after I insisted I should be the one to finish the mission. Un-Chul is more of a man than you will ever be. He *wanted* to take the bag. He's a hero."

I considered him for a long moment, sizing him up and down with my eyes, letting a sneer form. "OK. So, you let a wounded Comrade step in and take over your assignment. A man suffering and in shock and you let him fulfill your duty. So, where is he now?"

"What do you know about duty?" he spat. "Nothing. You abandoned your duty and your country."

"This isn't about me. This is about you and how you're not willing to die for the cause. No. You're too soft. Is that it? Too scared."

"I told you already—"

"Quiet. I don't need to hear any more excuses. It's clear you had a plan all along to sneak off to Mexico in hopes of living out the rest of your days far away from the misery of your homeland. Tell me where Un-Chul and that bag are."

I had him. His jaw muscles twitched, and his breathing grew sharper and deeper, his pride wounded beyond recovery.

Robinson cleared his throat, pulling my attention toward him. "What are you saying to him?"

I shot Robinson a look that said, "don't interrupt me," then returned my focus to the man on the other side of the bars.

"I don't care if you think the people on that plane are innocent or not. I do want you to understand that the courts will see it as mass murder, pure and simple. You'll be sent off to the worst jail, probably Guantanamo—you've heard of Guantanamo, haven't you? It's where the Americans send all the enemy combatants. It's in Cuba. A different country. Therefore, they don't have to follow US law and treat prisoners there with the same rights they have here. There's very little oversight from what I hear. And lots of other terrorists you can play with. I hear they like Asian boys, think they're cute and submissive. They like to share them, multiple times per day, if you know what I mean. Sounds fun, doesn't it?"

Mr. Lee's movements became stilted and robotic. His breathing was audible as he drew in breaths through his gritted teeth.

I proceeded slowly, enunciating each phrase and pausing to let it sink in.

"You will have one chance and one chance only to seek and gain asylum in the United States or an Allied nation, if you prefer. That opportunity will come only if you cooperate fully and completely. Any hesitation on your part will disqualify you."

Again, I waited. This time, after a few beats, he raised his head and said, "I don't believe you."

Robinson interjected again, demanding that I tell him what was going on. I translated the gist of our exchange and Mr. Lee's two-word answer. "What doesn't he believe? That we'll grant him asylum or that we know he planted the bomb? I need more details."

I signaled for Robinson to step out in the hallway with me. Lewis followed.

"Chances are, he understands English perfectly. So, let's keep our conversations out of earshot," I said just above a whisper. "He's playing the odds. By being disbelieving, he is buying himself some time to sift out the nuggets of information we actually have versus what we claim to have. He knows time is working against us, so he's angling for a deal by misdirecting the conversation." I took sixty seconds and caught them up with more details on what I had covered with our prisoner. Both men nodded, grim-faced and serious.

"How are you going to get him to tell you where he put the bomb? And how we can verify his claim?" Robinson asked.

"Well, the first video helped me establish credibility. Any luck finding video of the big guy anywhere?"

"Not yet, but my guys are trying."

"Well, then, the only thing I have as leverage is to keep threatening him with a one-way ticket to Gitmo."

"What if we offer to send him home? You said it yourself, back in my office, the North Korean regime won't tolerate mistakes, let alone defection. We tell him that we're going to send him home after being caught trying to defect into Mexico. See how he takes that news."

I considered Robinson with a nod of my head. "That's good. I like it."

"What if we don't find that device and the plane blows up?" asked Lewis. "He seems set on stalling as long as he can, so that's a real possibility, isn't it?"

Robinson flashed a reptilian smile, like he was hatching some diabolical plan.

"What's that look?" I asked.

"We need to shake this guy up. I say, we press on him for a while longer. If he doesn't offer any credible info, we let him go."

"What?" Lewis and I asked simultaneously.

"Look. We can send some trumped-up charges and photos to the Mexican authorities before we release this guy. Let him get a taste of a Mexican prison. Then we save him and offer to get him back to the US if he cooperates"

The thought was devious, but it made me smile, too. "I like the sound of that. I mean, the idea of letting him spend some time in a Mexican prison. I hear they're pretty sketchy."

Lewis guffawed. "That's an understatement. The one just over the border here is full of the worst Mexico has to offer. All their coyotes, drug runners, pimps, and cartel enforcers who get caught at the border are either kept in Tecate or in Tijuana. Both are cesspools. If you want to make him sing to get out of a worse situation, this is your place."

I thought for a beat. "OK. Let's set it up. We have no time to waste. Do you know people over there?" I asked Lewis. "Could we make this happen in the next hour?"

Lewis raised an eyebrow. "I have a good relationship with my counterparts on the Mexican side, sure. I'll get on the horn and set things in motion."

"Let's find something that happened on their side of the border recently. Something with major implications and lots of media coverage. Like one of those coyotes who abandoned a truckload of people and let them die in the desert. Tell them we have that coyote's boss, the big man behind it all. Tell them to watch out for a Korean guy trying to sneak back in to do it again and give them the full description of his car."

Both Robinson and Lewis nodded.

Lewis cocked his head and said, "Better yet, there are several teenage girls from one of the working-class neighborhoods who have gone missing recently. Suspected human trafficking for the sex trade. We send the Mexican police a tip and he'll land himself in that prison. Should be interesting."

Robinson turned to Lewis. "Your contacts on the other side of the border will cooperate with us and let him out before he's harmed, won't they?"

"If I ask, they will. Colonel Rodriguez from the Baja station owes me a favor. I'll call it in to nail this scumbag."

Chapter 24

M*inistry of National Defense, Yongsan-gu, Seoul, South Korea*
June 6, 11:16 a.m.; June 5, 7:16 p.m. California Time

"Jamkkanman," he whispered into his phone as he marched double-time to his corner office. *Just a minute.* The General exited another tense debriefing on the situation with the airliner. Half the men in the room wore military uniforms, the other half business suits and ties. Nothing new had been discussed, and his presence was not essential. He excused himself pointing at his phone.

His tone was professional, revealing nothing to his subordinates or counterparts regarding the identity of the caller. Culturally, it would be shameful to leave an important meeting to talk to his wife. That would be even more unbecoming of a high-ranking officer. After closing the door of his expansive private office, he continued. "What's wrong?" he said, trying not to bark at her. This was the third call in less than sixty seconds. It was obvious that there was something urgent. After thirty-seven years of marriage, even a man can learn not to ignore his wife when she has something important enough to interrupt during business hours.

The General's wife possessed both unfading beauty and an indominable spirit.

"I'm worried," his wife said. She offered no apology for interrupting his workday, as would be customary in a such a situation.

"You pull me from a strategy session to tell me you're worried?" he huffed.

"Stephanie called again. She said Jeong Tae told her he is working on a security breach at LAX, but now is not answering his phone."

"Don't worry. I already arranged Jeong Tae's release. He is a free man."

"That's not what I mean. I already knew you did that much."

"What do you know? And how?" His tone was laced with curiosity.

"I know you, Tae Seong. I know how you think."

"What's that supposed to mean?" The surprise in his voice expressed more hurt than he was prone to show under normal circumstances.

"I knew you would be concerned about your reputation and how having your son in trouble could tarnish it. With your campaign ready to launch, you would make sure it couldn't happen again. So much easier when it's in a foreign land and the local media is not there to record and comment on every detail."

While she wasn't the stereotypical Korean wife and mother of their generation—she had never allowed herself to be the silent trophy wife of the rising star—she had never called him out for his actions while at work.

The General paused. When he answered, it was just above a whisper. "I did what I had to do for our son."

She clicked her tongue on the roof of her mouth with a "tsk" sound. "And for yourself. Please don't patronize me, Tae Seong. You know me better than that."

"OK. Maybe it was somewhat self-serving. But I also had Jeong Tae and my grandchildren in mind. It's not good for children to have a father in prison."

"No, it's not," she agreed. "It's also not good for a presidential candidate to have a son arrested on the day he launches his campaign."

General Noh huffed again. "It's not like that. Not completely."

"Oh, no? Are you certain?"

"When you spoke to Stephanie this morning, I felt more than just a twinge of guilt. I realized that you have a relationship with her. I don't. She trusts you and you care about her. Suddenly, I felt like an outsider in my own family. So, I called her. It was awkward ... for both of us. I could sense that she was as uncomfortable as I was. I regret that."

"What are you going to do to fix it?"

"Now is not a good time to worry about . . ." The General started to speak but stopped. His wife was, as usual, putting the needs of the family first. She had always said that everything else in life falls into its proper place when one had his or her priorities straight.

She continued, her voice calm and soothing. "I know how you have fretted about the situation for years. I know the distance between you and our son is eating you up inside."

"Why do you say that? It's untrue. I'm at peace because I have tried."

She paused a beat so he could reflect. "Is that why you felt awkward talking to your own daughter-in-law? Is that why you watch your friends so longingly when their grandchildren come to visit?"

"I don't know what you're talking about."

"Yes, you do. I see how you react. You're just too proud to talk about it."

"Pride has nothing to do with it."

"That's not true. It has everything to do with it. Your pride in your position and your reputation and your accomplishments is the reason you don't have a relationship with your son."

General Noh said nothing. The seconds ticked by, each feeling like an eternity. When he spoke, instead of arguing, he simply replied, "I know. You're right."

There was a pause. When Mrs. Noh began to speak again, her voice was choked with emotion. "Then do something about it while you can. Becoming president will mean nothing if you lose your son. This may be your only chance."

"I've done what I can do."

Mrs. Noh was not one to argue with her powerful husband. Not unless she knew she was right. When it came to family matters, she did not back down. "Is that why Stephanie feels like Jeong Tae is being set up for failure? She fears that because he has been put in charge of this investigation, he will be the one to blame when that plane explodes. Is that the sum of your efforts? Have President Jang release him and make him the scapegoat for a doomed assignment?"

"He will not fail." The General's voice was soft, but full of conviction.

"What if he does?"

"Do you think I had an alternative? The US President said he would only release Jeong Tae if he promised to cooperate with the investigation. Then he changed it and said he should be the one to lead it since he has the most experience with North Koreans. What more can I do?"

"You'll figure it out."

Chapter 25

Tecate Port of Entry Station
June 5, 7:39 p.m.

Mr. Lee had regained his disinterested façade by the time we returned to his holding cell. He tried to look tough and defiant.

In the Korean language, there are three basic levels of speech to show deference, familiarity, or lower social status, usually based on age, rank, or accomplishment. In the beginning of our conversation, I wanted him to feel respected and important, so I had used the highest form of verb conjugation. After a short while, I switched from honorific to the more familiar middle form, showing that I felt we were equals. With his contempt and defiance, I felt it necessary to speak more commandingly. This is when I changed to "pan-mal," or "half words," where the conjugations are either dropped off or abbreviated. Using this low form of speech showed him that I did not hold him in high regard and that I was in a position of dominance or authority over him.

"That's right. We saw the video of you driving a stolen airport truck, exiting through the employee gate on the west side." I waited a beat. "I assume that is the body of the smaller guy. No way was he getting up."

He squinted at me again, but the contempt was starting to look more like fear.

"You're out on your own now, aren't you? You're running away."

He averted his eyes for just a split second, but it was enough for me to know I was on the right track.

Since Robinson had received some intel from his team during our flight down, I thought now would be a good time to bring up what we had learned. I pulled out my phone and opened the photo we had received and turned the screen so Mr. Lee could see the image of smoke billowing from what remained of a building in an older commercial neighborhood.

"How long did you think it would take us to connect you to the fire at that warehouse? I guess you figured you'd be over the border by the time we figured it out, right?"

Mr. Lee's shoulders rose and fell with the intake and expulsion of a deep breath. The tire was flat; the wheel now resting on its rims.

From there, I went with gut instincts, but also knew I was going out on a limb farther than I wanted with some of my assertions. I knew he understood me, despite the differences in dialects between North and South Korea. "I know you recognized me in the plane. I know the bag you hauled into the plane was heavy. You struggled with it as you lifted it on the loader." I kept watching him. He was trying hard to maintain a stone-faced expression, just as I had done earlier, and I hated him for it. "I know had an explosive device in that bag, probably C-4. It's the only way it went undetected."

Mr. Lee said nothing, but his facial muscles betrayed him.

"I know you moved it out of the plane so the scanners could not find it. Nor could the dogs. Our people searched the cargo area thoroughly and found nothing, so I know you did something with it. What did you do? Where is that bag right now?"

I paused to give our suspect a moment to reflect on what I'd said. His eyes were downcast at first. When he leveled them to meet my gaze, there was a latent defiance, but it was withering. "I don't know," was all he said. Nonetheless, I could see a shift in his posture and in his countenance. I had hit a nerve.

"You are on U.S. soil, trying to cross an international border after planting explosives on an airplane destined for Seoul, Korea. This is not a good situation for you. Failing to cooperate will only make things worse. Remember, things are much more lenient in the United States than in Korea. In Korea, the situation will be much different, much more immediate. There is truly no mercy for such a person." I stopped to let that salient information seep in. He had been trained to resist interrogation. That much was obvious. Despite his training, however, as the minutes rolled on, involuntary muscle twitches betrayed him. He was suppressing his rising anxiety. I broke the long silence. "If you cooperate here and now with the US authorities, we can petition to avoid extradition to Korea and save you from a much harsher punishment."

"The bag was in the truck. It burned." His voice was raspy, just above a whisper.

"You're lying. There was no sign of a suitcase. Our investigators checked."

Robinson nudged me, imploring for the translation with his eyes and facial expression. I translated in a whisper while "Mr. Lee" digested my last words. Robinson suggested I prick his conscience with talk of all the innocent people, especially the children, on board that flight.

I returned my focus to our suspect on the other side of the bars. "You're lying to me. I know it and I know you know it, so stop the games."

I studied his reaction. He kept his head low, but his body grew perceptibly more rigid. His movements became stilted and robotic. He sucked in another breath, more audibly this time. "I don't know where the suitcase is. Un-Chul took it."

"Is Un-Chul the big guy?"

He nodded.

"His arm was broken. How could he have taken it?"

"He's a strong man. Well trained. Very determined."

I translated for Robinson because he kept nudging me. This made Mr. Lee smile, though he tried to hide it. He obviously understood English well enough.

I gave Mr. Lee a hard stare. "Let me remind you, this is your one chance at freedom. You can go free only if you cooperate fully and completely. You tell me now where that bag is, and help us land that plane safely or you will lose that chance forever."

He raised his head and said, "I told you. I don't know."

"Mr. Lee, this is your only chance."

He looked down, then brought his eyes up to meet mine. "I don't know where the bag is, but if I know Un-Chul, he put it on the plane."

"How?"

"I don't know. But I am willing to bet my life on it."

"OK. Good," I said in English so Robinson could understand. "Un-Chul put the suitcase back on the plane somehow. Mr. Lee is willing to bet his life on it. So now all we have to do is find it and disable it." I nodded as I clapped my hands once and turned for the door.

"That won't do you any good," Mr. Lee added.

"What do you mean?"

"The explosives are controlled by a cell phone that I hid in another bag. The signal is unbreakable."

I stopped in my tracks and turned back to face the prisoner in his cell.

"It'll blow up no matter what you do."

My stomach tightened and a chill flashed through my body. Everything froze. My thoughts went immediately to my students, especially those two little eight-year-olds. Through gritted teeth I said as I lurched towards the bars that separated us, "You're going to tell me everything we need to know to save the kids on that plane."

Chapter 26

Tecate Port of Entry Station
June 5, 8:13 p.m.

I spent half an hour questioning our suspect and promising him a better life in America if he cooperated. Despite my attempts to build rapport, he remained aloof. The few times he spoke, his speech was so full of vitriol and contempt for all things Western and capitalistic, it made me realize the depth of the brainwashing that takes place with North Koreans, especially among their military operatives.

This man was a soldier who had been indoctrinated from a young age to believe that the leaders of North Korea had all the answers for all of life's problems. His role was to defend, protect, and maintain the honor and sovereignty of the Democratic People's Republic of Korea against all enemies. He was steeped in the socialist dogma, or at least he comported himself that way. Everything he said ended with a criticism of the two countries I called home or with some reference to one lowly breed of animal or another. I would have been amused had I not been under so much time pressure.

His deportment improved somewhat as our conversation went on, as I had hoped it would. However, no useful information came, no clues, no big picture sketch during any of his diatribes. Each question was answered with more of the same berating of our culture and lifestyle, but without the answers I needed. He didn't know how to defuse the bomb. He didn't even know where or how or *if* his partner had succeeded in stowing it on the plane. That much I believed. But when I questioned him about the other operatives and where they were and what roles they played, he got cagey. When I asked about who the mastermind was, his eyes darted almost imperceptibly. When I demanded answers about how to find those who might know, he repeated that he knew nothing more.

I didn't believe those parts. Maybe he didn't know everything I wanted to know, but he knew more than he was telling me. With each non-answer and with each phony line, I grew more impatient. The vision of those two eight-year-olds with their innocent smiles and playful laughs haunted me. I was letting them down and this man was sentencing them to destruction.

I leapt to my feet and approached the bars, grabbing two of them and glaring at Mr. Lee.

Lewis and Robinson had left us alone, ostensibly because they couldn't understand the conversation. I suspected they were monitoring things through the tiny camera in the upper corner of the room. My suspicions were confirmed when they barged into the room. Lewis walked straight toward me. I let go of the bars and took a step back.

"Mr. Lee," Robinson announced. "You are free to go."

I protested, the anger rising to new levels. Lewis stared down at me as he positioned himself to box me into the corner.

"We don't have sufficient evidence to hold him any longer. I'm sorry."

"But what about—"

Robinson shot me a look that froze me. It was the look a wolf gives one of his packmates as he takes his position in the enclosing circle.

The two MP's entered the room and unlocked Mr. Lee's cell and escorted him out of the room. Lewis, with his intimidating glare, gave me the willies, even though I knew what was going on. I didn't really have to act. My nervousness was genuine. Once the MPs had opened the cell and marched Mr. Lee out of there, Lewis cracked a fiendish smile and winked at me. His demeanor up to that point was convincing. I acted like I wanted to fight through his blockade to get to Mr. Lee, but Lewis' meaty paw held me in place. Lee shot me a contemptuous, gloating look of victory as he practically bounced out of the room. The MPs escorted him to his car and waited for him to get in and start the engine. A Humvee blocked him from being able to turn right and head north, back into the US, then followed him as he turned south toward the border crossing station.

I was exhausted and irritated that I couldn't get him to speak, that we had to resort to this kind of trickery. It wasn't foolproof. None of us knew whether this ruse would work as we hoped. "How long till they pull him out, do you think? That guy is our only link to finding a way to save those passengers."

Robinson and Lewis exchanged a glance, then Robinson spoke. "Your guy is being very resistant with you. I bet he won't be so tough after an hour or two in there." He pointed over his shoulder toward the Mexican side of Tecate.

"Just watch," Lewis said. "His whole attitude will be different when we get him back here." His deep baritone voice and his in-control manner soothed my rankled nerves and made me feel like less of a failure.

The three of us navigated through the hallways until we stood near the glass entrance doors of the station and watched Mr. Lee's taillights as he reached the front of the line, which was now much shorter.

In the twilight, it was difficult to make out what was happening. Lewis held a miniature pair of binoculars to his eyes, pinching them between his long forefinger and thumb like a toddler holding a piece of candy. He called out the play-by-play.

"He's handing over his documents now. The guard is leafing through the passport, handing it back. OK, he's through."

I could just make out the gray car sliding past the guard station. As soon as Mr. Lee rolled onto Mexican soil, two motorcycle cops pulled out in formation, lights ablaze. One whizzed around to the front of Mr. Lee's Ford Focus and the other stayed in the rear. Halfway down the block, two more joined the convoy, taking up positions on either side of the small gray sedan.

The three of us watched as he got out of the car, hands waving in exasperation. He yelled in protest, but that only got him a gun pointed at his face and some rough handling as he was body-slammed against the hood of the car and cuffed.

Lewis handed me the binoculars. It was a pitiful sight, really. Nothing, it seemed, would go right for Mr. Lee that day and his expression showed how mystified he was.

"Let's see how Mr. Lee likes Mexican prisons," said Lewis. "Chances are, he'll be begging to take your deal and spill his guts. Give it an hour or two."

My reaction was one I wish I didn't relish so much. It's deplorable to wish atrocities upon another human. But that man was a major conspirator in a plot to kill hundreds of my countrymen, including my young students, and disrupt the delicate balance of power in an already tenuous region of the world. Who knew what would happen on the world stage if that plane blew up? He had brought what was coming upon himself.

"He'll be in that Tecate prison just long enough to get a taste for what his new life would be like." Robinson was matter of fact about it. "Sergeant Lewis' Mexican counterpart promised to keep an eye on things once Mr. Lee is in his custody to make sure he is primed but not seriously injured. Then, we'll go in and give him another chance to cooperate, dangling the carrot of extradition to the United States with the possibility of a reduced sentence for good behavior. What do you think about that?"

"I have never wanted something so devious to work in my favor more than this." We were in unchartered territory, looking to solve a major homicide before it happened using the one and only piece of evidence we had time to collect. We were using dubious means to reach the only acceptable outcome.

"Unfortunately, we don't have time to wait until later tonight, when things promise to get really interesting," Lewis said. "But I would imagine that he'll get a pretty good idea how bad it can get during his brief stay."

A prisoner transport van arrived moments later, and we watched poor Mr. Lee get hauled off by the Mexican cops.

Robinson's phone rang in this pocket. As he listened, his facial features hardened, and his eyes squinted. "That's not good," he said. "I can't believe a man like that wasn't stopped and questioned." He listened for a moment. "That's true...but still." Another pause to listen. "Talk to everyone. Every ticket counter agent in that terminal and at every gate. Ask every security guard, TSA agent, baggage handler, shopkeeper, hell, question every janitor on staff. Someone must have seen this guy. We have to know where he went."

"What's going on?" I said.

"The bigger guy you beat up—there's a glimpse of him on one of the cameras in the baggage loading area. He's hobbling, dragging a bag that appears to be really heavy, just like you said, one arm tied or taped to his body." His face was contorted in disbelief.

"What's wrong?"

"This guy with the busted arm is nosing around near the landing gear and no one stopped him because he's shining a flashlight and is wearing a grounds crew uniform. Then he disappears and so does his bag. He's gone. Just like that."

"What do you mean, he's gone?"

"I mean, he disappeared. Or, more accurately, two minutes' worth of recording disappears. Yeah, a two-minute gap. Enough to climb up into the wheel well with the bag. And nobody saw anything. Unbelievable."

"What's the time stamp on the video?"

"1:17 p.m. Then it jumps to 1:19, just like that." Robinson snapped his fingers, still shaking his head.

"What time did flight 134 actually take off?" I asked.

Robinson tapped his screen several times in rapid succession. "1:44. Almost two hours behind schedule." He tapped some more and put the phone to his ear and turned away for a moment. When he finished the call, a ding on his phone announced an incoming message. "OK," said Robinson as he opened the picture. "Here it is. Do you recognize this guy?"

He turned his phone to me and played a short video clip. I saw, clear as day, the big guy's face, twisted with pain as he shuffled along, dragging the same weighty black bag I had seen earlier. I had to tip my cap to their notion of bravery and loyalty. It far exceeded that of the common man. "Holy cow. That's him. This is unbelievable. I shattered this guy's elbow and destroyed his solar plexus. How is he able to even move?"

Robinson, a grim expression shadowing his face, answered. "Good question. This is all we have. These thirteen seconds."

I turned back to where Mr. Lee had been arrested. The van was just pulling away from the curb. I had maybe two hours to prepare myself to make the most of my next meeting with him. Those two hours would be like an eternity knowing what hung in the balance.

Chapter 27

P*rocuraduria General de la Republica, Tecate, Mexico*
June 5, 9:51 p.m.

The sharp report of a club banging against the metal bars erupted, pulling Yong Byun back into the moment. Voices barked out commands. The kicking stopped. The men around him froze. Keys jangled and the bars of the jail cell rattled as the door slid open. Angry shouts of authoritative voices echoed against the cinder block walls and the concrete floor, just inches from his ear.

The startling noises were the sounds of salvation.

"Get back. Let me through." There were several voices, each calling out similar orders. "Get back, I say. Make room."

A strong hand pulled on his shoulder, rolling him onto his back. Yong Byun opened his eyes to see the concerned face of a uniformed officer who knelt over him, checking his eyes as he held Yong Byun's jaw. Three other officers pushed the crowd away. A sea of demonic, grungy faces peered at him through squinted eyes.

A wave of relief flooded Yong Byun's mind and body as the man said, "Come on, hurry. Get up. You're coming with us."

Yong Byun didn't care who this new officer was or where he was taking him. He just wanted out of this hellhole. Things had not gone well during his short stay in the Tecate prison, and he knew they would have gotten much worse had these guards not shown up.

Two of the officers pulled him to his feet and steadied him while the others continued to hold back the angry mob. The evil intent in these men's eyes gave him the shivers. His imagination was conjuring up increasingly frightening scenarios, one after another. Hard as it was to envision, he felt it was only a matter of time before he was forced into far worse punishment than what he had just received. Staggering, he gladly obeyed the man who had pulled him out of the crowd. The cell door clanged shut behind him as one officer led the way, and another pushed him from behind.

The shouting continued. His cellmates complaining and the guards rebuking. Yong Byun's head felt like it was full of rice, heavy and thick and discombobulated. A coppery taste stung the insides of his mouth. He coughed out his own blood onto the sleeve of his shirt, which was already wet. The stink of it made him queasy.

Jeers and catcalls abounded as he was led away. Every derisive and foul Spanish insult Yong Byun knew assailed him. He guessed that the words he didn't know were equally as abusive.

Even in his darkest imagination, Yong Byun had never pictured spending time in a place so horrific and so full of the depraved. The smell alone had almost been enough to make him vomit. And the body cavity search conducted by the jailhouse staff as he was booked on charges he didn't understand was a level of humiliation he had never before endured.

His first experience being arrested was a new low for him. But things only went downhill from there. An hour in lock-up with a cross section of humanity he didn't know existed had shaken him to his very core. His sense of security in the world had been ground to dust.

He had no clue what would happen next. And he didn't care, so long has he didn't have to return to pit from which he had just been rescued.

"The Attorney General fears you won't survive the night," said Lieutenant Hector Suarez, after introducing himself. He and the other three officers and Yong Byun had entered a corridor that was sealed off by solid doors that unlocked as they approached and locked as soon as they closed behind the group. The seven-meter-long corridor was dark, illuminated by a single low-wattage bulb shrouded in a steel cage fifteen feet over head. He spoke English slowly and clearly so Yong Byun could understand.

Yong Byun, whose eyes were as large as saucers and whose face was bloodied and bruised, simply acknowledged the comment by saying, "OK."

The grungy walls with their dark stains streaking down from the ceiling seemed to absorb every ounce of light and hope in the area. They entered a chamber with sealed doors on all four sides. Suarez snapped steel handcuffs around Yong Byun's wrists as he pulled his arms one at a time behind his back, then pushed a button. A second later, a latch clicked, and Suarez opened the door in front of him.

"You are being transferred to protective custody at the Attorney General's Office," Suarez continued as they moved through the next set of locked steel doors. Each passage brought them to a slightly less dank and gloomy hallway where the population looked less animal-like and marginally more civilized. Nonetheless, hoots and taunts and whistles assaulted his already-over-wrought senses. The nausea still threatened as he stumbled forward on unsteady legs.

At long last, they ascended a steel staircase tucked into a corner and entered a room that was fully lit and that had windows. Yong Byun caught his reflection against one of the panes of glass. An Asian man who, underneath the emerging bruises, looked white as a ghost stared back at him. He faltered as two new officers appeared from behind a closed door to his right. It opened to the outside. Each grabbed one of his elbows, muttered to the men who had escorted him, and half-dragged him out of the building and into a waiting panel van with police insignia stamped on the side. The two back doors yawed open, waiting for him. Suarez followed and closed the back doors once Yong Byun was secured to a steel bench along one side of the van. The two beefy officers sat facing him on the opposite side.

The process was reversed a few minutes later, after a bumpy ride full of twists and turns. Suarez swung the rear doors wide, hopped down to the ground, surveyed his surroundings, and motioned for the others to follow. He watched with curiosity as Yong Byun was man-handled out of the vehicle, up four steps and into a stucco building freshly painted the color of creamed coffee.

Once inside the building, Suarez switched to Spanish since Yong Byun had indicated he could speak his language, but he kept it simple and slow as he addressed another uniformed officer at the counter behind the small square of bullet-proof glass halfway up the wall. Suarez glanced occasionally at Yong Byun as he spoke through the speaker in the window. "The Americans will be here shortly. There is some confusion regarding this man's arrest warrant. They say the charges pending in their country are far more serious than the ones in this country," Suarez said with a shrug to the officer on watch, an employee of the court rather than the police department. "They believe they have first right of conviction. We'll see if that is the case. I'm turning him over to you for processing. He is not to be released until the Attorney General authorizes it. Understood? The Americans will be here to question him in just a few minutes, they said."

Kim Yong Byun understood most of what was said, enough to know that it was possible he could return to the United States. While this provided him little comfort, he was glad, nonetheless. The brutality he had endured over the past hour was enough for an entire lifetime.

Suarez led him into a small room. Behind a set of bars, a simple mattress with a clean sheet, a steel toilet, and a steel sink looked inviting in comparison to where he had been.

"You will wait here for the Americans," Suarez said as he locked the gate and exited to room.

Unfathomable as it may have been to him even hours prior, Yong Byun was happy to be locked away safely in this new cell.

Chapter 28

M*inistry of National Defense, Yongsan-gu, Seoul, South Korea*
June 6, 1:58 p.m.; June 5, 9:58 p.m. California Time

General Noh Tae Seong stood in front of a plate glass window in his office, overlooking the rows of cherry blossom trees that lined the perimeter wall of the National Defense Ministry's compound. The splendor of their blooms long gone, their spectacular annual apogee nothing more than a memory. The locals, as well as tourists from around the world, gathered each Spring to celebrate the vibrant colors and sweet fragrance that only lasted a few days.

Similarly, General Noh had experienced a glorious Spring, polling higher than any other potential candidate and garnering public support for his sustainable peace plan. His campaign would tout maintaining peak military readiness while building a strong economy to bring continued prosperity for every South Korean. That message resonated with the majority of voters. Recent tensions with the North had rattled many. General Noh had been the official spokesperson for the military during the crisis, assuring the public that their troops were well trained, equipped with the latest military technology, and perfectly positioned to thwart the enemy, should they attack. Aided by video clips from the recent joint military exercises with U.S. troops, his popularity and public image were at an all-time high, a perfect backdrop to announce one's candidacy.

The looming jetliner crisis, however, had the potential to be like the wind that blew the cherry blossom petals after their moment of glory. General

Noh's bid for the presidency, though splendidly promising just days ago, seemed destined to wither and blow away like the iconic flowers.

An airliner exploding over Seoul threatened more than just the many lives that would be lost. It would single-handedly lay waste to months of preparation, late-night strategizing, and tedious brainstorming that had already been invested in General Noh's potential run for the Blue House.

Having his son mixed up in such a catastrophe would annihilate his chances of victory and, in the opinion of many citizens of South Korea, the hope of achieving a lasting peace with their Communist neighbors based on their military might and not on concessions to the dictator in Pyongyang.

The press was busy grousing around for details about the man wearing the Dodger's jacket. How soon before they discovered Jeong Tae's involvement? Anything short of a miracle and he would be implicated in another scandal.

Beyond the compound's perimeter wall was Itaewon-ro, a heavily traveled thoroughfare in this area of Seoul that was popular with the foreign tourists. Filled with all manner of shops selling all manner of wares at bargain prices, the busy commercial district epitomized the success of the free market in his country. Vendors sold goods for a profit and customers benefited from the low prices brought about by open competition. It had its drawbacks, but the market thrived in an atmosphere of freedom where hard work and business savvy translated to success.

Across Itaewon-ro stood the War Memorial of Korea, a constant reminder to those who worked in the Ministry of Defense that theirs was the responsibility to protect their countrymen, their economy, and their way of life from attack by their hostile neighbors on the other side of the Demilitarized Zone.

This day, the sixth day of the sixth month, had significance. Memorial Day in Korea. The day the nation commemorated those who fought and died to resist the communist aggression from the North. The war started in 1950 and continued even today. A signed ceasefire, not even a treaty, was all that kept the two countries from continuing the violence. A cessation of fighting without the benefit of a surrender or peace accord was all that stood between the opposing nations. In other words, there was no official end to the war.

Nowadays, the struggle was more political as far as the world knew. For many families, including General Noh's, that had been divided when the border went up, the continuing conflict was deeper and more personal. The irony of the date South Korea's enemies had chosen to send a plane full of explosives into the crowded capital city underscored the ideological chasm that separated the two countries sharing the peninsula. The North Korean regime hated the South and wanted to suppress its rise in the global community.

Today, rather than becoming a candidate, General Noh would take action as a military leader and focus on the safety of the passengers on that airplane.

The role of a leader was difficult when intel was limited. Jeong Tae was working covertly with the US authorities but communication from him was sparse. General Noh was relegated to the role of spectator to some degree. He couldn't control nor direct the hunt for the perpetrators. The only thing he could do was wait and trust his only child.

Fortunately, the press had been contained. They knew nothing of a bomb onboard. The plane in Los Angeles had passed rigorous reinspection before it was cleared for take-off, so the moment of tension had passed, and they were on to something else. But if that plane exploded, the press would snoop until they discovered every tantalizing tidbit about what led to the disaster. Surely Jeong Tae's involvement would be suspect, and surely they would broadcast every shadowy detail. There was much to fear if this happened.

A knock on the door startled the General. He turned and called out, "Duhl-eoh O-seyo." *Enter, please.*

Mr. Park stepped in and cleared his throat. His face was taut, and his movements were jittery. Something was terribly wrong.

"Yes, Mr. Park. What is it?"

"Bad news. That foreign correspondent from MBC News—you know, the pretty one with the long legs—just aired a report from Los Angeles speculating that a flight from LAX to Seoul may be carrying a suitcase full of plastic explosives."

General Noh froze in place, staring at Park. "Where did she get her information? We need her source."

"She won't reveal her source but says that it is someone 'close to the investigation.'"

Both men remained silent for a long moment. Beads of sweat formed on General Noh's brow. "This is unacceptable. We have no confirmation from our intelligence community and here she is broadcasting rumors."

"It's running on other channels, too. The press is clamoring for a response from the Blue House. They demand to know what we know and what we're going to do about it." Park paused, eyeing the General with apprehension.

The General's facial expression was inscrutable, a stone face.

Park continued tepidly. "A press conference has been arranged. President Jang will address the crisis, then turn it over to you to respond and share what you know. In thirty minutes. It's the only way to get out ahead of the story and minimize the damage."

"But...how can I share what I know when we have no solid information? We also have no solution. It would be unwise to unveil an unsubstantiated threat without discussing our response to it."

"But any lack of action would be portrayed by the press and interpreted by the public as weakness and incompetence. As a military leader, you need to show strength. Of course you can't talk about specifics, but you put our military on high alert. Send tanks and troop carriers into the streets. Scramble fighter jets to fly over the city. Make your response visible. You know from past experience that this kind of action will calm the people. They want to know that our armed forces are ready to protect them. This is your opportunity to be seen as a decisive and courageous leader."

General Noh cocked his head toward Mr. Park. "Is it on social media platforms, as well?"

Park nodded in the affirmative.

General Noh grunted and turned to face the window again. Several moments passed. "Our response must be measured, appropriate. The official word out of Los Angeles is still that the aircraft was thoroughly inspected and cleared for departure. We cannot react because a news outlet demands it."

"But this is your moment to shine, General."

"I need to hear from Jeong Tae first. How could I act on something this important in a vacuum of knowledge? He is our only operative in the field at the moment. I will base my decision on his assessment, not some news reporter's story."

"Fine. Call him. Get all the information you can. Just be ready to face the cameras at Cheong Wa Dae in thirty minutes."

"Cheong Wa Dae in thirty minutes? I don't have enough time to get over there."

"I'm sure they can delay a few minutes for you."

Cheong Wa Dae, also known as the Blue House—South Korea's equivalent of the United States' White House—was a compound built in the traditional Korean architecture that housed the executive branch of the government. It sat roughly five miles north of the complex that housed the Ministry of National Defense and General Noh's office. With traffic congestion that always clogged the city's streets, it could take anywhere from thirty to sixty minutes just to get there, which left him with no time to prepare himself properly.

"Come," said Park, gesturing for the door. "We must hurry. Your car and driver await." Park pulled the door open. "Don't forget to call Jeong Tae."

General Noh heaved a deep breath and shook his head, staring into the distance at the majestic mountains that created a natural fortification for the city of Seoul. Fifty kilometers beyond lay the DMZ.

Park cleared his throat again. "General?"

"Yes, yes. I'm coming."

Chapter 29

P*rocuraduria General de la Republica, Tecate, Mexico*
June 5, 10:15 p.m.

While he waited for what would come next, Kim Yong Byun couldn't help but relive the trauma he had just experienced. It circled around his mind despite his best efforts to channel his thoughts elsewhere.

His time in the Mexican prison was the most harrowing of his life. From the moment he was thrust into general population, he was forced to make choices, the outcomes of which he had no way of predicting.

The first choice was where to place himself when he was shoved into the pen. After catching his balance, he had to decide quickly which side of the lockup to move to. The holding cell was no more than seven or eight meters left to right and maybe six meters front to back. There were at least a dozen men already in there. A tall, mangy man with long hair stood out from a group that occupied the left side of the cell. All looked mean and angry.

On the right side, the most prominent figure was distinguished by his muscles, tattoos, and scowl. The others behind him seemed to have similar features, as if there had been a sting operation at the gym. As he drifted toward the muscle-bound men on the right, one of the men from the left side said something like, "Be careful of who you make your friend." At least, that's how he translated it in his head.

Yong Byun stopped short, feeling like he was stuck in a veritable no-man's land. Laughter erupted from both sides. He heard derisive words like, "Who's the China boy?" "He doesn't belong here," and "where did this one come from?"

He froze as they jeered and taunted, asking him, "Who's going to be your friend?" It became clear to him that the occupants of the cell were more or less divided down the middle behind these two presumed leaders. It seemed that each man in the cell had chosen one of the two groups. Tensions were high, like a war was about to break out and if he chose the wrong side, he would tip the balance and escalate things to bloodshed.

Yong Byun's head was on a swivel, roving from one side to the other while his eyes darted from one man to the next. His heart was racing, and his palms were sweating. He worried that he might faint. And then what would happen?

He turned to face the door of the cell and backed himself against the wall, right in the middle.

Laughter erupted for a fleeting moment. Then an angry voice on his right demanded silence. On the left, the tattooed leader spat on the floor and said, "That's no good. Pick one side or the other, China Boy."

The long-haired man, now on his right, stepped forward. "Don't even think about it. He's ours."

The trolling group of miscreants behind him tightened their circle around their leader and glared across the cell at the opposing group on Yong Byun's left. Yong Byun had to make a decision. *Which group do I fall in with? What happens next? If a fight breaks out, what becomes of me?*

"Wait," he cried, throwing his hands out like a traffic cop bringing cars to a halt. In faltering Spanish, he pleaded, "Please don't do this. Not because of me. I don't want to start any trouble."

"He speaks," said the leader of the long-haired group.

A fresh chorus of jeers from both sides broke the rising tension.

"He knows Spanish?" said someone from the other side.

"It's not very good," said another.

"Sounds like a little kid," said someone else.

"I don't know what's happening," said Yong Byun. "But don't do this because of me. I'm nothing special."

"Oh, really?" said the leader from the muscle men. "You look special to us. We don't see too many China Boys like you around here."

"Except the ones in the factories," said one of his cohorts.

"Yeah, that's true. You from the factories?" asked the leader.

Yong Byun faced another decision. He surveyed the faces on his left, then on his right. They all seemed to be holding their breath, waiting to hear what he said next.

"Yes, I am," he said with all the confidence he could muster.

The leader of the muscled men drew his mouth into a tight crease. "My sister works at one of those factories. You the owner?"

Yong Byun assessed the question, stalling long enough to make his next decision. He repeated the word "owner" as if he was translating it. "No, I'm not the owner, but I work with him."

The man nodded his head and turned up his lip as if he were a human lie detector, assessing Yong Byun's words. "If you're not the owner, then what do you do there?"

Another tough choice to make with only a split second to make it. "I'm an accountant. Did I say that right? Accountant? I prepare tax reports."

Yong Byun felt the tensions between the two groups ease. "An accountant?" said the longhaired leader. "Yeah, you look like an accountant." As he said this, he jabbed an elbow into the man next to him, who went along with the joke and laughed out loud.

"What did you do to get here?" asked a man standing next to the other leader.

Yong Byun turned slightly to face that group, his mind racing to come up with something that might sound legitimate for an accountant. "How do you say it? I...uh...in English, they say 'tax evasion.'"

There was discussion amongst the two groups. Both sides seemed amused by his response.

"Tax evasion, huh?" said the big muscle-bound leader on the left, an evil grin on his face. "You lie. They don't bring people who evade taxes here. Not to this prison. What did you really do?"

Yong Byun cursed himself. *That was stupid*, he thought. From what he could surmise, his fellow prisoners were probably awaiting charges ranging from assault to kidnapping to drug trafficking. How could he be so dumb as to say, "tax evasion?"

One of the men in the back, whom they had referred to as "coyote"—the infamous and unscrupulous businessmen who crammed dozens of desperate peasants into bobtail trucks and left them in the desert to cross the border into the United States on their own after collecting huge fees from them—seemed to have a particular problem with Yong Byun's lie. "No, no," he said, adding several other words which Yong Byun guessed were curse words. "You are not in *here* for tax evasion. Maybe you're guilty of that, but you didn't come here because they caught you cheating on taxes."

The tension amped up again. Every man in the cramped cell seemed to grow more agitated as the coyote spoke.

Yong Byun cringed when the coyote's eyes met his. A silent signal had been given that he was about to regret what was coming. His heart skipped erratically at the thought of what might happen to him if he didn't appease the man somehow. He wished he could evaporate or shrink to the size of a rodent so he could escape this awful place. Or an insect, even a cockroach. He would do anything to get out before this mob turned on him.

Yong Byun's mind raced faster than his heart as fear took hold. There was only one way to gain respect and placate this group. "You're right. Even though I may be guilty of cheating on taxes, that's not why I'm here." He surveyed the faces staring at him. These men seemed ready to pounce on the "China Boy" because, he assumed, they viewed him as soft. A tense hush spread among the prisoners. They hung on every word as he hastily concocted a plan to win a modicum of respect.

Yong Byun spoke deliberately, buying himself a few precious seconds to put his story together in his mind. "No, they didn't catch me for that." He paused again, knit his eyebrows together, and allowed the darkness inside to come out. Nothing could be more convincing than the truth. He just had to play it right. His eyes widened and his countenance grew hard and a wicked grin pulled at his mouth. "I burned a man alive. In a truck that I stole. Not far from here."

The reaction of his fellow inmates was priceless. Their esteem for him rose instantly, he could tell by the way their expressions changed.

Hushed murmurs spread through the two groups as they considered his confession among themselves.

After a moment, one of the men called out from the back. "Why should we believe you?"

Yong Byun, whose face was still consumed by the malevolence of what he had done, turned an icy stare toward the man. "Maybe you can still smell the smoke and the gasoline on my hands."

One of the men from that side of the cell approached him warily, sniffing. Yong Byun held out his hands. Even though he had washed, he knew there was likely still a faint trace of it.

The man nodded to his Comrades. "I can smell it."

Others did the same, each confirming the truth of what Yong Byun had said. A sort of reverence for him replaced their cynicism and malice. One of the men next to the long-haired one asked him why he did it.

"That man failed. He could not do the job he was assigned. He jeopardized our operation. He had to die, and I had to send a signal to the others that there is a steep penalty for failure."

A collective "ooh" rose from the group. Yong Byun felt that his stature among these men had gained new elevation. There was silence for a moment, then whispered chatter among them. He leaned back against the wall, sucked in a deep breath, and congratulated himself for his quick thinking. Maintaining the dark look on his face, he hoped, would gain him additional respect. It would not be good to let his guard down now—or ever, not in a place like this. Even criminals had a code of dignity. His deed, though he loathed himself for it, had brought him a measure of esteem from his cellmates when he needed it most.

A delicate truce emerged as the group processed what he had said.

But that peace didn't last long.

The whisperings became more animated. He couldn't understand it, but he could sense a shift in their demeanor. They weren't afraid of him; they were angry with him.

The leader with the muscles and tattoos listened to the rapid-fire report from a man who moved in close and uttered something to him with his hand in place to block his mouth from Yong Byun's view. The man's dark eyes showed contempt. The leader pointed his chin at Yong Byun, indicating "go ahead."

"You, China Boy, came to our country and burned one of our men alive?" The hostility in the man's voice sent a chill through Yong Byun, stealing away his short-lived confidence. "So, now we know who did it."

The man, who appeared to be in his late twenties, moved closer to Yong Byun, his eyes narrowed, and his mouth twisted up tight. His stained tank top showed off his chiseled physique. "I knew that man, the one you killed." The man turned towards the others, meeting their gazes one by one as he spoke through gritted teeth. "It happened a few days ago. Before sunup there was a fire outside of town. Maybe you heard about it?" Some of the other prisoners shrugged while others nodded. "Women were screaming. Children crying." The young inmate resembled a prowling tiger, pacing in an arc before his victim. "My uncle, he heard it all He knew the man you killed, too. Lives in the same neighborhood. The one you killed worked at your factory. He worked there a long time. He worked very hard."

This man was stoking a fire of indignation, uniting both groups of prisoners against Yong Byun. Yong Byun imposed calm on his nerves as the man continued, pacing as he spoke. "But you people don't pay very much. He didn't do nothing wrong. Nothing but ask for a raise. Nothing but make a complaint that his wages weren't enough." The man telling the story stopped when his gaze met Yong Byun's. He hissed as he finished. "The man you burned alive was a good man, a family man. Why would you do that? Why would you leave his children without a father?"

Yong Byun's sense of acceptance fled like a prairie dog sniffing a predator in his territory. He wished he could drop down into a burrow and hide, but there was no burrow, no place of resort. His insides went cold, and his breath grew quick and shallow. What had he gotten himself into? Why did he choose to tell them that? How could he get out of this?

"You think you're tough? You ain't nothing." The coyote stepped forward. "Let's see how tough he is. There's no gasoline here, no lighters, no matches.

Let's see what you do now, tax man."

Talk of him choosing a side was abandoned, as the majority of the men in the cell closed in around him, forming a semicircle, with Yong Byun pressed up against the back wall.

The coyote jabbed his finger in the air. "You foreigners come in here and change everything. You hire our people as grunts and bring in your own people to run things, keeping all the money for yourselves. Think you're all important. Think you're helping the poor Mexicans. You ain't helping nothing. Then you burn one of our people? That ain't right."

Yong Byun swallowed hard—or tried to. There was nothing to swallow. His mouth was as dry as the Tecate landscape. "I didn't kill anyone you know. I promise." The words faltered as his voice cracked. His pronunciation was terrible because his tongue wouldn't move right.

The huddle grew tighter around him. Their stink was stronger than ever. Their breath, their body odor, the stench of cigarettes and beer and sweat stuck in the threads of their clothing blended together in a sickening potpourri. Yong Byun's stomach tightened, and he thought he might vomit.

Their faces showed menace, their words conveyed fury, their scents displayed raw connection to the world's cruelties.

The man who knew the victim struck first. A balled fist that felt like a granite club unleashed a powerful blow to Yong Byun's gut. He double over, coughing and gasping and staggering. The crowd whooped and cheered on the assailant and panted for more.

More came.

Another hammer-like wallop smashed into his ribs, forcing out what little air was left in his lungs. Yong Byun was sure he had a cracked rib or two. He struggled to breathe. His legs wobbled and the room began to spin. As he fell sideways, one of the men caught him and pushed back up, causing him to stagger toward the other side of the circle. Another pair of hands pushed him even harder back to the opposite side. He was pinballed around until a third strike landed on his cheek, sending him crashing against the wall. From there, he bounced off another body, then landed on the dirt-caked concrete floor. It smelled grotesque.

Laughter erupted, along with more hoots and howls.

As he lay there, more abuse was piled on him. First, he felt warm spit land on his face, one glob after another. Then he felt a sharp jab in the back of his leg, followed by another one in his chest. The crowd calmed and snickered in unison as if anticipating a grand finale. That's when he heard a zipper being unzipped. He soon felt a warm, wet sensation on his face and shoulder. Soon his shirt was soaked in urine. Yong Byun tried to move out of the stream but was held in place by heavy pressure from the other men's boots weighing down on his legs and torso.

That's when he heard an authoritative voice booming in the distance, growing closer, and the banging of the club on the bars of the metal cage.

Salvation came as two pairs of hands grabbed him by the elbows and the belt and hoisted him up amid a hail of Spanish scolding and commands to keep back.

* * * *

Yong Byun shook his head to bring himself back to the present.

He didn't know what awaited him, but certainly it would not be as horrible as staying in that prison another hour.

Yong Byun lay on the thin but clean mattress. There were no windows and only one door in the room. It was the heavy steel kind with a peephole centered between the left and right sides, about five and a half feet up from the ground. One rectangular light fixture pulsed overhead, shielded by a steel cage, casting bluish-white light that filled the four-meter by two-meter room.

He closed his eyes to clear away the fear and anxiety, trying to replace those thoughts with a game plan. Since his mission had failed and now his escape plan had also failed, Yong Byun was struggling to figure out a winning strategy.

He waited in the barren room for what felt like an eternity. Then he heard voices beyond the door but could not understand what was being said. The fear once again rose inside, an acrid taste forming in his throat. His mouth went dry as his heartbeat quickened. The unknown stirred such palpable distress.

When the door finally opened, Yong Byun startled at the sight of General Noh's son. His last bastion of hope banished.

He swung his legs over the edge of the bed and sat up. Doing so made the room spin and his stomach flip. Sharp pains in his head, back, legs, and torso overloaded his brain. The cracked rib shot agony through his core, stealing his breath. He did his best to hide his discomfort, but sensed his attempt fell short.

Noh strode across the room and stopped at the bars that separated them, scowling. No words were spoken.

Mr. Noh held him in his steely glare for an uncomfortable amount of time. Finally, he spoke in Korean. "Mr. Lee, if that's really your name, you are very fortunate that we had not yet returned to Los Angeles. You're also lucky that the Mexican authorities decided to cooperate with us, at least so far. They are eager to try you for human trafficking. They say you have been taking young girls and selling them across the border. They don't appreciate that sort of thing. Not when the girls are only eight and nine years old."

Yong Byun didn't feel all that lucky, but he knew better than to speak. Instead, he turned his head downward and to the side, refusing to acknowledge the truth of anything the South Korean said. He did not want to give his enemy the satisfaction.

Mr. Noh continued. "Of course, if you aren't in the mood to cooperate with us, we'll let them take you back."

Yong Byun hesitated, not sure what to believe. It seemed he was at the mercy of two undesirable masters. His mind raced, filled with uncertainty and distrust.

"OK, then. It seems you don't want to cooperate. That's fine." Noh turned and started for the door.

Yong Byun had another decision to make. It seemed to him a choice between prostituting himself one way or the other. Given what he had been through during his brief stay in the Mexican prison, cooperating with the Americans seemed the less reprehensible alternative. "Fine."

Noh paused as he gripped the door handle. "Fine? Fine what? Fine you'll tell me everything I want to know? Or fine you'll go back to the prison and await your fate?"

"I'll talk," Yong Byun said, still facing the floor.

Noh stuck a key into the lock, swung the barred door open, and launched himself at Yong Byun, extending his right fist into Yong Byun's midsection. The force of the blow knocked him backwards against the bed, forcing the air from his lungs. Shockwaves crashed his nervous system. Yong Byun gasped for air, physically unable to breathe, mentally spinning through space. Fear, helplessness, and an intense desire to avoid further pain swept through him instantaneously. He curled into a ball as he fought to regain the ability to draw in air. The urge to vomit overpowered him and he lurched all over the clean sheets.

Noh stood over him like a lion over its prey, fists clenched and jaw muscles pulsing. His dark eyes left no room for misinterpretation. If Yong Byun didn't cooperate, more violence was on the way. "No more games. No more lies. No more hiding anything. You tell me everything you know, starting with where to find someone who knows how to disable that bomb. Tell me now or you'll go back and spend a very long time in that prison cell. I'm sure they'll treat you with all the dignity you deserve."

Chapter 30

Procuraduria General de la Republica, Tecate, Mexico
June 5, 10:17 p.m.

My frustration level was so high it was all I could do to not rip this guy's head off. I wanted to pulverize him. All the energy and tension of the day had reached a boiling point and it felt like I might let loose in a whirlwind of flying fists and feet. Precious hours had passed, and we hadn't gained any actionable intel. This Mr. Lee had told us many things we didn't know, but nothing that would help us prevent a disaster in the air.

The first confession he had made was that his real name was Kim Yong Byun. Small progress, but it was something to build on. It's always better when they're not hiding behind a false name.

Mr. Kim had paid the price for his earlier noncooperative stance by spending time in a Mexican jail and by absorbing a punch to the gut delivered at about 75% of full strength. As I stood over him, feeling a bit like an alpha male silverback, a sense of futility swept over me. My outburst would likely yield little, if any, forward progress toward our goal.

But it made me feel better, if only for a moment.

I dropped a clean set of clothes and a wash rag on the bed next to him and commanded him to get himself cleaned up. I then exited the cell and locked the barred door. His every movement as he changed his clothes and washed his face and rinsed his mouth was as deliberate as could be. When he finished, I held open a plastic garbage bag for him to drop in his stinky soiled clothes. I took it to the door and placed it in the hallway.

As rationality settled back in, I was painfully aware that the clock was ticking. My two eight-year-old students' faces popped back into my mind.

Mr. Kim's turtle-like pace allowed me time to impose tranquility on my impulses. I regained my stone face. Control was imperative in this situation. I couldn't control him if I couldn't control myself.

But that clock kept ticking.

The first thing Mr. Kim did once he was cleaned up and had recovered from the nasty blow to his gut was smile a devilish smile and cough out a sinister laugh. "You recognized me," he hissed. "In the airplane. From that night." He was wheezing but trying to hide it.

I retreated half a step. "Not at first, but it came to me later." The sudden anger and hostility in me receded like a wave that had crashed on the beach, replaced by curiosity.

The smugness that he exuded would have left one thinking he was the one who had landed the first punch. It amazed me that changing his clothes and washing the vomit and urine off his face could so quickly restore his over-confidence. "That night, between the fences, was your high point. Look at you now."

I was dumbfounded but tried to hide it. I cocked my head as the memory of his face peering at me from behind a rock gained clarity. "You survived." A statement, not a question.

"Yes, I did. And so did several other teammates. Thanks to you, we were able to complete the first phase of this mission." The satisfaction on his face reignited the anger in me.

"What are you talking about?"

"Phase I: Gain passage to South Korea with our falsified passports and documents. Phase II: Gain employment with Korean Air Lines and learn about their aircraft, security protocols, and, most importantly, their vulnerabilities. Phase III: Seek a transfer to one of the West Coast hubs, like Los Angeles—"

"Hold on. You snuck across the border that night? That night led to this?"

"I did. Our whole forward team did, too. Other teams crossed at other times. It was all thoroughly planned and carefully executed." He flashed that devilish smile again. "The fact that you were the commander on duty was no coincidence, you know?"

A queasiness gripped my insides and worked its way up to my head. I found myself dizzy as I realized the full extent of what he said and the far-reaching effects that event continued to have on my life. I leaned against the wall behind me for support.

Mr. Kim continued. "Yes, we knew about you. General Noh's son. It was like—how do they say it here? —buy one, get one free. It was genius. General Noh is shamed and drops from the race and twenty-five of our operatives cross the border, including myself."

"Twenty-five? No, there were not that many—"

"Yes, twenty-five. Hiding inside fake rocks and in underground chambers, waiting for the commotion to start."

"It was all a set-up."

"Yes. A glorious victory for the true Korea and a good omen for the rest of our mission."

"The rest of your mission," I repeated weakly.

His smirk was unnerving. I could feel the balance of power in the room shifting and knew I had to regain control quickly or I'd lose more than just face. I'd lose the chance to save lives. I wanted to send him back to that Mexican prison.

"Yes. It is a grand mission with a glorious outcome."

"If twenty-five of you came across the border ...where are the rest?"

"I admit I do not know where all of them are. I only had a supervisory role for the baggage handling detail at LAX. When I called out a mission abort, each member of the team is to follow his own set of instructions, known only to that individual, for such circumstances. I do not know anyone else's Plan B."

"So, your Plan B was to come to Mexico? Then what?"

His face twisted, and he sucked in a deep breath. "No. I had to change my plan."

"Change? Why?"

"I cannot return home ..."

"Of course you can't." My wits were coming back. "You failed in your responsibility. Punishment is certain. Shame is guaranteed."

His head drooped, though I could tell he was trying hard not to allow me to see him defeated. "I am responsible for the outcome. At least in their eyes. But truly..."

His voice tapered off. I didn't jump in because my mind was busy churning through multiple possibilities. Still leaning against the wall, I stared at a spot on the floor ahead of me.

Mr. Kim continued his narrative. "I worked very hard these past six years. It was not easy to gain the promotions I needed in order to acquire the access cards to every area in the baggage handling system. Then I had to work harder to get transferred to Los Angeles. It took me two years to reach supervisor level. That is how I was able to get my Comrades into position."

"Of course," I muttered, still processing all of the moving pieces. "But where are the others? There were only three of you that I saw. That leaves twenty-two more. Where are they?"

That smirk returned along with the spark of devilish delight in his eyes. "So many questions, Mr. Noh. Questions that I cannot answer. Not because I don't want to, but by design. I am not privy to all the secrets and the tactics. I only know what was supposed to happen today in Los Angeles."

I shook my head, trying to formulate the next question.

Mr. Kim continued. "You must appreciate the enormous amount of planning involved in our operation in order to understand how meaningless it is for you to know about the explosives," he calmly chided.

"But I need to disarm that bomb."

"Again, you don't realize what you are saying."

That infuriated me, but I let it pass. Instead, I made an insincere compliment about the genius behind the plan and bade him continue.

Mr. Kim ran his tongue along the inside of each cheek, clearly feeling superior, as he chose his words. "I am not the technical expert. I apologize that my knowledge about these things is superficial at best," he said. "All I know is that each of the bombs have special detonators that are connected by Bluetooth to smart phones with GPS. Once the planes reach the airspace over Seoul, they will be set off."

"Wait a minute," I said, holding my hand out like a traffic cop. "What do you mean *planes*—plural?"

"That's right, Mr. Noh. I am explaining the whereabouts of the other twenty people who crossed the border with me that night. There are multiple planes," he said calmly, as if I should have already known that.

"How many?" I said, tensing and clenching my fists again.

"Five. Scheduled to arrive within thirty minutes of each other." He cocked his head at me when he said it, like he relished my reaction.

"You see," he continued, "one plane would not mean much. Two planes, even, is not very dramatic. Three is good. Four planes is the same number as the 911 hijackers. Five, though, is a bigger number. Five planes lighting up the sky above Seoul—boom, boom, boom, boom, boom. They will explode over the city as they approach the airport. Each flight path goes over the city, a very densely populated city, I might add. There will be many casualties, on the planes and on the ground. There will be great destruction—offices, apartments, churches, roads, historical sites. It will be a spectacle—glorious and beautiful. Then will the world come to know our resolve. Five planes will be enough to make everyone understand that The Democratic People's Republic of Korea, the true Korea, is powerful, sophisticated, and capable of many great things."

I spun out of my chair to alert Robinson of this vital new piece of information.

Chapter 31

P*rocuraduria General de la Republica, Tecate, Mexico*
June 5, 10:35 p.m.

When I returned from my debrief with Robinson, inwardly I was more anxious than I had been before. Outwardly, I imposed calm. With all the grace I could muster, I thanked my one and only source for the vital information he had provided regarding the additional four planes. I explained that if we were able to save those planes, he would be rewarded handsomely.

The ice between us started to thaw. Mr. Kim's kibun was reforming. He seemed to feel appreciated and important, which fueled a verbosity in him that I had not seen. That got him talking, and me listening, trying to be as patient as I could. But each passing minute felt like it was extracting essence from my soul. Lives were hanging in the balance. I just wanted to disable those bombs and be done. I was tired of listening to his blather about the greatness of the DPRK and the genius of their plan. Knowing all those people were in peril was a heavy burden and I was tired of carrying it. Getting home and giving my wife and kids a hug would be all the reward I needed.

My angry side told me I should unload on this guy and dump him in a gutter in Tecate. My fists kept flexing involuntarily. As the thought of punching him in the face rolled into my head, I had to back it out and let my rational side take over. I had to keep myself together and continue placating the only person who could help us.

The intended outcome of my softer approach and his time in the Mexican prison was actionable intel. We weren't there yet, though Mr. Kim was more forthcoming than he had been at the onset of the interrogation. Sensing an imminent breakthrough, I focused on building trust and rapport.

"Thank you for sharing what you know about the explosives and the detonators on those planes. I'm very impressed with the level of technical skill required to implement such a sophisticated plan." I was working hard to say things that would continue to soften him up. His response was muted, but positive. His head nodded slightly. "I, like you, don't have that level of technical expertise, but I would guess that all we have to do is scramble the Bluetooth signal on each plane and all of those bombs will be rendered useless."

Mr. Kim flashed that lopsided smile again. "I was told it is very difficult to scramble the Bluetooth signal. In most cases, it takes very specialized equipment, which, most certainly, they would not have onboard those planes. Thus, the bombs are virtually fail-safe. There's nothing you can do. No way to stop what is going to happen."

While I never want to believe that there's nothing I can do to solve a difficult problem, I had to marvel at the ingenuity required to devise such a sinister contraption. All that brain power had been wasted by our North Korean brethren. Instead of improving life for the starving masses in their own country, they spent their precious resources and intellect trying to destroy as many enemy lives as possible. It was an unfathomable equation for me.

My operational instincts kept pressing me forward, blocking my outrage and indignation. I focused on the next step. I needed to find the whereabouts of the masterminds behind the implementation or the computers that housed all this technical information. Nothing else was relevant.

Again, I had to tread lightly. I had to keep this quasi-friendly cooperative groove going. Admittedly, this was not my forte. I was trained primarily for combat, hand-to-hand and small arms combat at that. Negotiation and psychological profiling were only a minor part of my training and I had far less experience with either one. Some, but not a whole lot. Mostly, I was in the room observing when North Korean defectors were brought in, back in the day.

I had learned some as a spectator, but more from coaching youth. Whatever psychological tools I possessed had been earned during my years of teaching Tae Kwon Do. Dealing with kids, especially teenagers, had prepared me more than I would have ever expected for my interactions with Kim Yong Byun.

"I noticed you had no electronic devices with you when you were arrested. Why is that?"

He smiled again, but not the same wicked grin from earlier. This one was more resigned. "I knew they would track me. I also got rid of the car they provided."

"That makes sense," I said. I felt there was something useful just under the surface. I had to figure out how to pry it up. "If you got rid of the car, what did you drive here?"

"I left their car in a Walmart parking lot and bought the one you saw from someone selling theirs in the same lot."

"Cash, I assume?"

"Yes, cash."

"You have that kind of money, do you? I thought all your money was controlled by your superiors." I hoped this would keep him talking.

"Yes. Someone else controls my money."

"Then how did you come up with the cash to buy a car?"

"It was easy. I took it from the control house."

"The control house?" Now we were getting somewhere. "What is that?"

"That is where all our mission command group were stationed."

"Of course," I said, nodding like that's what I expected to hear. "How many of them were there?"

"It's hard to say," said Yong Byun, looking as if I'd thrown him off track.

"Where is the control house?"

He eyed me suspiciously. "It's in Garden Grove. But it will be useless to you. They would have certainly abandoned it by now. Plus, I took all the money."

"How much was that?"

"A little over $90,000."

"I'll make a deal with you. OK?"

Mr. Kim looked skeptical but nodded.

"You give me the address to the control house, and I guarantee that you won't have to go to prison. And you can keep the $90,000." I spoke with conviction, though I had no idea whether I could actually deliver on that promise. That decision was way above my pay grade.

To my surprise, Yong Byun rattled off an address in Garden Grove. I thanked him and excused myself from the room.

Robinson was in another room down the hall, working his phone. He ended the call he was on and promised to call the person back. I gave him the address and told him we needed to get someone over there right away. He nodded and asked how things were going. I gave him a brief summary and told him that I had finally made some progress and would keep the conversation going.

Robinson tapped his watch. "We don't have much time until that plane is ready to land."

"I know," I said, checking my watch. "Just get on the phone and get someone to that address first, then I'll tell you the rest."

Robinson punched the screen on his phone a few times. Probably calling up a number from his contact list. After he ended the call he said, "OK. The FBI has a group of agents on their way over there right now. What else did you get from our guy in there?"

I proceeded to give him the abbreviated version of our conversation. When I mentioned the promises I had made in order to get the information we needed, Robinson just shrugged. I took that as an indication none of them were a problem.

Checking my watch, I said, "It's approaching three o'clock in the afternoon in Seoul. The peak of the evening rush hour is in less than three hours. What have you and your team learned about the other four planes and their arrival time?"

"We've narrowed it down. Looks like they're heading in from San Francisco, Seattle, Honolulu, and Dallas," he said.

"Better get someone in touch with Korean Air, too. Let them know that those five planes need to be held up until we figure this thing out. They cannot be allowed to land—anywhere."

"Already done. The first plane should have been yours, which would have landed at 5:40 pm local time, that's 1:40 am here."

"When is the next one supposed to land?"

Robinson grimaced. "5:55. But it's being held up. They're not sharing details, just ensuring they to stay airborne with a military escort guiding them around the peninsula."

I closed my eyes to restore calm. "I need to get back in there. Anything I need to know before I do?"

"We can't find the big guy, the one with the broken arm. He disappeared somewhere. See if our guy knows where he went?"

"He insists he doesn't know. The guy got out of the truck, like I said, a couple of gates to the north, and told Mr. Kim he would finish the mission."

"All we've got is that thirteen seconds of video. No way to know where he went."

"I know where he is."

"How could you know that?" said Robinson.

"Since his episode in prison, Mr. Kim is being much more, shall we say, compliant? I think it's OK to believe what this guy is telling me. This group is extremely dedicated to their cause and motivated by a level of indoctrination you and I will never fully grasp. I would bet the big guy found a way on to that plane, the one with my students on it. Most likely he's holed up in the landing gear compartment."

Robinson looked flummoxed. "Impossible."

"Is it? I remember a couple of news stories not so long ago about some Cubans who stowed away in the landing gear of a plane."

"Yeah, but they died of hypothermia."

"I don't think the big guy cares about the cold. He told Mr. Kim he would find a way to carry out the original plan."

"There's no way," said Robinson.

"There's always a way. If someone is dedicated enough, they can always find a way."

Robinson closed his eyes and shook his head like I'd tapped a raw nerve.

"OK. I get your point," he said, shaking his head. "What do we do now?"

"We pray those FBI guys find something useful at the control house."

Chapter 32

Port of Entry Station, Tecate, California
June 5, 10:49 p.m.

I was spent. Every ounce of mental and physical energy had been poured out over the past two hours trying to get every bit of pertinent information out of our prisoner. Interrogating someone is not as easy as it may look on TV. Keeping the upper hand, applying consistent and increasing pressure, maintaining composure, building trust one question and one answer at a time while processing every piece of data collected—from words to tone of voice to inflections to facial expressions to nervous twitches—requires extreme focus. That much focus for that long, especially when thousands of lives are on the line, takes its toll on a person's physical and mental energy.

I had managed to keep Mr. Kim talking and answering questions. It was fascinating, but I wished he could speed it up. I was less interested in the details of their mission and more interested in how to prevent the bombs from going off. But since he was sure there was nothing to be done, he kept telling me everything he knew in exchange for my promises of his release.

He told me about the code they used. Every night, he would stop at the same Korean market on his way home to his apartment in Garden Grove. The market owners, he said, were a nice middle-aged couple who had no idea they were helping the North Koreans. Each day, a woman who claimed to be Yong Byun's wife would call in a grocery order. The nice lady who owned the market would bag it and have it ready for him, not knowing that each item in the bag had a meaning. For example, a jar of anchovies might be the signal to go to the hardware store where an order was ready for pick up. A bag of turnips meant to prepare certain documents and deliver them to another team member. The color of the turnips and whether they had been pickled or not determined which documents and which team member. Each evening there was a task to perform that was transmitted via the items in that day's grocery order.

Mr. Kim was proving himself to be more valuable than he initially led on to be. After he gave us the location of the safe house in Garden Grove, the FBI raided the place. Even though Mr. Kim was right about them having cleared out before the FBI could get there, the FBI discovered two thumb drives and an assortment of documents in two fireproof boxes hidden in the crawlspace beneath the house. Those two boxes also contained personnel files, financial records, employment documents, and medical histories for thirty people, including Kim Yong Byun.

The contents of those thumb drives were quickly uploaded to the FBI's secure servers and dispersed to field agents with Korean language skills. Within fifteen minutes, analysts found hundreds of files and dozens of pictures, which took time to translate and analyze. The FBI called on every Korean-speaking agent around the country to drop everything and assist. They also communicated their findings to their counterparts in Seoul, thus informing them officially of the dangers they faced and gaining assistance in the translation effort.

Through their combined herculean efforts, we learned valuable, if not disconcerting, new revelations in a relatively short period of time. The documents outlining the entire mission, code named "Chammae Boksu," indicated the departure and arrival times, as well as the flight numbers of the five planes heading for Seoul, each to be laden with explosives and detonators similar to the one Yong Byun had described to me. One had departed San Francisco just half an hour after our plane's scheduled departure. Another had taken off from Seattle an hour and ten minutes after ours. The Dallas plane had left two hours earlier. The flight from Honolulu had departed three and a half hours after our plane was supposed to leave. It had taken off two hours before the flash drives were found. All five planes were in the air, destined for my home country. All five planes were originally scheduled to land between 5:34 and 6:17 p.m. local time at Seoul's Inchon International Airport. The LAX plane would now land one hour and ten minutes after the arrival of the first flight.

According to Mr. Kim, none of those planes would land. None of those passengers would reunite with their families, or attend their business meetings, or catch their connecting flight. Chammae Boksu's masterminds planned to prevent all of that and more.

Beyond the loss of all those passengers, the thought of fiery hunks of metal falling throughout the city, raised the prospects of much higher casualties. The number of people that would be killed or injured in the maelstrom could be staggering. Secondarily, the explosions and the shrapnel would inflict significant infrastructure damage, which could slow commerce to a halt and do major damage to South Korea's economy for months, if not years, to come.

Add to that the severe psychological toll and trauma inflicted on the innocent bystanders, plus the irreparable damage to the nation's fragile sense of security, and the overall costs of their maleficence would become an incalculable but devastating sum.

The outlook was horrific. My father and his cohorts in the upper echelons of the Korean military and government would face the most monumental crisis since the Korean War. I tried to think like a general, like one whose job it was to protect the nation. I knew what I would do, therefore I knew the decision my father and the President would have to make. It was sobering and unthinkable. Their choices were limited: shoot the planes down or force them to circle over the ocean until they ran out of fuel. Either way, the two thousand passengers aboard those planes were dead.

But the alternative was worse. It was a global geo-political nightmare.

The FBI also learned that each plane was to carry approximately fifty kilograms of C4. Those bags would be heavy. Or, perhaps they used more than one bag. We had no way of knowing.

A fifty-kilo bomb was enough to level an entire city block if the explosion was aimed just right. Even if it wasn't, just the shock and awe of planes blowing up in the sky would be enough to send a ripple of fear throughout the world. North Korea obviously aimed to take a prominent position in the Axis of Evil.

Add to that the outrage when the world watched all of this on television. Surely, the US President would have his itchy trigger finger on the button shortly after witnessing one of America's strongest allies attacked in cold blood. Recent saber-rattling and rhetoric would escalate even further. Brinksmanship would give way to one-upmanship. The possibility of another global conflict loomed large and inevitable.

Robinson's brief report informed me that my father had already scrambled the fighter jets.

My father's decision was ominous, but at the same time, obvious. He and the other military and political leaders would have little time and few alternatives to debate.

I stood against the wall of the interrogation room as I listened to our prisoner, staring at Mr. Kim and wondering how he could be so calm.

The temptation to send this piece of scum back to the Mexican prison to get his just deserves was nearly overwhelming. But I had made a promise. Mr. Kim, while trying to stay true to his cause, had kept his part of the bargain and had told me everything he knew. Like it or not, I was convinced that he had come clean. The information he had given us had led to more grim discoveries, so I knew he had kept his end of the deal. I also knew that a mid-level guy like him wouldn't be given any more knowledge than was absolutely necessary for him to perform his duties.

The time was approaching for me to keep my end of the bargain and give him what he wanted most: to become a free man.

The thought made my stomach tighten and my blood pressure rise.

I pushed those thoughts aside. Before I concluded our session, I had to know more about the night that altered my life.

"Thank you for your cooperation, Mr. Kim. There's one last thing I need from you before you become a free man. I need you to go to the grocery store in Garden Grove with me, the one you frequented each day."

"They close at ten o'clock. Isn't it later than that now?"

"It is, but FBI agents have made the owners aware that you need to speak with them. They have agreed to cooperate even though they know nothing of the problems you've created."

He nodded but said nothing.

"While we wait for our transport, I wonder if you would humor me and tell me about that night in the DMZ, the night you and your Comrades shot up my team and infiltrated our country."

His eyebrows shot up and the corners of his mouth pulled tight as he considered my request. He seemed amused by it, but more than willing to share his heroics. "You were on patrol. We knew that," he said in a hoarse voice.

"How could you know our schedules and assignments?" I said.

"It's not that hard to figure out. Your command ran like clockwork. Very predictable."

I said nothing. What could I say? I gestured for him to continue.

"I was on patrol along the border near Chorwon. You were stationed at Yeoncheon, just a few kilometers to the south."

I signaled with my hand in a rolling motion for him to move it along faster.

"Those of us who volunteered for this mission did not come from privileged families. We wanted to make our lives better. Doing duty along the DMZ and taking on very dangerous tasks was one way to prove ourselves. Our families would be provided extra rations if we performed our tasks well."

Deep in my heart, I understood the draw. Protecting your people is a noble calling. He and I had both answered that call. I also understood the desperation from defectors I had interviewed. "Pretty dangerous assignment, especially when you consider that I shot most of your team that night. What kind of reward did their families get for that?"

"That I wouldn't know," he said. "That is not up to me."

I shook my head and kept plowing forward toward the information I really wanted. "That family was just a decoy, weren't they?"

"In a sense, yes. They had been caught trying to get through the barriers. Our team leader was told to send our least threatening soldier to intercept them. He befriended them and told them he would help them escape. But they had to follow his instructions precisely. Instructions were passed to them daily. Secret messages were provided to them in a variety of ways. I don't know all the details. These people were led to believe that he would help them escape. The time came, the signal was given, and that soldier met them at the designated spot. He let them through the fence and said he would distract the other guards long enough for them to get away."

"Your leaders filled them with false hope?"

Yong Byun paused, cocking his head slightly as my words sank in. "They were given the opportunity to play a role for the greater good."

"Clever how they twist things."

"They performed convincingly, and you came to their rescue, as predicted."

While there was more to explore, I didn't have time to satisfy my every curiosity, so I went straight to the heart of the matter. "Why didn't you kill me?" This was the crux of it for me. Ever since Yong Byun revealed that I was targeted because of my father, I suspected the reason. But I wanted to know for sure.

"Easy. You were to live. That was the order given. If you died, you would become a martyr, a hero, and your father would win the Blue House without a contest." He waved his hands dismissively.

I said nothing.

"We were told to shoot everybody else," he continued. "I believe we were successful, were we not?"

A cold hollow sensation ran through me as I thought about what he said. That young family were sent out as bait in a trap and my team mercilessly slaughtered, but I was kept alive as political leverage. "So, while the other soldiers had me pinned, you and the other twenty-four exfiltrated across the opening and killed the rest of my men."

"That's right. It was designed to discredit you, to raise questions as to why you would attempt something so foolish."

"So you could also discredit my father?"

"Your father is a threat to the Supreme Leader. His harsh words about bringing the North to our knees were not taken lightly."

"I see. So, you lured me and my patrol into the fences and ambushed us to discredit him."

"Yes. The plan was designed to bring shame to your family."

"Shaming me, shamed my father and ruined his attempt to run for president." This sickening thought hit me like a sledgehammer to the gut, stealing my breath for a moment. "Was I targeted today, as well?"

Mr. Kim cocked his head and narrowed his eyes. "I don't know for sure, but it's possible."

My fists balled up and my muscles tensed as I thought about the sixteen students, their mothers, and Jin Sook aboard that doomed plane. I breathed in deeply, trying to engage my brain before my weapons, as I had been taught, but the rage was building and I feared I might strike him again, only harder this time.

Just then my phone rang. The call was coming from Seoul. My rage cooled instantly as I wondered who it might be. Curious, I answered in a calm, polite tone and heard a familiar, though tense voice say, "Jeong Tae, this is your father."

Chapter 33

Port of Entry Station, Tecate, California
June 5, 11:01 p.m.

The rage was gone, replaced by an odd mixture of emotion. I felt a familiar sense of connectedness with my father, absent for so long. At the same time, a sense of melancholy stretched across all those wasted years. But more than anything, I felt his sense of urgency and desperation. He needed me to complete the mission I had started, and he needed information from me that he could pass on to the rest of the nation. He wanted me to be able to say, "Don't worry, everything's going to be all right."

But I couldn't.

I didn't say much, not with Yong Byun in the room. I just listened and gave short responses, assuring him that I was getting closer to a solution.

Then he said something that jarred me. "I watched much of your interrogation with the North Korean. You did very well."

"Uh, how did you manage to do that?"

"The feed from the camera in the room. We were patched in."

"I had no idea—"

"There is no time to waste. You must now use him to find his controllers. Surely one of them will know where the Bluetooth signal codes are located."

"How can you be so sure?"

"Redundancy. It's a North Korean staple. As is tight supervision and reporting. They will be expecting him to go to ground, so take him there. Take him back to his apartment and the market. Find those people and get the codes we need to break the connection."

All I said was, "Yes, yes. I'm working on it." I found it interesting that he felt the need to affirm the course of action I had already laid out.

"I want you to keep in touch with me. Whatever resources you need, I have available. They will be at your disposal, just a phone call away."

"Thank you," I said politely. "That is very helpful." I eyed Yong Byun as I spoke, wondering what he was thinking.

"One more thing. I know it was not your fault."

I paused, thinking that was an out of place comment.

"Last time, my candidacy. I heard him say it. They targeted you to get to me. And it worked. Not your fault. I am really sorry about...everything."

Yong Byun was looking at me, so I had to shake my head to fight back the emotions. My father's tone was soft and apologetic. I was startled and touched. I had never heard those words from him. "It's all right," I said.

"Jeong Tae," my father added in a soothing parental voice that took me back to my childhood, "Your country is counting on you. I know you can do this. I trust you."

As I fumbled the phone back into my pocket, a warm fog had filled me, slowing every thought and every movement to half speed, like a slow-motion replay. The feelings were both penetrating and unburdening. As my brain fought through the haze to process the meaning behind those few simple words from my long-estranged father, my coordination faltered, and I dropped my phone on the floor. Yong Byun's eyes grew wide and his eyebrows arched upward.

I wanted the pleasant sensation to last. I wanted it to spread backward through the past six years of uncertainty and shame. I wanted to talk through all the tangled cobwebs of our dormant relationship. But duty called and snapped me out of the moment.

"It's time to go find your friends."

"They're long gone," he said.

The uncertainty in his eyes told me otherwise. "I doubt it. I think you just don't want to see them again." I opened the door and asked the MPs standing guard if they would unlock the cell.

The MPs said that they could not because they had their orders. Unless it came from the Attorney General, they would not release him. It would take time, they explained, especially at this late hour, to obtain his consent. I realized there would be some sorting out to do before we could board the helicopter and be on our way.

"I can hardly blame you," I said to Yong Byun when the door closed again. "But today you're going to do the right thing and save thousands of innocent lives. It's going to make you feel better about yourself and make your freedom that much sweeter."

In the other half of my brain, thoughts about my family stirred. I knew Stephanie would be worried since I hadn't spoken to her for several hours.

"We're going to have to wait for all the paperwork to be done before we can go see them," I said to Yong Byun. "I'll be back to collect you." I stepped out of the room and walked down the hallway, dialing Stephanie as I went.

"What's going on, JT? I've been worried," she said as she answered.

"I can explain more later. I'm working with the TSA to apprehend a suspect—"

"A suspect? I thought you were just giving them advice about security—"

"Well, it's a bit more complicated than that. I don't have time to go into all of it." I paused. My feelings were still tender and muddled. "I need you to know that I love you. And the kids. I'd do anything and everything to keep you safe. I need you to know that." My voice was uncharacteristically choked with emotion.

Now Stephanie was the one who paused. "Are you sure you're OK?"

"I'm sure," I said, with much more confidence and conviction than I felt. "I . . . I don't know, I just had to tell you that. It's been a weird day."

"Tell me about it."

"What do you mean?"

"Let's see. First, I get a panicked call from Jin Sook. Then I see you being crammed into a police car on TV. Thankfully, they never showed your face and haven't identified you."

"I thought once the plane left the news would stop caring."

"Yeah, but they don't have much else to talk about today. Just more about the tensions between North Korea and the US. But the strangest part of my day was when I got a call from your father. In five and a half years of marriage, he has talked to me exactly one time before today. That's why I know there's a whole lot you're not sharing with me."

"I know," I said. "I'll tell you all about it, but not right now. Too much to do."

"Well, at least your mother has told me something."

"My mother?"

"Yes, she got it out of your father and thought I should know what's really going on." She stopped. "I want you to know that I believe in you. If anyone can save those planes, it's you."

She never ceased to amaze me. The way she conducted herself under stress and her calmness and faith in me lifted my sagging spirits. I told her again how much I loved her, then headed back to the room where Yong Byun was jailed. Before I got there, Robinson met me in the hall. "We need you in here," he said, pointing to a room further down the corridor. "Come with me."

We entered a large rectangular room with an oblong table. A conference phone with a starfish-shaped microphone/speaker sat on top of it. I could hear voices conversing through the speaker. Robinson interrupted and said, "Mr. Noh is now with me."

A group of men and women on the other end of the line introduced themselves. I couldn't remember all of their names, but I recognized the fact that two of them were also Koreans—an Agent Kim and Agent Kwon. They were leading the translation team that was working to decipher the cryptic instructions from the thumb drives.

Agents Kim and Kwon detailed the information they had been able to glean from the drives. Much of it corroborated what Yong Byun had told me, so they sped through those parts. One of the thumb drives, they said, contained a detailed explanation of how to arm the C4 packs, how and where to load them in the cargo hold, and how to set the detonator. Each detonator was hooked up to a cell phone via a Bluetooth connection. GPS and altimeter apps had been specially tweaked to send a signal via Bluetooth to the detonator when the plane entered the airspace over Seoul. If, for whatever reason, the plane didn't go over the city, the detonator would activate when it dipped below one hundred meters.

The cell phone was to be packed in a separate bag. The two bags were to be as nondescript as possible. A plain black roller bag purchased at Walmart or Costco—the type that dozens of other travelers would be using.

The logic was clear. Hide the bomb and the timer in plain sight, make it difficult to track and find. Make it a two-step process to further prevent their enemy's ability to thwart the plan. It was devious and ingenious. Nearly foolproof.

Agent Kim spoke English very well. I assumed he was second generation by the fact that he had virtually no accent. "The information on the first thumb drive confirms everything Mr. Noh learned. The plan to place five bombs on five different planes is detailed with flight numbers and departure times. We're tracking their locations now using satellite."

"That's right," said Agent Kwon in a lovely female voice touched with a delicate accent. "Each bomb was to be concealed in a thick Teflon casing. To a scanner it might look like a case for transporting collectible glassware items or fine art. It is not uncommon for people traveling internationally to deliver such goods to family or friends or businesses using a similar casing." Agent Kwon paused a beat in case there was a question before moving on. "Each bomb is set to explode over the city. The range of the coordinates covers the typical flight paths for aircraft coming from North America. Wherever they blow up, there will be a large civilian population directly below."

"Murphy Griggs, Deputy Secretary of Homeland Security." The voice broke in with an official tone and demeanor. "Let me remind everyone on this call that South Korea is a staunch ally of the United States. Let me also remind you that Seoul is one of the planet's most densely populated cities. Let me spell it out for you: this could lead to all-out war. We're dealing with a major crisis here that I'm sure we would all rather avert. So, how do we disrupt the connections to the detonators?"

"It's simple, sir."

"Is that you, Hank?" said Griggs.

"Yes, sir."

"Everybody, this is Hank Stevens, Head of Cybersecurity at the NSA. "Go ahead, Hank."

"The only way to save lives is to disable the bombs. The only possible way to do that is to scramble the Bluetooth signal between the cell phones and the detonators. It's simple if you have the right equipment."

"Somehow, Hank, I believe there's a caveat coming," said Griggs.

"Of course, there is. It's highly unlikely any of those planes have the proper equipment onboard." The guy sounded too young for his title but extremely knowledgeable. He spoke with a sort of confidence that comes from expertise.

Murphy Griggs interjected. "What kind of equipment are we looking at here, Hank?"

"Bluetooth is set up to use a wide band of frequency channels and uses FHHS to keep the strongest possible signal between—"

"In layman's terms, please," barked Griggs.

"Oh, yeah, OK. Um, let's see. What that means is that the paired devices can hop between frequencies thousands of times per second and with seventy-nine channels to choose from, it's like impossible to send out enough interference to break the connection unless you have some specialized equipment."

"We're going to assume, Hank," said Griggs, "that they don't have that equipment on the planes."

"Yeah, that's a good assumption to make. So, let's see. The only other way to disengage two devices connected via Bluetooth is to know the pseudorandom sequence they are using to perform what's called Adaptive Frequency Hopping. Without the right equipment, knowing and disrupting the pseudorandom sequence is the only way to effectively and permanently jam the frequencies and break the connection."

"Mr. Noh," said Griggs. "Can you get those pseudorandom codes Hank's talking about?"

Chapter 34

Cheong Wa Dae, Jongno-gu, Seoul, South Korea
June 6, 3:30 p.m.; June 5, 11:30 p.m. California Time

Outside, the weather was idyllic. Blue skies were framed between lush green trees and the distant mountains and dotted with puffy white clouds. Weather-wise, it was shaping up to be a spectacular day. In early June, temperatures and humidity in Korea did not reach the high levels they would later in the month and throughout most of the summer.

Early that morning, during his routine speed-walk through the massive governmental complex that housed his office, just north of the Han River, which ran through Seoul, General Noh soaked in the peaceful atmosphere knowing it couldn't last. Soon enough, a stiffening breeze off the Yellow Sea would bring with it stormy weather. Later in the month, thick clouds would replace the billowy, cotton ball-like ones that decorated the sky that morning. By the end of June, the Korean Peninsula would be enveloped in monsoon season with its drenching rains and soaring temperatures. In a few short weeks, the pleasantness of Spring would give way to the months-long sauna known as summer.

Within the walls of every office in his building, as well as those of the Executive Branch, a similar pattern was evolving. Atmospheric pressure was rising, brought on by the spiraling bomb crisis had obliterated what could have been the perfect day for a press conference to announce one's candidacy for the nation's highest office. Metaphorical pleasantness had given way to unyielding heat, much like the changing weather.

CHAPTER 34

As General Noh gazed through the window of the Press Hall, on the grounds of the Blue House, the irony of nature's tranquility was not lost on him. Decked out in his full military uniform, complete with an impressive array of medals lined up along his breast pocket, he paced the room that served as his "other office" on the occasions when he held meetings at or near the executive headquarters. He had just spoken to the nation on TV, answering some, but not all, of the press corps' questions about the imminent danger the country faced.

President Jang, who started the press conference, had skillfully narrated the threat as it was understood, then turned things over to General Noh to discuss details about the planned response to the brewing crisis. While avoiding specifics that would alarm the public but using the smokescreen of "in the interest of national security," the General had, in his commanding way, assured his countrymen that he and the military were doing all they could to keep the public safe.

With the press conference behind him, it was time for another debriefing. Pressing a button on the desk phone, General Noh was conferenced into a meeting with the Joint Military Council. As the discussion progressed, nothing but grim alternatives emerged. Lives on the ground were weighed against the lives on the plane. Those on the plane were certain to die, but those are the ground need not be endangered. The welfare of the many in the city must outweigh the welfare of the much smaller number onboard. It felt like such a dastardly decision.

The joint chiefs had discussed a short list of available actions to reduce the loss of life and minimize physical damage to the country's infrastructure. Of course, each alternative had a military bent to it, as none of his compatriots seemed capable of conjuring up anything short of an aggressive, tactical solution. Despite his thirty-five-year career in the Army, not once had General Noh contemplated the things this council had discussed. Although the Korean War had never officially ended, the fragile sixty-five-year peace was all but shattered. The men in that room were pounding on their war drums so loudly it made clear-headed thinking next to impossible. The pressure to mount an immediate and full-scale attack on North Korea was nearly overwhelming.

In his calm and commanding way, the General had stifled such talk. Instead, he insisted, they focus on the more immediate problem—doing everything possible to save the lives of those on the inbound airplanes. "There must be a technical solution," he said. "While there is still time, we focus on getting the right people in here, people who understand Bluetooth technology and signal processing. We aim for a peaceful resolution first and keep our military options open in case we're not successful."

While he agreed that they could not allow these planes to enter South Korean airspace until the explosives had been neutralized, he found the pursuant discussion bleak. The focus quickly reverted from figuring out how to save the lives of the innocent passengers to, instead, punishing the enemy.

Two competing and highly inventive ideas emerged. Since F-16 fighter jets had already intercepted the planes and were escorting them around the southern tip of the Korean Peninsula, approaching Incheon International Airport from the south rather than from the east, the Air Force Commander suggested having the pilots overshoot Incheon and fly their commercial jets below the radar, aimed straight at Pyeongyang. A competing idea was to just fly at low altitude directly over North Korea and try to get as close as possible to the capital before they got shot down. Either way, General Noh's compatriots were intent on doing harm to those who intended to harm them.

The thought of using commercial jets, filled with both foreign and domestic civilians, as kamikazes to bomb the enemy was unique, but reprehensible. Equally as unfathomable was shooting them out of the sky. Escorting them out to sea where they would eventually run out of fuel and succumb to gravity and then the unstoppable detonations was the least objectionable, but still distasteful. Political fallout aside, that was the one solution that represented the most realistic minimized-casualty scenario available to the security council given the time constraints should Jeong Tae fail in obtaining the pseudo random codes.

If he failed, the planes would run out of fuel. Their demise would be unseen, and the destruction minimized to the planes and their passengers.

This outcome was still awful to contemplate, but better than the alternative intended by the enemy.

The calculations showed the inbound flight from Dallas would be the first to drop. It had enough fuel to last just over three hours at typical cruising speed and altitude. The aeronautical experts had been busy crunching numbers to find the optimal speed and altitude to elongate the flight. They estimated it could go as much as an additional fifty minutes. That gave the team roughly four hours to work with.

As the discussion concluded, General Yoon, the Air Force Chief of Staff, announced to the council that two dozen F-16 Fighting Falcon jets that had been scrambled after the previous meeting had intercepted the incoming jumbo jets. Five teams of three jetfighters would escort the five passenger planes over the Sea of Okhotsk, before they reached Japanese air space, and lead them to the Yellow Sea, keeping them to the east of the island chain of Japan. The other F-16's would patrol the airspace over the country, focusing on the coasts, the northern border, and the Capital city.

Minister Yim of the Ministry of Science and Information Communication Technology had responsibility for all things technical. He informed the group that his team was busy working up a solution that could be broadcast to a member of each flight crew. The team was mapping out easy-to-follow instructions designed to walk someone with intermediate technical abilities step by step through the process of jamming the Bluetooth signal. Unless they had the pseudorandom codes, it wouldn't be a complete jam and it wouldn't last very long. The imperfect solution would be based on whether the captured North Korean had told General Noh's son the truth about how the detonators were set up and whether the devices were indeed linked via a standard Bluetooth configuration. Even if they were, because Bluetooth uses Frequency-Hopping Spread Spectrum technology to switch between seventy-nine channels 1600 times per second, Minister Yim was not confident enough to predict a successful outcome. At best, he said, without the codes they could only disrupt the connection for a short period of time.

"With precision timing and coordination," he explained, "there is a chance the plane could descend through the one-hundred-meter trigger zone during the estimated seven-second disruption window. This, however, presents two problems. The first is the speed that would accompany such a steep rate of descent. Would the plane have enough time to pull up and enough runway to stop? The second unknown is whether the altimeter alert on the phone would kick back on and detonate the device. It could work, though, and that's something, at least."

Minister Yim, for all his knowledge and experience, had not allayed any fears, his optimism breathed new hope into a gloomy situation.

The only fail-safe solution, he warned, was to get the pseudorandom sequence for each device pairing. "Just get me those code files, wherever they are, and we'll talk through the disarming process one-by-one with a member of each crew."

After the call, General Noh paced in front of the floor-to-ceiling windows, hands clasped behind his back. No longer did the scenery outside hold any interest. It was the storm inside that demanded his attention. The Republic of Korea had never faced such a threat. The threat itself was inconceivable. The choices left to the leaders were unfathomable. As a military leader, his job was to protect innocent lives. Today, that job seemed impossible.

Throughout history, many great leaders had been forged in the fiery furnace of conflict, where the choices made in the heat of the moment would only be judged as prudent after all the facts were learned and assessed. The question was whether the world and the history books would ever know all the facts surrounding the decisions that had to be made in this crisis.

The burden of leadership was staggering.

General Noh would have to make heart-wrenching decisions while contemplating the thousands of lives that hung in the balance and the many more thousands of loved ones who would be devastated by their demise.

As a general, he had grown accustomed to the responsibility for people's lives. But this was an entirely different level, a level few ever experienced. The term "sacrificing for the good of the many" took on new meaning.

Unless a miracle occurred, this day would surely go down as the most fateful day in Korean history, as well as in General Noh's personal life. If, by the grace of God, all of the passengers on all five planes and all the lives in jeopardy on the ground were spared, it would be the most blessed day in Korean history that no one beyond the group in that conference room would ever fully appreciate.

There was a tremendous load riding on Jeong Tae's shoulders, a load at least equal to that of the General.

General Noh stood, strode across the room, and locked the door. When he returned to the desk, he didn't sit in the high-backed leather chair. Instead, he knelt by it and spent twenty minutes in fervent prayer.

Chapter 35

Over the Yellow Sea, West of Incheon, Korea
June 6, 4:42 p.m. Local Time; 12:42 a.m. California Time

Two and a half hours before its scheduled arrival in Seoul, Captain Hong Moo Gwang, the pilot of the Korean Air flight from Dallas-Fort Worth, had received a call on the emergency frequency from the Air Chief Marshal of the Korean Air Force. The emergency frequency insured that neither the crew nor the passengers could listen to the conversation. He had been informed that a squadron had been dispatched to divert his aircraft and escort it on an alternate route to Incheon International Airport. Though the information provided was scant, Captain Hong, a former Air Force pilot, obeyed without question. It was a highly unusual request that certainly held national security implications.

As the aircraft approached the northern end of the island chain that made up Japan, three fighter jets appeared first on radar, then through the windscreen. The squadron leader instructed Hong to fly in a south-westerly direction two hundred kilometers east of Japan's eastern coast. Hong asked why.

"Sir," replied the younger fighter pilot. "It is for the safety of those on the ground. We cannot allow your plane to fly over inhabited land until we are sure it's safe."

The Boeing 747 was loaded nearly to capacity with 401 passengers and 16 crew members. Hong's posture stiffened. The co-pilot shot him a wary glance and adjusted his headset. Tension flooded the cockpit. An F-16 shadowed each wing and a third one followed a kilometer behind. It was a tactical formation with a message: If they didn't comply, their plane would be blown out of the sky.

Hong followed instructions to reduce power and climbed to a higher elevation. The air currents up there would reduce fuel consumption. The Chief Air Marshal came back on and provided a brief overview of the situation. "I regret to inform you that we have obtained an intelligence report stating that North Korean infiltrators may have loaded an explosive device aboard your aircraft. A smart phone is set to relay a signal to the detonator based on GPS coordinates or altitude. That is why we cannot allow you to fly over inhabited areas."

Again, the pilot and co-pilot looked at each other, eyes wide, faces taut.

The Air Marshall ended the conversation with a simple pronouncement. "We have our technical teams working on a solution. We'll radio when we have something."

Captain Hong was told to announce to the passengers that they were being rerouted and, therefore, their arrival into Seoul would be delayed. He was instructed not to share the information he had about the dangers they faced. No need to upset the passengers or crew members.

Chapter 36

Onboard Bell UH-1N Helicopter over Orange County, California
June 6, 12:47 a.m.

The Mexican authorities were true to their word and released Mr. Kim into our custody, but it took much longer than expected. Sergeant Lewis apologized profusely for the time lag. As soon as Yong Byun was signed out of the Attorney General's holding cell, we piled him into Lewis's Jeep and made our way back across the border.

Thirteen minutes later, Robinson, Yong Byun, and I were in the helicopter lifting off.

We each used the hour-long flight to catch up on our rest.

My sleep was interrupted less than thirty minutes into the flight by my phone vibrating in my pocket. It was my father, calling from his office at Army Headquarters in Seoul. I looked at the Huey's onboard navigational screen to get oriented. I realized we were speeding over the darkened hills of Riverside County, southeast of Los Angeles. Our destination was John Wayne Airport in Orange County where a car would be waiting for us. The FBI agents in that car would take us to Yeo Chae Market, the Korean store in Garden Grove where Yong Byun picked up his groceries each evening. That was my starting point. I didn't have much to go on, but I hoped the owners would share with me whatever information they could about Yong Byun's supposed wife. She, I was convinced, would be in the area and quite possibly the linchpin in this whole operation. My hunch was that she and maybe others would lurk around, waiting for a chance to collect Yong Byun and bring him in. Her fate would be tied to his. Of this I was almost certain.

Since Mr. Kim had informed me that the Alpha team was based in Orange County, supplying all other teams with instructions and codes, I knew the technical guru would be connected to the "wife." They seemed to be the ones controlling the technical and logistical aspects of all five teams. As the overlords of the operation, it would be their task to "tie up loose ends," one of which was our friend, Mr. Kim. I guessed another part of their job was to oversee the return of each and every team member involved in the operation to the homeland.

When I answered the call, my father's tone of voice was all business. This was General Noh, the highest ranking general in the Korean Army, who had called me, not my dad. I knew things were dire, and that others were listening to this conversation because his mannerisms were much different than during our prior call. He was performing for whatever crowd was listening. He was also gambling, betting all his political capital on the son that had cost him a chance at the presidency in the last election cycle. To the others in top positions in Korea, I was a court-martialed former squadron commander living in what amounted to exile.

No greeting, no small talk. He launched directly into a brief synopsis of the high-level meeting he had just attended. *Wasn't this stuff classified?*

The call ended three minutes after it began. He reiterated the need for the pseudo random sequences for each Bluetooth device and said his team was working up easy-to-follow instructions in Korean and English that a member of the flight crew on each plane could use to disable them. Without those, we had no hope of saving the nineteen hundred passengers and crew members on those planes.

The last thing my father said was, "One hour and forty-five minutes of fuel on the inbound flight from Dallas. Good luck."

The clock was ticking. I had until 3:15 a.m.

The only words I uttered were at the end when I simply said, "Yes, sir. I understand. We are en route to intercept the Alpha team as we speak. I'll report on my progress upon contact with the enemy."

I wondered what the others listening to our conversation were thinking.

There were no guarantees that a) we would actually intercept the team in question or that b) if we did, they would know or have access to those codes.

That meant my new friend, Kim Yong Byun, who sat wedged between me and Robinson in the back row of the Huey's cockpit, would be a key component to the mission's success. I was using him as bait. However, since the FBI had discovered the two thumb drives, we had a cache of pictures. They had uploaded them to a shared drive, which I accessed on my phone.

"Is this him? Is this your tech guy?" I asked Mr. Kim after jabbing his ribs with my elbow to wake him up.

"I don't think so."

"How about this guy?" I continued swiping through the collection the FBI had uploaded.

Mr. Kim used the same answer each time until we came to a handsome, yet boyish, face. He motioned with his hands for permission to hold the phone. I passed it to him. With his hands cuffed and secured to a belly chain, he looked awkward trying to hold the thing and manipulate the screen. But he was eventually able to position the phone so he could use his fingers to zoom in on the face. "This is the only guy who was allowed to use the computer in our apartment. Just him. It was password protected and no one else had the password. He only stayed there one or two nights per week. I don't know where he was otherwise, but I always guessed it was at the control house in Garden Grove."

I took a closer look, but the face was not one I had seen before.

"He had a laptop and a bag full of all kinds of gadgets and wires and things like that. I didn't know what his responsibilities were exactly, but I can assume that he's the technician. Or one of them."

"Do you know where he might be?" I asked, holding very little hope of getting the answer I wanted.

"No. Each man had his own set of instructions to follow after their part in the mission was completed. We were never to share that information with anyone, not even with other members of the team."

Robinson was looking over Yong Byun's shoulder. Without understanding the language, he seemed to know what we were talking about. He gave me an inquisitive look and without a word started tapping furiously on his phone's screen. "I'm sending that photo to my team," he said through the chopper's comm unit. "They'll run facial rec on this guy right away. We'll see what we come up with."

"He could be anywhere by now. That's the problem. We've got to work up an alternate solution in case we can't find this guy."

"Working on it," Robinson said with a frown. "We'll run it through every traffic camera and CCTV feed in the state. With the FBI on our team, that can be done instantaneously."

"Let's hope he's not holed up in some secret location for the next few weeks or months, waiting this thing out," I said. I realized that sounded incredibly pessimistic, so I added, "But that's not likely." But in my head I was thinking, "*That's what I would do in that situation.*"

"The odds are long." Robinson looked out the window, slowly shaking his head. "Let's pray for a miracle."

We all sat in silence with our thoughts and worries. The lights below us grew closer together and more intense as we moved from desert to suburban sprawl to metro. Wide concrete thoroughfares carried a surprising number of cars for that time of night, their headlights spread in front of them like luminescent antennae. Those in their cars were oblivious to the turmoil brewing in the skies. Lights from streetlamps and shopping centers and business parks twinkled below while I thought about the proverbial needle in the haystack.

An idea struck me. Call it inspiration. I texted Stephanie, knowing she would still be awake, waiting for answers. I asked her to do me a couple of favors. She responded as I knew she would and said "Gladly."

The pilot chimed in. "Sirs? We'll be landing at John Wayne in five minutes."

I furiously tapped a list of items and instructions and pushed the little up arrow, regretting the need to get my wife mixed up in this thing.

After a swift and smooth landing, we hopped out of the chopper, bent at the waist as the rotors tussled our hair and clothes. I pulled Yong Byun by the elbow and pushed his head down as I led him to a dark blue Ford sedan that waited for us twenty yards away. Two young Asian men wearing holsters and ties greeted us with firm handshakes and serious looks.

After giving the driver the address of the Korean market, we piled into the Ford and charged out of the airport and onto the empty streets of Santa Ana. The GPS informed us that it would take sixteen minutes to cover the eleven-mile distance between us and our destination. But at the speeds the driver was doing, I knew we'd be there much faster than that.

During the drive, Robinson spoke to various members of his team and I got an update from the two Korean FBI agents working on the thumb drives. They had been in contact with Agent Kwon, the woman from the conference call, who was leading the work on the captured files. We just barely had time to brief each other on the new information we'd learned before we arrived at the market.

It was nearly two o'clock in the morning when we drove past the strip mall where the market was located. Way past closing time, but the place was lit up. As instructed, the driver drove several blocks, then turned into the neighborhood behind the market and worked his way back. I told Yong Byun to get out and walk to the front of the market. The owners were expecting him.

I hopped out and went to the back door, where my coded knock was answered on cue by a kindly older gentleman wearing a sweater and thick-rimmed glasses. So far, so good. Instructions were being followed. He showed me through the storage area to the main store. I stopped there and was met by the familiar smells of kimchi, dried fish, and fresh vegetables. The small market was crammed full of dry goods, packaged noodles, snacks, and canned sweet drinks, just like the ones I remembered from home. I felt like I had stepped out of California and into Seoul.

From my vantage point, I could see through the front glass doors out to the parking area. I watched Yong Byun approach cautiously. He wore a hooded sweatshirt with the hood pulled down to hide his face. A short middle-aged woman with artificially black hair pulled into bun at the back of her head was sweeping the floor near the counter when he entered. She gasped, certain he was there to rob the place. Her hands went up, causing her broom to clatter as it hit the floor. Her eyes darted to the pocket of his sweatshirt. Yong Byun pulled the hood back and smiled so she would recognize him. She studied him for a moment, then turned and looked at me. I darted along the back aisle, then up toward the counter along a row of produce, staying out of view of the glass doors and two long windows in the front of the store.

The woman shook her head as I approached. "Who is your friend?" she asked warily. "Are you in some sort of trouble? Why did you request to pick up your groceries at this late hour?"

I spoke up from the second aisle, still out of view of the front window. While pretending to browse for snacks, I introduced myself as a local Tae Kwon Do Instructor, leaving out any details about the purpose of our visit and explained that I was Mr. Kim's Sabum, or coach.

She quickly corrected me and said, "Oh, you mean Mr. Lee. He is a regular customer here. We look forward to his visit each evening." Turning to Yong Byun, she said, "This is very unusual. You didn't come at the usual time, so I worried. I came back to the store when you called me. So late. Very strange. Is something wrong?"

Yong Byun was quick on his feet. "No, no. Nothing's wrong. I'm returning from a tournament in Sacramento. We caught the last flight, which got delayed. Noh Sabum-nim was kind enough to give me a ride from the airport. But my wife insisted I pick up her order."

"Yes, I see," she said. "Your wife called several times to check on you. She was very upset that you had not come by." She bent down and retrieved two plastic bags, hauling them to the top of the counter by their handles. "There you go. Just as she requested."

Yong Byun thanked her for her trouble and promised that it would never happen again.

She cocked her head and waved a dismissive hand, ready to move on from the ordeal. "You never mentioned that you are learning Tae Kwon Do. What level have you achieved?"

Without missing a beat, Yong Byun responded, "Sa-Dan Black belt." This indicated that he had studied the martial art for at least four years and had acquired a significant level of combat skill. As he said it, he shot me a loaded look that told me he wasn't fibbing.

If this was supposed to intimidate me, it failed. Jin Sook had made it a point on our Do Jang's website and on our brochures that I was a "Sa Seong," a Grand Master holding the ninth level of black belt.

The nice lady behind the counter looked appropriately impressed at Yong Byun's pronouncement. "That is quite an accomplishment, Mr. Lee. I presume you did well in your competition." Then she looked to me with new-found admiration.

"Yes, ma'am. Thanks to Noh Sabum-nim."

"You must be higher, no?"

I gave a half smile and a half nod, showing the appropriate amount of humility. This was not lost on Yong Byun, who held a long blink in acknowledgement.

"So, my wife sounded upset?" Yong Byun asked.

"Yes, of course." she said, glancing at the clock on the wall behind her. "Her first call was right on time. She usually calls around 6:30. Tonight, she called every thirty minutes to check on you."

"Did she say anything else, like where to meet her?"

A puzzled look crossed her face. "No. Why? What's going on with you two?"

This was going in the wrong direction, so I interrupted. "Can I see your phone?" I said. She gave me a curious look, then handed me the handset set. I thumbed the buttons to look for incoming calls. There were a handful from the same number. Indeed, someone had called roughly every half an hour since 6:30 p.m. I called Robinson, who sat in the car less than forty meters away. "You have the tracing equipment ready?"

"Sure do. Why?"

"I have the woman's number. I'm going to dial it now."

Chapter 37

Cheongwadae Complex, Jongno-gu, Seoul, South Korea
June 6, 5:00 p.m.

Every national and international news outlet was clamoring for more information. Their primetime newscasts needed the latest update on their breaking stories, each given a different, yet similar headline: "Crisis in the skies." "Danger Above." "Incoming." "Enemy Attack."

President Jang had acquiesced to the pressure and called another news conference to give them the latest information. Once again, the President said he would start things off with an overview and then turn it over to the General for the specifics.

"They're going to need more than generalities," said the President over the phone. "It would be wise to be upfront with them. Give them the illusion of transparency by sharing enough to satiate their need for the latest, most current information. But do not give them so much as to create panic. That will only make the situation worse."

The time had arrived. Each station would cut to the President at precisely two minutes after five o'clock. Before exiting his office, General Noh popped two antacid pills in his mouth and chewed the chalky capsules in seconds.

Despite the fact that he had no confirmation from his son, General Noh decided to trust that his son would be successful in his pursuit of the alpha team leaders in Southern California. There were no other new facts that would make this situation look or sound any less terrifying to the general public.

The President wrapped up his brief synopsis of the facts as they currently stood, thanking the press for keeping the nation informed and up to date. Before turning things over to General Noh, he pleaded with Koreans, especially those in and around Seoul and Incheon International to please stay indoors until the crisis was over.

General Noh stepped up to the bank of microphones lined up across the wooden podium with the Presidential seal emblazoned across its front. It was time to face the throng of reporters and state the problem, allude to the solution without giving away strategic or tactical information, and show appropriate concern while projecting an air of genuine confidence that the course they were on was the best one available under the circumstances. It was a tightrope act, higher and more dangerous than any he had performed in his long career. The press was like a school of piranha, ready to rip and tear the flesh off anything that smelled like food.

"Thank you for your attendance here today. Undoubtedly, you will have many questions. Please hold them until the end of my brief statement. At that time, I will provide whatever answers I am able to without compromising our strategic or tactical plans. The top-ranking security council personnel, as well as many of our allies, are working hard to resolve the current situation.

"Many of you have heard the reports coming out of Los Angeles about a potential terror threat to one of our Korean Air Lines passenger planes. Regretfully, I am here to confirm those threats are real, based on intelligence obtained by our best field operatives. We have recently learned that four other planes have also been targeted. Our intelligence community is working to establish the credibility of those reports. They have been working closely with the FBI and TSA in America. At this point, we are proceeding as if the threat is real and that five planes in total may be carrying explosive devices." An audible gasp rose from the assemblage of reporters.

General Noh continued without a pause. "Because of the work of our intelligence officers, we are able to take steps to minimize loss of life and destruction of physical assets. The borders of our nation remain fortified and secured. Our people remain safe." The attendees whispered among themselves, many of them scribbling notes or typing furiously as they listened.

"Our best and bravest pilots flying our fastest and most technologically advanced fighter aircraft are patrolling the skies above to protect our country. No doubt many of you have seen and heard our jets flying overhead. Other military assets remain, as always, vigilant and prepared to meet and repel any threat to the safety of our people and the sovereignty of our nation."

The General continued, explaining that the situation was evolving as new information came in. He promised to call another press conference to keep the nation informed.

As he backed away from the podium hoping to dodge any probing queries, a senior reporter with a reputation for diligence and honesty stood and bowed. "Sir, how long have you known about these bombs onboard these planes? That news story from Los Angeles aired over twelve hours ago?"

"We learned about it shortly after the last plane departed United States airspace. In an effort to avoid confusion and panic, we have been working with the Americans and others to verify the nature and veracity of the threat. Since that time, we have been working tirelessly on a solution to minimize the loss of life."

Another veteran reporter threw her hand in the air before the General finished his sentence. "The reports out of Los Angeles indicate the American TSA inspected the baggage aboard the flight from LAX to Incheon. If they re-inspected the bags, how can there be a bomb on board?"

"That is the main reason it took so long to verify the threat. We and the American officials believed that the threat had been nothing more than an elaborate hoax. Upon re-inspection, there was no trace of any type of explosive material anywhere inside that plane."

She followed up. "What happened with the man they arrested in Los Angeles? The one who had access to the plane's cargo area?"

"That man was taken into custody, searched, questioned thoroughly. During the interrogation, it was discovered that the man was working undercover. He alerted the American officials that he may have seen something suspicious. That is what led to the call to re-scan the luggage onboard and delay the flight."

Then the moment he had dreaded arrived. A pesky female reporter known for being astute and asking razor-sharp questions of politicians, stood, bowed, and fired away.

"General Noh, what are your intentions with those five planes? Is it to simply allow them to run out of fuel somewhere over the ocean? Or have you ordered those fighter jets to shoot them down if they approach Korean airspace?"

Noh Tae Seong closed his eyes as he gave a slight bow. "Those are very good questions. The safety of those planes is obviously a concern. As I mentioned, we have a team of experts working rapidly to find a way to bring those planes and their passengers safely home. Our technology experts have identified possible solutions. We are working with great urgency to apply those solutions. Whatever course we follow will seek the highest likelihood of success and risk the fewest number of lives. However, until we have a safe solution, those planes will not be allowed to enter Korean airspace."

The reporter jumped right back into the fray. "How long can those planes stay in the air, sir?"

"As you know, each plane carries enough fuel to make the long journey across the ocean plus enough to stay in the air for several additional hours. Depending on its origin, that may be anywhere from three to eight hours. Our experts are working on solutions to allow these airplanes to land safely." He did not mention that the first plane would fail in only two hours.

Another reporter asked, "Why not instruct them to land somewhere else, like Japan?"

The General nodded slowly. "We will not jeopardize the safety of our citizens, nor our neighbors or allies. There are no locations remote enough that have an airstrip long enough to land a 747. That's why the planes must remain in the air while we strive to implement a technological solution."

Hushed whispers filled the crowded room. General Noh stood straight and tall, cleared his throat, and spoke with conviction and confidence. "Ladies and gentlemen, this crisis represents a serious threat to those onboard the aircraft in question, but not to our national security. Our priority is to save lives and protect our border. We are working diligently to that end. Thank you for your time. I must get back to the business at hand."

The General made a quick exit through a doorway to the side of the raised podium and was immediately met by Mr. Park, his campaign manager.

As the two marched down the wide corridor away from the press conference, Park said, "All in all, not a bad performance. I wish we had had time to rehearse prior to your taking the stage. These appearances are critical to public perception and should not be squandered. Please work with me before you do that again."

The General stopped in his tracks and turned on his heels to glare at Mr. Park. "That was not meant to be a 'performance.' That was a press conference to address the most serious threat to our country since the invasion of 1950. Please do not talk to me about my 'performance.' I must focus on my job and my job is to protect our homeland."

Mr. Park shook his head dismissively, which produced a deeper scowl on the General's already-stormy countenance. Park held his gaze. "If you want to become the President of this mighty republic, you need to start by leveraging every opportunity you have in the public eye. Performance in front of your voters should be a high priority for you right now, despite the urgency of the moment."

General Noh glowered at the smaller man, then continued marching towards the conference room where the other joint chiefs were gathered, doubling his pace. Park had to practically run to keep up with the older man. "I will not be made to look like one of those attention-mongering politicians. Governing a nation, especially during a crisis, is a serious matter. It requires thoughtfulness and diligence, not the ability to woo the crowd. I'm here to serve my country, not act out some scripted role for the cameras."

Mr. Park held his peace, remaining behind the hard-charging general as he skipped the elevator and vaulted up the stairs two at a time, his hard-soled shoes booming like thunder on the metal steps in the concrete stairway.

Chapter 38

Yeo Chae Market, Garden Grove, CA
June 6, 1:42 a.m.

Robinson told me to wait for his signal before I pushed the "dial" button.

The FBI agents in the Ford were on speaker phone with their technical team. Before I dialed, the agents verified that the number in question was indeed a mobile phone, as suspected. Of course, it was unlisted. Most likely a "burner" phone with rechargeable minutes.

"OK," said Robinson. "Go ahead."

I pressed the button and heard the familiar beeps as the numbers were processed.

Using a StingRay device, the technical crew searched for the cell phone Yong Byun's controller had used to call the store and make her daily order. They started by scanning the cell towers near the store, then moving further and further away from our location by pinging towers in an increasingly large radius. They traced the last known location to a parking lot at LAX but informed us that the phone had been powered down for hours.

As suspected, the call went straight to a default recording that told me the subscriber I had reached did not have a voicemail box setup and that I should try my call again later.

Hope began to fade. Our success depended on us finding these people.

Robinson and the FBI agents had moved the Ford to the parking lot of a building directly across the street while we waited for the trace to complete.

This way they could maintain visual contact with the front door of the market. An unknown number of law enforcement agents in an unknown number of locations monitored an unknown number of inputs to track developments and communicate them to each other and to Robinson, who kept me in the loop on anything pertinent.

Yong Byun and I remained in the store, waiting for the phone to ring. I kept myself out of sight of the front windows, but close enough to keep watch. The store owners, who had come back at this late hour as a favor to Yong Byun, were ready to go home. We had made their long day longer and stolen their precious rest time by insisting that the items on his list were of vital importance to him and his family. They were kind enough to let us stay, but their patience was growing thin. The conversation had stopped, and the woman no longer seemed interested in Yong Byun's plight. There was nothing for her to do but sit behind the counter watching the phone while her husband puttered around in the storage area, occasionally calling out, "Are we ready to go yet?"

I explained to the woman the urgency of reaching Yong Byun's wife by telling them she was not well. There were both mental and physical health challenges. "You must understand," I said after a several awkward minutes of staring at the phone, "that since my friend lost his phone on our trip, he hasn't been able to talk to his wife to make sure she's all right. I can't use my mobile phone because once she has my number, she will never stop calling it. That's the way it is with obsessive compulsive behavior. But it's very important that he makes sure she's well."

That softened the woman's countenance, buying us some additional time by means of ramping up the sympathy. After thinking on what I had said for a moment, the woman turned to Yong Byun and said, "It all makes sense now. The daily phone calls, the small orders with very odd items. The insistence that you come here in the middle of the night like this." She wagged her head. "I had no idea what you were dealing with, Mr. Lee. I'm sorry."

A hundred questions ran through my mind, and a hundred more concerns for those in the doomed airplanes. My head was practically spinning as I wondered how extensive the North Korean presence was here in Southern

California. How many "guards" had they posted to prevent defection? What sized team would they send to gather Yong Byun and the others? How well trained were they? Or had they already left the US? That was not out of the question, but it would effectively end our chances of saving those passengers.

For those of us tasked to deal with North Korea defectors, our experience had taught us much. If my father was right, the North Korean personnel handlers would expect Yong Byun to "return to ground" out of fear of reprisal. Punishments for disobedience, though not broadcast, were widely known to be brutal and swift. If any member of the team were to fail, the whole team would pay the price. Therefore, I expected Yong Byun's handlers were close, possibly even watching the store. That's why I stayed back from the window. I had told Yong Byun to do the same, but he gave me a look of disbelief and kept close to the phone. He looked out the glass front doors constantly, causing me to think that maybe he was contemplating making a run for it.

As I watched Yong Byun fidget, I wondered to myself what the North Koreans hoped to gain by this operation. It seemed so carefully planned while at the same time being completely irrational and fool-hardy. Did they not think the Americans would detect them? Did they expect terror tactics to cause South Korea to capitulate and allow them to continue testing nukes? Was that what they wanted? Or did they expect this horrific stunt to somehow get the sanctions against their impoverished nation lifted?

The clock was ticking. That much I knew. Texts kept coming into my phone with updates. The flight from Dallas, because it had the furthest distance to travel, would be the first to run out of fuel. It had also departed before any of the others. It had until 3:15 a.m. My watch showed it was ten minutes after two o'clock.

I beckoned Yong Byun over to where I stood, then walked to the far end of the store. I whispered instructions to prepare him for the task ahead. Assuming the woman who was supposed to be his wife would return his call, he needed to tell her a story about his escape and what he did with the dead body and the warehouse and the car. He would beg her for a quick extraction, telling her he didn't feel safe, not after blowing up the warehouse. I reminded him that his life and his freedom depended on his ability to persuade her to come to him. "Obviously, this conversation needs to happen out of earshot of her," I said, tossing my head towards the shop owner behind the front counter.

He nodded his understanding and said he would do it, but his face was pallid and his movements rigid and awkward. Something had shifted in him. With other pressing matters on my mind, I dismissed it as nerves and went back to my train of thought.

I wondered how long this woman would ignore the calls. Half an hour had passed since our first attempt to contact her. Certainly, she would be monitoring incoming calls. My guess was that she wouldn't be asleep, not with their mission still incomplete. She must be in full panic mode by now. None of the planes had blown up and all were at least an hour past their scheduled arrival time.

Because our first three attempts to reach her went straight to voice mail, I was beginning to feel an oppressive gloom closing in on me. Each delay increased my anxiety. I needed something good to happen *now*. I—we—needed to find this woman and learn what she knew. I was pinning all my hopes on her as the one with the operational knowledge. She would know where I could find the information I needed to save those doomed passengers. It was just a matter of extracting it from her. And I had a plan for that.

She could have been anywhere. Time was working against us, as it had all day. Every minute we had to wait raised my anxiety level that much higher. Waiting had never been one of my strong suits. I was always a man of action. I preferred to be moving, doing, working. Proactive, rather than reactive. But, in this case, I had no choice.

Out of an abundance of caution, I paced along the back aisle in case the North Koreans had a surveillance team watching the front. The 9mm Glock 17 handgun loaned to me by Robinson had a round chambered and a full clip. Plus, I had two additional clips in my pockets. I flashed the piece at Yong Byun periodically, in case he got any unwise ideas.

As I waited, a text came in from Sunny, my father-in-law. "Call me," was all it said. I explained to Robinson that I had to make another call. I thumbed to Sunny's cell phone number on my favorites list.

"Listen to me," he said without a greeting. "I spoke to a contact of mine in Seoul. I know what's going on. You need my skills."

Those few words, and the conspiratorial tone he used, caught me completely off guard coming from my laid-back father-in-law. I was at a loss for words. The only ones that tumbled out were, "Your *contact in Seoul*? What are you talking about?"

"I don't have time to explain. I know people. That's all you need to know."

"Your *skills*? What...? No way, I can't ask you to get involved in this. It's too dangerous."

"Dangerous? Are you kidding me? Do you know what kind of supply runs I did for the Allies in Vietnam?"

I guess I paused too long. I realized right then that I really didn't know what he did over there so many years before I was born.

"We'll talk later," he said. "My contact told me about the bombs and the need for some sort of code to disable them. Have you got the alpha team leader yet?"

I was blown away. Sunny, the guy who wore Aloha shirts and flip flops, had just summarized reams of classified data into the pivotal missing element of my mission.

He continued. "I can help. I understand you've got one of them in custody."

"Yes, that's right."

"Let me question him. I have certain . . . skills that should help you get the information you need," he said.

My perception of this man I had known for so many years had just been blown out of the water. I didn't know how to react. I stuttered. "I've already questioned him."

"How much useful information did you get?"

"We got enough to figure out there are five planes, not one, and how the detonators work. He says he was not privy to much beyond the scope of his duties. So, we didn't get mission-critical intel, like how to stop this attack."

"All right. You really do need my skills then."

"Why? He seemed to be telling me the truth." I was starting to sense the skills he was alluding to. I had them, too.

"Maybe, but I seriously doubt he told you everything he could have told you."

"Skills?" I said, still trying to wrap my head around this revelation.

"I never really used them myself, but I saw some, shall we say, 'questioning' going on more often that I care to recall. I watched closely, if you know what I mean. It's been a long time, but you never forget that kind of stuff once you've seen it."

"What are you saying?"

"Let me at him. I'll get you the details you need. That way there's no blood on your hands. It keeps Stephanie and your family safer. I'm sure you'd agree, it's better that way."

Once again, my wife's surfer-dude dad showed wisdom far beyond his appearance. "You're right. But I also don't need you to get mixed up in this. Because of my dad and his clout, I'll be granted immunity." I only hoped that was true, but I said it with conviction. "I know what to do."

"I saw the list of supplies you sent to Stephanie. Most of them were in my warehouse. "Just bring your guy up here and I'll help you."

"No, no. I really don't want you to get any more involved. I've got another idea." Just then the store's phone rang. "I've got another call coming in. Gotta go. I'll call later."

My heart leapt. This was the break we needed. I hoped and prayed for the best, knowing what was at stake.

As instructed, the shop owner answered after the second ring. She exchanged pleasantries, explained that she and her husband had come back to the store when "Mr. Lee" called and explained the situation. "He seemed so worried because he lost his phone was unable to reach you all day. He came here later than usual, hoping I had a message from you. Then he called me two hours later and asked me to let him use my phone to call you back. He's so nervous. Won't you please talk to him?" After nailing her lines, the kindly shopkeeper handed the phone to Yong Byun.

Yong Byun followed the outline, explaining that there had been an accident that had delayed him. He told his pretend wife how worried he was when he found the house empty and how he needed to talk to her so they could patch things up. He needed her to pick him up at the market.

When the call ended, Yong Byun looked at me, shaking his head, eyes wide with fear.

That sinking feeling worsened as I read a text from Robinson. "She's here. In the building across the street from your position."

I was half-way to the back door when I heard the glass of the front door shatter.

Chapter 39

Onboard Korean Air Flight from Dallas-Fort Worth to Seoul

June 6, 5:27 p.m. local time; June 6, 2:27 a.m. California time

Four hours after receiving the initial communication from Seoul, the Dallas-Fort Worth inbound flight was rounding the southern tip of the Korean Peninsula. Captain Hong received the welcome phone call from a top technology expert at the Ministry of Science and Technology. He listened intently, asking questions occasionally, and jotted down notes on a pad of paper kept near the pilot's seat.

After ending the call, Captain Hong turned to his cockpit flight crew and outlined the strategy as it had been explained to him and asked for a volunteer to go belowdecks with a tablet computer to disable the explosive device.

Since the First Officer was a thirty-something-year-old with a penchant for the latest electronic gadgets and devices, he was elected to be the one to attempt to jam the Bluetooth signal between the terrorists' phone and the explosive device.

First Officer Kim wore a blank expression as he sauntered through the cabin to the back of the plane, nodding calmly at any passengers who made eye contact. It was important that they think this was something routine. He took the small service elevator down to the cargo hold to get as close to the two devices as possible so as to have the maximum amount of jamming power.

Once in the cargo area, he pulled out his cell phone and tapped the screen to connect with the experts at the Ministry of Technology. Using his tablet computer, Kim opened the app he had been told to download and set it to work. The app sent out a stream of digital interference across a wide spectrum of the 2.4Ghz signal.

First Officer Kim used the sleeve of his uniform to wipe sweat from his brow as he tapped on the tablet's screen. He listened carefully to the team as they walked him step-by-step through the process. Officer Kim repeated each set of instructions as they were relayed to him. The steps involved complex, high-level programming.

"OK. I've completed the command prompts. I hit 'Enter,'" said Kim into his headset. "There is a long list of words and characters scrolling down my screen, but how do I know if we've succeeded?"

One of the technology team members in Seoul sucked air in through his teeth. "I don't really know. I've never dealt with military-grade signal without the lab equipment.."

An array of pulsating squiggly lines on the tablet's screen was the only indication that anything was happening.

"How do I know for sure it's working? All I can see is a screen full of colored waving lines," said Kim.

"Then the app is running," said the one of the government gurus.

Even though there was nothing more they could do, the technical team in Seoul maintained phone contact with Officer Kim. One of them explained how the app was able to sniff out the devices' MAC addresses.

"So, once it finds the right MAC address, the bomb is disabled, right?" asked Kim.

"That's right," said a mature, reassuring voice. "You've done well."

The truth that no one wanted to relay to Officer Kim was that there was no guarantee of successful jamming of the signal without the link key that paired the two devices. Only the person who set up the connection between the cell phone and the detonating device would know the exact pairing sequence.

Without the type of sophisticated hardware available on the ground, there was less than a twenty percent chance of making this work. Nonetheless, for the sake of Officer Kim's peace of mind, this vital fact was never shared. The current set up was the best they could do to save the four hundred seventeen lives onboard that aircraft.

At that moment, another voice came through the open line to the team in Seoul. It was the pilot, but his voice was obscured by the harsh blare of an alarm.

"This is Captain Hong. The low fuel warning system has come on," he said. "We have less than sixty minutes to land this aircraft."

Chapter 40

G*arden Grove, CA*

June 6, 2:30 a.m.—45 minutes of fuel remaining in the first plane

I should have seen it coming. All the time we were waiting and calling from the store, Yong Byun's North Korean handlers were maneuvering into position. One shot from a silenced high-powered rifle is all it took for them to staunch the leak of vital information. A loose end tied up. By not following his prescribed escape plan, Yong Byun had been flirting with death all day. He knew they would want him dead. I knew it, too. I just never thought they would be so swift and so brazen.

Watching Yong Byun's head explode into a spray of blood and brain stunned me to the core. Paralyzed by a wave of anguish and sympathy, I stood as if my feet were bolted to the floor. The visceral reaction to something so shocking is natural and unavoidable. One's brain does not know how to process something like that. But allowing one's innate inclinations to take control in combat situations is often the difference between life and death, success and failure.

My soldier's training kicked in and I pushed all of that human emotion out of the way.

The mission was always far more important than one man's life.

Thoughts of my students on that doomed plane rushed into the void, replacing hopelessness and confusion with an action plan.

First, I assessed my situation. Feeling exposed and vulnerable, I dropped below the line of sight, using the stocked shelves as cover. Crouched down, I sprinted as fast as I could until I was through the back door to the storage room. As I ran, I called Robinson. "Stay in the car," I barked. "Don't move. Don't do anything or you're all dead and they'll be gone."

I burst out the back door and took a hard left, sprinting past the back doors of several businesses until I reached the end of the building. Not wanting to catch the attention of the shooter, I crossed the narrow aisle of asphalt that ran along behind the stores. With the building blocking me from view, I jumped the low back wall of the parking area and ran to the opposite side of the road behind the strip mall. I was in the shadows of the streetlights, beneath the canopy of mature trees that lined the residential street which paralleled the main road. I ran another half a block, behind the back of a car dealership, then slipped through the next parking lot until I was back at Garden Grove Boulevard, a full block east of the market. No way they would look this far down for signs of motion.

Without hesitating, I bolted across all six lanes of the nearly empty street and into the parking lot of an office building, only adjusting my speed a little to avoid the one car on the road at two o'clock in the morning. Keeping up my sprint, I made my way back to the building across from the market where I was sure the shooter had been, hoping he was still there.

In the darkness, I moved like a panther into position behind a truck in the corner of the parking lot adjacent to the two-story building across from the market where Yong Byun lay in a puddle of gore. The building was painted a burnt orange color. There was a one-meter-high cinder block wall covered in matching orange stucco that separated the parking lot from the sidewalk running alongside the boulevard. A smattering of cars took up a few spaces in the row of parking spaces just on the other side of that short wall, facing the street. One of those cars was the blue Ford with Robinson and the two FBI agents frozen and hunched down. Another handful of cars was parked pointing toward the two-story building. Thumping music and multi-colored light spilled out of a karaoke bar on the ground level. That was the likely reason for the cars in the lot at this late hour.

The other tenants on the ground floor of the building—a nail salon, a boutique clothing store, and a golf shop—all had signs in Hangul, the Korean alphabet. Only the bar had lights on. The few cars in the lot told me it was nearly closing time and not many customers remained inside, perhaps waiting for taxis because they were too drunk to drive.

Above those retail establishments were offices with windows that looked out over the parking lot and the street. The signs in the windows indicated they were offices for a law firm, an insurance agent, a CPA, and a travel agency. Most of the window coverings were closed. The ones in the travel agency were not completely. Long white vertical blinds hung across a large plate glass window overlooking the parking lot and directly across to Yeo Chae market.

The long white blinds were rustling.

I took off running, staying low and out of the line of sight. I came to the pathway along the front of the building. A wide stairway between the clothing store and the karaoke bar led to the second floor. I launched myself up the stairs, taking them quickly but stealthily, making almost no sound as I went. At the landing, I paused to listen before turning down the suspended hallway which ran across the back of the building. Each of the second-floor offices were accessed from this walkway.

The travel agency was the second door down. I slinked past the first office, an insurance agency. Matching vertical blinds adorned a window before I reached the second door. Its window coverings were partially open, allowing me a view into the space. I could see an empty desk in the front. A framed doorway with no door separated the small reception area from the main office space behind. I could just make out one of my targets crouched near the window in the back. It was a woman. She must have been so preoccupied putting something away that she had no idea I was there. *Perfect.*

I tested the knob. It was unlocked. I slipped the Glock out from waist band of my cargo pants. I checked the magazine, unlocked the safety, and said a prayer.

With the gun in my right hand and the doorknob twisted in my left, I took a deep breath, planning out the sequence of movements that would follow. I did a quick count to three, then in one motion, pushed the door open and hurled myself into the room. I dove forward and slightly to my left, tucking and rolling to a half-wall that separated the front reception area from the open office space behind it where my targets were.

A rustle of hurried movements gave away their surprise. I popped to one knee, aiming the Glock in the classic two-armed position as I swept the rectangular space to locate the first target. The vertical blinds swayed from the sudden movement. The two targets had leapt to opposite sides of the room. Most likely, they were expecting hesitation. Someone with less training than myself may have lost the edge in this scenario, but I didn't flinch. The man was to my right, a straight shot. I squeezed off two rounds, both of which hit the mark. One hit his right arm, causing him to drop his weapon. The second hit his shoulder, throwing him back against the wall behind him.

High-pitched screams from the bar below filled the air.

I ducked behind the half wall in a crouch as the woman fired off several shots. Chunks of drywall and white dust rained down on my head and back. I sprang to my feet and took aim. I fired the first shot in her leg. The second one in her the shoulder. She flew back against the blinds, clutching at them as she fell to the ground. Her weight, slight as it was, brought the whole contraption down on top of her, hitting the side of her head as it fell. But she didn't drop her weapon. Without delay, I charged at the woman and kicked the weapon out of her hand.

I moved to the man, secured his gun, and patted him down to make sure he didn't have another one concealed. He did. It was strapped to his right calf. A Berretta Nano, the compact version of the gun he had held. A smart choice as a back-up. I hopped up and approached the woman, the Glock steady in my hand. My sites were on her the entire time I checked the guy and as I closed the three meters between me and her.

The panicked screams and crying from the bar-goers downstairs intensified. It sounded like the late drinking crowd had spilled out into the parking lot.

I quickly did the same to the woman as I had to her counterpart. She also carried a Nano around her lower leg.

As I was dragging her over by her fallen Comrade, Robinson and one of the

FBI agents stormed into the room, guns drawn.

Once the two of them assessed the situation, Robinson signaled to the other guy to secure the weapons from the ground. He did. I could hear his partner outside trying to pacify the crowd by saying that there was nothing to worry about. Robinson radioed in, requesting a clean-up team and back-up.

My two victims groaned, almost in unison, as I rolled them onto their stomachs next to each other. I dropped to my knees, landing a kneecap into the small of each of their backs. Robinson tossed me two sets of handcuffs, which I ratcheted firmly into place in a matter of seconds. I then rolled them over on their backs and karate chopped each of them in the abdomen to preempt any counter attacks they may have dreamed up. With the two of them gasping for air, I used my thumbs to press down on the bullet wounds in each of their shoulders.

"Tell me now how to deactivate the bombs on those planes." I was barely able to control the fury in my voice. My jaw was tight, my teeth clenched, and my words tumbled out with bottled emotion.

Neither of them answered, so I pressed harder, which brought agonized howls from each.

"Tell me now or I start peeling off your skin." I pulled a composite combat knife from its sheath strapped to my calf and gave them a knowing smile as if to say, "Yeah, that's how I knew about your hidden weapons." I flicked open the blade and tested its sharpness by slicing through a piece of paper I pulled off the desk next to us.

Both sets of eyes widened.

Robinson stood over me with his gun pointed at the woman's head. I asked him to come around and hold their legs and feet down. I didn't want to get kicked. He gave me an inquisitive look but complied with my request.

I then repositioned myself so that I had a knee just below each of the North Koreans' sternums, right on the solar plexus. While gasping for air, it is very difficult to maintain enough tension in the abdominal muscles to keep the weight from completely inhibiting the diaphragm's ability to draw in air. Desperation sets in very fast when one can't breathe. The shock from their injuries wasn't helping matters for them. Their toughness was leaching out rapidly. It would only be a few moments before they would begin cooperating.

I hoped and prayed that they would do so quickly and that they had the information we needed to disable those bombs before it was too late.

Chapter 41

Onboard Korean Air Flight from Dallas-Fort Worth to Seoul
June 6, 5:27 p.m. local time; June 6, 2:27 a.m. California time; 42 minutes of fuel remaining

With a sigh, the pilot radioed the control tower. "Incheon control, this is Korean Air 5821."

"Go ahead 5821."

"We are low on fuel and request permission to begin final approach."

"Negative 5821. Permission not granted at this time."

"Incheon, we are below minimum safety levels. If we do not initiate our approach in the next fifteen minutes, we risk the ability to carry out a successful landing."

"Roger that Korean 5821. We are awaiting clearance from the National Security Chief."

"My First Officer is in contact with the Ministry of Science and Technology. They have done everything they can to jam the signal. We must land, Incheon, or we will end up in the ocean."

"Roger that Korean 5821. Still awaiting word. Stand by."

An agonizing seventy seconds passed before Incheon Tower returned. "Korean 5821. This is Incheon Tower. Negative. Maintain high-altitude holding pattern until further notice. A more robust solution is being developed. One with a higher probability of success."

"But Incheon, my First Officer is in contact with the ICT. They have sent him instructions to disrupt the signal. We must descend while he runs interference."

"Yes, Captain. We are aware. However, that solution is not a perfect one. The President's Chief of Staff has asked for more time to work on a better solution. Please await further instruction."

"We will be dangerously close to shutting down our engines, Incheon. Dangerously close."

"Roger that. We are aware of your fuel situation. However, the President has asked for more time. Captain, this is for the safety of everyone on board as well as people on the ground. Please be patient."

"Patient? How can I be patient with these alarms and with empty fuel tanks?"

"You have forty-two minutes' worth of fuel. Hang tight. We'll get you on the ground as soon as we are able."

Chapter 42

Garden Grove, CA

June 6, 2:41 a.m., 34 minutes of fuel remaining in the first plane

These two were harder to break than Mr. Kim had been. Neither would say a word, even as I pressed on their wounds and knelt on their diaphragms. They resisted me with everything they had. Even with my knife blade waving in front of their faces, they didn't yield. They held contempt in their steely eyes, jaw muscles twitching. I knew they hated me. I also knew they had been indoctrinated from a tender age to hate all things Western, capitalistic, and opulent. South Korea's success in the world was decried as gluttonous, despicable, and even fictitious. That seemed to be what was fueling their defiance.

I kept checking my watch. I knew the Dallas plane must be getting close to the end of its fuel supply. My father had told me it would run out at 3:15 a.m. my time, giving me only thirty-four minutes. Realistically, that meant I needed to get the information out of them in fifteen, max, to have enough time to convey the codes to the IT team so they could relay them to the flight crews in the air. I was stressed, and my prisoners knew it. I was acting far too erratically and compulsive. The sweat beading up on my forehead and upper lip giving away my anxiety.

I had to figure out a better way. Neither pain nor the threat of further pain was working. But with the clock running, I was feeling extreme pressure building.

The setting wasn't the best, either. In an unsecured location such as we were in and with two federal officers as witnesses and a crowd gathered out in the parking lot, they must have guessed it was safe to call my bluff. Rightly, so.

That was a smart move on the part of the North Koreans. Their training likely included a course on the Bill of Rights and how to use it against us. Funny how they could learn about that and think negatively towards a nation that espoused and protected individual rights and freedoms—or at least claimed to. My time living around US soldiers and in the country had shown me that many of these rights were under attack from multiple angles.

I viewed my actions and demeanor from the perspective of these two captured combatants and realized my anger was getting the best of me. I wasn't thinking straight, and they were picking up on it. How could I expect them to cough up vital information so quickly when surely they had been taught, trained, and even threatened to never reveal the details of the operation. I seethed but hearing the klaxon sound of approaching sirens in the distance, I was forced to back off.

The incoming police presence and the murmuring of the gathering crowd outside forced me to think quickly. My opportunity to save hundreds of lives was slipping away. I thought about my conversation earlier with my father-in-law. He said to use whatever means necessary. I took that literally, knowing that if the police showed up, there would be even more eyeballs to witness what I had in mind and even more delays as the conglomeration of law enforcement worked through the layers of bureaucratic nonsense to figure out what to do next. We'd be forced to wait for an ambulance, then forced to wait for the sedatives and pain killers to wear off before we could speak to the then-protected terrorists.

The passengers onboard those flights didn't have that kind of time. Another glance at my watch reminded me how little time I had to save that first plane. I needed to take action and I needed to do it right away.

A thought crossed my mind, causing me to snap my head to face the TSA Director. I jumped to my feet, pointing toward my victims. Agent Ahn, who had accompanied Robinson and I in the car, nodded his understanding and stepped into their view, his FBI-issued Glock 19M cocked and ready.

"Director Robinson, may I have a word with you privately," I asked.

He followed me into the empty reception area. "I need to question these two—alone. Can we arrange that?"

"I don't know," he said, furrowing his brow as he thought about what I was asking. "The first thing we need to do is get them medical attention."

I wagged my head and sucked in a breath to show my incredulity. "You're the Director of the TSA. You have a direct line to the Secretary of Homeland Security, do you not?"

"Yeah, sure. What are you getting at?"

"Can't you order an ambulance staffed by your own people to come pick up our suspects and take them someplace where they'll get the treatment they deserve?"

"Mr. Noh. This is the United States of America, not some lawless bush league frontier. We have laws to protect people's rights—"

I cut him off. I didn't have time for a speech on the virtues of the criminal justice system. "Don't you have laws that protect the rights of people whose lives are in imminent danger? I know you have rights for criminals. What about rights for innocent victims?"

"What you're asking me is against the law. I could lose my job for a stunt like that."

"You should lose your job if you let all those people on those planes die without doing everything in your power to save them."

"That's just it. It's not in my power—"

The sirens outside grew louder. "Never mind. I understand your position. Let me just ask you this: Are you willing to sit back and let this become a huge international incident? Can you imagine what your President will do when he finds out North Korea infiltrated this country and put bombs on the planes of a strategic ally? Can you imagine him not calling for a full-scale military strike? Can you imagine him laying off the impulse to nuke them to oblivion? We're looking at an incident that could alter the world as we know it. Hell, it could end the world if China gets involved and starts launching nukes, too. You know they whole-heartedly support North Korea, don't you?"

I held Robinson's gaze, but he said nothing. He just shook his head slowly and shrugged.

"OK," I said. "Let's just get these guys in the car before they bleed to death."

"We can't—"

I was taking control of the situation and he needed to know it. I was playing by a different set of rules that he would have to come to grips with later. "I know you have your procedures. This is one of those cases where we have to alter the procedures out of urgency." My eyes were filled with rage. "In the end, the means will be justified."

He inhaled and held it, slowly nodding his head as he let the breath out. He didn't say anything.

"Just help me get them to the car before the cops arrive," I said.

"I can't do that," Robinson said, standing still and looking defeated.

"You're right. You can't." I pulled out the handgun he had given to me and instructed Agent Ahn to drop his weapon, away from the North Koreans. He did so. I motioned for him to come closer with his hands in the air. I spun him around, grabbed his handcuffs off his belt, and pushed him face first into the wall. I grabbed one of his wrists and one of Robinson's and cuffed them together. Then I grabbed the second set of cuffs that every agent carries and cuffed their other wrists, so they were back-to-back.

Robinson gave me a knowing look and said, "Hurry, would you?"

Wasting no time, I spun on my heels and practically jumped toward the two prone figures on the carpet.

Ahn started to protest, but Robinson stopped him.

"Mr. Noh has been duly authorized," Robinson said. He didn't finish the thought.

Ahn looked out-of-sorts but stopped struggling.

I suppressed a smile. Robinson and Ahn looked pathetic. Robinson squinted at me, and said, "God help us all. You'd better make this right, Mr. Noh,"

I nodded my silent commitment to finish what we had started. "I will do everything in my power to save those passengers and prevent the outbreak of World War III."

Before leaving, I rummaged through drawers and cabinets until I found a roll of duct tape. A strip of the magical grey adhesive went over each mouth, Robinson's and Ahn's. Then I wound it several times around their ankles. That would show the next group of law enforcement that they had been forcibly removed from the situation and had nothing to do with what I was planning.

Chapter 43

Laguna Niguel, CA
June 6, 2:42 a.m.

"Gramma, what's all that noise?" Sophia appeared at the bottom of the stairs, rubbing her eyes. Her hair was tussled, and her face scrunched up.

Anna Choi, wrapped in a robe and wearing warm slippers, forced a wan smile for her granddaughter. "Oh, I'm just getting a few things together for your grandpa," she said, ignoring the real question.

"No, Gramma, where is Grampa and Mommy going?"

"They are going to your daddy's gym."

"Why? It's so late."

"Because your father needs them to take care of something there but doesn't have time to do it himself."

"Daddy went to Korea with the Tae Kwon Do kids." Sophia's little face twisted in puzzlement.

"Yes, dear. But he needs these things down at the gym right away, so Mommy and Grandpa need to hurry."

"Oh. But why so late at night, Gramma?"

"Well, dear, all I know is that your daddy said it was very important that these things be at the gym right away. I guess someone there needs them." Anna had crossed the room and knelt down in front of her three-year-old granddaughter using her body to block her granddaughter's view of the array of kitchen knives lined up on the counter. "You and me and Matthew are going to have a good time together in the morning. But first, you have to get a good night's sleep. OK?"

"OK," said Sophia.

Anna at smiled at her granddaughter and patted her shoulders. "Let's get you back upstairs and in your bed, shall we?"

Sunny appeared from the side door, breathing hard. "I've almost got everything ready. Did you get the—? Oh, I mean, where's Stephanie?"

Anna forced another smile directed at her husband as she turned toward the sudden sound. A motion of her head indicated that he needed to keep the young ones in mind.

Sunny nodded his head, but continued to quickly gather his keys, his wallet, and his phone. While Anna distracted Sophia, he slid the knives into a duffle bag.

No matter what the trouble or the cause, the Choi family stuck together. Neither Anna nor Sunny were strangers to situations like this. But they were older now and there were more unknowns than ever. More to lose, as well. The Choi's avoided trouble and kept to their own business. Tonight, however, they would do all in their power to aid their son-in-law, who found himself in an impossible situation. It was the right thing to do, but it still brought a high level of tension.

"Upstairs," said Anna, answering Sunny's question. "She said she had to change her outfit. You might want to do the same."

Sunny looked down at his flowered button-up shirt and cargo shorts and shrugged. "Why? No need to impress these people, right?"

"I don't know. I thought you might want them to take you seriously." Anna raised an eyebrow at Sunny who looked momentarily deflated.

Sunny cocked his head, as if to consider her words. "Nah, I prefer the element of surprise." Even in stressful situations, his instant, sunny disposition and unflinching comfort with who he was remained a pillar of strength in the Choi household.

Stephanie appeared at the top of the staircase, looking stunning as ever. "I'm ready to go." She wore black stretch pants, a long-sleeved dark grey athletic shirt, and black running shoes. Her hair was pulled back in a ponytail.

"If looks could kill ..." her father said.

"I wish it was that easy," she said, glancing at the worried look on her mother's face.

"You two need to let Jeong Tae take care of this situation. He's the military man."

"Ex-military," Sunny corrected. "As am I. There's no difference between us."

"Just thirty years and twenty pounds of muscle," she said with a grin, stealing a page from Sunny's book and trying to lighten the mood.

Sunny was known for his humor, but also for his penchant for helping anyone in their time of need. This night, he dropped everything and rushed to the aid of his son-in-law. And Stephanie was just like her father. Stubborn and capable in her own right. With all the training she had done with JT, she was more than just a pretty face and toned body in a ninja-like outfit. She exuded strength and confidence but was also filled with kindness and compassion.

"Mommy, why are you dressed up like that?"

"Don't worry, baby. Daddy said for us to take a few things to the Do Jang. That's all."

"Then why are you dressed like that?" Sophia repeated her unanswered question.

"It's comfortable, sweetie."

"Oh." Sophia's facial expression still showed concern.

Stephanie bounded down the stairs, knelt down, and took her daughter in her arms for a long embrace. "Grandpa and I are just going to run a few errands that Daddy needs us to do. We won't be long. Go back to bed now, OK?"

Sophia pulled back and looked at her mother with concern.

Stephanie headed off the next question by saying, "I'll bet Grandma will make pancakes for you in the morning if you're a good girl and go back to bed."

Stephanie kissed her daughter's cheeks and stood.

Anna pulled Sophia's little hand into hers and said, "Say good night. You'll see her in the morning."

"OK," said Sunny. "Let's get going."

Sunny and Stephanie each grabbed a loaded duffle bag.

"I love you, too," Anna called out as the door closed.

Anna closed her eyes and mumbled a little prayer as she heard the throaty purr of Sunny's big Chevy truck rumbling out of the garage, followed by the sound of Stephanie's minivan's ignition awakening its engine. "Lord help them and the people on those planes.

Chapter 44

Garden Grove, CA

June 6, 2:49 a.m., 26 minutes of fuel remaining in first plane

I dragged the two bleeding terrorists one at a time by their armpits, struggling the whole way, to the door. Dumping them in the little reception area, I escorted Ahn and Robinson into the back room and used more duct tape to secure them as best I could to one of the desks. It was a hurried job that they would have no trouble breaking, but it would at least show that they were not in on my scheme.

Returning to the front room, I helped the two resistant detainees to their feet. Pushing them out the door and past the darkened window of the insurance agency. My prisoners stumbled as I guided them down the steps. This was understandable since the woman had a bullet hole in her thigh, but it was still slowing me down. The gauze and cloth I had found in the office and wrapped around the wounds were soaked through with blood. She had a pronounced limp and caught her breath with every movement. I finally gave up and swept her off her feet in my arms and carried her like a baby down the stairs and across the parking lot to the car. She was too weak to protest. Her body was rail thin and light as I'd imagine a mannequin to be. She couldn't have weighed more than a hundred-ten pounds. Before I did that, I aimed my weapon at the guy and motioned him onward.

Yes, they needed medical attention. Yes, their faces were sallow and their movements clumsy and weak. Most likely they were in the beginning stages of shock, but I really didn't have time to make a fuss over their physical well-being when the lives of so many innocent people lay in the balance. These two were the most likely sources of the information I needed to prevent those bombs from going off, so certain protocols went out the window.

I also couldn't ignore the approaching sirens. I barked at the guy to move it along faster. He stumbled along and I kept barking like a drill sergeant. The small crowd outside the karaoke place gasped in horror as they saw the blood and the condition of my two detainees.

Since these two hadn't cooperated in front of witnesses, I needed to isolate them. I did what I could to not put Robinson in a tough spot, but it was inevitable. Without the information they were clinging to, heartache and tragedy would reign. I could think of no other way to get the information I needed in the narrow window of time that remained.

As I approached the blue Ford parked at the base of the stairs, Agent Kim, the driver, was standing at the rear of the vehicle and gave me an odd look. I put the woman down on her feet next to the back door on the driver's side but continued to prop her up by the elbow since her hands were still cuffed. I nodded to Agent Kim and said, "It's OK. We need to get them out of here in a hurry, so we're going to take them in this car."

Agent Kim's mouth twisted up, like he wasn't sure what to say. Finally, he said in English, "Shouldn't we wait for an ambulance?"

"No time," I said. "They've got to be transported immediately."

"But—"

"But nothing. Keep a gun on that one," I said throwing my head in the direction of the injured man.

Kim pulled out his service weapon and took aim, still looking bewildered.

I yanked the back door open and shoved the North Korean woman into the driver's side of the back seat as quickly as I could. I fixed my aim on the guy. He stood unsteadily near the trunk. Manhandling him into the back door on the passenger's side, I slammed it shut.

Painfully aware of the passage of time, the approaching sirens, and the crowd of onlookers, I rushed to get out of there as fast as I could.

Racing back to the driver's side, I thanked Agent Kim. "That'll be all," I said as I kneed him square in the crotch. He dropped to the ground in instant pain. I wrenched the weapon from his hand and dragged him out of the way, then opened the driver's door and checked for the keys. They weren't there, so I got back out and searched Agent Kim's pockets until I found them.

The sirens were almost upon us. I could see them approaching on the boulevard, coming from my left, preparing to turn right onto the side street where the driveway entrance was located.

I slipped into the driver's seat and shut the door, hit the lock button and started the engine with a roar. The few spectators standing in front of the karaoke joint jumped out of the way as I backed out of the parking space then threw the car into drive and smoked the tires out of the parking lot.

I put the siren on. I was heading away as two cops turned on to the side street, then into the parking lot. I caught two confused looks but kept my foot on the accelerator. Another police car was turning left into the parking lot of the market across the street. I navigated through and around the approaching cars, not pausing for anything.

Tearing down Garden Grove Boulevard in the dark blue Ford sedan, looking for Harbor Boulevard, I was glad there was no traffic. An on-ramp to Highway 22, which would lead me to Interstate 5, which would lead me to Highway 55, which was the fastest way to my Do Jang, just a block or two away. I prayed that there would be a similar clear path all the way to Costa Mesa.

As I turned onto the onramp, I yanked all the wires out of the dash-mounted radio. I figured they could potentially use the signal to track the vehicle. Of course, there were probably other transponders in the vehicle to monitor where I was going, but I didn't have time to find or disable them. I only needed a few uninterrupted minutes, I hoped, to extract the information I needed.

Despite my speed, I sensed the sands of the hourglass in my head continuing to drain.

As soon as I was on the 22, I called Stephanie. "I'm on my way. Have you prepared everything I asked?" I spoke in English and I spoke fast. I didn't want to make it easy for my passengers to comprehend.

"Yes," she said. "It's all ready. We're on our way there now." Her voice had that no-nonsense quality to it, like a battle-hardened warrior. I knew at some point I'd need to talk her through the events that had transpired and the decisions I had made, but I was surprised at how calm and focused she sounded. Sunny must have talked her through things.

"OK. Thanks. Just drop them and leave. Trust me, you don't want to be anywhere near when I show up. So, please, return to your parents' house."

"My dad insists on helping you."

"I think it's best if I do this on my own. No need for you or him to be accomplices."

"Go ahead and try to make him leave. You know how he is. What are you going to do?"

"Please don't ask me that question. I've got to go." I paused before hanging up. I could feel her trying to make sense of everything and her need to keep the connection between us. "I have some very ugly work to do and very little time to do it."

Her voice was quiet, but her spirit was strong. "Please be careful."

"At this point, Honey, it's more important that I'm successful than careful."

"OK. Then be successful. Please."

I ended the call and focused on my driving. I was exceeding the speed limit by a good margin, passing the few cars on the road in a blur, and only slowing slightly for the turn-off to Highway 55.

Admittedly, it was a thrill to drive that fast with impunity.

As I raced down the wide-open highway, a chill ran down my spine. The woman in the back had ruthlessly taken out Yong Byun, just as I was starting to like him. A shadow passed through me along with the image of his blood pooling on the floor of that store. He, like anyone else stuck in a hopeless circumstance, just wanted to live a better life, free of the oppression he had grown up with. There was light at the end of his long, dark tunnel. He had come so close.

I also felt bad for the shopkeepers who would not be returning to their home anytime soon. Their long day wasn't over yet.

As I neared my Do Jang, I turned off the lights and siren. I pulled into the employee parking area behind the strip mall where my gym was located. As suspected, there were no other cars there at that late hour. That meant no witnesses to what I was about to do.

I pulled the car right up close to the back door, leaving just enough room to swing it open. I jumped out, unlocked the rear entrance to my office, surveyed the area to make sure no one was watching, then hauled my prisoners out of the car one at a time, dragging them by their shirt collars. As I dropped them on the floor, I gave each a half-kick to the gut. This was to keep them incapacitated, which would keep me safer and them more compliant. They gasped for air. After dumping them in the cramped office space behind the actual gym, I closed the car up and locked it.

There was going to be some hell to pay for the time we had already lost. But I had to control my fury until I got the information I needed.

Chapter 45

Over Incheon Harbor, West of Incheon, Korea

June 6, 6:09 p.m.; six minutes of fuel remaining in the first plane

Permission to land had not yet been granted and time was running out. Tensions ran high in the cockpit. The fuel gauges indicated six minutes until empty.

The co-pilot raised his voice, uncharacteristically. "We need to land. We have to trust that Mr. Kim can jam the connection. We have only a few minutes before this Jumbo Jet becomes nothing more than a huge glider."

"If we try to land, those F-15's will shoot us down."

"Doesn't matter. We're dead either way. I say we try it."

Captain Hong nodded and held the mic button on his headset. "Incheon Tower. This is Korean Air 5821. We're coming in for landing. We are out of time. Do you have a runway clear for us?"

"5821. Please await further instruction."

"Negative Incheon. We are out of time. We must attempt a landing now or we will all die."

"5821. I read you loud and clear ... 5821, hold on, please."

A short eternity passed as the pilot and co-pilot exchanged anxious glances and fiddled with the instruments in front of them, trying to bleed out some of the nervous twitches.

"5821. This is Incheon Tower. The entire airport has been cleared. Your First Officer has been instructed to re-run the signal disruption protocol when you reach two hundred meters altitude. You have seven seconds to finish your descent once he starts the protocol Proceed to runway 02 Niner Left."

"Roger that, Incheon."

Captain Hong noted runway 02 Niner was the furthest from the terminal, out to the west where there were fewer buildings and less visibility from the two major highways leading to Yeong Jong Do, the island southwest of Seoul and directly west of the port city of Incheon the airport inhabited. Another chill swept through his body as he realized how many lives were at stake. He winced as he considered again that the passengers and flight attendants were clueless as to what was going on. The Ministry of National Security felt it was best to keep them in the dark to avoid panic and to allow the flight crew to focus completely on the task at hand. He had complied and had given them frequent updates regarding the delayed landing, explaining that there was a problem at the airport.

The pilot said a silent prayer as he lined up his massive jet with the appropriate runway and continued his descent. "Incheon, we're coming in on a bearing of 331. Altitude of two thousand meters."

"Roger, 5821. We see you. You're clear to land."

Captain Hong navigated into position for final approach, watching both the fuel gauge and the altimeter carefully. "Final approach, Incheon."

"Descending. Officer Kim? Are you ready?"

"I'm here and ready," said First Officer Kim. "On your mark, Captain."

A short pause. "Current altitude 500 meters, 400, 300."

"Initiating protocol, sir,"

"God help us," said Captain Hong.

"Godspeed, 5821. Everyone here at Incheon is praying with you."

"One-hundred-fifty meters."

Then there was nothing.

The massive fireball could be seen from miles away. People in cars on the two main highways that crossed over the water to Yeong Jong Island saw it. Workers on the docks and on the boats in and around the harbor saw it. Passengers and employees who had been evacuated to a location two kilometers from the terminal, the airport-based fire and rescue crew, and everyone in the flight control tower saw it.

Where there was a massive incoming aircraft just a moment earlier, there was now an ominous black and orange cloud splaying out in a south-to-north orientation. The hull of the plane disappeared in the blink of an eye. Four hundred and seventeen lives extinguished simply because they chose to fly on the wrong plane on the wrong day. They were considered the enemy by a reclusive, impoverished nation ruled by an unhinged regime looking to prove they were not to be trifled with anymore.

The pieces of the wreckage continued to approach the runway at over 250 miles per hour. Most of the larger chunks didn't go far, splashing forcefully into the gray waters of Incheon Harbor, kicking up waves a dozen feet high and plumes of water vapor that extended like angry balls of steam hurling toward the runway, before raining with hurricane force down on the pavement. Hundreds of the smaller pieces pitched toward the southern shores of Yeong Jong Island, crashing into the rocky jetty. Some made it to the runway where they skittered across the concrete as smoldering attestations to the violence that had occurred.

Chapter 46

C*osta Mesa, CA*

June 6, 3:04 a.m.

As I reentered my little office space through the back door, a dark figure appeared in the doorway between the gym and the office. My breath caught in my throat and my stomach dropped. But my survival instincts, pounded into me during training, along with a shot of adrenaline kicked in. I bounced to the balls of my feet in a defensive stance, hands in front of my face and body, ready to parry or strike.

How could I have been so blinded as to not clear the area first? In my haste to get the North Koreans out of the car and into the Do Jang without being seen, I hadn't paid attention to my inner senses or my learned security protocol. Someone was in my space uninvited and I had to deal with the threat.

"Easy now. It's just me."

The lights came on and I relaxed. It was Sunny, complete with his customary flowered shirt. He stepped into the room and surveyed my prisoners with a dark, impassive expression. Then Stephanie stepped through from behind him. The look in her eyes was absolutely terrifying. "You heard the news, didn't you?"

"What news?" I asked.

"The plane from Dallas blew up as it approached the airport in Incheon."

My insides froze. My breathing stopped. And an overwhelming sense of failure washed over me. "How?" I said as I checked my watch. "They still had ten minutes' of fuel. How could they try to land without the codes?"

Stephanie looked at me with a mix of sympathy and toughness, a resilience in her eyes shone through. She wagged her head. "No time to think about that. There are still four other planes to save."

"Yes, that's right. No time to worry about what we can't change," said Sunny. Looking over his shoulder at his daughter, he continued. "Move that car now, as we discussed. We don't want them to track it here."

Stephanie looked at me. "Keys," she said with her hand out, palm forward next to her face.

I fumbled them from my pocket while calculating what Sunny said. He was right. And I realized he was a few steps ahead of me. Stephanie caught them midair, then shot daggers from her eyes as she stepped over the handcuffed, wide-eyed terrorists. The tables had turned on them unexpectedly. With the blood of four-hundred souls on their hands, many of them women and children, Stephanie had morphed into some sort of vigilante. "You know what you have done," she sneered in Korean as she moved toward the exit door. "Tonight, you're going to wish you had stayed at home."

With that, she slipped out the back door and disappeared into the dark. A moment later, I heard the engine of the Ford sedan roar to life and a shriek from the tires as she goosed the gas.

The prisoners' focus snapped back toward Sunny much the way the cuff of the latex gloves he was putting on snapped against his wrists. He glared at them. I had never seen a look anything close to that from Sunny before. It was completely out of character from the guy I knew. "Are you ready for this?" Sunny said with an icy smoothness that sent chills up my spine, and I wasn't even the object of his anger.

With no regard for their comfort, Sunny and I dragged and prodded and pulled the two terrorists across the floor until we had them leaned up against the side wall where they could get a good view of the table he had set up. I gave them each a slap on the face. Not because I'm cruel or love to inflict pain, but because I wanted them focused on us—on my words and Sunny's display. I had something to say and he had plenty of things to show.

Each story I would tell, and each implement he would show, would be intentional and purpose-driven. There was no reason to be subtle or two-faced. I had a mission, and I was determined to accomplish it. My mission, my purpose, was higher than theirs. They had to know this. Their purpose had been to destroy. Mine was to save. I explained this to them in clear, concise words.

I thereby established moral authority and explained that I would allow my "friend" to use his tools however he wanted to in order to extract the information we needed to save the lives on those planes. There was no need to enunciate the time crunch we were under. I tapped my watch with my index finger and Sunny went to work.

Sunny moved with an unexpected expertise and stayed in his role as a menacing character like I had never witnessed before.

The first thing was duct tape. Sunny ripped off a piece of the grey adhesive and pressed it forcibly over the mouth of the woman. "Ladies first," he said with a sadistic smile. He applied tape to their mouths to both make it harder for them to breathe and to prevent them from communicating.

Next, he wrapped the guy's feet together with duct tape. At Sunny's signal, I pinned his arms to his torso and leaned him forward so Sunny could apply several wrappings around his midsection. This is when I noticed the lack of musculature on the guy. I knew he was thin, but as I held him up, he felt even more skeletal than he looked. He offered no resistance, just dark eyes burning with a mix of hate and distress.

We did the same for the woman. They both looked sufficiently restrained and miserable. At this point, Sunny stepped forward and made a big display of laying out all manner of sharp objects. Hacksaws, ballpeen hammers, long pointy nails, an awl, needle-nosed pliers, a corkscrew, an assortment of drill bits, a battery-powered drill, and my favorite—a compact welding torch with a bottle of propane attached to it.

I loved the fear in their eyes. I'm not a cruel person by nature, but I despise bullies. And these terrorists represented the ultimate bullies, having targeted innocents in their quest for power and respect. So, I had no compunction dealing with their ilk in the only language they understood: force and fear. There's nothing like an immense show of force when dealing with someone who has gone to great lengths to inflict pain and suffering on thousands of non-combatant civilians—people just trying to live their lives, make a living, enjoy time with people they love. Couple the show of force with a display of potential torture implements to add that psychological edge and getting information out of a hostile bully becomes a much easier task. And quicker, I was hoping.

Chapter 47

B*lue House, Seoul, South Korea*
June 6, 6:35 p.m.

As President Jang Ho Shin concluded his solemn remarks in front of an overflow crowd in the Presidential Press Room at the Blue House, General Noh stood behind him along with other members of the Cabinet. The South Korean President had delivered the bad news about the explosion that claimed the lives of four-hundred-seventeen people. His tenor was somber, his countenance stoic, his words sincere. There was no bravado. President Jang was not one to beat on the war drum. The ongoing effort at every level of the Administration, he assured the public, was focused on saving as many lives as possible aboard the remaining four planes while mourning those who had been lost. He revealed this fact without going into detail.

During the first four years of President Jang's administration, he had earnestly sought a path for peace and reconciliation between the two nations that shared the Korean Peninsula. General Noh believed in the same principles and had been a staunch ally of the President's proposals and efforts. His soon-to-be-launched presidential campaign would be based on a similar platform.

General Noh hadn't stopped working to resolve the current crisis since the pre-dawn phone call from Stephanie. He hadn't eaten. He hadn't prepared a single line of what he would utter shortly.

There had been no time to prepare any type of strategy—military, diplomatic, or otherwise. An appropriate governmental response would be forthcoming, after a continued, all-out effort to save the passengers on the other four planes. The President was absolutely correct: there had been no time to think about anything else. And General Noh had been involved in every meeting, every call, every discussion since this crisis erupted sixteen hours earlier. Nothing else had occupied his mind as much in the past thirty-five years.

Already, General Noh had been assailed by many within the Cabinet and the Joint Chiefs to retaliate against North Korea swiftly and decisively. Anything short of that, they told him, would be viewed by the world and by the enemy as weakness. Weakness would only breed more hostility and invite more violence, according to the other members of the Joint Military Command. If there was one thing that marred his esteemed military career, it was the constant demands to strike first and assess other options later. So many of the commanding officers he worked with closely held that frustratingly shallow mindset.

Protecting a country wasn't always about armaments and ordnance. Skill with words and knowledge of human psychology were often weapons better suited for the type of warfare today's world demanded.

The General turned to his top aide and asked him to get his son on the line as soon as his speech was over.

The press conference had been called moments after the explosion of Korean Air flight 5821 was televised. President Jang felt it was his duty to speak words of comfort and to call upon the citizens of both North and South Korea, as well as the international community, to avoid jumping to hasty conclusions and calling for immediate military action. During his brief remarks, he assured the nation and the world that suitable measures would be taken, once he and his council had time to deal with the current crisis, gather all available intelligence, and evaluate the best path forward.

President Jang bowed slightly in deference to General Noh as he pivoted a quarter turn from the lectern to face him. The President invited the General to give a brief synopsis of how the crisis was being managed from a military and tactical standpoint. The President warned the buzzing press corps that there would be no details regarding future response to the tragedy. General Noh would not be able to discuss any potential military response but would give a high-level overview.

Following the President's call for calm, General Noh stood at the podium. He gazed out over the bank of microphones at the assemblage of reporters. While everyone in the room was anxious and agitated, he also saw the concern etched into their expressions. Those gathered seemed to share a sense of reverence for those lost and one of trepidation for what was to come. General Noh began by adding his condolences to those of President Jang and continuing the sense of reverence he had invoked.

When he spoke, his melodic bass voice lacked its usual vigor. His tone was strained, nearly to the point of being raspy. The skin of his face sagged, showing the signs of stress and worry. Dark circles under his eyes gave away the sleeplessness of the preceding night.

The General cleared his throat after his canned opening statement thanking the press for being there, for conveying to the public his and the President's and the council's deepest sympathies for the victims of this terrible tragedy. He thanked the news channels for airing the President's speech and expressed his heartfelt condolences to the families and loved ones of those lost to this senseless tragedy.

The rest was unrehearsed and unscripted. He paused his remarks, shifting gears from what was conventional and somewhat obligatory to what was in his heart. Using that moment for both effect and for word selection, he spent several seconds looking out over the audience, taking in the myriad cell phones positioned to capture every word. Many of the reporters balanced laptop computers on their knees and typed furiously as he spoke. A dozen or more cameramen trained their lenses on him in anticipation of some startling new revelation about how Korea would respond.

General Noh seemed to sense that his people looked to him now like the citizens of Great Britain looked to Winston Churchill during the London Bombings in World War II. Although no leader wished for this sort of crisis as a proving ground, General Noh didn't shy away from it, either. The General cocked his head to the right and began to speak, slowly and clearly. "Now is a pivotal time in our nation's history. Never before have we seen this type of terrorism target our land or our people. While the mighty military under my command is vigilant and remains ever prepared to defend our Homeland, our beautiful country, we Koreans are a peace-loving people. War and invasion have been a near constant throughout our history, yet our people have never been guilty of the first offense. We have never acted out of aggression. We do not attack our neighbors. We do, however, defend ourselves, our families, our lands, and our way of life. Always, our goal has been to live in peace. Always, our aim has been to exist in harmony with our neighbors and with the world.

"Because we cannot fathom the evil and malfeasance behind this terrible act of senseless violence wrought upon the helpless and defenseless, we will neither tolerate it nor replicate it. Our response will be appropriate. It will be restrained, aimed at those who were behind the planning and execution of this unconscionable deed. The common people of the Democratic Republic of Korea will not be called upon to suffer the consequences of the acts of their leaders if, indeed, it is discovered that their leaders instigated these atrocities as has been rumored. At this point, that is all the reports are—rumors. Every resource available will be dedicated to finding and bringing to justice the perpetrators of this crime, but only after every available resource has been expended to save those whose lives remain in jeopardy. That is our first priority.

"Rest assured, my fellow citizens, that our military stands at attention at this very moment, ready to protect and defend our borders, our airspace, and our coasts. Our allies stand with us, ready to assist. Any and every aspect of our military resources is under the command of President Jang as the elected leader of this sovereign nation.

"Many have asked and many more wonder what the future holds. The past eighteen months have proven historic in terms of diplomatic progress with our neighbors to the north. At this point in time, we have no confirmation that the leadership of the Democratic People's Republic of Korea instigated, sponsored, or approved this attack. We are working diligently on the diplomatic front to ascertain the origins of this deadly chain of events."

General Noh paused and surveyed the crowd. The silence in the room was deafening. Maintaining his calm and authoritative tone, he continued.

"If, after extensive and thorough research and fact-finding, it turns out North Korea is responsible in any way for this tragedy, we will respond appropriately, as President Jang has said. Everything regarding our relationship with North Korea will be reevaluated in the weeks to come, including the talks scheduled for later this month at Panmunjeom.

"I know you all have many questions. So do I. So does President Jang. So does every member of the Security Council, as well as our allies and the rest of the world. We are in the midst of gathering data, hard evidence, and intelligence in order to provide context and understanding. After we have had sufficient time to analyze all of this information, we will gather you together again for another news conference such as this. We will answer as many questions as we can at that time, so long as those answers do not compromise our nation's security.

"In the meantime, please know that the entire leadership apparatus of this great country is engaged in doing all we can to keep you, the good people of this good land, safe and secure. We value peace. We value freedom. We value human life. To these ends, we have pledged every ounce of our energy, our capacity, and our diligence. We are working hard toward as successful an outcome as humanly possible given the circumstances that face us. We ask for your patience and understanding as we return to the urgent work at hand.

"Please pray with us for those who are gone and those who are suffering. Pray for us that we may help those still in peril. Thank you. That is all for now."

Chapter 48

Onboard Korean Air Flight 134, LAX-ICN

June 6, 9:14 p.m.; 3:14 a.m. California Time

Jin Sook Lee, the assistant instructor at JT's Do Jang, was unable to stay in his seat, nervous energy making it impossible for him to sit still. With his legs bopping up and down constantly, he was annoying even himself. He walked down the aisle to the restrooms in the back of the plane. Most of the people were asleep or engrossed in games or movies on their devices or were reading. There were a few, however, who looked awake and concerned. He smiled as he passed by, as if he knew something that would provide assurance.

The sum of all of his observations brewed into a sense of impending disaster. A two-hour delay of their departure. Tons of ground crew personnel scurrying about. Police cars on the tarmac. The onboard internet had been shut off for hours. Some of the kids had seen the arrest of an Asian guy wearing a Dodger's jacket just like the one Noh Sabomnim had been wearing at LAX—a fact that JT had conveniently forgotten to mention during their phone conversation. But the kids had noticed it and were more than concerned. A couple of hours ago, the crew had abruptly turned off the navigational video, the one that showed the plane's path as it traveled across the Pacific. It was cut off as they approached Japan. No explanation was ever given other than "technical issues." The plane had also turned southward sharply when it should have been going almost due west. The eastern coastline should have been visible by now with the twinkling of the first artificial lights below. Flying into Seoul at night was an experience many expatriates relished because of the plethora of red crosses atop the churches dotting the landscape. It heralded one's arrival home. Tonight, however, the view was just an expanse of black water below.

The thing that really set Jin Sook's nerves on edge was the presence of the fighter jets. Maybe other passengers hadn't noticed them, but he did. In only a momentary glimpse as the passenger jet banked hard to the left, he saw them in formation off the port side of the plane. They quickly retreated as the 747 made its turn to the south.

The flight attendants went about their routine, but it was apparent to Jin Sook that something was off. There was a tightness about them, and he caught the furtive glances among themselves as they moved through the cabin asking passengers if they needed anything. He overheard one flight attendant explain to a passenger two rows in front of him that there was something on the ground that had to be resolved before they could be given clearance to land, so the pilot had routed them back out to sea until further notice.

Jin Sook looked at his watch. His patience was reaching its end. The plane should have been on the ground three hours ago.

Chapter 49

Costa Mesa, CA

June 6, 3:15 a.m.

I didn't relish what lay ahead. I only wanted a few vital bits of information and I wanted them quickly. Sunny, on the other hand, was in a zone like never before. He was ready to get started.

At the same time, the two North Koreans seemed to be wishing they could sink through the floor. There was a sour smell emanating from their side of the room. I recognized it: the smell of fear. And we hadn't even done anything yet.

I checked my watch again. The next plane, the one with my students, had less than forty-five minutes' worth of fuel. I wasn't sure if that would be enough time. Interrogations, even enhanced interrogations, take time. There are both psychological and physiological processes involved in breaking a person down. The more they've been trained and the deeper their commitment to whatever the cause they're representing, the longer it takes. Things like physical strength and mental stamina, of course, play a part as well. I had heard that the Americans had stretched some interrogations out over the space of six days. The Russians, on the other hand, held the dubious honor of both the longest and the shortest such information gathering sessions. These records, like so much that goes on in the geo-political underworld, was known solely within the clandestine community.

I had to figure out how to leverage my advantage while also determining how to exploit their individual and collective weaknesses. What a task. And only forty-four minutes to accomplish it.

Knowing what I knew about the way the North Korean regime operated, I figured these two needed to understand that their lives were never going to be what they had imagined when they signed up for this mission. So, I began a detailed, but fast-moving monologue explaining to them what I had learned in my eight years of dealing directly with the North Korean military, both leaders and soldiers, and more to the point, what the defectors and asylum-seekers had shared.

I needed these plotters to know that their dreams were now irreparably shattered. Whatever recognition they may have been hoping for in the form of extra rations, nicer living conditions, or better jobs outside the country where real money could be made had been hopelessly snatched from their grasp by the high-minded carelessness of their leaders. I reminded them of something Yong Byun had admitted during his interrogation. "You're all being used as pawns in a very dangerous game. You mean nothing to your leaders. Look at what they made you do to your partner, Yong Byun. They make you kill a Comrade who steps out of line. Think about it. Whoever sent you has total and complete deniability. You realize that, don't you?"

They were working hard not to crack. I got empty, far-away looks, but I kept going.

"There is no link between you and them, nothing that can prove their involvement. You will be painted as rogue agents and radicals. You'll be described as 'traitors to the cause of peace,' 'escapees trying to thwart the reconciliation with the South.' Your failure will be on your heads. That's why they sent you here with a plan that was always doomed to fail. Always. You were nothing to them before, but now that their poorly-conceived plan has failed, you are toxic. Anyone who comes near you will be destroyed. Your lives have been carelessly discarded. You've been used like experimental lab rats, sent on an errand the so-called Supreme Council hoped might work. These are the same people who have treated you and your families like dirt for generations."

Words are not normally my forte, but in that moment, I felt like my words were working for me.

I continued by telling stories that I was intimately acquainted with from both personal experience and experiences my father had shared with me in private. The names, dates, locations, and granular detail I used were likely familiar to someone like them who had been recruited to infiltrate the South.

While I hoped my stories were having an impact, I continually reiterated that not only were their hopes dashed, their lives were essentially over. Building a true sense of hopelessness, according to Sunny, was the first step in getting a captive to talk. Physical pain worked, but only after the mental barriers that created the initial resistance had been torn down.

Failure, I reminded them, was not tolerated by the Supreme Leader nor his Supreme Council. Blowing up one plane was perhaps a victory, but it would be considered a small one because it didn't create a shower-storm of fiery debris on top of the residents of Seoul. The death toll, while unacceptably high by civilized standards, was a fraction of what Pyeongyang wanted.

I cleared my throat as Sunny tinkered with the sharp instruments.

"Because the leadership in South Korea, like my father and the entire security council, are now aware of your diabolical plot, those planes will not be allowed anywhere near Korean airspace. They will simply fall out of the sky, landing far out in the ocean where no one can see. There will be no shock and awe in the skies over Seoul. No live newsfeed, no cell phone video footage going viral. Therefore, there will be no earth-shaking terror killing tens of thousands." I checked their eyes for comprehension. I could see something shift in the woman. She knew more, it seemed, than the other guy.

"Yes," I explained, "it will be a tragedy to lose the passengers aboard those planes. An extreme tragedy for those affected and for the nation, but not the type of theatrical knock-out your leaders were no doubt looking to score."

I let that sink in, but I didn't have the time to wait for all the puzzle pieces in their minds to click into place. I had to keep building my case, trying to weaken their resolve and motivation.

"Failing to blow up the other four planes over their intended targets and land the ultimate sucker punch your superiors thought they were going to land is nothing short of a colossal failure. Five downed planes is only enough to make your efforts appear juvenile, a hollow imitation of the 911 perpetrators, a copy-cat crime that lacks originality and, worse yet, any damage to the country's infrastructure. It will be a glancing blow at best, one that would make life for your fellow countrymen even worse than it is currently. The rest of the world will react with condemnation and further sanctions. I can assure you of that. Nothing good will come of your efforts to kill innocent people."

As I talked, I had removed their shoes and socks, flicking and pinching the soft spots near the arches of their feet, as if testing for the most tender place on each foot. I could see the woman trying to divert her eyes. A slight tremor shook her slender frame. I had struck a chord within her and she was clearly uncomfortable.

"Needless to say," I said as I grabbed the corkscrew and inspected its sharp tip. "You will not be welcomed home. There will be no praise, no medals, no rewards. Each of you, and most likely all of your loved ones, will suffer an ignominious death." I needed to drive home that point by reminding them of several would-be defectors who had failed in recent history. I brought up the spectacle the state-run media had made of each. Their eyes widened. I'm sure they didn't expect me to know the inner workings of their hermit nation. Each of these little factoids would be another deposit in my asset column.

I bent the top of one of her feet backward to expose the ligature that ran along the arch. Pressing the corkscrew against it, the woman flinched and tried to draw her foot away from me. I held her foot firmly in place with one hand and twisted the corkscrew until I drew blood. The guy's eyes grew almost as wide as hers. She was doing her best to suppress the yelps of pain, but a few emanated despite her efforts. I could see all hope beginning to fade, replaced by terror.

"I'll keep digging in here until I reach the plantar fascia, a big, long ligament. This thing will tear it apart, making each step you take very painful for the rest of your life." Her countenance slumped even further.

Watching them deflate, much as Yong Byun had earlier in the jail cell in Tecate, bolstered my confidence that I was making progress. I was in unchartered territory and not at all comfortable with it. Torturing another human is not in my nature but sparing the innocents on those planes took precedent.

While I spoke, Sunny made a show of preparing his collection of hardware. He wanted to intimidate them, instill that dark sense of hopelessness so vital to unlocking guarded secrets. I told him before we got started that I thought I could manage the interrogations so as to keep the blood off his hands, so to speak. Nonetheless, his background theatrics played a strong supportive role.

I mentioned a name that I was sure they would recognize. I also gave the corkscrew a quarter turn. These were either spies or military officers who had been caught in recent years trying to gain intelligence from South Korean military sources, infiltrating a Western financial institution, meeting with ranking officers of a high-tech firm with ties to military equipment manufacture, or in one case, South Korea's Presidential Security Service. These spies had failed and had been publicly shamed, their names and faces dragged through the twenty-four-hour state-run news cycle repeatedly before they disappeared, never to be heard from or spoken of again. The executions of the so-called "traitors'" families were never publicized through official media channels, of course, but the gruesome killings were made known through word of mouth by eyewitnesses—a disarming tactic used by governments around the world to control the masses. "Leak" information about what happens to those who step out of line, then deny any involvement or knowledge of the atrocities.

Each name I mentioned brought a flash of recognition, followed by an increase in the tension in the room. Each twist of the corkscrew broke down a measure of their resistance. It was like adding a ten-kilogram plate to each side of a barbell as a weightlifter held it overhead. The mention of these names seemed to cause their collective psyche to sag a little more, leaching a measure of hope or strength. I didn't have to bring up any details. I just dropped each name and twisted. By the third turn of the corkscrew, the woman was shrieking.

Chapter 50

C*osta Mesa, CA*

June 6, 3:17 a.m.

Stephanie Noh was not entirely at ease driving a stolen FBI vehicle. Her dad was certain they would be tracking it, despite JT's efforts to disable such capabilities. She had to hurry, but not attract any undue attention. Speeding recklessly was not a great option but driving casually wasn't either. At that time of night, with few cars on the road, she decided ten-to-fifteen miles over the speed limit was an acceptable compromise.

At that rate, she was able to make it to the crowded Long-Term lot at John Wayne Airport in roughly eleven minutes. This, she and her dad had agreed, was the perfect place to hide a car. Following his instructions, she used the hand towel she had stuffed in her waistband to wipe down every surface of the car. Trying to imagine where JT might have left prints, she worked the door handles inside and out, the steering wheel, the gear shift, the seat belt latches, the radio, the wires he had pulled, and the window buttons. Every hard surface received attention.

Satisfied that the car was free of any damning evidence, she locked the keys in and took off in a crouch between the parked cars in the lot, darting from row to row, in case there was anyone in the area that she wasn't aware of. Once clear of the parking lot, Stephanie ran to the arrivals area. She caught a taxi driver taking a nap. Startled awake, the driver muttered something she couldn't understand then unlocked the doors. She jumped in the cab and was greeted by the ripe aromas of body odor and halitosis. She paused, taken aback by the assault on her olfactories, then asked him to take her to the Home Depot in Costa Mesa, where her minivan sat waiting in the darkest corner of the parking lot. This was the spot Sunny decided they would hide her car. It was out of the way enough so that she would not run the risk of crossing paths with any law enforcement. A taxi, he said, would not attract their attention.

Before starting the engine, she checked her phone. No messages—text or voice. Stephanie's thumb hovered over the "favorites" screen where both JT's and her dad's numbers were displayed. The digital clock glowing on the van's in-dash screen showed 3:32 a.m. According to what JT had told her, the next plane would run out of fuel in twenty-seven minutes. JT's students, many of them the children of friends, neighbors, and fellow churchgoers, were on board. She shook her head and put the phone in the cupholder. Best not to disturb them.

She squeezed her eyes shut and said a prayer.

Shifting into Drive, Stephanie headed toward the Do Jang. The streets were virtually empty. The fog was rolling in from the mighty Pacific, lending an eerie glow to the orange street lamps and the neon lights of the small businesses that lined Harbor Boulevard as she pulled out of the parking lot.

Two turns later, her phone lit up and buzzed against the plastic lining of the cupholder. It was her dad.

"Appa," she said. "The car is in the long-term parking lot now. Should I meet you at the Do Jang now?"

"Yes. Come quickly. Your husband is doing very well. Not bad for his first go-round in wet work." Sunny sounded out of breath, tense. "It shouldn't be too long until he has the information he needs. In any case, he wants you and me out of here. I fear we don't have much time before the FBI come, even with the diversion. After they get the car, they'll see on the GPS tracker where he's been. They'll come here next."

"On my way. Let's get you out of there."

"Yes, meet me at the back door. Hurry."

Out of an abundance of caution, Stephanie took the next right and made her way to the Do Jang on the main thoroughfares. It didn't feel as covert as taking the back roads, but since time was of the essence, it made the most sense.

Chapter 51

Costa Mesa, CA

June 6, 3:35 a.m.; Thirty minutes of fuel remaining in the LAX-ICN plane

My tactics were working. The woman was quivering uncontrollably after only three turns of the corkscrew. I had one knee firmly on her calf muscle and my left hand gripped her ankle so she couldn't squirm or kick. Sunny held her other leg. Her eyes rolled to the back of her head and her face was white as a sheet. Her howling tugged at my heartstrings for a fraction of a second. But then the thought of the families of the passengers and crew helped me sweep away any sympathy that I might have been tempted to entertain.

Despite the fact that I hadn't touched him, the guy looked to be in no better shape than her. Dark stains had formed under his arms. His eyes were big as saucers. Sweat dripped from strands of hair stuck to his forehead.

I stopped twisting for a moment to show them that I was not a sadist.

"Anything you want to tell me?" I asked.

Through terror-filled eyes, the two exchanged a meaningful glance. It felt to me like there was something to the silent communication. Perhaps it was just some sort of non-verbal encouragement, but I couldn't have that. I decided right then that the two of them needed to be separated, so I stood up, dropping the woman's foot and glared at the guy. She let out a muffled howl when I pushed myself up off her foot.

I walked a few steps and opened the door to the darkened gym to make sure the blinds were drawn. They were, so I dragged the woman in there by her heels. The sharp implement dangled for a second or two, then fell out on the floor. A steam of blood began to flow, so I grabbed the duct tape to cover the wound and slow it down. While I was at it, I used an excessive amount of tape to strap her ankles together. I rolled her onto her stomach, pulled her legs back, and used even more duct tape to hog tie her. Any movement of her arms or legs would put pressure on her windpipe. If she struggled to get loose, she would likely strangle herself.

When I returned to the back room, I could see the abject fear in the guy's eyes. He tried to hide it, but it was there. Sunny gave me a nonverbal que and stepped toward her. I had left the door open on purpose. I wanted her to hear what was going on. I had also positioned her just so, allowing her to get a look at the table full of implements, but not at her comrade.

"Trying to be brave, are you?" I said. "Let me remind you, there is no sense in withholding information from me now. The best you can hope for is a quick end." I studied his face for any hint of comprehension. This message had to resonate, but it hadn't yet hit its mark, so I continued. As I spoke, I pulled another sharp instrument off the table, deliberate in my movements as I twirled it in my hand. Sunny shook his head at me, so I set it down. I moved to the drill and picked out one of the long bits used to counter-sink screws into wood. The bit had a tip that protruded from the end, then broadened slightly, exposing a fiendish, razor-like cowling edge. I secured the bit into the chuck and squeezed the trigger. A gratifying mechanical whirr emitted as I hefted the power tool in my hand, feeling its weight and balance.

Again, Sunny shook his head and said in Korean, "No good. Save it." His lips curled as he showed me a bottle of ammonia-based cleanser and a lemon. "These will intensify its effect. But wait."

Sunny studied the items on the table like an experienced shopper deciding on the right shoes to complete an outfit, surveying each with an expert's eye. When he came to the end of the table, he hefted a car battery and some wire. He signaled for me to hand him the Xacto knife, which he then used to strip the insulation from the wire, exposing the raw copper strands.

I smiled at our male prisoner seated right in front of me. I needed him to think I was enjoying this. "If you insist on withholding the information we need, things are going to start getting really bad for you. We are here to save lives, possibly yours as well as those you intend to murder. You can choose to cooperate with us before we get started on you, or you can choose to find out if you're as tough as you think you are."

I stepped to the doorway and kicked the woman's feet to make sure I had her full attention. Her eyes were hollow. She was trying to put herself in a trance, a technique often employed by well-trained operatives to remove themselves from the pain. They mentally detach themselves from the situation and bury the vital secrets of their superiors deep in their mind, layering lies and nonessential half-truths on top of the vital information their enemies seek. Sometimes they do it so well they confuse themselves and are unable to disentangle the truth from their own fabrications. I couldn't allow this to happen. The freshest pain was in her foot, which is why I chose to whack the bleeding one.

That subtle recognition of her attempt to entrance herself was like adding one more twist to the coil inside of me. She, I realized in the moment, she was the linchpin, the one with the deepest knowledge, the highest rank.

Crouching next to her, I picked up the corkscrew and poked the tip of it into the soft flesh of her underarm. She pulled back, cutting off her own airway, and I knew I had interrupted her internal ritual.

"I think you understand that things will be much different than you might have imagined from here on out. First, your government will deny your very existence. You will have brought shame and disgrace and a mountain of intense scrutiny to your struggling nation. You know all the illegal markets that have sprung up over the past several years? You're familiar with them, right? People are sneaking into China, buying things like electronics and beans and appliances and fresh fish and selling them for profit back in their cities and villages in the northern sectors of your country. A privileged few make it further south where the prices for such goods rise. You're aware of this, are you not? You or your family members may have profited from this sort of activity or gained some level of luxury by means of such illegal trade. Am I right?" I was rewarded with a nearly imperceptible fluttering of the eyes. "I can see that I'm right," I continued. "The most likely result of your attempted plot today is that those markets will be completely shut down. The Chinese will enforce tighter controls over their border with your country. They cannot afford to piss off the Americans.

"When the investigations conclude that your country was behind these attacks, you better believe all foreign money and food that is now coming into your country and helping your desperate citizenry will dry up. Conditions will worsen, and your countrymen may face another famine like the one in the 1990's. Is that what you want?"

Again, I let my words sink in as I toyed with the sharp tip of the corkscrew. "How long can North Korea support its people with its own crop production? Without rice coming in from other countries, your domestically produced rice will feed less than fifty percent of your population. You know that. Who decides who lives and who dies?"

I made eye contact with the guy through the doorway. "Who decides the fate of millions of your people? I'll tell you. You do. You can act right now and save those who will die a slow death by starvation as a result of your actions."

I watched her eyes intently, allowing my voice to grow more somber. "Where are the codes to scramble the signal? Tell me now and save your countrymen."

No response. She stared straight ahead with eyes that were dead to the world. The trance was threatening to take over again. I raised my voice. "Hey! I'm talking to you." I slapped her wounded foot again and dug the corkscrew into her armpit just enough to rip open a small hole in her tender skin. Blood gushed and she cried out in pain.

The woman's body shuttered as a fresh wave of shock set in. The guy pressed his eyes closed and howled through the duct tape.

While I talked, Sunny had hauled the battery and the wires into the bathroom in the corner of my office, walking backwards so they could see what he was doing. He flicked on the light. The whir of the woefully inadequate ventilation fan filled the space. He slid open the shower curtain.

Yes, my gym had a small shower in it. A nice little convenience for which I paid extra rent each month. This night it was going to serve a higher purpose. Sunny turned the water on all the way. Cold, of course, and plugged the drain with the mousepad from my desk. The shower pan had about a five-inch lip on it. Not much, but hopefully sufficient for our purpose.

I quickly deduced his intentions and nodded my understanding.

Sunny removed a folded towel from the cabinet and placed it on the floor. That was where I was to stand, he said. He donned a pair of leather gloves for insulation and tossed me another set. Then he dropped the wire into the shower pan to electrify the water with somewhere around fourteen volts of electricity. Not enough to kill, but enough to cause considerable discomfort, for sure. I gestured my next move and he stepped aside.

On Sunny's signal, I turned to the woman. "Once again, ladies first." After ripping apart my elaborate hog-tie contraption, I grabbed her under the arms, feeling the gooey warmth of her fresh blood, and dragged her head-first to the edge of the shower. I maneuvered her upper body in one swift motion into the shower stall, mashing her face down into the shallow pool of electrified water that had accumulated, holding the back of her head and her neck firmly so she couldn't wiggle out of my grip. Her weakened body gave very little resistance.

My movements were calculated to be severe and dramatic, the kind of rough treatment that would steal away one's breath. I gave her no time to pull in any air before I pushed her face in the water. Today's ordeal had already snuffed much of the fight out of her. The loss of blood, the shock, the disappointment, my grim appraisal of their situation.

Her body convulsed as I counted to sixty in my head, then pulled her up. "Ready to talk?" I asked. Before she could answer, I shoved her face back into the water, once again giving her no time to pull in a deep breath. I noticed, and I think she did too, that the water was tinged pink. Blood from her shoulder and armpit wounds was mixing with the spray from the showerhead. I didn't hesitate. I put her face right back in it. This time, the count was to seventy-five.

"Now?"

Splash. She was in the water again, twitching and bucking. Only thirty seconds this time.

She came up gasping and spluttering water from her nose. Her whole body trembled uncontrollably. She nodded her head vigorously.

"Good. Tell me now how to disable those bombs."

I ripped the duct tape off her mouth. "I don't know," she coughed. "I think it's impossible."

"Nothing is impossible," I yelled. "Nothing. Now tell me." I pushed her face back underwater for another thirty seconds, then yanked her head back up.

"Only our mission technician knows," she cried. "He programmed all of them."

"Where is your mission technician?"

She pinched her eyes shut and struggled to turn her ahead away from me, toward the back of the shower. "I don't know. I promise," she rasped between ragged breaths.

Something dawned on me in that moment, something I had overlooked or ignored in my anger and haste.

I dropped her and let her twist and struggle from a face-down-in-the-shower position to an awkward half-kneeling, half-sitting position using her good shoulder to gain some leverage. Cold water continued to rain down on her, but she had knocked my makeshift plug away from the drain hole. She had also bumped the battery and disconnected the wire with her thrashings.

But I didn't care.

My attention was immediately fixed on the guy. I could see him swallow hard as I approached him. "You're the technician, aren't you?" I barked. "Makes sense. Weasley little guy like you wouldn't be good for much else. Now talk." I grabbed him by the legs and yanked him away from the desk he had been leaning against. It was so sudden his head hit the floor with a thud.

The scrawny little man tried to be brave. He gritted his teeth and held his breath and turned away his eyes as if to signal that he could handle whatever was coming.

Sunny had quickly moved to the table and now held the welding torch in hand. He fiddled with the nozzle and its ignition switch before attempting to light it. It roared to life right away and he adjusted the gas mix until he had a nice, steady blue flame jetting out of the brass tubing.

"Ah," he said in Korean. "Haven't done this for a while. I really don't like the smell of burnt human flesh, but duty demands we get answers. We don't have time to mess around." Sunny pointed the nozzle toward the guy's exposed feet. I held the skinny calves and pressed them into the floor with all my weight.

"Go ahead," I said to Sunny. "We need him to talk. Now."

The technician looked at me and began to kick and thrash with all the terror of a bleeding man in shark-infested waters.

Sunny flashed an evil grin. "I usually start with the toes and work my way up to more vital parts. It isn't pleasant. The smell is horrible and the pain, I would imagine, is worse." Sunny continued to adjust the flame to increase the length of it. "Good thing we have lots of towels. This is going to be messy."

I nodded to my father-in-law and he began to aim the flame toward the young technician's toes. The smell of burning hair began to waft towards our noses. "Awful, isn't it," said Sunny.

The technician's eyes, already wide, somehow grew another few centimeters in diameter. Ten seconds into his brave resistance, the skin on his pinky toe began to bubble as it scorched. The smell was horrendous. The poor guy was trying so hard to be brave but trying even harder to escape. I exerted my strength to hold his lower body still while Sunny held the flame in place. As the first lump of flesh melted off, exposing the off-white phalange, the man howled like a wounded dog and blurted, "Stop. I'll tell you. I'll tell you. Stop, please. I'll tell you." He sobbed the pitiful tears of a child who fears disappointing a parent. He was not about to take one for the team.

The woman, who was still groaning in the bathroom, suddenly became vocal and commanding. The problem was her voice held neither strength nor conviction. It was barely above a whisper. "Don't do it. Don't tell these dogs anything."

Sunny whipped around, pointing the blue flame at her. He walked toward her with the torch, but she continued. He waved the end of the flame across the sleeve of her soaked shirt. It was too damp to ignite but enough for her to feel the heat. Sunny set the torch down close to her body so that if she flinched it would topple over on her as he fastened a strip of duct tape across her mouth.

"Do the right thing," I said to the sobbing young man. I gave him a reassuring squeeze on the calves. Speaking to Sunny, I said, "Thanks. Let's hold off on her until we hear what this guy has to say."

Sunny stood and slammed the bathroom door shut so the woman could be neither seen nor heard.

I turned my attention to the computer guru writhing in pain under my grip. This poor kid had little, if any, military training. He was a nerd—pale and wispy. Any veneer of a tough guy gone; his whole frame shook. He wouldn't look me in the eye, but he started talking. I stopped him with an outheld hand, fumbling for my phone. I pulled it out and quickly found the audio record app and started it. "Please," I said, "tell us how to disable those bombs."

Seven minutes later, I had a voice recording from the technician that detailed the online location and password to a secured site where the pseudo random codes for the device pairings were stored. We logged on to it with my smart phone and accessed the life-saving sequences, which I was able to copy into the notes on my phone for easy distribution to the right people on the planes. The technical guru spelled out the steps necessary to disengage the Bluetooth connections, which would disarm each of the bombs. I had to give him credit. If what he was saying was true, he had an excellent memory and was as smart as anyone I had ever met. Anyone who can boil down complex tasks into easy-to-follow directions like that is on the genius level, I've discovered.

I bypassed Robinson for the time being and dialed my father. "Put me through to your IT guy, now."

"It is too late, son," he said solemnly.

Chapter 52

C*osta Mesa, CA*

June 6, 3:55 a.m.; Ten minutes of fuel remaining in LAX-ICN plane

My father's voice was uncharacteristically faint. The usual force and gusto were absent.

"No, that can't be." I tried to control my own tone, but my emotions were bubbling over. "The plane from Los Angeles must have at least another fifteen minutes' worth of fuel. It hasn't been that long."

"Yes, only fifteen minutes. They'll never make it. They're too far out to sea. We already lost a plane trying to land in Incheon. A true tragedy. Thousands of people saw it. We can't risk another attempt like that."

Even though we hadn't spoken for many years, I recognized the resignation in his voice. It scared me. This is the man who was always so self-assured; the one who always had an answer, no matter the question.

My thoughts were disjointed. They flew out of my mouth in clips, rushed, and with very little formality, which normally I would afford a man of his rank, despite our familial relationship. "Father, I have the solution. The mission technician, he gave me instructions on how to disengage the detonators. They need to know. The people on the plane. The pilot or somebody. I need to send instruction to the pilot. All of them. Please, patch me through to someone on that plane. The Los Angeles plane. Hurry. There's no time to waste. Hurry." Although I used semi-polite conjugations, it was still an odd feeling yelling a string of commands to the highest ranking general of the Korean army. "Trust me, father. This will save their lives."

"Without the codes, they're doomed— "

"I have them. I have the codes. Patch me through. Now, please."

"They're so far out..."

Someone on the line interrupted. "Sir, they're high enough that they can still make it if we patch the call through right now."

"Really?" said my father. "Is that true? Can they make it to Incheon?" His tone brightened immediately. "Stay on the line, Jeong Tae, while we patch you through."

Three minutes later, I was speaking with the captain of Korean Air flight 134 from Los Angeles—the plane my students were on. Apparently, my father had sent out a string of commands in the intervening minutes that told the fighter pilots to escort the jumbo jet back toward Incheon. I had the KAL pilot on speaker phone while I texted the audio file with the instructions. I skipped the long, formal introductions and just told him I was General Noh's son and was working with the TSA in America. He didn't need any more explanation of who I was or how I'd gotten the life-saving information I was in the process of sending them. "I have the codes you need. Please give the phone to your most technically savvy crew member. Hurry."

Chapter 53

Onboard Korean Air Flight 134, LAX-ICN

June 6, 3:58 a.m., Seven minutes of fuel remaining on LAX-ICN plane

The pilot turned to the navigator. "Officer Kim? Would you please do the honors? I believe you are better suited to do this."

Officer Kim, who had been listening in on the phone call with General Noh's son, snatched the phone from the pilot's hand as he spun out of his chair and headed for the cockpit door. He trotted down the aisle, his laptop computer under his arm, through the business-class cabin and down the stairs, careful to avoid the look of one grappling with four-hundred lives in the balance. He bounded down to the main cabin, then speed-walked down the port-side aisle toward the aft serving area, ignoring the anxious looks from passengers as he went.

Without ceremony or explanation, he gave a knowing glance to the two flight attendants, then moved aside one of the wheeled service carts, forgetting to lock the wheels after pushing it out of his way. It crashed against the bulkhead and would have toppled had one of the attendants not caught it and secured it. The lever on the hatch didn't release easily, so he had to give it a karate chop with the side of his hand. It finally popped up and he was able, with some force, to pry open the hatch, which led to an aluminum ladder fixed to a bulkhead beneath the service area wall. He scrambled through the undersized opening, aware of the increased engine noise coming from the space. He closed the hatch as he descended, then quickly moved to the luggage storage area belowdecks. Opening his laptop so it would wake up as he picked his way through the space, he looked for a place to set up.

Space was tight amid the specialized baggage holders, but so was time. He found a spot with enough room to sit and plopped onto the steel floor between two of the large, netted racks in a cross-legged position, balancing the computer between his knees as the machine whirred to life. He ran the pad of his index finger over the scanning bar to unlock the operating system. While the computer's screen displayed its welcome page, the navigation officer fumbled his earbuds into place, dropping them twice due to the shaking of his hands before positioning them into his ear canals. He then opened the audio file on the phone and listened to the instructions.

A strangely accented male voice spoke on the recording. The navigator couldn't place the region from which this guy had come, but he sounded smart and familiar with the technology.

The voice helped him open the command prompt screen and instructed him what to type and what to look for before entering the next command. Officer Kim worked as quickly as he could, his trembling fingers finally relaxing enough to function at a higher speed.

He listened intently as the unfamiliar voice hissed through the earbuds, a pained, somber tone that told Officer Kim that the man was under duress. He prayed that the voice was telling him the truth. He prayed that these instructions were not a hoax. He prayed that he and his fellow crewmates and the passengers would not meet the same fate as his colleagues forty minutes earlier.

After completing the first set of directives, Officer Kim noticed a small box pop up at the lower left corner of his computer screen. It was an altimeter. It showed 5029 meters when it first opened, but that number was dropping quickly. Another box appeared that showed two sets of constantly changing number marked by the symbols for degrees and minutes. It was a GPS reading of the plane's coordinates.

When he completed the next line of code as instructed, the numbers in the altimeter box showed 2850. He gulped as he realized how fast numbers were changing. At their current rate of descent, he had maybe a minute to disarm the bomb or he and everyone onboard would meet the same fate as Flight

5821.

Sweat beaded on his brow as he strained to listen and follow the prompts. Several times he had to pause, slide the progress bar on the phone backwards, and re-listen to sections of the recording to ensure he followed exactly. The indistinct words made it hard to understand some of the commands. Time and nerves were conspiring against him. He wiped his forehead and pulled in a deep breath. "Stay calm. It's going to work," he muttered out loud to himself.

The altimeter showed 1137 meters.

There was now twenty-nine seconds left of the recording. There was no time for replaying and double-checking for accuracy. He closed his eyes and listened hard.

The voice continued, assuring him that he was nearly there. Just two more things to do before the bomb was disarmed. Two things and maybe twenty seconds until they reached 100 meters above sea level, the trigger point on the detonator.

There were no sounds or beeps or flashes of light confirming that he was doing it right. No pop-up windows congratulating him on successfully completing each task and prompting him to continue on to the next level. Just the altimeter quickly counting down. 500 . . .400 . . .300 . . .200 . .

This was not like the countless online games he'd played. This was real life, and it was a look into a sinister plot aimed at killing him and the three-hundred ninety-three passengers onboard the jumbo jet.

Officer Kim exhaled when he completed the last command prompt and punched the "Enter" key. After a millisecond pause that felt like a lifetime, he was rewarded with a single, white-lettered word against the black backdrop. "Complete," the blinking word said.

The altimeter at the bottom left corner halted, displaying "00109."

He closed his eyes and began to count. A loud noise startled him. He swung his head in the direction of the noise and realized it was the landing gear. They were just moments away from touching down. A whoosh of air exited his lungs as he realized he'd been holding his breath for who knows how long. Relief flooded his system and he burst into a howl that was half celebration, half painful realization that things could have worked out much differently.

He scrambled to brace for the impact of the landing. He grabbed a handful of netting from the nearest cargo holder just in time to steady himself for the impact.

After the plane came to a stop, Officer Kim tried to stand. However, his knees buckled underneath him, and he nearly fell. That's when he noticed that his light blue shirt had dark patches around the armpits and chest. Officer Kim took a moment to gather himself, then stumbled back toward the ladder.

Anxious flight attendants greeted him as he emerged. They chattered to him about how unusual it was for a flight crew member to go belowdecks during flight. They asked him if he was alright and what was going on.

"Nothing to worry about," he lied. "Just had to manually reset one of the controllers."

Chapter 54

Costa Mesa, California

June 6, 4:02 a.m.

Sunny and I were working as fast as we could, even before Robinson called ostensibly to warn me that they were on their way. I didn't bother to ask him where they were on their way from since I didn't want to give anything away. I figured if he had accessed the tracking function the FBI's Ford, it would buy me about 11 more minutes. Not much time to clean up the mess, but it would have to do.

It was time to face the music. I wouldn't run away. I would just wait for them, knowing the powers that be would figure things out. Sunny and Stephanie needed time to clear the area. Nothing good would come about by having my wife and her father at the scene where several international rules of warfare and laws regarding the treatment of prisoners were categorically violated.

Sunny and I had managed to clean up most of the mess, wiping up all the blood from the floor and the blood-tinged water from the shower. All of the duct tape was removed from my prisoners. All of the paraphernalia Sunny had brought with him was re-bagged. I checked a locator app on my phone and saw that Stephanie was still a couple miles away.

I needed for her and Sunny to never cross paths with the FBI. I was ready to pay whatever price my treachery and law-bending would require. But I couldn't let either of them get caught up in any part of it. They needed to stabilize the rest of the family.

CHAPTER 54

Sunny, who had looked over my shoulder and seen the moving blip that represented Stephanie's location, said something that showed he was thinking much more clearly than I was. "Why don't I just take these bags with me? My truck is only a few blocks from here."

That made too much sense. Why didn't I think of the simple solution?

He just smiled at me as he placed a reassuring hand on my shoulder. "I'll call Stephanie and tell her to head back to our house." He moved toward the door, then stopped. "Don't worry, Jeong Tae. You did the right thing. It wasn't pretty, but it was the right thing."

Sunny took the garbage bag full of duct tape and blood-soaked towels in his free hand. The other arm had the loops of shopping bags lined all the way up to his elbow. He gave me an approving nod and a reassuring smile as he pushed his load through the door. I watched him hurry away, quickly melting into the shadows. He disappeared in a matter of seconds.

When the door slammed shut, I felt all alone, depleted. Sure, I had the company of the two North Korean terrorists, but they were in no shape to speak, laying there all unconscious and still.

My detainees had been prepped on what to say if they wanted freedom. If they played it right, they could circumvent the worst of the justice system and get out on good behavior after a few years at a federal prison, also known as "club fed." I hoped that their innate desire to live free would overcome their desire to do the bidding of the twisted regime that ran their country.

As I worked on disinfecting and bandaging their wounds, I talked of my wife and children and life in America. I spoke to them about the promises that had been extended to them via my father and the United States government, as well.

When I heard the cars pull up to the back door, I was kneeling next to the woman, adhering the last bandage in place on her shoulder. Color had returned to her face and with the help of a hair dryer I found in a gym bag under the cabinet, she was mostly dry. Although they had each lost a fair amount of blood, they seemed to be stabilized now that they were laying down and covered with white doboks, the uniforms my students and I wore during class. I hoped the doboks would help ward off further shock.

Robinson rapped his knuckles on the steel door just a few feet from me. I thought that was very mannerly considering what I had done to him.

Even though I expected his arrival, I froze. On the other side of that door lay an uncertain fate.

"Come on, JT. I know you're in there."

I finished applying the bandage, and stood, exhaling as I did. The ten feet to the door seemed like a mile. I opened it in a slow arc, showing my hands, and invited him in. He flashed me a knowing smile and gave a slight bow as he slid past me into the cramped space of my office. Three other agents of some ilk or other followed. They began examining every inch of the place.

"I don't know how you did it," he said, squinting at me. "And I don't care. That plane from LAX has landed safely. No explosion. No lives lost."

I didn't say anything. Instead, I nodded, bowed, and put the stone face back on.

Over the course of the next twenty-five minutes, the two North Koreans were strapped to gurneys and taken away in ambulances. I didn't ask where they were going.

The FBI agents scoured my office, the bathroom, and the main gym. They shrugged at Robinson and announced that they didn't find anything.

Based on a brief conversation with Robinson about how I got the information that ultimately led to the remaining four planes landing safely in Incheon, I hoped the Department of Homeland Security would follow through on the promises I had made to these two. There needed to be a path to redemption for the roles the two North Koreans played in saving so many lives because they had done the right thing in the end. They had lived their entire lives under the influence of a corrupted and unstable group of leaders, but I believed in their ability and willingness to change. I offered to be their sponsor if they wanted to seek asylum in either the United States or South Korea, since I had dual citizenship.

Robinson shook his head. "You *are* an optimist, aren't you?"

"I guess so. Most people will do the right thing given the opportunity and the right incentives."

"Is that why you brought them here? To give the right opportunity and incentives?"

"Exactly. Life is all about choices. Some people need a little more encouragement to choose the right."

Robinson looked at the blood smears on my shirt and pants and raised an eyebrow. I just shrugged.

"It all comes down to the path we choose in life. These guys all started out with the destination of a better life fixed in their minds. They come from a closed and backward nation where there's very little hope. Then this so-called 'Chammae Boksu' mission came along with its promise of a better life for them and their families. What would you have done?"

Robinson shook his head. "I guess for me it's hard to get into the mindset that says, 'Yeah, I'll go kill thousands of people so that I can live a better life.'"

"Look, I know it's screwed up. Their whole society is. Nothing we can do about it, really. Desperation breeds desperation and these kinds of things are the unfortunate results."

"Are you saying they shouldn't be executed for the four hundred lives they helped take?"

"No. I'm saying we'll never bring the true culprits to justice. I'm willing to bet that there is no clear connection between the masterminds and those who carried out this mission. Trying to press the issue would only further destabilize the region and the world. As far as punishment goes, these two will have a lifetime to ponder the consequences of their actions. Their families will suffer immensely, as will those of the victims."

"Hell of a thing they've done." Robinson glared at nothing in particular, his jaw muscles tensing as he spoke.

"Could have been worse had they chosen not to spill their secrets."

Robinson was about to say something else when his phone rang. His whole body stiffened, and he stood straight and tall when the voice on the other line introduced himself. He then retreated outside, not to return for several minutes.

Chapter 55

Costa Mesa, California

June 6, 4:27 a.m.

The first words of praise I had ever heard from him came at a point when I was not really feeling worthy of it. They were simple words, uttered for the first time in my recollection, spanning some thirty-five years. "I'm proud of you, son. Your work today was admirable—more than admirable, extraordinary."

Those words from my father should have lifted me out of the quagmire my soul had sunk into. I had never dreamed of torturing another person, but I had done it that day. Guilt and shame and the melancholy that accompanies the realization that you have committed some serious misdeeds against a fellow human being threatened to swallow me. I had stooped low enough to treat a woman with the same brutality as a man—something that ran counter to everything this same father who now praised me had taught me all my life.

Yes, many may say that the ends justified the means, but my heart took little comfort in that thought. I had stood on the precipice of committing cold-blooded murder in order to save sixteen-hundred souls. I had looked over the edge and caught a glimpse of the abyss. It chilled me to the core to examine what I contemplated doing had that plane full of passengers from Los Angeles, sixteen of which were my young students, exploded.

My father's reassurance aside, my self-reflections were dark and brooding. No one except me, Sunny, and those two North Koreans would ever know what took place in the back office of my gym in the wee hours that morning. No one outside of a handful of people would ever know how terribly close we came to experiencing another 9-1-1. The world at large would never realize that World War III, with the very real possibility of a nuclear strike, had been averted because the Geneva Convention had been summarily, but temporarily, dismissed for the purpose of avoiding such a chilling prospect.

But my father knew and that should have been enough. Nonetheless, I sat at my desk in the back of my Do Jang with my head in my hands for twenty minutes after the ambulances left.

Robinson sat across from me, just staring at the wall. Neither of us spoke. Neither of us moved.

I contemplated the path I had chosen that day, recalling the thoughts I had had in the airport eighteen hours earlier. My day had turned out much differently than I had expected, which matched the way my life had turned out compared to my high school and college-day dreams. Though I hadn't found the time to contemplate my future, I had come to a decision by the end of it all that there would indeed be a career change—soon.

I heard another car pull up to the back door. Robinson stood, slowly extending his torso to its full six-foot-three-inch stature. He tapped a pair of handcuffs fastened to his belt. "Sorry. Protocol. You know how it is?"

I nodded and rose with my hands held out in front of me, still staring blankly at nothing in particular.

"We'll get this all sorted out, Mr. Noh." He clicked the steel bracelets in place loosely just as someone began pounding on the back door. He paused, looked me in the eye, and spoke from the heart. "Our country owes you a debt of gratitude for all you've done here today. I'm sure the Korean government must feel the same, as well as the passengers and their families, blissfully ignorant though they may be. Along with the lives you've saved today, many careers, mine included, have been spared. Thank you. That may be as much as you ever get, but it's sincere."

I nodded again, not knowing what to say. I knew Robinson was right. No one else would ever formally thank me for the unsavory deeds I had performed. It would all be swept under the rug and the world would continue on as it always does, tumultuous and harried.

Gripping the door handle, Robinson added, “You’re a hero in my book.”

I smiled as I soaked it in. The path before seemed clearer now.

Epilogue

My wife was hurriedly re-packing her and the kids' bags. Mine were waiting for the Bell Captain by the front door of the fifteen-hundred square foot Ritz-Carlton Suite atop the luxury hotel at Marina Del Rey, just five miles north of LAX. I stood in front of the picture window, gazing out at the ocean, watching the planes taking off from the northern runway and climbing into the sky. The limousine Korean Airlines had hired to drive us to the airport would arrive in less than five minutes. Our first-ever trip in first class, the hotel, and all the food we could eat would be paid for by the airline as a "small token of their appreciation," though appreciation for what was never specified.

My students would complete the first day of competition without me. With Jin Sook coaching them and because of their diligent preparation, I was confident they would shine. My heart was still with them but now my head was in a different place. The rust that had accumulated over my true identity as a soldier and protector had been shaken off. A sense of duty was calling me down a different path, down a path more similar to the one I had originally chosen. As much as I loved my students and teaching them Tae Kwon Do, I knew I could never return to it with the enthusiasm and commitment those kids deserved. Nor could I ever enter the back office without recalling what I had done there. That location would forever be tainted in my memory.

My career had already come to a fork in the road. Job offers had already been floated out there, though few details accompanied these discussions. One choice was to return to my homeland and accept a position within the

Korean Army's intelligence corps as a lead investigator. My record was to be expunged as the details of what had transpired six years prior had been brought to light and my innocence proven. The other and even more intriguing option was as a liaison with the United States Department of Homeland Security, working with Alan Robinson, the soon-to-be-appointed West Coast Director of Airport Operations for the Transportation Safety Administration, to beef up security protocol at every international airport from San Diego to Seattle and from Denver to Honolulu. The specific assignment would be to identify, track, and monitor all known North Korean travelers. I would work closely with counterparts in Seoul and Beijing, mostly. With all the tension between the Hermit Kingdom and the rest of the world, and with the US's recently exposed security deficiencies, this would be a monumental and high-profile position.

I had a lot to think about.

One thing for sure, the pressure and heat from the near catastrophe had cooked up something good in terms of my family. Whatever malice or hurt or disappointment there had been before had, through this experience, been boiled off, replaced by something new and healthy.

The future was looking good all around.

Before You Go

Thank you for reading "Chosen Path." I hope you enjoyed the adventure and came away with an appreciation for the Korean people, the Korean culture, and the history of Korea while being entertained. The situation on the Korean Peninsula is a tenuous one with global implications. May peace prevail.

Authors like me depend on reviews from readers like you to gain visibility and help new readers find our work. I hope you will take the time to share your thoughts about this story. Follow this link: Review Your Purchases (amazon.com.

As a "thank you," I would like to offer you a gift. Please visit www.glen-robinsbooks.com to request a free copy of my next release.

My other books include:

Off Kilter

Off Course

Off Guard

Off Chance

Off Limits

Off Track

Coming soon: Born Into Espionage

Continue reading for a sneak peek.

Born Into Espionage – Sneak Peek

Prologue

I'm not proud of too many things in my life. The things I've done—that I've had to do—are not the kinds of things you talk about in polite company. Not that I keep polite company, mind you, but if I did, I would lie about what I do for a living. Or, better said, what I have to do to survive. I'm just fortunate to get paid for it some of the time.

Since my skills are second to none, having been reared and trained by two of the best in the business, my fees are high and my bank accounts enviable.

My parents taught me well. I learned to follow the "Golden Rule," but also to defend myself, my fellow countrymen, and the cause of freedom. Mine was an upbringing that by most accounts would appear fraught with conflicting values that are diametrically opposed, such as, "Love thy neighbor as thyself" and "It is better to kill than to be killed." I have had to do some things that others would consider heinous or horrifying. Those are the kinds of acts that fall more in line with "protect the innocent and defend the weak" than "turn the other cheek."

Living true to these values can be confusing, especially when you're orphaned at seventeen and have been hunted ever since by those who gave the orders to eliminate your parents. All my parents ever did wrong was question the motives of their superiors. And refuse one time each to do their bidding.

While being instructed by my parents not to lie, I was trained on the fine art of falsifying documents, such as passports and driver's licenses. They gave me several identities and explained when and how to create more. I've grown up in an elaborate web of half-truths and concealment for the sole purpose of surviving. My life, I was told, would be difficult but rewarding. My life's mission, they said, would be to remove evil from the world so that the good can flourish. I was to take out the wolves so the sheep could continue to live in peace, blissfully ignorant of the dark and seedy underworld of espionage into which I was born.

To some in high positions, my existence would be problematic. To some with direct oversight of my parents and their professional lives, it is not acceptable. To those who need certain, shall we say, "deeds" to be done, my existence is essential. To the relatively few people who know of me, I am sought after for varied reasons. Some want to kill me while others want to employ me to accomplish things that will make them and their superiors look good. Those same superiors who would not hesitate to sign the kill order to get rid of me.

I am a loose end that needs to be "tied off."

At the same time, I'm an untraceable, highly effective killing machine.

I'm an asset, but also an enemy.

It's just a matter of perspective.

If you're on the right side of the equation, I am a measure of protection. If you're on the wrong side, I'm an undetectable threat.

One of the things I *am* proud of is my physique. I've worked hard to build lean muscle mass so that I'm far stronger than I look. I can deadlift twice my body weight and carry it slung over my shoulder at a trot for a mile. Yet, I remain nimble and agile. I don't spend much time in a gym, however. I do calisthenics, yoga, Tai-Chi, and aerobic exercises to build and maintain my fitness level. I sprint up staircases at local parks or high schools with a forty-pound backpack while most people are asleep. I also do a lot of swimming because it stretches out the muscle fibers while strengthening them so I don't get all bulky.

I need to stay fit and lithe. My life often depends on it.

On top of all that, I have been blessed with cat-like reflexes and a predator's instincts. Some of that is a product of my upbringing—much of it, truth be known. I have even been trained since I was small to stalk like a panther, silent and stealthy. I could be in the same room with you and you wouldn't know it until it was too late.

So, yeah, I'm proud of what I can do physically.

I'm not too shabby on the mental acuity scale, either.

Much of my physical makeup is purely hereditary. I inherited my athletic build from my father, God rest his soul, and much of my grit and determination from my mother, may she, too, rest in peace.

Both of my parents were extremely bright people. They tested well, graduated with advanced degrees from prominent universities, and began promising careers before they were recruited. He was a former Navy Seal turned computer programmer and information technology architect. From him I learned how to gain access to information stored in almost any computer anywhere. She once qualified for the British Olympic gymnastics team, but injury prevented her from competing in the Games. Instead, she applied the same drive to her schooling and studied material science engineering and physics. Under her tutelage, I became proficient at math, science, and the art of manipulating the environment around me to my advantage. Because of her, I can build and dismantle explosive devices.

All that training happened a long time ago.

Things have changed. My life is not like anyone's that I have ever known or read about.

I am unique and so is my story.

I'm a twenty-three-year-old orphan.

And a lethal free-lance assassin.

A few days before my most recent assignment started, I drove my car off an embankment into a rain-swollen creek in the middle of the night during one of the most powerful storms the San Francisco Bay Area had experienced in recent history. The timing of my short stay in the East Bay was not coincidental. It was calculated based on the arrival of that monster system coming down out of the Gulf of Alaska and blasting the region with heavy wind and rain.

Of course, I drove off the road on purpose. I needed to lose a tail. I needed to be dead and I knew my story would make headlines because it would be so unusual. Faking my own death was my best chance of vanishing into the night. Beyond that, I needed the guy in the backseat to be dead even more.

The day after the accident, I was on my way to Tora Bora, Afghanistan, with stops in Washington, D.C., and London along the way.

I found and kept a copy of the news article covering my mysterious disappearance in my electronic journal. I also saved the video clip from the evening news.

January 7, San Francisco Bay Area News

Fremont, California – The Search and Rescue Team from the Fremont Fire Department was dispatched early this morning to the scene of an overnight accident in Niles Canyon for a potential rescue after a vehicle apparently plunged off the roadway during last night's heavy downpour. A missing section of guardrail was the only indication of the crash.

"There were no eyewitnesses, only a motorist who passed by sometime after the accident and reported seeing headlights pointing into the trees overhanging Alameda Creek," said Officer Reed Phillips of the California Highway Patrol during a press conference held this morning at the Fremont Station. "The CHP was dispatched to the scene at 4:09 a.m. The responding officer reported that he could see no driver and no passengers when he shined his flashlight through the windows of the vehicle from the bank of the creek. It's about a fifteen-foot drop from the roadway to the creek below and visibility was extremely poor due to the heavy rain and the dense foliage along that stretch of the road," explained Officer Phillips.

Due to the torrential rain that has been falling steadily for the past three days, the creek has swollen and is said to be six to eight feet above its normal level. "It is highly unlikely anyone survived that crash. The creek is running extremely fast with all this rain and the water is very cold. The windshield and driver's side window were both completely broken out upon impact. It appears that the driver and any passengers were swept downstream in the strong current."

According to the CHP, the ongoing effort is now focused on recovery. Despite the fact that the Fremont Search and Rescue team responded to the call for assistance and arrived approximately thirteen minutes later, they were unable to locate any survivors. After scouring the immediate vicinity of the crash for any signs of human life, the crew began searching downstream in hopes of finding whoever was in that car before it was too late.

Hopes of a successful rescue were dashed shortly after sunrise when the crew found the body of a middle aged man submerged and pinned against a metal grate under an overpass roughly two miles downstream. The victim has been identified as John "Jack" Maguire, a senior advisor and member of the President's security council on terrorism. He was scheduled to meet with the founder and CEO of ZuessNet Technologies to discuss forthcoming innovations designed by the company to aid in the war on terror.

The vehicle was a late model Tesla registered to a high-ranking employee of ZuessNet who was sent by the company to take Mr. Maguire from Oakland International Airport to his hotel in Santa Clara. The driver's identity has not yet been released, pending notification of the family. Maguire had arrived on a flight from Dulles Airport in Washington, D.C. at roughly 9:49 p.m.

-Sarah Ducas, Ryan Kwon, and Leslie Scow contributed to this story.

Born Into Espionage – Chapter One

I shouldn't exist. You might say my birth was an accident.

Many people wish I didn't exist. I can count some seventy-eight people who are now dead because of me. I bet they and those close to them wished I hadn't been born. But, then again, they were bad people who needed to die. In most of those cases, if I hadn't killed them, some other hired gun would have. I didn't write the contract, after all. I just delivered the desired result.

Four of those cases, including the guy in the backseat of the car I plunged into Alameda Creek, were personal. Call it revenge. Or vigilante justice. Or "paying the piper." Whatever the label, those four had it coming for what they did.

There will be more.

My mother and father were never supposed to meet. They were never supposed to communicate, collaborate, or consummate. But they did. That's why I'm here. Born into a relationship that was never supposed to be, my existence is not officially recognized anywhere.

The only paperwork that proves I am alive was fabricated by my parents. None of their colleagues nor their handlers in the CIA and MI6 learned of me until I was fifteen. Even then, it was accidental.

Before that, very few people knew about me.

One aunt on my mom's side and two of my dad's second cousins have been in on the secret from the beginning. They're eight and ten years older than he was, so they're more like an aunt and uncle to me. That's what happens when your father's parents have children later in life. These second cousins' children know me, but don't know how I'm connected to them. My parents wanted to keep it that way. That's the extent of my family relations, as far as I know. By the time I was ten, my parents ended my visits with all family members "for their safety and yours," they said.

During those early years, this small group of relatives provided a safe place for me to stay while my mom and dad fulfilled various assignments. My parents would drop me off in the middle of the night with one of my aunts, then disappear. Sometimes I stayed for a few days. Sometimes it was weeks.

More often than not, it would be me living alone with one of my parents for long periods of time. We spent the time learning and training. Games involving the capitols of every country in the world and the fifty states in the US helped me learn my geography. Speaking the language of a different country each day and eating the food from that country kept things interesting and fluid. More often than not, we would end up in those countries, eating the food and speaking the language for long stretches. That's how I became conversant in seven languages.

Being a former Navy Seal, my dad made sure I had all the skills he had. We would do fun things like have contests to see who could stay underwater the longest or who could climb a tree the fastest. As I grew, he kept track of my personal records in everything—how fast I could run a hundred meters and how long I could last at full speed. Same with swimming. He recorded my longest and highest jumps and got more excited than I did every time one of those personal bests was eclipsed.

It wasn't until recently that I realized he never actually measured any of my runs or swims. He could calculate distances by sight or feel or magic or something. I guess that's where I picked up the same ability. It comes in handy.

Without realizing it, I was taught parkour, the art of maneuvering through obstacles in any environment quickly and efficiently and without equipment. It involves running, jumping, climbing, tumbling, and danger. The level of danger grew as I did. That's why I liked it so much. That and the fact that my parents were so good at it that wanting to reach their level kept me constantly motivated.

Our games of hide and seek, especially with my dad, would sometimes last for hours. He showed me how to pick the best places, then praised my ability to conceal myself using whatever I could find around me. Eventually, I mastered the art of camouflage using grass, mud, and leaves. By the age of eight, I could stay quiet even while my dad walked within a few meters of my hiding spot. When he finally found me, I would be on the verge of tears sometimes, worried that I had been abandoned. He would comfort me by saying, "Someday you're going to thank me for this."

After it became too difficult to leave me with the relatives, I was home alone more and more. Because well-meaning adults who saw me buying food or other supplies would ask why I wasn't in school, the day came when my parents started to refuse certain assignments.

At the time, those refusals made sense. My mom in particular had strong, logical reasons for turning down work. They weren't desperate for money and they had become suspicious of the motives behind some of the tasks they were asked to perform.

But that's when the trouble began.

I was fourteen and in the same room when my mother told her handler at MI6 she would not be available to go on an extended assignment in the Persian Gulf. Her face was full of determination as she spoke, explaining to the person on the other end of the conversation that she had just completed a long assignment and needed rest. That look of steely determination I had seen so many times left her face toward the end of the call, replaced by fear, something I was unaccustomed to seeing.

Because we never stayed in one place for very long, except my aunt's remote cabin in the Harbottle area, we never had much. We were always prepared to leave at a moment's notice. At the end of that phone call, we left the cabin for the last time, faster than we had ever left any place. We were gone in two minutes. No explanation. No second-guessing. No hesitation.

As we hurried out to the carport, my mother stopped, placed her phone on a large rock that we often used as a place to sit and rest after our morning runs, and proceeded to smash it to bits with another hand-sized rock. She looked at my bewildered face. "They'll have traced it. We have to go."

Dark, ominous clouds filled the sky overhead, obscuring the sun, similar to what I felt inside. Each of us carried a duffle bag stuffed with clothes over our shoulders. We strapped our meager collection of belongings to the rack on the back of our Honda CFR motorcycle, donned our helmets and dark-colored rain gear, and climbed on.

A light drizzle began to fall. My mother drove to the paved road at the end of the driveway, explaining that it was important not to leave tracks that could be followed. I had expected her to go into the thick forest straight back from the house where we always went riding. Instead, we turned uphill on the windy, narrow road and she goosed the throttle. We almost never went that way. There was nothing in that direction. But as I thought about it, that made the most sense in the moment.

We both leaned forward and from side to side as we took one turn after another at breakneck speeds. After only a few minutes, she turned off the paved road onto a single-track trail. She reduced the speed but given the terrain and my unfamiliarity with this route, it still felt wild and reckless. The further we went, the more I could sense the tension in her body easing. She eventually slowed to a stop and we both climbed off.

She removed her helmet and ran her fingers through her long, black hair. "I shouldn't have crossed them. That put you in danger."

"But Mum, you always said to stand up for what you feel is right."

"Yes, I know. But sometimes you have to realize that the right thing for you may not be the right thing for everyone involved. In this case, I should have ...oh, I don't know what I should have done."

We were in unchartered territory. She never wavered in her decision making. She never doubted herself. And I never questioned her judgement. Not even at this point.

She must have seen the confusion on my face.

"I just didn't want to leave you alone for such a long time, especially with your father already on miserably long assignment."

For the first time I could remember, my mother shed tears. Her voice trembled as she spoke. Her hand shook as she covered her mouth and squeezed her eyes shut.

"It'll be all right, Mum. They can't hurt you."

She shot me a wide-eyed look. She pursed her lips to control the quivering.

The naturally dark skin tone of my mother's face was paler than I had ever seen it. "What makes you so sure?"

"Dad says you're the best at what you do. He tells me that every time you're gone and I begin to worry about you."

Those words seemed to affect her deeply. She paused, her head nodding slowly. A tiger-like ferocity returned to her dark eyes. "Your father's right, of course. I *am* very good at what I do. I've managed this far. I'll continue managing. Come now, let's not dither around here any longer."

She pulled her helmet back over her head and indicated for me to do the same.

"I'll not let them do anything to hurt you. And that includes taking your mother."

About the Author

Glen Robins enjoys a good adventure. If he's not participating in one, he's writing or reading about one. From a young age, he learned to love the outdoors. This love of adventure has spurred much of his writing.

Mr. Robins and his wife are both native Californians. They continue to live in the Bay Area. He currently has three grandchildren.

The characters in "Chosen Path," while fictional, have a basis in real life people that Mr. Robins has met. Their stories, experiences, and attributes have found their way into the characters and situations in this novel. The aim of this book is first and foremost entertainment. But a secondary goal is to help the reader gain an appreciation for the people, culture, and history of Korea and the importance of current events on the Korean Peninsula and how they have the potential to become a factor of global significance.

You can follow Mr. Robins and his adventures on his website: www.GlenRobinsBooks.com or by following him on Facebook (https://www.facebook.com/glenrobinsbooks/) or on BookBub (https://www.bookbub.com/authors/glen-robins).

You can connect with me on:

http://www.glenrobinsbooks.com

https://www.facebook.com/glenrobinsbooks

Subscribe to my newsletter:

https://dl.bookfunnel.com/v6h93ypyqa

Also by Glen Robins

My books are designed to be fun, fast-paced action adventure stories the whole family can enjoy. They're filled with intrigue and difficult situations, but not with profanity or salacious scenes. There's high-stakes drama and heart-pounding suspense, but no adult material that you wouldn't want your teenager to read.

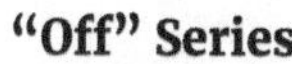

"Off" Series

Collin Cook is thrown off by tragedy.

Then he is targeted for the settlement money.

Then he is framed by the nefarious cyber-terrorist Pho Nam Penh.

Now he is being chased by Penh, the FBI, and Interpol.

His only allies are his two best friends, one of whom is a security expert with the NSA.

How will he survive?

How will he prevent Penh from destroying the global economy?

How will he triumph?

Have you been looking for good, clean action adventure stories? Ones you can read to or with your children or teens? You've come to the right place. The "Off" series is a fast paced, edge-of-your-seat type thriller series without all the smut.

Here's what readers have said about the "Off" series:

Customer Reviews

"A mind-blowing story of an innocent man involved in top level espionage and national security. My heart was in my mouth for Collin and Rob the whole way." – Erica

"Glen Robins' writing style is easy to read and is appropriate for any age. It keeps you reading and is very hard to put down. I will be looking for more of his books." – Judy

"I thoroughly enjoyed this series. The action was very good and I was certainly drawn into the characters. Good clean fun and non-stop action - along with international intrigue - loved it!" - mhawk

Get your copy of the "Off" series boxset today and delve into a good, clean action adventure story.

Off Chance

Lukas Mueller knows something is off. He just can't pinpoint it. His girlfriend goes missing, he goes searching, and the NSA comes investigating.

When his mentor, Pho Nam Penh, disappears, Lukas's nightmare begins.

Lukas goes from suspicious to suspect overnight.

With the NSA breathing down his neck, how can Lukas prove his innocence and assert his usefulness in the hunt for the world's worst unknown enemy, Pho Nam Penh? Does he have the grit and tenacity to pursue and ultimately conquer his foe?

Collin Cook's genius high school friend, now an MIT student on scholarship, gets unwittingly swept into the current of international cyber-crime and economic warfare that threatens to destroy lives, livelihoods, and entire nations. Staking his career on the pursuit of Penh, Lukas must decide whether to protect his friend, Collin Cook, or allow him to be the bait he needs to trap Penh.

Join Lukas Mueller on an epic journey to find justice, fulfillment, and peace. "Off Chance" is a companion novella to Glen Robins' high-octane "Off" series that thrills and entertains readers of all ages without resorting to the base and foul language and themes used in so many action adventure stories these days. If you like clean fiction that is fun and fast-paced, you will enjoy this entire series.

Get "Off Chance" today and begin a quest of your own.

Off Track

Trouble follows Captain Gordon Sewell. It always has.

He never seeks it. It just finds him.

Bad decisions, bad luck, and bad timing conspire against him, but he never gives up. Quitting is not in his nature.

When Collin Cook finds Captain Sewell, trouble is not far behind. Soon, the two men's fates are intertwined in a way neither could ever have imagined.

Rather than hide from trouble, Captain Sewell copes, adapts, and learns from it. After each setback, he musters the courage to press onward and upward.

Fortitude, tenacity, and a powerful survival instinct lead Captain Sewell through perilous journeys, gut-wrenching dilemmas, and mettle-testing voyages until he emerges scarred, but victorious.

Spoiler Alert:

"Off Track" is a companion novella to the "Off" series by Glen Robins. It launches you into fast-paced adventures without using the profanity and salacious content that is so common in thrillers. If you haven't read "Off Kilter," "Off Course," and "Off Guard" yet, you might want to do so before reading this novella so that you don't. You can save by downloading the Off Series Box Set today.

Come sit on the deck of Captain Sewell's boat and listen to him tell his story of the role he played in Collin Cook's epic saga. Get your copy of "Off Track" today and begin a new quest of your own.

www.ingramcontent.com/pod-product-compliance
Lightning Source LLC
LaVergne TN
LVHW041115080826
845145LV00007B/1820

* 9 7 8 0 9 8 6 3 5 1 7 8 5 *